CONTENTS

Nick

Chapter 1

Darcy's fingers almost stumbled when she looked up at the three men who had just sat down at the piano bar where she played. Great granny's garters, those were three of the best-looking men she had ever seen.

They were obviously related. All three were tall, dark, and handsome, each with chiseled features and full, sensuous lips. They shared the same unusual eye color, a unique silver-gray shade that contrasted sharply with their various shades of hair and sun-bronzed skin. Their hair was different, one sable and curly, one with wavy dark chocolate colored hair, and one with long, straight locks of a golden-brown color, but other than that they could have been triplets. The trio were all muscular, their shoulders so broad they nearly brushed each other as they sat at the bar.

Three times the hunkiness. Yum.

One of them in particular, the one with soft, wavy hair, eyed her seriously. She felt his gaze sweep over her, taking in her long, dark rust-colored curls and whiskey-colored eyes. When his gaze slid across her generous bust line, it almost felt as if he'd reached out and touched her. A shiver traveled down her spine.

Darcy's fingers trailed over the keys, lovingly creating the flow of the instrumental piece The Autumn Leaves as she watched the man watching her. His pewter colored gaze stayed on her even when he answered a comment from one of the men he was with. Something the one with the curly hair said made a small smile slide across his face, and she watched with fascination as a deep dimple danced in his cheek, softening the hard features.

Wow. Just looking at the guy made her toes curl inside her tan stilettos. Maybe this was going to be her lucky night.

The thought made her smile. That would be amazing. It seemed she had experienced nothing but bad luck lately. Last spring, she had lost her job teaching music because of budget cuts. She had tried but not succeeded to find another teaching job but finally, out of desperation, was forced to take the job here at Papa's Place. She'd caught her latest boyfriend cheating on her, and it seemed like her car was in the shop every other day. Her life seemed as though if something could go wrong, it did.

Wouldn't it be nice if something went her way for once?

The last poignant notes of the instrumental faded away and Darcy paused and smiled at the crowd. Leaning into the microphone, she asked, "Any requests?"

"How about Can't Help Falling in Love with You?" called a deep voice, and Darcy turned her gaze directly on the man with the silvery eyes. "Do you know that old Elvis classic?"

Their eyes locked momentarily as silent messages seemed to zing between them. Darcy broke eye contact finally and smiled warmly. "It's one of my favorites."

She played an introduction then began to sing in her sultry voice. She really did love this song. She let her emotions take over and poured herself into the rendition, closing her eyes for the last few bars. When at last she opened them and looked to where the man had sat, he was gone. And so were the men who had come with him.

Well, for gosh sakes. She didn't think she'd done badly on the song. Not bad enough to run off her customers, anyway. She felt the color mount in her cheeks. How rude. He requested the song and didn't even stay until the finish?

Darcy attempted to shrug off the hurt. Others were clapping; others had enjoyed it. What the hell was his problem, anyway? She noticed a new twenty-dollar bill in her tip jar. Humph, like money made up for the insult.

Things went downhill after that. A group of drunks took a table near the piano and started heckling her, gently at first, then becoming more venomous. The men at the table made remarks about her body, urged her to "take it off, baby," and leered at her openly. The women with them made comments about her taste in clothes and style and boasted about their best-looking body parts, comparing their ultra-thin bodies with her more voluptuous one. She handled them with her usual finesse but felt an ache building behind her temples.

Then came an older gentleman who kept requesting the same song over and over. "Let's hear Take the Ribbon from Your Hair," he'd holler again and again. She played the song for him twice but didn't want to bore the rest of the audience. She felt sorry for the old guy, but business was business.

Darcy normally enjoyed her job. Papa's Place was like a page out of yesterday, reminiscent of the Rat Pack days. The rich red leather and gleaming dark wood counters, bars, and tables were sophisticated and elegant. The crowd was normally fairly quiet, though some nights seemed to attract the crazies, especially those like tonight when a full harvest moon glided across the sky.

Last call was finally issued, and Darcy went into her closing performance of the night. By the time she finished the bar was nearly empty of patrons. She turned to rise from the piano stool just as an older man stumbled towards her, and the entire contents of his glass of red wine flew straight onto the bust of her ivory silk dress.

Darcy's mouth dropped open in surprise, and the face of the gray-haired gentleman in front of her registered shock. Darcy pulled the dripping off-the-shoulder bodice away from her chest and gasped.

"I am so sorry, madam. So very sorry. Please, let me help you." He fumbled forward with a napkin and reached for her breasts.

"No, no, that's okay. I'll get it." She jumped back defensively. The last thing she wanted tonight was some old man feeling her up. "No. I'll take care of it."

"At least let me pay for the cleaning." He reached for his wallet. "I insist."

"Fine. Thank you. Thank you very much." Her eyes grew wide when he slipped $50 into her palm. It was more than she'd paid for the vintage dress. "Really, that's too much."

"No, it was entirely my fault. I insist. Besides, that's better than a wet T-shirt any night." He winked at her, glanced briefly at her clinging wet neckline, and walked away.

Oh. She glanced down at the dress. realized the stain was spreading rapidly across the fabric and growled. "Good God Almighty."

She took the $50 and the rest of her tips and stomped behind the bar. She grabbed a bottle of club soda and a clean white bar towel and made her way to the employees' break room directly across from the kitchen. It was a small area where employees could sit and rest their feet. A large window looked out into the kitchen, and two small bathrooms were against the back wall.

Darcy scurried into the lady's room and pulled off the wet dress, spreading it across the vanity. She knew if she didn't work fast it would be ruined forever. And the last thing she needed right now was to spend money on clothing.

She poured the club soda on the dress then patted it with the bar towel. She eventually got most of the wine out and hung it over the automatic hand dryer so it could blow on the wet fabric. To kill time while her dress dried, she called her best friend, Sophie. Sophie was an artist and liked to work nights and sleep during the day, so Darcy wasn't worried about waking her even though it was nearly midnight.

"Hey, Snooks, what's up?" She sat on a bench and crossed her legs.

"Oh, girl, there's all kind of excitement going on. There was a big fight downstairs tonight." Sophie lived above a popular bar and lived vicariously through the bar's regulars. "What's up with you?"

"Well, it's been one of those nights." Darcy went on to tell her about the customer spilling wine on her dress, the hecklers, and the man with the magnetic eyes.

"Dang, girl, he got away?"

"Slick as a whistle."

"Wow, that's a mind blower."

"Isn't it, though. Hey, I think my dress is about dry. I'll see you tomorrow afternoon for brunch, okay?"

"Sure. See you then, girlfriend."

Darcy disconnected and rose to put on her dress. She had slipped the ivory silk over her head and just settled it on her hips when an explosive noise almost made her jump out of her stilettos. What the heck?

She pulled open the door to the bathroom and peeked out the window in the break room. She stood, opened mouth, unable to believe what she was seeing.

Three men, armed with assault rifles aimed at four of her co-workers, had their backs to her. Papa lay sprawled on the floor, his son Rico lying on top of his rotund body. Before she could even move, she heard a voice shout, "No witnesses," and then there was an eruption of gunfire. Darcy watched as the other two employees dropped to the floor one by one.

Chapter 2

Darcy stood frozen as she saw her coworkers mowed down. She heard their shouts of fear, their moans, their cries of pain. She stood helpless as Leo, the chef and her good friend, grabbed a huge knife and dashed towards the attackers, only to be cut down by a barrage of bullets. Darcy stuffed her fist in her mouth to keep from screaming.

Just as the killers turned to admire their handiwork, Darcy's brain began working again, and it shouted, "Run! Hide!" The last thing she remembered seeing was the face of the man who seemed to be the leader of the band of thugs just as he turned around. She'd retreated into the restroom and hid in a stall, hauling her feet up on the seat, pulling off her stilettos and holding them in her hand. God, she prayed he hadn't seen her at the same moment she'd seen him.

She was in shock. She couldn't stop seeing the images of Papa lying there tangled up with Rico. She saw dishwasher Danny's face spasm in horror as bullets slammed into him and couldn't rid herself of the sight of Leo, arm raised, riddled with bullets and falling in his tracks. And most of all, the look on the killer's face, so cold, so unfeeling.

Darcy heard the men talking, congratulating each other on their successful mission. Their voices became one big blur as she huddled on top of the toilet. They were bold enough to help themselves to the food the men had been putting up.

She thought they'd never go. Her legs cramped, and tears ran silently down her face. She was shivering all over. She fought down nausea, terrified of giving away her hiding place if she made any noise at all.

At last, she heard them leaving, then silence reigned, but Darcy forced herself to stay in place at least 10 minutes after they were gone. Then she slipped her cell phone out of her pocket and dialed 911. Still too frightened to speak loudly, she whispered the emergency and stayed on the line with the operator until she heard the voices of the police hollering, announcing their presence in the kitchen. She was still crouched on the toilet seat when the stall door slammed open, and she bit back a scream as her gaze clashed with the silver-blue eyes of the man who'd been at the bar earlier.

"Police, ma'am. Are you the woman who called in the murders?"

Darcy still couldn't find her voice, so she simply nodded her head frantically.

"Well, you're safe now. Why don't you come down from there?" He held out his hand, and Darcy hesitated, then took it. He helped her step down from the toilet, and her knees buckled when her feet touched the floor. She felt herself start to fall, but before she hit the ground, he grabbed her and pulled her to him.

"Whoa, there. It's okay. It's okay now." His voice was deep, smooth, and comforting. He held her trembling body in his arms, and she buried her head in his chest, listening to his heartbeat. Oh, God, he was alive. A living, breathing warm human being.

She didn't move for several moments, sheltering in his arms. At last, he pulled back and looked at her. "Are you ok?"

Okay? Was she okay? Hell, no she wasn't. She'd just seen her boss and co-workers shot down right before her eyes. She felt a burst of anger and jerked away from him.

"I'm not hurt if that's what you mean."

"We need to talk to you then. Let's go on out to the dining room." He took hold of her elbow and began urging her towards the front of the building. She turned her head to look at her fallen co-workers and the police officers milling around, but he hustled her on through the kitchen and sat her down at the first table they came to. He made sure she couldn't see the kitchen at all from where they were seated.

"I'm Detective Nick Baker. And you are?"

"Darcy Campbell." She twisted her hands in her lap.

"I'm so sorry for your loss, Ms. Campbell."

She knew it was standard procedure to offer condolences, but somehow Darcy felt like this man really meant it. Her gaze shot to his and he looked sincere, his eyes warming to a deep pewter hue.

"Tell me, Ms. Campbell, are you normally here this late after closing?"

"No, no I'm not." She went on to tell him about the wine, and her dress, and exactly what happened.

"Did you see any of their faces?"

Again, she saw his face. Thin, high cheekbones, square chin, squinty eyes.

"Just one of them."

"Would you be willing to come downtown and look at some pictures? See if you recognize anybody?"

Was he kidding? All she wanted to do was go home, have a glass of wine, and fall apart.

"Look, I know you're worn out, but we need to do this while your memory is still fresh." His voice was soft, his gaze intense. Huh, like she would ever forget that face. But at last, she nodded. She had to do whatever she could to help find Papa's killer.

"Good. I'll get us down there as soon as possible. Barnes, come in here." He stood and hollered, and a young officer almost immediately appeared in the room. "Stay with her until I'm ready to go."

And then she waited. And waited. She couldn't sit still and paced across the dining room, back and forth. The young officer stood patiently, watching Darcy pace.

It was more than an hour before Nick was ready to go. By the time they got to the station her head was pounding, her stomach nauseous, and her nerves shot. She felt weak, trembly. She wasn't even sure she could focus on the pictures Detective Baker presented to her.

There were so many faces in the books. Young, old, black, white, ugly, handsome. She turned page after page, growing frustrated after looking at hundreds of photos. She wanted to cry, to shout, to throw the books of pictures across the room.

And then she saw it.

It was him. The man she'd seen in the kitchen at Papa's Place. She'd recognize that cold, merciless face anywhere.

"That's him." She stated coldly. "That's the bastard that killed Papa."

Chapter 3

Darcy sat at her kitchen table, a coffee mug cradled between her hands. She knew she looked like hell, but she didn't care. Her auburn curls tumbled riotously around her sagging shoulders, violet circles underlined her eyes, and her complexion was so pale the baker's dozen of freckles across the bridge of her slender nose stood out like rust spots.

She'd let Detective Baker bring her home last night and then immediately shed her heels and dress and climbed into some old gray sweatpants and a ratty old T-shirt and was still wearing those same clothes.

After she'd changed clothes and greeted her black cat, Warlock, she'd poured herself a glass of wine and huddled on the couch. She'd turned the TV on but paid no attention to it, just letting the droning sound fill the air.

At last, when she was finishing off her second glass of wine, her emotions overwhelmed her, and she started crying. Huge, jagged sobs. She couldn't believe she'd witnessed such a massacre. Her friends, her coworkers, mowed down right in front of her eyes. So much blood. Who knew blood had such a putrid smell or that it was so thick when it congealed on the ground? The sobs just kept coming, racking her body with pain, contorting her face as she cried.

When the tears finally ran dry her head was throbbing. She'd tried to lay down, but it was useless. Sleep wouldn't come. Visions kept flashing before her eyes.

And Detective Baker's words after she identified the man kept replaying in her mind. "Are you sure?" he'd asked, a flat tone tinting his voice.

She'd nodded, looking him directly in the eyes. "I'll never forget that face, those eyes. That is definitely the man."

He hadn't said anything for a minute, just looked at her with an odd expression. Finally, he dragged a palm over his face and sighed deeply. "I'm going to tell you something that's going to sound scary... because it is."

Oh, God, that's the last thing she wanted to hear. She was still terrified from this evening's earlier events. She drew her shoulders back and squared her chin, preparing herself for the news he seemed reluctant to deliver. She knew it was bad.

"The man you identified is Dimitri Pasquale. He is the right-hand man to the head of a mob family. They, in turn, control the street gang known as the Bad Ass Banditos. We're very familiar with him. We've been trying to get him for years, but he's too slick. You are now the key to putting this guy away."

She kept hearing those words, pounding over and over again in her head. She was responsible. But what if she didn't want to testify? What if she didn't want to put herself in that position? My God, this guy was a coldblooded killer. Why should it be her responsibility to put the guy behind bars? The bastard had all kinds of men under his control. It would probably be signing her own death certificate.

The problem was, this dude really was a bad ass. He was, obviously, a killer. She'd seen that with her own eyes. He was also a big-time drug dealer and a slick character that had either great lawyers or great influence. Or both.

And now she was supposed to "put him away." Lord that would take courage. Didn't Nick Baker understand that?

She was not a brave person. Sure, she loved to take risks with color and style, she enjoyed skiing, whitewater rafting, and horseback riding, and she even liked zip lines. She wasn't afraid of a little danger, but this was different. This was a whole lot of danger and a whole different kind. Danger from the mafia. From a gang. From a cold-blooded killer. Not the nicest people in the world, to say the least.

When Detective Baker asked her last night if she'd be willing to testify against Pasquale, it felt as if her heart stopped beating. Of course, she should have been expecting it. She was the only witness. The only one who could put this villain away.

She didn't really have a choice. She couldn't pretend it hadn't happened. It was solely up to her to bring justice for Papa and the others. And she knew it—knew it was her responsibility, her fate, so to speak, to tell what she had seen.

But the thought terrified her.

She shuddered, recalling how she had put the detective off last night. Unable to respond to his question, she'd begged for a little more time to let it all sink in.

She'd expected him to pressure her, but he hadn't. He drove her home to the cozy, quirky cottage she'd inherited from her aunt without bringing the subject up again. He talked about the Cubs, and his family, including his two brothers who had been with him earlier in the evening.

When he mentioned his earlier trip to the piano bar, Darcy remembered that she was mad at him. He'd requested a song and left before she'd even finished it. If that wasn't a slap in the face. She'd turned an angry amber glare on him.

"Oh, you mean the men who walked out with you while I was singing the song you requested."

"I'm sorry about that. I got a phone call from my mother. There was an emergency at home. We had to leave immediately." His tone was conciliatory, but his look said more than his words did. Obviously, he would let nothing come between him and his family.

She guessed she could understand that. If she had any family left she would certainly put them above all else. Unfortunately, her father, a policeman, had been killed in the line of duty when she was just 10 years old. After he died, her mother went downhill, finding comfort in a bottle. By the time Darcy turned 13, her mom was killed by a violent boyfriend. That's when she went to live with Aunt Liz.

Aunt Liz. Thank God for her. She'd kept Darcy from being lonely, made her proud of her slightly plump body, was her biggest supporter, and taught her how to love again. Her aunt was an artist, a free spirit who encouraged Darcy's love of music and the unique. Then, suddenly, just two years ago, Aunt Liz had died in a car accident. The shock of her startling, unexpected death sent Darcy reeling. Now she had no family.

So, she could understand his loyalty to family. Kind of. So, she simply smiled and said she hoped everything had turned out okay. He'd nodded, and they continued on their way. They didn't speak any more until at last, he broke the silence.

"I really am sorry, you know. I hated walking out on you."

His sincere words had an odd effect on Darcy's heart, and she smiled.

Now she sat huddled on her curved red velvet sofa, Warlock curled up at her side. She knew her nose and eyes were red from crying, but she didn't care. She needed a shower but couldn't seem to find the strength to get up and go take one. Right now, she barely had the energy to breathe she felt so broken.

The doorbell rang, and Darcy tipped her head back and cursed. She didn't want to see anyone. It was probably just her busybody neighbor Georgia. Word of the shooting was probably out, and the neighborhood snoop wanted to get the dirt straight from the horse's mouth. She knew Darcy worked at Papa's.

Well, she might as well get it over with. Otherwise, Georgia would keep ringing. Darcy's car was in the drive, so the middle-aged spinster wasn't going to give up.

When she peered through the peephole, though, it wasn't Georgia's wizened face that she saw. Instead, Detective Baker stared back at her. Oh, crap. What was he doing here?

Darcy cast a rueful glance at her baggy clothes and ran a hand through her jumbled curls. Oh, well, it was too late to do anything about it now.

She opened the door and peered around the edge. Her breath caught in her throat when her gaze met his pewter eyes.

Damn, she shouldn't let herself be affected by his good looks. This man was not for her.

"Morning, Ms. Campbell. May I come in?" He smiled, looking impeccable in his black suit and silky white shirt. A lock of chocolate brown hair fell across his forehead, and she had to fight an urge to reach out and sweep it back.

Darcy stepped back and opened the door to allow him entrance. She saw his eyebrows raise as he took in her eclectic space. It was, admittedly, a little messy. The jacket she'd worn last night lay tossed across a bench in the entryway. The living room was crowded with chintz and gingham overstuffed chairs, a dress form she had turned into the figure of a maid that acted as a wine server, and her piano. Magazines were scattered about, and surfaces were covered with projects in progress.

"I hate to disturb you, but I need to talk to you." Nick turned a serious gaze on her.

Darcy's stomach sank at his words. She knew he was going to ask her for a commitment. Was she willing to testify against Dimitri Pasquale?

"Come in and sit down, Detective," she motioned towards a chair. "Would you like some coffee?" Anything to put off the discussion she knew was coming.

"I'm afraid this isn't a social call."

"I didn't figure it was. That doesn't mean we can't be comfortable while we talk, does it?"

She took her time brewing a fresh pot of coffee and fixing two cups after enquiring how he took his. Black, of course. She should have guessed. She added muffins to a plate then reluctantly made her way into the living room.

Once she was seated, he took a sip of his coffee and started speaking.

"Ms. Campbell," was all he got out.

"You might as well call me Darcy. I'm not used to Ms. Campbell. It just makes me more uncomfortable."

"Okay, then, Darcy, I know this is a frightening position you're in." He looked her directly in the eyes.

"Frightening. Yeah, that could be an understatement, Detective. It's terrifying. Completely, overwhelmingly terrifying." Her voice shook as she spoke.

"I do understand. But it's also necessary. We need you to put this bad guy away. You saw him pull the trigger. You are the only one who has the power to end his murderous ways." He leaned forward intensely. "We'll protect you, Darcy. I promise. Trust me."

She stayed silent for a long moment, staring into his silver-blue eyes until he finally spoke again.

"You know we can subpoena you if we have to. Even if we have to bring you in as a hostile witness."

She felt her chin jut up in defiance. She didn't like taking orders. Especially not from an arrogant man.

But then her shoulders sagged. She knew she had to do this. She couldn't turn her back and pretend it hadn't happened. Even despite the detective's threat she already knew she would testify.

"Okay. I'll do it."

He let out a long breath. "Thank you."

"And it's not because you threatened me," she retorted.

"I understand," he said seriously.

"Well, it's not. I'd already decided I would testify. It's the right thing to do."

He eyed her, a small smile playing across his lips. "I believe you."

"Well, you should, because it's true." She still sounded defensive. "Here, have a muffin." She practically shoved the plate at him. She'd made the orange-pineapple muffins herself yesterday morning and for some reason wanted him to enjoy her cooking skills.

He bit into the tasty morsel and could hardly contain a groan of pleasure.

"God, that's good. Thank you."

She couldn't help grinning in satisfaction. Her cooking skills were approved.

"I do have to ask you some more questions, though. Would you mind coming back down to the station?"

"What the hell. In for a dime, in for a dollar." She tried to sound casual, but couldn't hide the tension that spun through her. Lord, she was in for it now.

"Then we'll go. As soon as I finish my muffin."

Chapter 4

Darcy met Sophie for their brunch date later that morning. When she finally left the police station, she barely had time to get to the restaurant in time. She raced into the deli with her face flushed and frantic eyes.

"Thank God, you're here. I have to talk to you." She gathered Sophie in a warm hug.

"Good Lord, woman, I'm so sorry about the shootings. I've been trying to call you ever since I heard about it on the news." Sophie Adams squeezed her tight. "Are you all right?"

Darcy held her close and apologized for not charging her phone. Sophie was her dearest friend. The two women had hit it off immediately when they met in a yoga class. They had much in common. Both were orphans, though Sophie hadn't been lucky enough to have any family left. She'd grown up in foster homes until she turned 18. She'd worked and struggled to make her way through college then got a job teaching at the same school Darcy did. Now she was in the same position as Darcy—unemployed and scrimping by. While Darcy played in a piano bar, Sophie did custom frames, painted, and managed to sell some of her work.

"Girl, I'm so glad you're okay. I take it you were already gone by the time the shooting happened," Sophie commented as they slipped into a booth.

"I wish I had been. Let me tell you what happened."

For the next little while, Darcy filled Sophie in on all the events of the night before, pausing only long enough to give their orders and take an occasional bite of food. Sophie gasped and shuddered as Darcy described the happenings.

"You actually picked the guy out from a photo?"

"I did. And, to top it off, I have to testify against this Dimitri Pasquale."

"Dimitri Pasquale?" Sophie squeaked. "I've heard of him. He's a real bad guy, Darcy."

"Believe me, I know." Darcy's voice quivered as she agreed.

The two women clasped hands for a moment as the reality sank in.

"It will be dangerous, Darcy. Have you thought about that?"

"I can't stop thinking about it," she confessed. "But I have to do it, Soph. I have to...for Papa."

"Oh, girl, I wouldn't want to be in your shoes."

"Believe me, I wish I wasn't in my shoes."

They finished their lunch and hugged goodbye, holding on to each other a little tighter than usual. Less than 24 hours before, Darcy had feared she'd never see Sophie again. She loved her like a sister and that possibility terrified her.

Sophie headed east to her parking spot and Darcy headed west to her own car. It was a beautiful, sunny autumn day. One of those days that made her thankful she lived in Chicago and could enjoy all four seasons. She paused at the corner and waited for the light to turn then started across the street.

She was midway across the sleepy street when she heard the roar of an accelerating car engine. She turned her head and saw a black SUV careening around the corner, all the time picking up speed. What the hell? It was heading right towards her. Darcy lunged forward, but the car turned in her direction. She hurled herself towards the curb as the SUV missed her by mere inches.

She curled up, sprawled on her belly, her chin crashing into the sidewalk. Her teeth clashed together, and she felt a burning sensation speed through her jaw. Her skirt flew up her thighs, and her knees stung where the pavement scraped them.

A few people witnessed the scene and came hurrying towards Darcy's sprawled form. They all demanded to know if she was all right, but the breath was knocked out of her, and she was unable to answer. She felt herself attempting to suck in air like a fish on dry land.

She was finally able to speak and began to protest. "I'm okay, really, I'm okay."

"Lady, you could have been killed," a rotund, middle-aged man gasped as he helped her to her feet...

"I thought you were a goner," a teenage girl added. "He was coming right for you."

"I called the cops," somebody else put in.

"No, really, I'm all right," Darcy protested as she rubbed her raw chin. The last thing she wanted was to hang around here and wait for the police to arrive. She really just wanted to go home and go to bed, pull up the covers, and wake up to find this was all just a bad dream.

Instead, she waited for the cops, answered their questions, and denied their offer of medical help. She was impatient, upset, and a little in shock. How could all these awful things happen to her in less than 24 hours? Was she just having a string of bad luck or had somebody just tried to kill her?

She finally reached her home and stripped off her clothes. She doctored her scrapes and soaked in the tub while she sipped a glass of white wine. God, she was exhausted.

When she finally climbed out of the tub, she slipped into her favorite long white flannel gown and left her hair flowing free. She warmed up leftover soup and sat on her couch to eat it and watch a bit of TV before she crashed. She'd been awake for 37 hours now, and she could feel it.

She tried watching the news and found the shooting was the lead story on every channel she turned to. She couldn't stand to watch it and finally flipped over to an old John Wayne western. Before she knew it, she'd nodded off.

The banging on the door awakened her. She glanced at the grandfather clock in the corner and saw it was just 8:15, but she was still not happy to be disturbed. She stomped, barefoot, to the front door and peered out the peephole. Nick Baker looked back.

Aw, hell, what now?

Chapter 5

Darcy flung the door open and stared at the man. She had no desire to talk to this guy again today, even if he was the most delicious eye candy she'd seen in a long time. She was tired, she was sore, and she was in no mood for company.

"What is it now, Detective Baker?" She planted a hand on her hip, annoyance written all over her face.

"Good to see you, too, Darcy." He allowed a smile to play around his mouth. "I need to talk to you. Would you rather stand here with the door open with you in your...lingerie...or let me come in?" He eyed the flannel nightgown up and down.

"Oh, for Pete's sake. Come on in." Darcy waved her arm to motion him inside when Warlock decided to greet him as well. The black cat wound around his ankles and rubbed his chin on Baker's legs. Well, would you look at that. Warlock didn't like anyone, yet now he acted as if this was an old friend come to call. She tossed the feline a disgusted look. Traitor.

"Nice cat."

"No, he's not," she snapped. "Have a seat, Detective."

"I'm sorry to bother you again, Darcy, but I saw your name in a police report. Someone tried to run you over?" He settled into a red and white gingham-checked wingback chair.

"I'm sure it was just an accident," she answered.

"Darcy, this is serious. Yes, it might have been a coincidence, but it just seems too ironic. They could have been

30

after you. The witnesses said it came right at you. Did you get a look at the driver at all?"

Darcy shivered and pulled her bare toes under her gown. She didn't want to think about that possibility, though she had to admit it had been playing on her mind all evening.

"I didn't have time to see anything but the ground coming up to meet me." Her hand instinctively rubbed across the raw spot on her chin. "Besides, you said you were going to keep my identity a secret, right?"

"Yes, but a few people have to know. There could be a leak." His face scowled in concern. "Pasquale has long arms, and they might be squeezing somebody on the force."

"You mean...somebody might have told him my name?"

He leaned forward and rested his elbows on his knees. "Chances are slim, very slim, but it is a possibility."

The serious tone of his voice sent tremors along her spine. Surely no one had given her away already? It hadn't even been 24 hours.

"No, surely not. It's too soon, isn't it?" Her brown eyes deepened with worry.

"Maybe, maybe not." He watched as her face crumbled. "Hey, I'm not telling you this to scare you. I just want you to use extreme caution. I've got extra surveillance on your house, and you've got good, sturdy locks on your doors. Do you have an alarm system?"

She shook her head.

"Well, you will have tomorrow," he growled. She started to protest, knowing she couldn't afford it, but he held up his hand to silence her. "It's on the city's tab."

She had her doubts that the city would pay the bill but stayed silent. She was too terrified to argue.

"We'll get this guy, Darcy. He can't hide forever." She looked into his silver-blue eyes long and hard, wanting to trust him. But could she? Maybe she ought to just run away, put all this behind her. She had enough savings she could take off to someplace on the other side of the country, and nobody could find her.

And give up her house? Give up Sophie? Live life always looking over her shoulder?

31

She passed a hand in front of her eyes to wipe away a wave of exhaustion. It was all too much.

"Darcy." She felt his hand tugging hers down from her face and looked into his concerned gaze as he stood over her protectively. "We're going to get through this together. I promise."

Once again, Darcy spent a sleepless night. After Nick Baker left, she double checked the locks on all the doors and windows and tried to go to sleep, but her nerves were tight as bowstrings. She sat on the window seat in her bedroom and was comforted when she saw two patrol cars crawling down her street in less than thirty minutes. At least apparently there were cops watching her place.

Finally, near dawn, exhaustion won over, and Darcy fell into a deep, dark sleep filled with visions of gunfire and roaring SUVs.

Darcy didn't leave the house for the next couple days. She just stayed home and brooded about Papa and the others, about her own uncertain future and the danger she could be in. She only spoke to Sophie on the phone and jumped every time she heard a car door slam or a tree branch brush against the windows.

A man came and installed the alarm, so she felt a little safer, at least, but she also felt like a caged rabbit. The third day she got up determined to go on with her life. She couldn't let fear rule her.

Today she was going to file for unemployment, go to the grocery, and come home and make lasagna. She'd call Sophie, too, and ask her to come for dinner. Time to get back in the game.

While she was at the store, she remembered that tomorrow was Halloween, even if the weather was still warm and sunny. She picked up some candy for the many trick or treaters she always had and grabbed a gallon of apple cider. Halloween was one of her favorite holidays, and she wanted to enjoy it like imaginary ghosts and goblins were the scariest things in her life.

There was still no news about Pasquale. He hadn't been picked up yet, and according to Detective Baker, he hadn't been seen on the streets. She tried hard not to think about it, but she caught herself looking over her shoulder and constantly glancing in her rearview mirror. Was he out there? Was he following her? The idea sent chills chasing through her despite the warmth of the day.

Sophie came over, and they sat in front of the TV indulging in lasagna and watching chick flicks. They'd talked about watching old horror movies in honor of Halloween but decided against it. Darcy didn't need anything else to give her nightmares.

Darcy topped off her wine glass and leaned her head back on the sofa. It was good just to sit here and relax with her old friend.

"Want to spend the night? We could drink more wine, or I could break out the good stuff."

"Oh, I'd love to, Darcy, but I've got a date at 11:30. Jack works second shift at a factory, you know, so we planned to meet late." Her green eyes narrowed. "But if you need me to, you know I'll stay. I don't blame you if you're scared. I know I would be."

"No, no, I'm fine. Really." She reached out and gave Sophie a hug to prove it.

"You don't really look fine. You've got circles under your eyes, you're pale, and your hands shake every so often." She frowned, her warm brown eyes filled with concern. "I'll call Jack. He'll understand."

"You'll do no such thing. Now get up and go meet Jack." She pulled Sophie to her feet and gave her a quick hug. "I'm fine."

"Are you sure, Darcy? It's not a problem." Sophie ran troubled fingers through her short cap of raven locks.

"Positive. Now go, or you'll be late."

Darcy hustled Sophie out the door and watched her safely get in her car, then shut the door and lock it, leaning against the wood door with its stained-glass panel. Sophie was a good friend. Darcy loved her dearly, but she lied to her anyway. She assured Sophie she wasn't scared, but she was. God, she was scared right down to her bones.

Chapter 6

The morning was perfect for Halloween. A damp, gray fog engulfed the area in the morning but burned off by afternoon. The sun peeked out from behind the clouds, a cool breeze rustling fallen leaves along the street.

Darcy had decorated the house in traditional style. There were three jack-o-lanterns and a dancing skeleton on the porch, and a pair of headstones presided over the small front yard. A huge black spider climbed up its web on a porch column.

When Darcy went out to get the paper, she stopped and admired her little house. Every time she looked at it she thought of her aunt. Darcy had been devastated after the loss of her father and the virtual, then actual, death of her mother after his passing. Aunt Liz refused to let her loll in her misery, though had indulged her bouts of tears. She sat quietly with her when Darcy needed to be quiet, and was the best thing to happen to Darcy after her father's death. Darcy said a prayer of thanks for Aunt Liz and the role model she provided.

Halloween had been one of Aunt Liz's favorite holidays, and she always went all out. There always lots of decorations, Halloween baking, and great homemade costumes. Darcy remembered Halloween parties with groups of Aunt Liz's eclectic friends and suddenly felt extremely lonely. Oh, she had friends, but they were scattered across the country. Sophie was all she had near, and she was gone to a painter's workshop this week.

"Well, Warlock," she told the cat as she reentered the house, "it's just you and me this Halloween. Let's make the most of it."

She started by figuring out what costume she would wear tonight when the trick-or-treaters arrived. She went up in the attic and dug through boxes and bags of collected costumes and accessories. She finally decided to pay homage to Aunt Liz and picked the last costume Liz had worn, an Elvira-type skin tight black dress with jagged handkerchief hems on the skirt and sleeves. There was also a tall, pointed black witch's hat to match.

Perfect. Next, she mopped the kitchen floor, cleaned the bathroom, and kept the washer and dryer whirling. She even washed the living room windows.

Darcy stopped cleaning and dressed in her costume. She added heavy green eye shadow and painted her nails scarlet. She left her hair tumbling around her shoulders. A wart on her left cheek was the final touch. Now she was ready to greet trick-or-treaters.

She loved the kids' reactions when she opened the door in full costume, a selection of spooky music playing from hidden speakers on the porch. She was greeted with everything from giggles to screams, especially when she cackled wickedly as she welcomed them.

Devils and superheroes, soldiers and princesses all came calling. One little girl dressed as a hobo especially tugged at Darcy's heartstrings. Her big brown eyes looked sad, and she wasn't with other children, just her and her mother. Her voice was quiet as she requested her treat.

"Sure, honey," Darcy answered her. "But, tell me, why do you look so sad?

Darcy didn't expect her response. The little girl immediately turned and buried her face in her mother's legs and started sobbing.

"Oh, honey, I'm sorry. I didn't want to make you cry." Darcy felt terrible as she watched the child's shoulders shake. "I'm so sorry."

"It's not your fault." The mother was quick to assure her. "Her daddy was killed last week in a drive-by shooting. I was hoping going trick-or-treating would make her smile. Obviously, I was wrong."

Darcy felt herself choke up as the woman spoke, sadness, anger, and hopelessness all expressed on her beautiful caramel-colored face. Darcy quickly reached out and hugged the woman and child to her, tears brimming in her own eyes.

After the mother and daughter left Darcy felt down. Violence was everywhere, or so it seemed. A drive-by shooting. Most likely the father had gotten caught in the crossfire from rival gangs. One of them might even be the gang controlled by Pasquale.

The thought sent shivers racking through her. God, she'd be so glad once he'd been arrested. She would never feel safe until that monster was behind bars.

At eight o'clock she turned her porch light off and shut the front door. It was late enough that trick-or-treaters should be home, and she knew the official hours ended at eight. She had to admit there was a pall on Halloween this year.

Darcy stood in her living room thinking about the way this holiday felt different from those in the past. There was a weight pressing down on her shoulders, a cloud wafting around her. She felt a longing for the Halloweens she'd spent with Aunt Liz.

She was standing there thinking when a sudden crash resounded through the room. The picture window shattered as an orb came crashing into the room and glass splattered across the area. A jack-o-lantern landed at her feet, and the candle inside it flared into a blaze as its flame licked to life as it caught on the rug.

Darcy screamed and began stomping on the flames. She soon realized that was a useless attempt and ran to the kitchen and grabbed the fire extinguisher.

The fire finally died out, and Darcy fell back on the sofa. She scrambled to find her phone and the card Nick had given her. She didn't even think about calling 911. Her first instinct was to call Nick.

Thank God he answered on the first ring.

"Darcy, what's wrong?" His voice was tense, demanding.

Darcy babbled out what had happened. Her voice was almost incomprehensible, but somehow, he managed to understand her need.

"I'm on my way," was his immediate answer.

"Please, don't hang up. Don't leave me alone."

"I won't, Darcy. I'll put you on speaker while I drive. I'm only a few blocks away." Nick's voice was reassuring. "Where are you now?"

"I'm in the living room." Her voice shook, and her teeth chattered. Shock raced through her.

"Is the back door locked?"

"Yes."

"Then stay right where you are. Everything's going to be okay. It's adrenaline making you shake. It's natural. Don't be scared."

She let his rich, smooth voice wash over her. It was soothing, calming, full of confidence and reassurance. She clung to the sound of it as she waited the few minutes for him to arrive. When she saw him pull in the drive, she flung open the door and threw herself into his arms.

Chapter 7

Nick's arms automatically clasped her close. She buried her head in his chest, relishing in his strength, his comfort, and his security. It felt so good there for a moment she didn't want to leave the shelter of his embrace.

Then she noticed the man standing behind Nick. She sucked in her breath, her eyes widening at the sight.

Nick glanced over his shoulder as he reluctantly loosened his grip on Darcy.

"Oh, yeah, meet my brother Nate. He's a cop, too. Gangs division."

She recognized him then. The man with long, straight hair who had been with Nick at the bar that night. He waggled his fingers and nodded at her.

Darcy was taken aback by his handsomeness. He looked much like his brother but with a hipper vibe. Where Nick was dressed in his usual dark suit, which looked great, Nate wore faded jeans and a tight black T-shirt over his rock-hard physique. His eyes were as frosty blue as his brother's, but Nick was clean shaven, and Nate sported a lush, trimmed moustache. While their hair was almost identical in color Nick wore his in an almost military cut while Nate's was lush, sun-streaked and long and loose around his shoulders.

She really preferred Nick's looks, despite Nate's obvious sexiness. But what the hell was she doing? Now was not the time to be comparing the brothers' sexiness. Good Lord, it must be shock. Yeah, that was it. Shock.

"Tell me exactly what happened, Darcy." The sound of his voice brought her back to reality.

"Oh, okay. Oh, Nick, I was so scared. I'd just finished with the last trick-or-treater. Wow, she was a real heartbreaker. So cute, about five years old. Her mom told me her dad had been killed in a drive-by shooting last week. She cried, I cried, her mama cried." She knew she was babbling but couldn't seem to stop herself.

"Darcy, what happened to the window?" He looked towards the broken glass that lay scattered on the floor.

"Oh, yeah, well, I had just come in and shut the door and turned off the porch light. I was just standing here thinking when bam! There was this great big crash and glass flew everywhere. The rug caught on fire, but I used the extinguisher and got it out. Then I called you."

"Where exactly were you when the window broke?"

"I was standing right here." She moved into the living room just a couple feet from where the pumpkin lay. "I was just thinking, and then everything exploded."

"Okay. Why don't you go wait in the kitchen? I'll look around, and I've got backup on the way. Oh, looks like they're here now." Nick looked out at the flashing lights that pulled up out front as they cast eerie shadows against the wall.

Darcy agreed and slipped quietly out of the room as Nick opened the door for the other officers. She sat at the kitchen table and wrapped her arms around her chest as the shakes began to take over. A wave of nausea swept over her, and for a moment she felt faint.

"Hey, how you holding up?" Nate walked in to join her and sat across the table.

"I'm starting to fall apart I think," Darcy confessed. "Damn, I don't want to be wrapped up in all this."

"I understand. Nobody wants to get caught up in this kind of mess." Nate's voice was solemn. "But sometimes things happen that we just can't control. I'm interested in your situation, too, because Pasquale is definitely involved in the

Bad Ass Banditos gang. He's a big man in charge. He's into a lot of bad stuff."

"So I've heard. I just can't figure out why he came after Papa."

"It wasn't Papa they were after. It was his son."

"What? Rico?" Shock ran through her body as his words sank in. Rico seemed like a quiet, hardworking guy. He'd always been straight and kept his nose clean as far as Darcy could tell.

"Rico wasn't what he seemed. He was into the dark side. He dealt drugs. He laundered money through the restaurant. He was also greedy. He tried to pull one over on the Banditos."

"Rico? Are you sure?" She had trouble envisioning the young man with the receding hairline and bulging midline involved in such underhanded dealings.

"Positive. We'd been planning on busting him a day or two after he was killed."

Darcy sat and let his words sink in. It seemed so impossible.

"Darcy." She jerked as she heard her name called and looked up to find Nick entering the room, the pumpkin clutched in his gloved hands. Without a word he held it up and let her read the message that was carved into the orange flesh:

SHUT UP BITCH

Her breath caught in her throat as she read the words. There was no doubting the message she was being sent.

She stared at the orange globe. The words sank in and sparked a flame of anger. How dare they threaten her. She'd now been attacked in her own home, and that pissed her off.

She felt her spine stiffen. She looked straight into Nick's eyes and uttered, "Let's get this bastard."

He returned her gaze, and a grin spread across his face. "That's the plan, ma'am."

Crime scene investigators scurried around gathering what little evidence there was. When she was given the go-ahead, Darcy started cleaning up the scattered glass. Nick and

Nate found a large sheet of plywood in the garage and nailed it up over the gaping hole in the wall. Finally, Darcy went to the kitchen and put a pot of coffee on, and they gathered around the table for a well-deserved break.

"You guys must be hungry. Have some cake. I just made it this morning."

Both men accepted a piece of the flaky chocolate cake with chocolate frosting and dug in with enthusiasm. Darcy poured the coffee and finally collapsed into a chair herself.

"Now comes the big question. Is there anyone you could stay with tonight? I don't think you should stay here alone." Nick paused in enjoying his cake to eye her seriously. "It's not safe."

Darcy's mind immediately flashed to Sophie, but unfortunately, she was out of town. There was no one else that she could think of. She had some friends from her former job, but she wouldn't feel right asking them to put her up. She shook her head reluctantly.

"There's only Sophie, and she's away this weekend."

"I really don't like the thought of you staying here by yourself."

"I'll be fine."

A look of skepticism crossed his face.

"No, I will. I'm a big girl."

"Not that big."

Darcy shot him a hot glare while Nate grinned as they debated.

Darcy was about to make an angry retort when her cell phone rang. She pulled it out of the pocket of her witch costume. She glanced at the caller ID, expecting it to be Sophie, but instead it was a number she didn't recognize. She followed an instinct and put the phone on speaker before answering. Her voice sounded questioning as she said, "Hello?"

"Did you like my little present?" A slimy voice came across the line, and Darcy's eyes grew wide. Nick and Nate both came to attention, their spines stiffening.

"Who...who is this?" Darcy stammered.

"Who is this?" he mimicked. "Lady, I'm your worst nightmare."

"What do you want?"

"I want you to keep your mouth shut, got it?"

"About what?"

"Don't get smart. You know I'm talking about what happened at Papa's Place."

"How do you know I know anything about it?" She couldn't believe she was bold enough to ask the question.

"I know everything. There are no secrets from me."

"You sound pretty sure of yourself."

"I am. I have my ways. I can find out anything."

"Then you ought to know I won't have a choice in the matter. I'll get subpoenaed even if I don't voluntarily testify."

"Okay, play stupid, bitch, and see where that gets you. You don't have to tell them anything. You forgot, that's all."

"I...I'm not a good liar."

"Well, you better learn fast, lady, because if you don't, you'll be dead. Got it? If you testify against me, you'll die. And it won't be an easy way to go."

His voice was a hiss by the time he stopped talking...and then he was gone.

Chapter 8

First Darcy's face flushed scarlet, then the blood receded, and she turned milky white. Her vision blurred for a moment and a wave of nausea flooded over her. When she realized she was still holding the phone, she tossed it on the table like it was a venomous viper.

"Okay, Darcy, it's okay." Nick's voice seemed to come floating through a fog. "We're going to take care of you."

"Do you promise, Nick? Can you promise me I'll live through this?" Her brown eyes were huge and intense, and she reached out and grabbed his lapels. "I don't want to die."

"I promise I will not let you die. I'll die before I'll let you die." Nick's face was serious, his eyes icy and silver. "One thing is for certain now. You're not staying here alone tonight."

"I agree." Nate stepped up laid his hand on Darcy's shoulder. "Consider yourself adopted by the Bakers. Now the question is, where are we going to keep her?"

"And Warlock," Darcy hurried to add.

"And Warlock," Nick agreed.

"How about Mom's?" Nate suggested.

"Mom's would be great. I hate to call her now, though. You know she gets scared as hell when the phone rings after ten."

"Should we try the twins?"

"I think that would be best. After all, they are cops."

"Wait," Darcy interrupted. "Who are the twins?"

"They're our sisters. Our twisted sisters." Nick said with a smile. "You'll love them. They're about your age, and they love cats. In fact, they have two of their own."

"I'm not sure how Warlock will feel about that, but he'll just have to adjust, I guess. And hopefully, we won't be there too long."

"I hope not too, Darcy." Nick pulled his phone from his pocket and dialed a number. Apparently, the call was answered immediately.

"Hi, Nora." He greeted his sister then walked away to continue the conversation.

Darcy shook her head as if to shake off the confusion settling over her. Everything was happening so fast. Just a few hours ago she had been happily passing out candy to kids, and now she was preparing to evacuate her home. Panic started to swell within her.

"Hey, Darcy, it'll be okay. Don't flip out on us now. Keep your cool." Nate slipped his arm around her and hugged her. "You're a hero, you know."

"I don't feel like one. I feel like a cowardly wimp." She leaned her head against his chest and closed her eyes, trying to slow her breathing. He felt comfortable, soothing.

Nick walked back in the room at that moment and raised a single eyebrow when he saw her snuggled up against Nate's chest. "Okay, it's all set. Nora and Natalie will be happy to put you up."

For some reason, Darcy felt guilty for being in Nate's arms. She didn't know why. There was no spark there, despite how hunky and handsome Nate was, but feeling Nick's eyes on her, she felt uncomfortable.

"I better go pack," she muttered, moving away from the shelter of Nate's presence. She scurried from the room and ran upstairs and started packing. It almost felt as if Nick was still staring at her, a bit of hurt in his eyes. That was silly, though. They barely knew each other.

Darcy didn't even know what she packed but eventually made her way downstairs toting a suitcase and a duffel bag crammed with clothes, hair dryer, shoes, and laptop. She didn't know how long she'd be gone or what she needed, so she packed all kinds of things. The last thing she grabbed was Warlock, who she stuffed in his crate. She was immediately rewarded with a haughty look and a snarl.

"I know, Warlock, I don't like this any better than you do," she assured him. Throwing the duffel over her shoulder and grabbing the crate and suitcase each in one hand, she headed downstairs to leave her home.

"Just one more thing." Nick stopped her before she walked out the door. She turned and looked at him. "You might want to get rid of the wart."

Nora, Natalie, and Darcy sat around the kitchen table, lingering over coffee and muffins. Nora was off today, and Natalie didn't have to work tonight, so no one was in any hurry. Nora and Natalie had made Darcy feel so comfortable that she'd gotten up early and made the orange pineapple muffins as a treat.

She and Warlock had been here for two days. Darcy wasn't given a chance to feel uncomfortable or out of place. As soon as she walked in to the twins' condo, she was welcomed and made to feel right at home. Warlock had come out of his carrier and strutted around surveying his new kingdom and allowed Peaches and Cream, the twins' female cats, to sniff him then swaggered away to claim his place on the windowsill.

Darcy studied the twins across the table. They looked identical, except Natalie wore her hair in a short pixie cut and Nora's hair was shoulder length. They both had sparkling eyes like their brothers and the same dark hair as Nick. The family resemblance was amazing. They were a feminine version of their brothers, both fit and slim.

"You know, not only do you two look alike, you look just like your brothers." By then Darcy knew that the third man at the piano bar with Nick was also his brother. Noah was the youngest of the three boys and was, like his brothers, also a police officer. The entire family was cops. "There are really strong genes in your family."

"That's thanks to Daddy," Natalie noted confidently. "We all look just like him."

"Except we've got Mama's eyes," Nora added. "And Natalie and Noah have her curly hair. But we've all got the one dimple and high cheekbones like our dad."

"Daddy's a police officer, too. A captain." Natalie spoke through a mouthful of muffin.

"It's a tradition. Grandpa was CPD, too."

Darcy shook her head in wonder. "How does your mom stand it? The stress, I mean. My dad was a cop who got killed on duty. My mom fell apart afterwards. I can't imagine worrying every day about your entire family. I'll never get emotionally involved with a cop."

Both twins' eyes flew wide open, and they exchanged a conspiratorial look.

"Are you sure? Not even if it was a match made in heaven?"

"Not if it was the last man on earth," Darcy resounded stoutly. "Nothing could make me put myself under that kind of stress."

The twins looked at each other and inexplicably giggled. Darcy didn't get the joke. She meant every word she said. She was just about to emphasize her point when her cell phone rang. She didn't think to look at her caller ID because Sophie was due to call when she got back in town. It was probably her.

"I know where you are," was the first thing she heard after she answered the phone.

"What...what did you say?"

"I said I know where you are. You're staying with those cop sisters."

"Who is this?"

"Oh, you're going to play dumb again are you? Let me tell you something, lady. You can run, but you can't hide. I'll find you, and you won't be able to testify against me."

"Why don't you just leave me alone?" Her voice rose as she talked, and she felt herself begin to shake.

"Just keep your mouth shut, bitch, or I'll shut it for you...permanently." The words were snarled just before the line disconnected, and Darcy wrapped her phone in a death grip. The twins had come to stand on either side of her, both laying a comforting hand on her shoulder.

"Call Nick," Natalie ordered her sister. "Tell him to get his ass over here."

Chapter 9

"I won't go." Darcy clamped her lips together and crossed her arms.

"Darcy, you have to go. It's the only way to protect you."

"You want to drag me off to some lost-in-the-wilderness cabin and keep me there for God knows how long? I don't think so."

A frustrated scowl marred Nick's handsome features. "Look, do you want to die?"

His blunt statement was like a punch in the gut, and her cheeks paled.

"Because that's exactly what could happen if you stay here. And not just you. You're putting Nora and Natalie in danger, too. They're cops. They'd die trying to protect you, you know."

Darcy did know. The twins had sworn to keep her safe, but she knew she was hazardous to their health. She swallowed a big fat lump that had risen in her throat.

Nick knelt down before her and laid his hands on her knees. "Darcy, it won't be forever. Just until we arrest Pasquale. The cabin's only a few hours north of here. Nobody will know where you're at. Only my captain and my family."

Darcy didn't want to endanger the twins. She didn't have a job, so there really was no reason not to go. But the thought of being alone with Nick for days...and nights...just the two of them...well, the very thought made her breath catch in her throat. He was too handsome, too macho.

And she was too sex deprived to resist, she admitted to herself. She'd been without a man too long.

Of course, Nick hadn't even shown an interest in her other than professionally. What made her think he was even attracted to her sexually?

Darcy had never considered herself a coward, but she was beginning to realize she had a broad yellow stripe down her back. It was natural to be worried about Pasquale, she figured, but why was she so frightened to be alone with a man who had treated her with nothing but respect? A man who was a police detective.

"You can't be away from work, can you?"

"I've got some vacation time coming. I was going to the cabin anyway. I've already talked it over with my captain. There's no problem."

Darcy closed her eyes and fought a silent battle. She didn't want to leave Chicago; she had never spent much time in the woods. She liked being able to pop out for coffee or to get her nails done. She liked shopping and eating out and going dancing. She adored her house, she loved her closeness with Sophie, and she loved her life, at least when she had an income besides unemployment. Could she stand to leave it all behind?

Even more pressing, however...could she stand to be responsible for the life of Nora or Natalie? The two women had been nothing but kind to her. They'd made her welcome in their home, laughed and cried with her as they watched movies together, they'd offered to protect her. Regardless of her own selfish reasons for avoiding Pasquale, did she have the right to endanger the lives of the two sisters?

No. She couldn't put them in that position. She really didn't have a choice. She had to get away to keep Nora and Natalie safe.

Her shoulders lowered, and a look of defeat came over her face. "Okay. I'll go."

They were on their way before four that afternoon. Once the decision had been made, they didn't waste time. Once again Darcy packed up to hit the road. They made a quick swing past her place, checked out the repaired window, and she repacked. Next, they made a stop by Nick's place. She noted the minimalist atmosphere as she waited in his simply decorated black and white living room while he packed. It was as different from her own, cozy home as it could be. His only decorations were a few black and white prints on the walls, whereas she had rooms full of eclectic, colorful pieces.

Yet there was something sexy about the sleek, clean lines Nick had chosen. It was cold but sophisticated. Even if his kitchen did look as if it had never been used. It reminded her of him, dressed in his tailored black suits and crisp white shirts.

"Help yourself to a drink out of the fridge," he called from the bedroom.

Darcy walked into the kitchen and opened the refrigerator. There wasn't much food, basically just ketchup, mustard and a suspicious looking half-gallon of milk, but there were plenty of drinks to choose from. Soda, water, beer were all there. Darcy grabbed a soda and flipped it open.

"I'll take one of those, too," Nick spoke from behind her, and she whirled to face him.

She wasn't prepared for the transformation. Gone was the buttoned-up, serious detective. No suit, no tie, no white shirt. Instead, she gazed at a handsome hunk dressed in tight, faded jeans, a snug-fitting blue tee-shirt, and a blue and black plaid flannel shirt hanging open over the tee. His feet were no longer clad in black dress shoes, but instead, he wore black leather hiking boots.

He looked like a model who had just stepped out of an LL Bean catalogue. He looked somehow younger, more carefree and natural. He'd been amazingly sexy in his suit, but somehow, he looked even more appealing in casual clothing. She felt her breath catch in her throat, a trill running along her spine.

He turned a curious gaze on her, and she tried to cover up her hungry hormones. She let her hand fly to her chest and said, "You startled me."

"Sorry. Didn't mean to." His voice was gruff, but his smile softened his tone. "I'm ready to hit the road if you are."

Two and a half hours later Nick pulled into a grocery store in a small town in northwest Wisconsin. They were about a half hour from Eau Claire, in a heavily wooded, hilly area. The sun was slipping behind the hills, a pale twilight filtering through the air.

Darcy was surprised by how pleasant the trip had been. They'd driven quietly, soft country music playing on the radio. She was amazed they liked the same station. Nick talked about the cabin, which really belonged to the family, but he was the one who actually used it the most. From what he told her the cabin had been in his family for three generations. It was isolated and located up in the hills above a small lake. According to Nick, it was one of the most beautiful places in the world.

His voice warmed as he spoke of the cabin. He loved the place, she could tell.

"It is pretty far from the store, though," he admitted. "That's why we need to stock up on the basics before we get there."

Darcy stepped out of the SUV and stretched. They'd only stopped once on the way to get gas and use the restroom.

It felt odd to be in the grocery picking out food with Nick. They definitely had different tastes. They hadn't been there long before Darcy decided to grab her own cart and start filling it with her choices.

For every frozen pizza he put in his cart, she selected a fresh meat. Each time he added a bag of chips she added fresh produce. By the time she placed a loaf of French bread in her cart, he was openly grinning.

"I hope you like to cook," he said.

"I like to eat; therefore I cook." She cocked her head at him, a twinkle in her eyes.

"Well, I like to eat, but I don't like to cook. Therefore," he grinned wickedly, "I microwave."

"We'll see whose food gets eaten the most."

"You're on." He reached out to shake her hand and when their palms met Darcy felt a chill zip through her then a flash of heat that built swiftly. It started in her fingertips and blazed through her arm straight to her cheeks, detouring through her feminine parts. She gave his hand a brief shake and tried to pull hers back, but he clamped it in his and held on.

Darcy raised her gaze, and it locked with his. For a long, frozen moment in time, they stood there, hands clasped, her heart skipping erratically. Her breath fluttered in her throat, not reaching her lungs.

She finally managed to remove her hand from his and turned quickly to her shopping cart. What had just happened? She hadn't felt a surge like that in...well, she couldn't remember the last time.

"I don't know how many days we need to shop for," she muttered, scanning the contents of her cart.

"We'll get plenty. Better safe than sorry."

Better safe than sorry, she silently repeated his words. Good advice in more ways than one.

Chapter 10

The sun had set completely by the time they arrived at the cabin. She could make out a timber structure with a wide front porch and lots of windows, but that was about all. Nick pulled the car next to the house and hurried to unlock the front door, flipping on the porch light before returning and starting to unload the car. Darcy grabbed a couple of shopping bags and joined him inside.

This wasn't the rustic cabin she had expected. The living room ran the length of the house and had a full glass wall on one end. A river rock fireplace spanned one wall, and cozy furnishings were scattered about. The walls, the floors, and the ceilings were all constructed of wood with a warm, rich finish, and here and there soft rugs made pools of color.

"Wow. This is a cabin?" Darcy looked around appreciatively as she moved to place the bags she carried onto the granite island. "It's more like a mansion."

Nick laughed. "Not hardly. But when there are lots of people in a family, and most of them are men that are pretty good with tools, you can make something fairly special."

"Indeed," was all she whispered, still taking in the spaciousness of the place.

"We'll put these groceries up, and I'll give you a tour."

"Sounds good to me." She turned and went back out to the car to retrieve Warlock's carrier and a suitcase. One more trip for the last of the groceries and they were finished bringing stuff in, and then Darcy turned to putting away the provisions. Nick helped, pointing out where things went as he stowed their purchases. She couldn't help but notice the well-supplied pantry filled with canned goods and staples.

"My mom and the girls make sure to keep the place stocked up," Nick confessed. "Okay, now I'll show you where you can sleep."

They grabbed their bags and headed up the stairs with its beautiful twig railing and landed in a large, spacious loft with four sofa beds scattered about. She leaned on the railing and admired the open view of the floor below.

Nick waited just a moment then took off to the left and opened a door into an end room.

"This is where you'll stay," he informed her.

"It's beautiful," Darcy exclaimed.

Nick's eyes twinkled. "I knew you'd like it."

"I love it." She twirled around as she took in the brass bed, the colorful patchwork quilt, and a small wooden rocker in the corner. Apparently, Warlock liked it, too, she thought as she watched her cat turn in a circle before lying down in the middle of the bed.

"I'm on the other side of the loft," he told her. "If you ever need me during the night, just holler."

No, no way. She would not need him during the night. That was way too risky.

"Come on, I'll show you the basement then we can grab a bite to eat."

Darcy followed him downstairs and saw a finished basement that included a pool table and another huge bedroom and bath. Wow, her little house could fit in half this basement alone.

Darcy was still stunned when they returned to the kitchen. She couldn't get over the beauty of the cabin. It felt welcoming, peaceful and warm, safe and secure. She mustn't drop her guard, though. There was too much at stake.

"How about a grilled cheese sandwich and a can of soup?" Nick asked. "I can rustle that up."

"As tired as I am tonight, I'll take it." She flipped her braid over her shoulder and smiled wryly. "I'll make breakfast in the morning."

"Is that a promise?" he asked.

"I promise."

"That's a deal." He smiled warmly and started to whistle as he began buttering bread. She noted with shock that the tune he whistled was Can't Help Falling in Love with You.

After they finished eating, an awkward feeling fell over Darcy. They were going to basically be living together for at least a few days and she barely knew him. All she knew was she really liked what she saw. Nick was big and strong and hot as hell. Being isolated here with him was going to be...well.... challenging.

Darcy carried their soup bowls to the sink and rinsed them before sticking them in the dishwasher. She had to admit, though, she was intrigued by more than his looks. He was dedicated to his work, devoted to his family. And, she sighed, Warlock liked him. Warlock had been known to slash the cheek of one of Darcy's dates he didn't approve of. But he accepted Nick without question. She knew it sounded silly, but she trusted her cat's judgment.

There was just one thing stopping her jumping his bones, she thought as she ran a damp cloth across the countertop. He was a cop.

She'd never forgotten the night her father died. Darcy had been busily making him a birthday card, her mother in the kitchen icing his cake. Her mom had never been very domestic, but she tried hard. The cake she'd made was a five-layer chocolate cake, but unfortunately, it was only about three inches thick. Marie Campbell was busily piling on extra thick chocolate frosting trying to make the cake look taller when the doorbell rang.

Darcy hadn't paid much attention until her mother's scream cut through the air. When hysterical sobbing followed the outburst, Darcy had tiptoed from her chair and peeked around the dining room wall. Her mother was on her hands and knees, her chest heaving and her two large police officers hovering over her. She heard her mother say over and over again, "I want to die. God, take me now, I have nothing to live for."

Her mother had never been the same afterwards. She'd been so dependent, so reliant on Darcy's father that she simply was never whole again. It was like both her parents had died. Marie changed drastically. She became even more nervous and unsure. Never having handled finances before or held a job, she floundered. She turned away from Darcy, who looked so much like her father and tried to drown her pain in alcohol and other men.

Those were hard years for Darcy. Her mother barely functioned, rarely cooking, often drinking too much. There were times her mother brought men home. One night she'd awakened and found one of those men standing over her bed. She'd screamed in terror, and he left, but her mother slept through the whole thing.

And then Marie met Bruce. Bruce was good looking, big, and smooth. Marie seemed hypnotized by him. But he was mean. He was mean to her mom and mean to her. One night he punched her mother in front of Darcy and Darcy went wild, leaping at Bruce with her fingers clawed and fire in her eyes. Of course, as a 12-year-old Darcy didn't have a chance against a two-hundred-pound man. He tossed her off like he was batting a mosquito, sending her rolling across the floor and crashing into a buffet. When she came to, she found her mother dead and Bruce gone.

"Darcy." Nick's voice seemed to come through a cloud. Lost in her memories, she realized she'd been staring into space. "Darcy."

She shook her head and rinsed out the cloth she'd been using.

"Sorry. I guess I'm more tired than I thought. I think I'll go upstairs and unpack and go to bed." Darcy wiped her hands on her jeans and moved to leave. "Good night."

Nick didn't say anything, just eyed her for a long moment from under his thick, long lashes. When she was past him, he called her name, placing his palm on her upper arm. She paused, turning to face him.

"Sweet dreams," he murmured, a soft smile on his lips.

Sweet dreams. Not likely, she thought. Not with thoughts of her mother, Pasquale, and Nick himself swilling through her mind.

"Thanks. You, too." She managed a weak smile before hurrying from the room.

Chapter 11

Much to her amazement, Darcy slept soundly that night. The bed molded around her, seeming to cradle her in comfort. A soft breeze sighed through the slightly open windows, and she snuggled under the blankets. She didn't dream at all, sweet or otherwise. Her reserves had finally run out, and she gave in to deep, blissful slumber.

It was the quiet of the dawn that eventually woke her. No revving engines, grinding garbage trucks, or wailing sirens filled the air. No neighbors hollered back and forth, no doors slammed.

Instead, a soft symphony of bird song feathered through the air and other than that there was silence. She lay there blinking in the pale golden light, breathing in the tranquility. A sudden flare of curiosity flickered through her. She wanted to see this place in the daylight.

She didn't waste any time getting out of bed, immediately drawn to the balcony outside the French doors. Slipping a robe on over her nightshirt, she stepped out onto the wooden surface and gasped. She hadn't expected to see a view like this.

Below, the yard rolled away to a wide band of trees then descended on to a steel-blue lake that spread out like a bottle of spilled ink. A layer of fog lay just above the still surface of the water and golden-rose rays played across the gentle waves lapping against the shoreline.

Darcy was aware of the chill of the frosty morning but was too hypnotized by the view to withdraw. The autumn colors swirled before her, painting a patchwork of patterns and arrays of varying shades and hues.

She held her breath as a half dozen deer tiptoed out from the woods and began to drink at the edge of the lake. Deer, right there in front of her. They almost seemed close enough to reach out and touch.

She watched fascinated until the damp chill began to gnaw at her. She turned, tugging her pink fuzzy robe tighter around her and moved to go back inside. That's when she saw Nick.

He stood there staring at her. A plaid wool robe did little to disguise his physique. His shoulders rippled beneath the fabric. He worked out, it was obvious from the size of his biceps. A belt cinched the robe around a trim waist and sculpted legs covered in thick, black curls, ending in leather moccasins.

She froze at the sight of him. His eyes were looking at her intently. She couldn't help but lock gazes with him, her eyes widening as she took in the sight of him framed by the natural background.

A slow grin slid across his face as he assessed the rumpled look of her. Her hair was loose and tumbling, shining in the morning sun, her breasts unbound beneath the robe.

She was suddenly very aware of her boobs, a heaviness swelling their crowns. A low humming throbbed in her lady parts, almost building to a growl. Her amber eyes locked with his pewter ones and they stood for a long moment without speaking.

He was the first to break the silence.

"Good morning, Darcy. Beautiful isn't it?"

"Absolutely. Incredible." She brushed a breeze-tossed curl away from her cheek, finally breaking eye contact with him.

"I'll be happy to show you around more after that breakfast you promised me."

Darcy's eyes widened. She was supposed to be fixing breakfast this morning and instead she'd been eyeballing the view, including ogling the man who was supposed to be protecting her. Hell, someone was going to have to protect him from her and her overactive hormones if she didn't quit that shit.

"I'm on it, boss," she called back, tossing him a salute. She didn't want him to see the affect he had on her, so she kept it casual. "See you downstairs."

Darcy almost ran to her room she was so anxious to escape his macho presence. A quick, cold shower, then she slipped into a pair of comfy jeans and a soft sweater of turquoise blue. She slid her feet into a pair of soft ankle boots and did her hair in a quick braid. A swish of mascara and a touch of lip gloss and she was ready to face the day with Nick.

The cabin was even more impressive in the daylight. She couldn't help gawking at the space as she made her way to the kitchen. Everything felt timeless like it had been in this rustic setting forever. She was almost sidetracked again by the view out the window but forced herself to keep marching.

She was amazed by the modern kitchen in such a country setting. There was a huge island, a well-stocked pantry, and a six-burner gas stovetop. The kitchen inspired her. She loved to cook, and this space was a cook's dream. She quickly began whipping up a batch of Belgian waffles and crispy bacon.

Nick came into the kitchen, his hair still damp from the shower. Darcy tried not to eye his body clad in jeans and a flannel shirt. God, he looked hot.

He poured himself a cup of black coffee and sat at the bar while she bustled around. She was aware of his gaze on her the entire time. She almost wanted to scream at him to stop watching her. She turned a piece of bacon and gasped as the grease popped and burned her cheek.

"Ow!" She hollered and raised a hand to her cheek.

Nick was on his feet and around the island in a flash.

"Let me see," he commanded, pulling her hand down from her face.

"I'm okay," she protested.

He pulled her close and examined her face carefully. She held her breath as she felt her body pressed between his and the cabinets and his arms clamped around her holding her in place. His silver-blue gaze swept over her face, taking in its blemish-free surface.

"It looks okay." He spoke quietly.

"It is okay," she insisted, wriggling in an attempt to escape his closeness, but he didn't even seem to notice.

"You know," he continued as his eyes focused on hers, "my mom used to say a kiss would make any owie better." A smile played across his lips just before he lowered his mouth and placed a gentle kiss on her cheek. "She also believes freckles are places angels kissed."

Darcy's eyes fluttered as she felt his lips tenderly brush against her skin. Her heart tripped, and she felt a jolt clear down to her nether regions. God, if just a kiss on her cheek affected her this much, she couldn't imagine what a full on liplock would do to her.

"I've got to turn the bacon." Her voice sounded breathy to her own ears.

Nick grinned and stepped away from her. She moved around him and focused on the bacon. Damn him, anyway. He was playing with her, and she didn't appreciate it. He was supposed to be protecting her but what she wanted to know was who was going to protect him from her?

Breakfast finished, Nick encouraged her to grab her coat and come explore outdoors with him. She pulled on a leather bomber jacket and joined him in his survey of the acreage.

The land was amazing. To a city girl used to the urban landscape, it was incredible to walk amongst the tall timbers, to listen to the sounds of nature. The breeze soughed through the trees, almost seeming to sing. She followed Nick down the path through the woods, taking in the natural setting and the peace and tranquility. She paused to let a rabbit hop in front of her. This was a traffic jam here. So much different from the city.

She followed Nick as he followed a trail down to the lakeshore. There was a long dock that led on to the lake, a boat house on the right.

"I'll be happy to get the boat out and take you around the lake," Nick informed her, stuffing his hands in the pockets of his blue jeans. Darcy couldn't help but notice how the fabric pulled tight across his crotch. She changed the direction of her gaze, but the tingle still shot through her.

"That sounds great. How big is the lake?"

"360 acres." She couldn't miss the tinge of pride in his voice.

She cast her gaze upward as a flock of geese flew overhead, their honking filling the air.

"Let's go this afternoon when the fog is gone. You'll be able to really check out the scenery."

"Sounds good." The idea excited her. She loved boats, and the idea of cruising over the lake's smooth surface was quite the turn on. Like she needed anything else to turn her on, she thought grumpily. Just being close to Nick seemed to make her horny. And the last thing she needed was to hook up with Nick. He was a cop. A nightmare waiting to happen. She had to stop hungering for him and start acting like he was just an ordinary man.

Yeah, right.

Chapter 12

They spent the rest of the morning tramping through the woods. Nick pointed out interesting sights from his childhood, including where he and his brothers had built a clubhouse and the spot where they had hidden an injured deer and nursed it back to health. She could easily picture the three brothers working together to save the life of a young fawn.

They finally wound their way back to the house, and Darcy whipped up some stir-fry for lunch. Then Nick announced it was time for their boat ride. She nearly hopped with excitement.

It turned out there was both a motorboat and a pontoon boat stored in the boathouse.

"Let's take the pontoon. You can move around on it and see both sides."

Darcy agreed, and a few moments later they were motoring down the lake. She drew in a deep lungful of the sweet air, tipping her face up to the sun. The air was cool but rich with the aroma of the water and the surrounding hills. She heard birds calling and an occasional fish jump. Other than that, it was silent.

There wasn't any awkwardness in the quiet, though. Darcy and Nick both enjoyed the tranquility for several minutes before Nick spoke.

"Up here on the right, you'll probably see a beaver lodge. They usually build on this stream that connects to the lake. Keep your eyes open."

Darcy strained to catch sight of the natural construction and gasped when it came into view. Timber and stones were intricately piled across the mouth of the creek, water pooling behind it.

"Oh my gosh. There's a beaver," she whispered, staring in fascination at the brown rodent. "It's so big."

"Yeah. Beavers can grow to nearly four feet long, counting their tail. Uh, oh, he's spotted us. Watch."

Darcy saw the animal smack his broad tail against the water several times before disappearing beneath the water's surface.

"That's his warning system for his buddies. He let them know there could be danger in the area." Nick idled the boat and moved to stand beside her at the rail.

"And they really did all that by themselves?" she murmured, still studying the lodge.

"Yep. They're great architects. They'll store their food for winter in the water and in their lodge. Most lodges actually have two rooms, one for drying when they come up through the water to get in and one to socialize and sleep." Darcy listened to him talk, enjoying the smooth timbre of his voice. "You know, they say beavers mate for life."

Darcy felt color flood her cheeks as she felt his gaze on her. Damn, he shouldn't talk about mating. Now all she could envision was her and him.... mating.

"So they enter their house through the water?" She grabbed on to the additional information to attempt to change the subject. He nodded and continued to keep his eyes on her. Damn, he needed to quit looking at her like that. Like he cared about her, like he truly liked her. She didn't want that kind of relationship with him. She had no desire to have a relationship with a cop.

But who said she had to let emotions get involved? Maybe she could just use him to satisfy her sexually. The thought was strange to her because she wasn't really the promiscuous type. Yeah, she'd been with a few men, but she had to admit she'd had feelings for them and maybe even a little hope for a future together, but none of them had worked out.

But she'd never been one to just indulge in sex for sex's sake. And she knew she never wanted to live a life in fear like her mother had. She'd spent too many evenings with the nervous woman who relied so much on her husband. Living with a cop added way too much stress to life.

Darcy broke her gaze away from his and turned to study the horizon. She couldn't think about this right now. Her life had already been turned upside down. She didn't need any more complications.

Nick moved back to man the motor again, and they took off, Darcy turning her face to the wind and letting it whip away her confusing thoughts.

Once they returned to the house, Darcy escaped to her room. She used the time alone to talk herself down from her raging hormone overdrive. Nick Baker was just a man. A man who, admittedly, was delicious eye candy and who also seemed to have a pull over her. But now was not the time to indulge in sexual play. She needed to focus on staying alive long enough to testify against Dimitri Pasquale.

After a little while, she felt calmer and put in a call to Sophie. Her friend was worried about her.

"Don't worry, Soph. Nobody except you, Nick and his brothers, and his captain know where I am."

"I want to see you for myself. I don't like you being missing."

Darcy laughed out loud. "Sophie, honey, I'm not missing. You know where I am."

"Yes, but you left without me seeing you, making sure you were okay. I don't like it."

"I'm sorry. If I knew how to get you here, I would."

"I just hope this whole thing wraps up soon and things get back to normal."

"You and me both, sister, you and me both." Darcy sighed with frustration. She didn't tell Sophie that one of the main reasons she wanted to end this enforced "vacation" was to get away from Nick Baker. He felt almost as dangerous to her mental health as Dimitri Pasquale did to her physical safety.

Darcy ended the call with Sophie still grumbling about her absence. She needed to get downstairs and start dinner. A bit of pride made her want to show off her cooking skills since he'd made fun of her grocery purchases. Life was better when you ate real food.

That thought had her smiling as she entered the kitchen and saw Nick on the sofa in the family room watching the news. He greeted her and straightened up in his seat, popping his stocking clad feet on the coffee table.

He looked young and comfortable, like he didn't have a care in the world. And completely different from the formal, professional detective she'd first met. She was starting to like this new, homier guy.

"You look happy," he commented.

"I just got off the phone with Sophie. She's fussing, as usual." Darcy moved around the counter and opened the fridge. "She's upset because she can't see me for herself to make sure I'm really okay."

"She's a good friend, isn't she?" He actually sounded interested.

"The best," Darcy answered with a smile. She pulled a pack of boneless chicken breast from the fridge. Soon she had fajitas sizzling in a cast iron skillet and some chopped fruit with a honey and yogurt cream for desert.

She watched with pleasure as Nick dug into the meal. He ate heartily, truly enjoying the food.

"So, is that better than a frozen pizza?" She couldn't help picking at him.

"Oh my god, so good." He dipped his fajita into the fresh guacamole she'd made.

She couldn't help but notice how comfortable they were together. Conversation flowed easily even though she was constantly aware of his sexiness. He kept her laughing, and that made her relax. When he moved to help her clean up, she felt a flare of admiration flicker to life. Not only was he a good conversationalist, he did dishes.

After the kitchen was clean, they retreated to the family room and watched a funny movie on TV. He made popcorn before they started another movie and spent a quiet, comfortable evening together before Darcy said good night and headed to bed.

She felt happier than she had in a long time. In spite of the danger looming around her, she felt better than she had since the murders. She and Nick might be hiding out, but it didn't feel like it. It actually felt like they were simply spending time together and enjoying the environment and the serenity of the natural beauty of the Wisconsin woods.

If only it really was actuality. A shiver ran down her spine as she swallowed a big dose of reality. No matter how good the situation felt she needed to remember they were not here for fun. She needed to remember this was a matter of life and death.

She swallowed as she let herself into the bedroom. Now that was something to think about.

Chapter 13

Warlock woke her up the next morning as he stood on her chest and kneaded her flesh. His purr was a loud rumble, his head rubbing against her chin.

"Are you trying to tell me it's time to get up, fella?" She scratched his black head and ran her hand down the length of him and up and over his tail. He arched in appreciation, and she did it again to please him. "Okay, let's get this day started, big guy."

Darcy showered and dressed and began what was to become a routine the next few days. She fed Warlock then started breakfast. Soon she had breakfast on the table, and Nick came in from outside and joined her. They ate, cleaned up, and headed back outdoors. They hiked the hills or explored the lake. In the afternoon they had lunch then went back outside. One day they even had a picnic lunch high on a hill overlooking the lake.

Darcy found herself feeling more and more comfortable around Nick. It wasn't that she found him any less sexy. Not at all. But she felt more in control. Nick was a perfect gentleman, and she only had to worry about her attacking him, not fighting off advances. She managed to keep her own libido under control, so they hadn't had any clashes yet.

The evenings were spent reading and watching TV. Nick often built a fire for them to relax in front of, and a couple of evenings she made mulled cider. The peace and serenity were just what the doctor ordered as far as Darcy was concerned. She felt herself unwinding and chilling out.

One day they woke up and the sky was gray, the winds whipping around the corner of the house. She didn't think anything about it when he decided to stay in that morning, and Darcy started a load of laundry while Nick hung a shelf in the dining room. She was busily folding a load of whites when the doorbell rang.

Darcy froze. It seemed like such a foreign sound after being completely isolated. My God, what if Pasquale had found her. She started to panic then remembered—killers don't ring doorbells. Her heart settled down a little bit, but Darcy still didn't move out of the laundry room. She had no idea who was out there.

Until she heard a familiar voice. No, it couldn't be Sophie, not here. But it was! Oh my god, Sophie was here.

Darcy raced out of the laundry room to wrap her around her best friend. The two girls squealed and hugged and jumped up and down as if they'd been apart for months instead of days.

"My God, I can't believe you're here. How did you get here?" Darcy gasped.

"Courtesy of Nate Baker." Sophie's elfin face broke into a smile, and she waved her hands like a TV game show model.

That's when Darcy saw Nick's brother standing next to Nick, a goofy grin on his handsome face. "You have one stubborn friend there, Darcy. She wouldn't stop badgering me until I promised to bring her up here."

"I told you I needed to see you for myself, to make sure you were someplace safe." Sophie's small chin jutted out with determination. "You know when I want something I get it."

"But you never even met Nate, did you?"

"Well, not before yesterday."

"Sophie, girl, I love you." Darcy chuckled and hugged her friend close. "Come on in. Let me make you some coffee."

The four of them gathered around the kitchen island. Darcy served coffee and they sat and talked. Nate brought news that Pasquale was off the radar and assumed to be out of town. So how much longer would she need to hide out? No one seemed to have an answer to that question.

Sophie was impressed with the cabin. Despite the gray skies she oohed and aahed over the scenery. "It's like a whole different world."

"I know. You should see it when the sun's shining." Darcy couldn't hide the pride in her voice. It almost sounded like she'd taken ownership of the place. It's a good thing she didn't see the grin slide over Nick's face as he listened to her talk.

Darcy and Sophie worked together to make a lunch of chili and grilled peanut butter sandwiches, and after lunch the four of them sat down and played cards for a bit. After the women trounced the men in euchre, Darcy and Sophie headed upstairs to see the rest of the house.

"Can you believe it? This is my room." Darcy spun around the spacious room. "And look at that view."

"Not exactly what you expected when they decided to drag you into hiding, huh?"

"Not exactly. I didn't expect to love it so much."

"And what about Nick?"

"Nick?" Darcy fiddled with the curtains on the French doors.

"Yes, Nick. He looks at you like he wants to eat you up." Sophie plopped onto the bed and propped her head on her hands. "Do you like him?"

Darcy tilted her head in thought for a moment before she spoke. "I do. I like him very much, but..."

"But what? You like him, he's hot, and he's employed. That's a lot better than some of the guys you've dated."

Darcy lightly smacked Sophie's arm. "Hey, look who's talking. But seriously, Soph, he's a cop. A cop. That's not for me."

"Come on, Darcy, nobody said you had to marry the guy. But can you imagine the fun you could have. Woohoo, talk about the horizontal mambo, the bedtime boogie. It'd be a great way to spend the time here."

Color flamed in Darcy's cheeks, and her mouth went dry at the images Sophie's words drew in her mind. Lord, she really did want the man. But could she really just have sex with him and not let her heart get involved? Something told her that wasn't going to happen. He was too dangerous to her emotions, too hazardous to her mental health.

"It's not going to happen, Sophie. You might as well get that thought right out of your mind." Darcy's voice was almost grim as she made the declaration. "I am not going to sleep with a cop, especially not Nick Baker."

"Methinks the lady doth protest too much," Sophie teased back. "I hope you don't mind if I feel differently. I might decide to take on his brother Nate."

"Really?"

"I might. He is just as hunky as Nick, you know."

Darcy noticed a pink flush creep across Sophie's ivory complexion. There was something about the softness in her eyes, the defensive tone in her voice that made Darcy look a little harder at her friend.

"I know he's not after anything permanent and neither am I. You know I have no desire to get married or anything like that. And from what I've seen, neither does Nate. Sounds like the perfect friends with benefits arrangement to me."

"Are you sure, Sophie? I have a feeling the Baker boys are enough to threaten any woman's heart."

"I'm a big girl. I can handle it." Sophie sounded confident, but Darcy saw the doubt in her eyes.

"I hope so. Just remember that old saying about playing with fire." And Darcy knew she didn't want to get burned.

Chapter 14

Darcy hugged Sophie tight when she and Nate got ready to leave. It seemed like she was letting everything familiar go when Sophie walked out the door. As much as she enjoyed being here at the cabin, she missed her life. She missed her house, her gym, and her favorite restaurants and bars. She felt like she was in limbo not knowing how long she would have to hide out here. When would she get her life back?

She felt depressed after the other couple was gone, and Nick seemed to sense it. He even offered to cook dinner.

"That's sweet, but I'm not in the mood for frozen pizza."

"No. I was thinking I could whip up a batch of my famous beef stew. It's the one other thing I know how to fix that doesn't involve the microwave. How's that sound?"

"Sounds good." She smiled her agreement, but it didn't reach her eyes.

Nick began puttering in the kitchen, and Darcy wandered around restlessly. She finally flopped down on the sofa and turned on the news. A curvaceous blonde meteorologist was speaking seriously about a winter storm headed across Wisconsin. This could turn into an ice storm, she warned. Gusting winds, freezing rain, and falling tree limbs and power lines.

Nick heard the feminine voice floating through the air and paused in his cooking to listen.

"She says it will probably blow in tomorrow evening. I think we ought to run in to town in the morning and restock on perishables like milk and bread, just to be on the safe side. I've seen these storms before up here. They can get pretty fierce."

"Sure, that sounds like a plan," she agreed but felt her spirits fall even farther. Seemed like the weather was matching her mood.

Darcy had to admit Nick's stew was delicious even though it was spicy. She'd made toasted cheese sandwiches to go with it, the way Aunt Liz always had, and by the time supper was over she was stuffed. They cleaned up the kitchen together, and then Darcy excused herself to go to her room.

She took a shower then curled up in the big comfy chair by the window and did her nails. Her thoughts dwelled on home and how long she would have to wait to be there. Even after Pasquale was caught, would she be safe? He had long arms that still might be able to reach out from prison.

Well, that was a depressing thought.

Darcy read for a while then climbed into bed. She fell into a troubled sleep, disturbing dreams haunting her slumber.

Next thing she knew she was face to face with Pasquale. He sneered at her with his sharp features, a gruesome grin slashing across his face. He held a huge gun in his hand and started firing it around the room. Then Papa was there, his body slammed with bullets, dancing with every shot that hit him.

God, no. Stop. Stop shooting. Sophie appeared next, joining in Papa's morbid dance, her beautiful face contorted with pain. When Nick came onto the scene, Pasquale laughed maniacally and took aim at him.

Darcy screamed and screamed and screamed. She rushed towards Pasquale desperate to stop the slaughter. That's when he turned towards her and raised his gun.

"Darcy. Darcy, wake up. You're having a bad dream."

She continued to struggle, screaming yet again. She fought and scratched and pounded with her fists. Nick tried to wake her, shaking her and calling her name. When she woke suddenly her eyes flew wide open, and she was gasping for breath. The sheets were kicked off her sweat soaked body, and her nightshirt was wrapped around her waist, exposing her black lace panties.

Darcy recognized Nick and immediately threw herself into his arms.

"Nick, oh Nick, you're alive. Thank God."

Nick held her close, burying his nose in the tangled curls that fell around her neck.

"Of course I'm alive, silly. It was just a dream. It's okay, it's okay." He swept her hair off her forehead and placed a tender kiss on her brow. "Don't be afraid. I'm here, honey."

Her body still trembled, and her breath came in gasps. She held onto him for dear life. It had seemed so real, so genuine. She ran her hands through his thick hair just to reassure herself he was really there.

Next thing she knew he was kissing her, his lips gentle at first then hungry and seeking. His taste was intoxicating, the feel of his mouth hypnotic. His arms pulled her close, and she felt her unbound breasts flatten against his chest, the nipples hardening automatically. She slid her arms down to grasp his brawny shoulders. He was only wearing a pair of boxer briefs, so his upper torso was bare, the skin sleek and satiny. Her hands glided over his smooth flesh, almost burning with each touch.

Nick cradled her to him, his lips exploring her mouth with his tongue, swirling around the velvet canyon. His hands crept down her spine, caressing and stroking her back. Then his lips moved to play across her neck, tickling the hollow and teasing her jawline. Every place he tasted felt on fire, and he left a blazing trail across her skin. She tilted her head back and gave him the freedom to travel sensuously down her throat, shivering with response.

She placed her hands on either side of his face, cupping the whisker-stubbled cheeks. Lord help her, she was falling down a deep, deep well into a maelstrom of emotions. When his hand dropped to her exposed thigh, she felt a groan escape her lips.

Darcy ran her hand down his chest, feeling the muscles ripple beneath her touch. Her palm slid across his nipple and the tiny bud toughened beneath her fingers. She could feel the beat of his heart and relished in the feeling of life.

His hand slid slowly up her thigh, igniting bursts of sensations, and her body cried out for more. It had been too long since she'd been with a man, too empty, too lonely. Now all she wanted was to be with this man, to make love with him, and lose herself in him.

His fingers crept up to touch the silk edge of her panties, and she whimpered. He moaned and moved to cup her ass in his palm, squeezing and fondling the plump cheek.

She knew making love with Nick would be special, probably an experience like she'd never had before. And she wanted that, wanted that with a burning desire deep within her soul.

But then she remembered who she was with. Nick Baker, a cop, a man who put his life on the line for other people every day, a man who couldn't promise to always be there for his family. Yea, sure, she could indulge in this goodness, this pleasure for the moment, but what about tomorrow? What if she fell in love with him? And she had a sinking suspicion she would.

Oh, she did want to fall in love, but not with a cop. It was a heartbreak waiting to happen. She had to stop this now before it was too late. Yes, it would hurt but not as much as losing him later would.

"Nick," she managed to say. "Nick, wait."

His silver-blue eyes looked at her, studying her expression seriously. "What is it, babe? What's wrong?"

"I can't do this," she whispered. "I can't." Tears swam in her amber eyes. She couldn't tell him it was because she was afraid she'd fall in love with him. She couldn't tell him it was because he was a cop. He'd made no mention of a long-term arrangement, and she didn't want him to think she was out to "trap" him.

Nick paused, a confused expression on his face. She didn't blame him; one minute she was crawling all over him, the next putting up stop signs.

"I'm sorry, Nick. I'm just not ready for this." Her voice cracked as she confessed her fear.

He drew in a deep, shuddering breath then kissed her gently on the forehead. "It's okay. Don't be sorry. I shouldn't have taken advantage of you in your vulnerable condition."

"No," she protested. "I was enjoying it just as much as you...probably more. I just ...got cold feet. It would be too awkward."

"Okay. But do you mind if I reserve the right to try and change your mind?" He smiled softly and slid his arms from around her. "I've had a taste of you now, and I'm hungry for more."

She was grateful that the room was dark so he couldn't see the color flame in her cheeks. Cause truth be known, she felt exactly the same way. The next few days were going to be hard.

"Are you okay now? Do you think you'll be able to sleep?" Once again, her gaze locked with his. All she could manage was a quick nod. Otherwise, she'd beg him to stay, to hold her while she slept.

"Okay. Good night then, princess." He dropped a kiss on top of her head and left the room, Darcy staring after him.

Lord, she needed strength. Help her get through this with her heart in one piece.

Chapter 15

The next morning dawned cold and gray, a stillness in the air that felt almost eerie. Darcy lay in bed, reluctant to get up. It was tempting to just snuggle in under the covers and stay there.

Her mind traveled back to the night that had just passed and the feel of Nick's lips tracing across her skin. She was glad he had given in gracefully when she asked him to stop. She knew a lot of men would not have pushed the subject, some might even have held back. She'd seen the bulge in Nick's boxer briefs; she knew it hadn't been easy for him to let go.

Now she had to face him. She groaned and threw her arm over her eyes. She'd be damned if she let this attraction destroy the peace she'd found here. She was determined to act normal and ignore the magnetism drawing them together.

Drawing her determination around her, she got up and dressed in jeans and a pink turtleneck and a white hoodie. She swept her hair into a ponytail and prepared to face Nick like nothing had happened between them.

Nick was already in the kitchen starting the coffee. He tossed her a casual good morning and went back to concentrating on his task. Thank God, he must have decided to take the same route as she had this morning. Good, they would just go on acting like they'd never tasted each other.

"We need to get into town before the storm breaks," he commented as he took a seat at the bar.

"Not a problem. I'll just whip up some scrambled eggs, and we'll get going."

They ate breakfast then headed out. Darcy was relieved there wasn't stress between them. They talked about what they wanted to buy and planned for the worst. "Don't worry. If we lose power the generator will kick in," Nick reassured her. "And we've always got the fireplace."

Darcy wasn't worried. She felt safe with Nick and knew he could handle an ice storm. They had to be here anyway. It's not like they had anywhere else to go.

Nick tuned the radio into a station playing golden oldies rock and Darcy applauded. She loved the old songs. She'd grown up on them. When Rag Doll by the Four Seasons began flowing from the speakers, Darcy couldn't help but sing along. Soon Nick joined her, and they harmonized perfectly much to her surprise.

"You're a great singer," she said. "I didn't know you sang."

"You should hear me in the shower," he chuckled.

Hear him? Hell, she'd like to see him in the shower. For one moment she let her imagination run free, visions of a naked Nick with water sluicing over his golden skin and dripping from his hair.

She coughed, almost strangling. Damn, she had to quit that shit. That was not the way to keep this relationship casual.

Nick turned alarmed eyes on her and reached out and patted her on the back. "Are you okay?"

After a couple more choking noises she nodded, eyes watering. Geez, she had to quit thinking things like that; now it was endangering her health. She'd almost choked.

They drove through the forested hills and came into town. Once again, they hit the grocery, but this time they shared one cart. The store was busy with people stocking up for the storm, shelves quickly emptying of bread and milk. Their own cart was full when they rolled up to the cash register. The cashier, an older lady with curly silver hair, glanced up and a look of recognition lit up her face.

"Nick. Nick Baker. How have you been? How's your folks?" The lady talked fast and nonstop. "Oh, and this pretty lady must be your wife. You finally got married, did ya? Looks like you picked a winner. And, little lady, you definitely got yourself a prize. Girls around here have been chasing the Baker boys forever it seems like."

"This isn't my—" Nick started to say, but Margie, as her name tag read, talked as fast as her fingers flew over the register keys.

"Well, it's good to see you. It's been too long since any of you Bakers have been around. Is your momma doing okay? I swear, she is the sweetest woman. That'll be $72.83, please. I wonder when we'll get a visit from the seniors. Your parents haven't been around in a coon's age."

Nick fumbled for his wallet and tried to speak again, but Margie didn't have time to listen. She continued on with her rant. "You Bakers need to come around more often. You know all the town folk miss ya. Now, here's your change and I hope to see you again soon. Nice to meet you, Mrs. Baker." And then she was waving goodbye at them and greeting her next customers. They left the line and headed for the SUV.

Darcy's cheeks were still flaming by the time they had the groceries loaded and were back in the vehicle. The thought of them as a married couple upset her equilibrium. She didn't know why she felt so uncomfortable by the idea; it was just a silly mistake. Margie had simply jumped to a conclusion. But that didn't make Darcy feel any less disturbed about being proclaimed Nick's wife.

Nick laughed out loud as he looked at her as he pulled out of the parking spot. "I thought you were going to explode when she called you my wife."

"What made me want to explode is you didn't set her straight."

"I tried. She wouldn't let me get a word in edgewise."

Darcy knew that was true, but she wasn't ready to let him off that easy.

"Come on, you question killers and rapists. You mean you couldn't speak up to one little old lady cashier?" She put as much sarcasm in her voice as possible.

"Confronting Margie about something is scarier than busting a killer," he chuckled. "She used to give me gumballs and correct my grammar. I've never talked back to her."

"Well, now she thinks you're married. What are you going to do about that?" She tried to sound stern but was distracted by the image of Nick as a boy. She bet he had been a real charmer.

"I'm not going to do anything about it right now. Margie's been trying to fix me up with locals for a dozen or more years. I can use a break." A smile played across his lips as he made the declaration.

"That's just wrong, Nick." She shook her head, amazed that he was so willing to give up his single status. "I don't want to be part of your lie."

"Oh, lighten up, Darcy," he shot back. "Besides, what's so terrible about the thought of being married to me?"

Darcy felt her mouth fall open then snap shut. She didn't know what to say. Was now the time to confess her feelings about cops? Or should she just brush him off?

She didn't know if she was ready to explain her feelings, so she decided to go the other route. "What makes you think it would be so great?"

He turned his gaze on her for a moment and raised an eyebrow. "It seems like there are several women who like the idea."

"Well, some women are willing to settle."

"Settle? Settle?" Nick's voice went up in volume. "I'm a great catch. I've got a good job, I'm not addicted to anything, and I'm a pretty nice guy. And, I've been told, I'm not bad to look at."

"Phew, the smell of arrogance is pretty strong in here." She commented with a tiny grin playing across her lips.

"That's not arrogance. It's confidence," he retorted. "Seriously, though, why are you so abhorred by the idea of being married to me?"

Darcy didn't say anything for a minute. Did she really want to tell him the truth? She didn't like to talk about her dad's death. She had been as close to him as it was possible for a daughter to be to a father. But she didn't know what else to tell Nick except the truth.

Chapter 16

"It's cause you're a cop, okay?" She finally spat out the words. "My dad was a cop. He was killed in the line of duty when I was just a kid."

"I'm sorry, Darcy. I didn't know." His voice was soft, shocked. "Were you close?"

Close? Darcy knew she had never loved anyone more than she'd loved her father. She didn't know if close was quite the way to describe her relationship with her father.

"He was my best friend," she answered at last. She couldn't hide the catch in her voice.

"I'm so sorry, Darcy. What happened?" She could tell he wasn't just asking to be kind. He really wanted to know.

"It was just an ordinary traffic stop. Nothing special. He pulled somebody over because they had a taillight out. He walked up to the window on the driver's side, and the driver just shot him. He didn't have a chance." Her voice took on a cool tone as she tried to disconnect from the memory, but it wasn't really possible. The pain stabbed her heart whenever she thought about it. She closed her eyes against the burn of tears and swallowed hard.

Nick shot her a glance then pulled the SUV off the road. Before she knew it, he had gathered her up in his arms and was kissing the top of her head. He didn't say anything, just held her, and it was more than she could stand.

"My mom was totally dependent on Dad and just fell apart when he was killed. She started drinking and seeing all kinds of men. One of them beat her to death when I was 12." She didn't seem to be able to stop the words from pouring out, sobbing as she ranted.

"Ah, Darcy, you went through more than any little girl should have to endure." His smooth baritone rolled over her, soothing and comforting. She buried her face in his shoulder and wept like she hadn't cried since she was a child.

She finally managed to get her emotions under control and slowed her sobs to hiccoughs. She couldn't believe she'd fallen apart like that. He probably thought she was a big crybaby. She pulled away from him and ran her fingers across her nose.

"I'm sorry. I didn't mean to fall apart like that," she sniffed.

"I think you've been holding that in for a long time," he said as he opened the console, pulled out some tissues and handed them to her.

"I think you're right."

He moved over and put the car in gear. "We need to get back on the road to beat the storm, but Darcy, we'll talk some more when we get home."

Not if she could help it, she thought mutinously. She'd ridden enough emotional roller coasters for today.

By the time they pulled in the drive at the cabin sleet was pinging off the windshield. The wind had picked up and nearly swept Darcy off her feet as she helped tote groceries inside. She put groceries away then hurried up to hide herself away in her own room. She surfed the web for a while and talked to Sophie on the phone but eventually had to give up and go back downstairs.

She found Nick in the kitchen staring hungrily into the fridge.

"Looks like you're ready for supper," she commented as she came into the room. "How's goulash sound?"

"Sounds great to me," he agreed enthusiastically.

"What, better than frozen pizza?" she couldn't help teasing him.

"I admit it, you've got me spoiled."

"Well, tonight I'm putting you to work. Know how to chop onions?"

"I'm a fantastic onion chopper."

"Then get to chopping, buddy," she ordered, grabbing an onion and tossing it at him.

"Yes, ma'am," he consented while she grabbed some garlic and started heating a saucepan. They worked together with her singing along to the radio and him playing dutiful assistant. It felt funny to see Nick as subservient. His big, forceful personality was hidden, replaced by an easy-going relaxed guy now and then tossing out comical quips. Darcy was surprised she didn't feel uncomfortable after the emotional scene this afternoon, but amazingly enough, she was perfectly peaceful.

Outside was anything but peaceful, however. The wind howled, hurtling icy pellets into the bank of glass windows. It howled mournfully around the corners of the house, occasionally adding a high-pitched wail that sounded like a woman screaming. It was scary sounding, but the inside of the cabin was so warm and bright Darcy could ignore the wind songs.

A fire crackled in the fireplace, and the spicy scent of goulash and garlic bread filled the air. Warlock curled up on the sofa, lying on a soft, plaid afghan. The wood floors gleamed in the soft light, and golden oldies music filled the room.

The food was hot, flavorful, and filling, perfect for a cold, windy night. They indulged in red wine with dinner and sat long after they were finished just talking about a variety of subjects. Nick told stories of his childhood and the mischief he'd gotten into with his brothers and sisters. She talked about adventures with Aunt Liz and Liz's wide variety of friends.

They finally started clearing up and doing dishes. They were almost done when Darcy heard the rich voice of Elvis beginning to pour from the radio. It was Can't Help Falling in

Love with You. Her gaze flew to meet his eyes to see if he heard it.

She found his gaze locked on her. They simply stared at each other for a moment then Nick moved to take her in his arms. He started to dance with her, crooning the words to the love song in her ear.

Darcy fell under his spell. She wrapped her arms around his neck and allowed him to guide her through some sensuous moves, losing herself in the moment. The warmth of his body seeped into her, and she felt herself drawing closer and closer to the heat. She let her head fall onto his chest and breathed in the scent of him, a mixture of soap and musk that swirled around her senses.

Nick swayed his hips to the rhythm of the music and Darcy could feel a growing swell against her. Her breathing quickened, and Darcy felt her nipples harden as they were pressed against his chest. They moved together fluently, like they were a matched pair. Darcy felt herself beginning to hope the music would never end.

It felt as if she were melting into him. She couldn't tell where he stopped and she began. She was suddenly lost in a cloud of fantasy, of motion, and music. She was floating, only the embrace of his arms holding her on earth.

Despite her wishes, the song began to come to an end. She slowed with his movements and started to return to reality.

And then he kissed her.

Chapter 17

And kissed her...and kissed her. He kissed her gently, passionately, tasting the intoxicating sweetness of her, drinking it in. At first, she was so shocked she couldn't react. Then response set in and she found herself kissing him back. His lips were like velvet, warm and smooth as they explored her lips. Her lips that were hungrily seeking his, opening so he could slide his tongue in the dank cavern and dance with hers.

Nick's arms held her even closer, his lips sliding across her jawline, finding the hollow behind her ear. His tongue teased her, flicking and tasting her skin, and she felt her knees threaten to buckle. She wrapped her arms tight around his neck to support herself and let her hands delve into the depth of his hair.

The sensations that swam through her blinded her from all sensibility. She forgot he was a cop, a man she had no desire to become involved with. She forgot she had basically sworn off men after her last disastrous relationship, and she'd lost her common sense.

It wasn't until his hands slid down her spine and gently cupped her ass that reality set in. God, she wanted him desperately, but she needed to resist—she couldn't do this.

A moan broke from her lips as she forced herself to pull away from him. God, it was hard to stop kissing him, experiencing the magic of his mouth.

"Nick, I can't do this." She sounded breathless, unconvincing.

Nick paused, obviously trying to catch his breath. He looked into her eyes, and that was almost her undoing. She couldn't deny the pain that shot through her chest.

He took hold of her hands and walked to the couch. He sat, then pulled her down on his lap.

"Let's talk," he said, his arm falling around her waist.

Darcy took a deep shuddering breath and laid her head on his shoulder, avoiding his piercing eyes.

"Angel, I don't blame you for feeling the way you do. The only relationship you have had with a cop ended traumatically and changed your life forever." He started out slowly, all the while stroking her rusty waves. "But you've been so brave, so courageous. You've come out strong. You're not a weakling, baby."

"I know," she whispered.

"But you don't trust yourself. Your brain's telling you one thing, your heart another. Your brain's jumping way ahead. It's determined that if we get together, you'll end up married to me, following in your mother's footsteps, just waiting for future catastrophes to descend on us.

"Honey, I hate to tell you, but I haven't asked you to marry me. You're looking for trouble before it gets here. I want you. You want me. That's what it boils down to." He tipped her chin up to face him. "Are you going to deny us that because of what might be one day? Because of problems that may never arise?"

Darcy looked into his eyes, the intense silver-blue seeming to pierce into her soul. Live for the moment, live for today, she'd always told herself. But now she was backing off on those beliefs. She was afraid of an unknown future, of what might happen. That wasn't like her.

He was right. She knew he was right. She had no idea if a night of making love with him would lead to a permanent life together. She was running away from a problem that didn't exist.

But something inside of her told her that once she fell into Nick's arms, she would never want to leave them. There had been something about him from the very first that intrigued her, called her to him. Like a snake charmer magnetizing his prey, she was being pulled in, lured closer and closer to disaster.

Lord, she wanted him, though. Every nerve in her body twanged with desire. Every cell hungered for his touch, to be kissed by him. How could she say no?

That's when she made her decision. She wasn't going to live in fear of what might come. She wasn't going to deny herself this one thing she wanted so achingly. Especially when the specter of Pasquale hung over her. All seemed well and safe here in their private little world, but the reality was she was the target of a killer, a madman who wanted her dead. When they went back to the real world, which they had to do soon, she might be finished. He or one of his henchmen could kill her any day. It wasn't just Nick who could die young. She might not live to see next month.

That stark reality slapped her in the face. Did she want to die without knowing the intimacy of being with Nick, without sharing that magical journey with him even if it was only one time? No, no she didn't. She wanted his touch, craved his body, yearned to feel his bare skin burning against hers.

She looked him deep in the eyes and raised her hands to slide them through his hair.

"No, Nick, I'm not going to deny us this night. I want you."

He tenderly kissed her lips, once, twice, three times.

"Are you sure, angel?" His voice was full of questions, his eyes full of concern.

"Positive," she whispered and then she pulled him to her, kissing him passionately, sliding her tongue into his mouth, swirling and venturing through the damp canyon.

Nick groaned and gathered her closer to him as she sat on his lap. His hands were on her back, one behind her shoulder blades, one cupping her hips. Her breasts crushed into his chest, nipples budding. She felt a flood of moisture spring between her legs.

One of his hands slid upward into her wealth of curls, tugging her head slightly back to give him access to her slender neck. He nipped a trail down her throat to the hollow on her shoulder, his tongue flicking over the sensitive skin there.

Darcy grabbed his shoulders and pulled them both down on the overstuffed couch, her back flattened against the seat cushions. She ran her hand beneath the hem of his tee-shirt and stroked his firm, satiny skin.

Nick matched her actions and worked his hands down her front, lingering over the swollen nipples then sliding underneath her top. His palms sizzled over her skin, seeming to brand every place he touched. When he pushed at the material to expose her pink lace bra, she helped him pull it the rest of the way off. His hands quickly undid the snap of the bra, and her naked breasts looked golden in the light from the flickering fire.

"You are so beautiful, angel," he moaned, studying her body. "So incredible. I need to taste you." With that, he lowered her back, and his lips took a jutting nipple into his mouth, suckling gently at the flesh. His tongue lashed across its peak, twirling and skimming across it.

Darcy clenched her hands in his hair, arching her back with desire. When his teeth nipped playfully at the bud a spasm of pleasure and pain shot through her core and landed deep in her uterus. She couldn't stop the cry that burst from her lips.

Now he was working at her jeans, unzipping the fly and undoing the button. Darcy grabbed at his hands and slowed them, pushing them away so she could tug at his shirt and remove it. God, he was so handsome, his shoulders so broad, his abs ripped.

He grinned and went back to working at her jeans, sliding his hand beneath the tiny bikini panties she wore. His fingers slid across her abdomen, awakening a surge of flutters in her pelvis. When he began to tug at her pants, she lifted her hips to help ease their removal. At last, she was free of the confining garments and let her legs fall open freely.

Nick ran his hand down her thigh then back up it. He swirled around the head of her labia, teasing, playing until she thought she was going to drown with desire. At last his fingers plunged between her pouting lips, slipping and sliding in the pooling juices there. He found the magic button and ran his thumb over it, circling the throbbing blossom. His finger dipped into her moist cavity, then a second one eased in beside it.

The sensations streamed through Darcy, pouring over her like ribbons of colorful satin wrapping her up in a cocoon of feelings. She was drawn inward, twisting and turning, and then suddenly exploding like a caterpillar erupting as a butterfly. Wings of ecstasy carried her high, higher, bursts of light everywhere, and then brought her floating down, gently spiraling back to earth.

Chapter 18

"I've never seen anything more beautiful in my life." Nick's tone was awed, reverent. "You are so special."

Darcy reached up and brought his lips to hers. They were far from finished here. Now her hunger was even more keen, more intense. Her hands slid down his abdomen and began tugging at his jeans, impatient to get them off. Nick complied and helped slide them down his long legs, and then his boxer briefs disappeared too. The sight of him naked, bathed in dancing firelight, took her breath away.

His skin was golden, his physique sculpted. His dick sprang from between his legs like a burnished hammer.

His dick. My God, Darcy realized, it was huge. Long and thick, a droplet of white crowning its mushroom shaped head. She reached out and wrapped her hand around its length, rubbing the moisture with her thumb.

"I want you," she groaned. "I want you now. Inside of me."

A long moan escaped from Nick's throat as he kissed her. He left her lips and reached for his jeans, slipping a foil packet from the pocket and tearing it open. Darcy reached out and took the coiled latex from him and slipped it along his oversized cock then lay back and held her arms up.

He covered her with his body, the heat searing through her. She felt the head of his pole sliding against her wet lips, his hand guiding it up and down the wet canal. She was moaning and writhing with desire by the time he finally entered her.

The head slid in slowly, giving her flesh time to stretch and capture him. Then he plunged in the rest of the way, and Darcy cried out with the thrill of it. He was so big, he filled her so completely. He set the rhythm, and her hips instinctively matched it.

He took her arms and raised them above her head, clasping both her wrists in one hand. Then he began to ease out of her, just to the edge, before driving his cock in up to his balls. They slapped against her, playing backup to the sensual sounds escaping from them. He gave his hips an extra grind, and she couldn't bite back a scream of delight.

Together they climbed the mountain then came plunging off the cliff. Darcy felt her mind leave her, sailing into its own world full of stars and spangles. Joy, sheer unadulterated joy ran through her veins and just as she exploded she heard Nick let loose a guttural cry, and his cock quivered inside of her.

Neither one of them spoke for a long time, just lay there with Nick collapsed half on top of her while they caught their breath. At last, he raised up and looked at her.

"You're magical, like a fairy princess."

"No, it's you who has mystical powers."

They cuddled and gave each other little kisses, Nick scattering pecks across her cheekbones, her eyelids, and her forehead. She buried her nose in his neck, breathing him in and filling her senses with the scent of him.

It wasn't long, though, before their passion rekindled and they were making love again, this time slowly, exploring each other's bodies with haunting leisure. Soon she was orgasming again, flying, and then half an hour later, once again she burst into flames, heat shooting through her like molten gold.

When at last they drifted off, cuddled right on the rug in front of the fireplace and covered with an afghan, she slept the sleep of the sated. Every time she started to rouse she felt his arms tighten around her and she nestled closer to him, seeking and finding solace and comfort. She didn't remember when she'd slept better.

The world was completely silent when Darcy's eyes flickered open. She rolled over, bumping her butt into Nick's groin and his arms automatically tightened around her. She blinked at the mystical land visible through the wall of glass. Sunlight glittered on an ice-covered world that lay still and pale. Every tree branch, every blade of grass, each tiny little twig was cloaked in its own sparkling coat of ice. The sun beamed back off it, creating a world of silvery enchantment.

"Hmm, beautiful," she heard Nick murmur sleepily.

"It is, isn't it? Like a fairyland encased in jewels."

"Oh, were you eyeing the view outdoors?" He chuckled and held her close. "I hadn't looked that far."

She turned back towards him and kissed him, lingering over his lips, running her tongue along the edge of his mouth. He didn't even have morning breath. He tasted just as delicious as he had last night.

They made love again, slowly, sweetly. Darcy knew she was lost. Being with Nick was unlike being with any other man she'd ever known. He made her feel safe, protected, but sensuous and dangerous.

Darcy stretched luxuriously and moved to gather up her clothes. "I'm going to go take a shower. Care to join me?"

"Try and stop me," he growled and playfully chased her up the stairs.

Darcy felt good, so she baked. She always liked to cook when she was happy. First, a tasty frittata for breakfast along with fresh berries, then she whipped up a batch of chocolate chip brownies. She spanked Nick's fingers as he snitched one while it was still warm. He sucked the gooey crumbs from his fingertips then leaned over and gave her a smacking kiss. Darcy licked her lips afterwards, enjoying the taste of chocolate.

They played a game of Trivial Pursuit then decided to explore the frozen world outdoors. Darcy bundled up and held Nick's hand as they ventured onto the ice-covered hills. Her first steps found her feet slipping and sliding, and she ended up grabbing his arm and holding on for dear life.

They walked the hills, every step crunching on the ice-covered ground. A brisk breeze whipped around them, and Darcy's cheeks soon turned pink, but she didn't want to turn back. It was too enchanted, too peaceful.

They ended up down by the lakeshore, standing with arms wrapped around each other's waists, gazing at the ice-edged water. A feeling of peace surrounded Darcy, serenity settling over her like an old comfortable blanket. She listened to the stillness, watching the waves ruffling the water. They stood there for a long time while the sun slid slowly towards the west, a blaze of color coming alive on the horizon beyond the water.

She shivered at last, and Nick pulled her closer. "Come on, princess, it's cold out here. Let's head back inside."

Once indoors she shed her outerwear and started to make dinner, but Nick apparently had other ideas. He came up behind her while she had her head stuck in the fridge and wrapped his arms around her, snuggling her to him. His lips burrowed under her hair and trailed a track of burning kisses along the back of her neck. Aw, God, now a whole different appetite was awakened and demanding attention.

Nick spun her around and kicked the fridge door shut with his foot. He backed her up against the kitchen island, his hands wandering across her body, his lips kissing her again and again. Darcy melted like a piece of ice and allowed Nick to remove her jeans and panties and set her up on the cold surface of the island. She leaned back against the broad counter and let her legs dangle off the other side.

Nick picked up each leg bent at the knee and sat her feet on the granite. He pushed her legs apart and drank in the sight before him. Darcy moaned, and he reached out and traced a finger along her lips, then bent down and touched her swollen bud with his tongue.

Darcy spasmed when she felt the warm tip of his tongue on her most sensitive area. Her hips bucked but his hands came up to hold her down while his tongue played across her clit. It flicked and swirled relentlessly, until Darcy exploded, juice squirting freely across his lips.

She lay there panting, recovering, holding his head to her breasts. She felt like a virgin who'd never had sex before, so foreign were the feelings he aroused in her. Only he could make her fly, soar to the stars and back. She knew she was in trouble. Damn, she should have guarded her heart more carefully. Now she knew it would break when they parted as they must someday.

She tried to hold back the tears, but she couldn't stop the burning, couldn't halt the wetness building up in her eyes.

"Darcy, darlin, what's wrong?" Nick questioned her urgently. "Did I hurt you?"

"No," she sniffed. "Not yet, anyway."

Nick pulled back and eyed her. "And what's that supposed to mean?"

Darcy tried to bite back the words. She was being silly, overdramatic, but she couldn't help herself. Finally, the words burst from her.

"I'm afraid, Nick. I'm so afraid." She wrapped her arms around his neck and cried like a baby.

Chapter 19

"Hush, hush now, princess. What are you afraid of?" Nick sat her up, smoothed her hair back off her forehead and dropped a gentle kiss there. "Is it Pasquale?"

"No." She shook her head adamantly. "It's you."

"Me. Why me? I would never hurt you."

"No, not physically. But I told you I don't want to get involved with a cop. It's a heartbreak waiting to happen. But I'm afraid now it's too late."

He turned away for a moment and ran his hands through his hair in frustration. When he swung back around he had a hard look on his face.

"I can't help it, Darcy. I am a cop. I'll probably always be a cop. But, dammit, that doesn't mean I'm going to get killed tomorrow. Hell, look at my dad, he's been in for almost 40 years and never had to fire his gun in the line of duty. Most cops live!"

"But some don't. My dad didn't, and that changed my life forever. My mom loved him so much she fell apart without him."

"Darcy, honey." He pulled her to him. "You are not your mom. Your mom was weak, dependent. She never learned how to stand on her own two feet. But you're not your mom. You're a strong, independent young woman. You know how to take care of yourself. You are courageous and brave; you will never have to depend on someone else to take care of you."

He stopped talking for a moment and looked down at her tear-streaked face, brushing the hair away from her damp cheeks. "Darlin, there are no guarantees in life. Love doesn't come with a guarantee of forever, and it sometimes comes when you least expect it. You have to grab on to that love and take it for everything its worth. That's life. No guarantees. You could be eaten by a bear tomorrow and be gone, but I don't want to miss a minute of sharing life with you while you're here, even if it is just one more day."

She couldn't help but giggle at his analogy. "Really, Nick, eaten by a bear?"

"Well, you know what I mean. Let's enjoy this time together, babe. It's precious."

She kissed him and felt her insides melting again. Damn, she liked him, maybe even loved him. But she couldn't deny the feeling of dread dwelling deep within her.

They did eventually eat a light supper and drank a couple glasses of wine then wound up in Nick's bed. They made love multiple times, trying different positions and discovering new pleasures. Once they did it doggie style with Darcy on her hands and knees, Nick behind her. She truly liked this uninhibited position because it allowed her head to twist and toss about, and his balls spanked her ass with a noisy rhythm. Her boobs danged freely so Nick could grasp them and pull on the nipples, and he rubbed her clit as he pumped away at her. It was incredible and when they were finished Darcy collapsed on the bed.

"Stop. I give. We've got to stop before I have a heart attack," she gasped, her breasts heaving as she tried to catch her breath.

Nick leaned on his elbow and looked at her, his eyes twinkling. "Really? You're done already? Quitter." He tugged a lock of her hair playfully.

"Quitter or survivalist?" she queried with a raised eyebrow.

"Okay, maybe we do need a break. But it's hard to stop loving you." He breathed the words as he nipped gently at her lips. Her eyes took on a dreamy hue as she tasted him.

"Hmm. Maybe I have just one more session in me."

They slept nested together, her head resting on his arm. Darcy slumbered peacefully, Nick's thigh thrown over her leg. Nick snored lightly, deeply asleep. Darcy was dreaming. In the dream, they were here at the cabin, and it was summertime. They were in the lake, and they were naked. Her wet hair streamed down her back, her hands holding on to Nick's shoulders. Hmm, a sweet dream.

A sweet dream that ended abruptly when a crash exploded through the night. They both shot up at once. What the hell? Even Warlock leaped up from his curled position at the foot of the bed, hair standing on end.

It sounded like breaking glass.

Darcy's heart thundered in her chest, and her hand clutched Nick's arm.

"My God, what was that?" she breathed.

"I don't know. Maybe the weight of the ice broke one of the tree limbs, and it crashed through a window. I'll go see."

"No. Don't leave me."

"It'll be okay, darlin. Wait here. I'll be right back."

She held her breath as Nick climbed out of bed and pulled on his jeans. He hesitated, then reached into the nightstand and took his pistol out. "Just to be on the safe side. It could be a bear."

"Oh, Lord, a bear?"

"Probably not, but better safe than sorry. I'll be right back," he said then slipped silently from the room.

Darcy crouched on her knees, trying to control her shaking. She reached out and grabbed her robe from the bench at the end of the bed and slipped into it, pulling it close around her shivering body.

It seemed like Nick was gone forever. What was taking him so long? She strained to hear any sounds from downstairs, but silence was her only reward. Should she go check on him? What if he'd fallen or gotten cut on the broken glass?

She waited a few more minutes then made up her mind. She needed to go down there and check on Nick.

She had just climbed out of bed and slid her feet into her slippers when the bedroom door burst open. Nick stood there, weaving back and forth, blood pouring from a gash on his head. His eyes were unfocused.

And he wasn't alone. A man stood directly behind him, a gun rammed in Nick's back. Another man was visible in the shadows behind him.

Her heart stopped as she stared at the man with the gun.

Dimitri Pasquale flashed her evil grin.

"Hello, Darcy. Surprised to see me?"

Chapter 20

An angry rage swept through her as she looked at the injured Nick.

"What have you done to him?" she demanded, her hands balling into fists.

"Who, Nicky boy here? Just a tap really. Just a little love tap."

"He's bleeding." She moved to rush to the semi-conscious man.

"Ah, ah, ah." Pasquale waved the gun in her direction. "Stay back if you don't want him to have a bullet in his head."

"No!" she cried. "Don't hurt him."

"If that is what you want, then you will have to do what we say. Me and my man Tank here." He waved his hand and the second man stepped forward. He was ugly. Dark hair surrounded a broad face, his nose seeming to flatten across it. His eyes were squinty, enveloped in cheek fat, his neck as thick as a ham. The man was stocky and round, but short. Clad in a green sweatshirt and green sweat pants, he looked like a waddling Christmas tree.

Quite the contrast to Pasquale. Half Italian/half Chinese, Dimitri was tall and whipcord slender. His features were finely cut, and he exuded an air of arrogance and superiority. Silky black hair crowned his proud head.

Darcy stood frozen. God, she and Nick had gotten so comfortable here in their isolated cabin they had forgotten about Pasquale. A fatal mistake.

"What do you want?" Why hadn't he just killed them and gotten it over with. He had the perfect opportunity.

"Oh, you know what I want. But it doesn't have to be right now, does it? Maybe I want to have some fun first."

Fun? What would this madman consider fun? She had a feeling she didn't want to know.

She did know, however, that she had to stay calm, no matter what. She had to pull herself together, to take any and every opportunity to turn the tables on these guys. Or die trying.

Of course, if she didn't figure this out, she would be dead anyway.

She squared her shoulders determinedly. She would figure this out.

"Right now, I'm hungry. How about you, Tank, are you hungry?"

"Hell, yes. I'm starving."

Pasquale smirked. "You're always starving."

"You're damn straight."

"Well, Darcy, what are you going to do about it?"

"I'll fix you something to eat."

"Excellent idea."

Once again, he jabbed the gun into Nick's back and swung him around. "After you, Darcy."

Darcy pulled the belt of her robe snug and marched past Dimitri, her hand brushing against Nick's limp fingers. Wait. Had he squeezed her hand?

Pasquale fell in behind her and Tank waddled along behind. They made it to the kitchen and Dimitri half dragged, half pushed Nick into a bar stool at the island. His head immediately fell forward to his arms resting on the granite countertop. Darcy walked around the island and opened the fridge, staring inside.

She wanted to poison the men. Lord, she wished she had some arsenic. She wouldn't hesitate to use it. Anything that would put these two out of commission.

"It's almost dawn. How about bacon and eggs?" Dimitri spoke as he sat next to Nick. Tank took the seat on the other side of the injured man.

"Scrambled okay?" she enquired dryly.

"That would be fine."

"And some coffee," Tank demanded.

"Oh, coffee, definitely."

Darcy's hands shook as she put the bacon in the skillet. Her stomach heaved, and she had to bite back bile.

"How about some extras in those eggs. Maybe some onion and peppers and some cheese." Tank called his order from the bar.

Darcy didn't answer, just turned and took an onion from the cabinet. She pulled open the drawer and got a knife to cut it with. For one long moment, she thought about slamming the blade into Pasquale's chest, but she knew she couldn't get them both. Instead, she turned and began to clean the onion.

"How did you find us?" she demanded.

"Oh, it wasn't hard. Not when you have friends in the right places." He smirked. "I really shouldn't tell you, but since you'll not be able to tell anyone, I guess it doesn't matter. Captain Baker's secretary Sharon can be very helpful when you have the right persuasion. Keeping her son safe seemed to work."

Darcy's stomach fell. Nick's father's employee. How sickening.

"You are quite attractive, Darcy. It's a shame you have such a big mouth. Now, thanks to you, I need someplace to hide out. It just makes sense for it to be here, I guess. I mean, who would look for us at the very place you're tucked away all safe and sound. It's genius really."

Darcy pulled the coffeepot off the burner and turned to pour each man a cup. While she was facing the island, she took the opportunity to study Nick. He was pale, the red blood spilling down his forehead a sharp contrast to the white countertop.

And then she saw him wink.

Oh my God. Had she really seen that? Was he just pretending to be out of it? Hope burned in her heart.

"At least let me wipe the blood off his head," Darcy pleaded.

"Will that make you happy, Darcy? Okay, fine. Clean his head up." Pasquale rolled his eyes, sighing as he said the words. "I don't know why you should bother, though. He'll be dead soon...and so will you."

Ice surrounded Darcy's heart as she heard his words, spoken casually as if he were talking about the weather. She barely disguised her gasp of horror.

She grabbed a clean rag and moistened it with cool water then hurried back to Nick. She patted at the blood, examining the gash just above his hairline. When she lay her hand on top of his where it lay on the bar, she felt him tense. He wiggled his fingers ever so slightly, letting her know he was coherent. Thank God. Suddenly she didn't feel so alone.

The next move was up to her. She didn't know what it would be, but she was determined to take a chance. If she didn't, they would die.

"Come on, make it quick. I don't want you to burn the food.

Darcy finished cleaning the blood off Nick's face, giving it a gentle pat as she turned back to breakfast for Pasquale. She got the eggs out of the fridge and began cracking them into a bowl. Using a fork, she whipped them heartlessly, her nervous tension exploding in the motion.

She poured the eggs into another skillet and turned her attention back to the bacon. It popped and sizzled, snapping hot grease hitting her cheek. The sudden burn gave her an idea. Would Nick be ready to back her up? She could only pray.

Darcy took the tongs and started to pull the bacon from the pan, "accidentally" bumping up the heat under the pan of hot grease. She took her time placing the bacon strips carefully on a plate covered with paper towels.

Darcy hesitated, waiting for the perfect moment. When she heard Pasquale tell Tank to get ready to chow down, she was almost finished, she made her move.

Grasping the cast iron skillet full of scalding hot grease, she turned and raised the arm holding the pan. She let the grease fly across the island straight into Pasquale's face. His squeal of pain rent the air, and his hand flew up to cover his scalded eyes.

The second after she threw the grease, Nick came alive. He leaped up and drove his fist directly into Tank's face, sending the man flying across the room to land on his ass. Nick turned to grab Pasquale's pistol from the bar at the same moment Tank drew his gun. Both blasted simultaneously, the noise exploding in the space. Darcy screamed and watched as Tank crumpled, a blot of red expanding across his chest.

Then she turned to hug Nick but was shocked to see him, too, falling to the floor, blood pouring from a wound in his abdomen.

Before she could comprehend what had happened, she felt a presence behind her and spun around. Pasquale stood there, his face blistered and scalded, his mouth warped into a pained position. His hands reached out, grasping for her throat. She didn't hesitate.

She raised her arms and brought the skillet crashing down on his skull.

Chapter 21

The hospital room was noisy. The machines hooked to Nick's body bleeped and pinged, the nurses outside the ICU talked and hustled back and forth. Darcy thought it would be quiet here, but that wasn't the case. Every noise sounded painfully loud. The nurses' footsteps should have been silent but seemed to echo through the room. She wanted to shout at them to shut up when she heard the sound of laughter floating in from the nurses' station.

She hadn't taken her eyes off Nick for hours, not since he'd been settled into his hospital bed.

She thought back over the time that had passed before that. Her voice had shaken as she called 911 and tried to explain the situation. She'd finally just begged for help and worked on Nick, trying to staunch the blood. She had to take care of Pasquale, too, securing his unconscious form in case he woke up. He couldn't be allowed to get away. She tied his hands behind his back and wrapped an extension cord around his ankles and waited for the police and paramedics to arrive.

What she had feared most had happened. Nick had been shot, and she didn't know if he would live. Not only had he suffered a gunshot wound that had ripped through his abdomen and his liver, his head injury was just as life-threatening. His skull was fractured, his brain swollen. How he had managed to take on Tank still amazed her.

Tank had died at the scene, and Pasquale had been taken away in cuffs to the hospital. Nick had been in ICU almost two days now and had never regained consciousness. He'd had surgery as soon as he came in and again when they discovered they'd missed a bleeder in his abdomen. His face was so pale, so still, except for the occasional twitch of pain. Tubes ran everywhere: oxygen up his nose, IVs in his arms, and she knew a catheter was hidden away beneath the white blanket.

She was alone for the first time since Nick had been brought to the hospital. His brothers, Nate and Noah, had been here since shortly after he came out of his first surgery. Their mother was still recovering from surgery herself, and his father opted to stay with her but had called frequently. The twins had shown up yesterday evening, and they had all huddled together to wait. Now the others had gone to the cafeteria, but Darcy chose to stay here with Nick.

Her eyes felt gritty and burned from lack of sleep. Her back ached from sitting hunched over in the chair or bending over his bed, talking to him, rubbing his hands. She knew she looked worse than a cat that had been out in a thunderstorm. She'd managed to throw on some jeans and a sweatshirt before coming to the hospital, but her hair still tumbled crazily around her shoulders. Circles ringed her eyes, and her skin was pale.

The exhaustion was finally catching up with her, and she found herself nodding off in the chair. She couldn't help it; she had to take just a little nap.

She awoke when she heard Nick calling her name. At first, she thought she was dreaming but then flashed to reality. She scrambled for the bedside and breathed his name.

"Nick. Aw, Nick, you're awake." A single tear tracked down her cheek and fell on his chest. He tried to sit up but winced and immediately fell back, his face contorting with agony.

"No, lay still. You're hurt." Darcy gently pressed her hand against his shoulder.

"You're alive." He breathed the words with satisfaction.

Darcy caught her breath. The doctors had been worried about his memory, but it looked like it was good.

"Yes, thanks to you, I'm alive."

A faint smile flickered across his face.

"Love you, Darcy."

The words were a mere whisper as his eyes fluttered closed again. Had she really heard him say that? Her eyes widened as her hand flew to her abdomen. Her stomach fell, an icy shiver slithering through her. This is exactly what she had feared.

Darcy knew she had to act fast. She hurried to the nurse's station and reported that Nick had momentarily awakened and seemed to remember what had happened. The nurse quickly called the doctor and went to check on Nick. While she did that Darcy tucked into the bathroom, scribbling out a note on the back of an envelope she found in her purse. She slipped back into the room where the doctor and nurse were hovering over Nick and laid the note on the chair where she had spent much of the last forty or so hours.

She paused at the doorway and looked back at Nick lying so still in the bed. She blinked tears, silently mouthed the words, "I love you, too, Nick," and slipped from the room. She should be able to get a cab to the bus station and head home from there.

Darcy stood by her living room window and stared out, watching the falling snow swirling in the breeze. It was a little after five, but already the sun was disappearing, and shadows crept in around the edges. The world shimmered before her tired eyes, and she watched listlessly as a taxi slushed down the street. True, this was the first real snowfall of the season, normally an event she loved, but it seemed lackluster compared to previous years.

Of course, everything seemed lackluster since she came home. She didn't find anything exciting or fun anymore. Every day seemed to drag by, each one longer than the last. She tried to keep busy; she didn't think there was a surface in the house that hadn't been scrubbed or polished. She'd been applying for jobs, but nothing actually appealed to her.

Restlessness roamed inside of her. Nothing seemed to satisfy her; nothing seemed to soothe the edginess that surrounded her. The holidays were fast approaching. Darcy normally loved this time of year, but now she didn't feel the same zest for the coming festivities that she usually did.

The weather had matched her mood the past couple weeks. Gray and often overcast, it rained most days, and the wind moaned around the windows. If this was a sign of the winter to come, she wasn't going to enjoy it, that much she was sure of.

Even Warlock seemed effected by her mood. He prowled restlessly around the room, occasionally emitting a discontented meow.

Darcy took a sip from the cup she held in her hand. She'd made herself hot chocolate, hoping to comfort herself and ease her taut nerves, but it didn't seem to be working. The cocoa tasted fine but lacked its normal magical relaxation powers.

As she watched the shadows deepen her mind drifted to thoughts of Nick, but she shoved them away. It felt like she spent an awful lot of time trying not to think about him. Sophie had informed her he was recovering nicely and was at home now. Sophie was the only one she talked about it with. She refused to talk to any of the Baker family. If she didn't talk to them or see them, they didn't exist, right?

It was hard to see Nick's name come up on her caller ID and not answer it. She wanted to hear his voice, to be sure he was all right. She yearned to see his silvery eyes and longed to taste his sweet lips.

But she was determined not to give in to her cravings. It was for her own good, she lectured herself. It hurt now but not as much as it could later if he didn't live through his next encounter with a killer.

She'd sworn she wouldn't marry a cop over a decade ago. For years she promised herself that she wanted nothing to do with any police officer no matter what. He could be the best-looking man in the world, and she wouldn't want anything to do with him. She hadn't figured on being isolated with such a man, left alone with him for days. She hadn't imagined getting to know him so intimately.

He'd said she was brave, courageous, independent. That she wasn't like her mother. Her mom had only been eighteen years old when she fell in love with Darcy's police officer father. She'd just lost her parents in a car accident, and Darcy had arrived by the time her mom was 20 years old. Her mother had never worked outside the home, never taken care of the financial end of things. Darcy had to admit her mother had been rather helpless.

But her pain had been real when Asa Campbell had been killed. Her fear had been palpable...and contagious. Darcy had felt it, lived it. She'd watched her mother disintegrate into a helpless wreck. She watched her descend into a world of drugs and alcohol. Lord, she did not want to live like that. The only way she knew to prevent it was to avoid Detective Nick Baker at all cost.

Thanksgiving was day after tomorrow. She always spent it with Sophie. She wasn't in the mood, but those pumpkin pies wouldn't bake themselves. Dispiritedly, she turned towards the kitchen and began to preheat the oven.

Chapter 22

Before she actually started cooking her phone rang. She carefully checked the caller ID and saw it was Sophie, so she answered it.

"Hey, lady, what's up?"

"Hi, girlfriend. Hey, I wanted to talk over an idea with you."

"Okay, shoot."

"Well, you know how you and I usually have Thanksgiving together with a couple other teachers? I was thinking, let's not do that this year. A friend of mine is hosting dinner for some folks who are down on their luck and has asked me to help serve. She said she could really use some extra hands, so I suggested you. What do you say?"

"You mean people that are more down on their luck than we are? Wow, I feel sorry for them." Darcy tried to inject some humor into her voice, but she was afraid it fell flat.

"Ah, come on, Darcy. We're not so bad off. We've still got roofs over our heads, vehicles to drive, plenty of warm clothes, and each other. What more do you want?"

A flash of guilt shot through Darcy. Sophie was right. They were much better off than some people. So what if she was longing to see Nick Baker? That was by her choice, and it was the right decision.... wasn't it?

"Okay, okay, I'll go. By the way, who is this friend of yours that's being so generous?"

"Oh, just a lady I met recently. She's wonderful. You're going to love her. Her name is Nancy."

"Well, tell Nancy I would love to help. What time should we be there and where is it?"

"Great. I'll pick you up at eleven and we'll go in my car. Oh, and go ahead and bring your pumpkin pies and the rest of the stuff you usually make. The more food the better."

Darcy hung up and turned back to her pies. At least she had a little bit of purpose now. Feeding the hungry. That was a good thing.

Thanksgiving Day dawned sunny and bright, beams dancing over the snow-covered ground. Darcy got out of bed early and made a last-minute batch of macaroni and cheese and some extra cookies. While the mac and cheese was baking she hopped through a shower and dressed in a forest green sweater with a deep cowl neck and soft gray flannel slacks. She chose a pair of black ankle boots and pulled her hair into a festive chignon. She might feel blue, but she didn't have to look it.

Sophie arrived, and they piled her back seat full of baked goods then took off for their destination, Christmas carols playing on the radio. They drove to a neighborhood not too far away and pulled up in front of a huge Victorian house. Darcy climbed out and grabbed a couple of food containers and started up the walk,

That's when she saw the twins appear on the porch, Nate and Noah right behind them. Darcy's footsteps paused, her mouth falling open.

"Sophie, you lied to me," she hissed.

"I didn't. I just didn't tell you it's Nick's mom that's hosting this party.

"I'm leaving."

"Don't be ridiculous, Darcy. There's no reason to run away like a coward."

Darcy's backbone stiffened. A coward? She was not a coward. My God, she had taken on a killer armed with just a cast iron skillet. There was no way she was a coward.

The four Baker siblings greeted them warmly urging them inside. Darcy was led into a spacious foyer featuring a wide wooden staircase and gleaming hardwood floors. They headed through a massive dining room then wound up in a spacious kitchen full of activity.

A plump little woman hurried over to them as they entered the room. Darcy knew at once this was the mom. Her eyes were the same unique color as her children's.

"I'm so glad you could make it."

"Mrs. Baker, I'd like you to meet Darcy Campbell." Sophie made the introductions then stepped back.

"Please, you girls call me Nancy, both of you. Darcy, I've heard so much about you I feel like I already know you." She reached out and pulled Darcy in for a quick hug.

Then they were swallowed up in the excitement of the preparations. Dish after dish of delicious creations were carried to the dining room table. Stuffing, mashed potatoes, sweet potatoes, green bean casserole and huge bowls of salad took their places. Homemade cranberry sauce and cheese balls lined up, and all sorts of desserts came at the end.

"My goodness, how many people are coming?" Darcy asked.

"We never really know," Nancy answered her. "This is the fifth year we've done this. We invite people the kids have met while on duty, many of whom have run into bad luck. The ones that are just down and out. Sometimes they bring others with them. We'll keep serving as long as the food holds out.

Darcy jumped in with the other women and set out food and welcomed people as they came in. The three-car garage held several tables, each covered with a white cloth. The guests came in the front door, piled their plates with food, then ate in the heated garage. When they were finished, they moved on, and others took their place.

The event was full of laughter and good cheer, the guests grateful for the bounty. Nate and Noah and the twins made sure everyone had everything they needed and handed out small gifts to the folks as they left. Gloves, scarves, and wooly hats were for the adults, but there were toys and candy for the children.

Darcy was having a wonderful time, but part of her couldn't help wondering where Nick was. She hadn't seen him since she got here. Did he know she was here? Was he avoiding her? The thoughts plagued her as she filled glasses and sliced pies. She was determined not to ask, and nobody seemed to volunteer the information.

The crowd abated around four, and the family settled down to eat their own Thanksgiving meal. Norman, the senior Baker, offered grace and everyone attacked the food like they were starving. Still no Nick. Where was he? She felt uneasy just waiting for him to appear out of nowhere.

Chapter 23

And then he was there. He walked in to the dining room and stood there, his eyes immediately finding Darcy and watching her intently. A hush fell over the dining room as everyone waited for her to react. She knew her cheeks were berry red as they all surveyed her.

"Nick," was all she said at first, the fork still dangling halfway between her plate and her mouth.

"Darcy." He continued to stare at her from those silvery-blue eyes. "I'm sorry I wasn't here earlier. I was on forced bed rest at my mother's insistence. I wasn't told you'd be here." He shot a steely glare at his siblings and his mom.

"And I didn't know I was coming here until I got here." She turned a stern eye on Sophie who calmly continued scooping corn pudding into her mouth.

"It seems like we've both been duped."

"It appears that way."

"Well, we're all here now so why don't we just enjoy our dinner?" Nate declared jovially. "Sit down, Nick. There's plenty left."

Nick sat but he ate very little, and Darcy found her appetite had completely disappeared. She just wanted to get out of here. Looking at Nick and not touching him was too painful, too excruciating to endure. Finally, she laid her fork down, dabbed her mouth with her napkin, and stood up.

"Excuse me, I need to get some air." The words came out in a twisted groan, and she dashed from the room, grabbing her jacket on the way.

Once outside on the porch, she dragged in deep gulps of air. She was shaking, trembling. Damn Sophie. How could she put her in a position like this? She walked over to the porch swing and plopped down, blinking back tears.

A moment later the front door opened, and Nick stepped out. God, he looked good, even with the new scar that blazed across his forehead. It was all she could do not to throw herself into his arms.

He walked over silently and took the seat beside her. Darcy gasped as his thigh brushed against hers. Touching him was almost a physical pain.

For a long moment they sat in silence, swinging gently, avoiding each other's eyes.

"Nick."

"Darcy."

They spoke at once then both chuckled nervously.

"Go ahead, Darcy. What were you going to say?"

"No, you go first, please."

He hesitated a moment then reached out and took her hand. "Darcy, these last couple weeks without you have been hell. Not knowing if you were okay, if you were thinking about me as much as I was about you. It was almost as if you'd died."

She knew the feeling. This is what had been wrong with her. Missing Nick, longing to hear his voice, to see his gentle smile. Not feeling his arms around her or hearing him breathe while he was sleeping. It was almost as if he were dead.

But he wasn't, and that was the difference. He was alive and well and going on with his life. Going on without her.

"I understand you're scared, baby. I know you're afraid that something will happen to me. But don't you know I feel the same about you? What if you fell down the stairs and broke your neck? What if you walked in front of a bus? What if you got cancer? Do you think it would hurt me any less if you were gone than it would you if I died?"

"But I don't go around asking for those things. You being a cop, you're putting yourself out there every day. You're a

116

target just waiting to get hit, Nick. I would worry and fear every single time you left the house. That's no way to live." Her voice broke with desperation, her throat clogging with tears.

"And we'd celebrate every time I came home." He pulled her head down on his shoulder and dropped a kiss on top of her hair. "Besides, without you, I'm only half alive. Think about it. How did it feel to you while we've been apart? Were you happy?"

She couldn't lie. She shook her head, unable to speak.

"Is that how you want to live, babe? Do you want to only feel half alive all the time?" He used his finger to lift her chin and force her to look in his eyes. "Or do you want to live life to the fullest, love the most, to celebrate every minute we have together? To me, it's worth the fear. It's a small price to pay for a lifetime of happiness."

Did she dare give in to temptation? To go against her lifetime vow to never fall in love with a cop? Or did she allow herself to love freely and fully and not let old hurts haunt her?

After a long moment of thoughtfulness, she felt herself give in. She didn't want a life without Nick in it. It was too painful, too empty. She told herself she wasn't a coward. Well, now was the time to prove it.

She raised her lips to his and kissed him thoroughly, indulging in the taste of him, so warm, so alive.

"Let the celebrations begin," she murmured, tears running down on her face. Only this time they were tears of happiness. Fear was gone, doubt was gone. Only love remained.

Nate

Chapter 1

She'd only taken three steps out of the store when Sophia Cruz felt her feet slip on the icy sidewalk. She did a complicated dance for a moment before her feet flew straight up in the air. A startled squeak emitted from her throat as her body tipped and formed a 45-degree angle in midair. She hovered there for a second before crashing down on the hard-packed-ice-coated concrete. The air whooshed from her lungs as the back of her head smacked the ground. For a second, she actually saw stars whirling before her eyes.

She gasped for air that refused to come. Her wide brown eyes opened even wider, blinking repeatedly, pain exploding behind them. As her vision cleared and her first full breath entered her lungs, she saw a face floating above her. And quite a handsome face it was.

Dark hair tumbled around chiseled features. A well-trimmed mustache perched above full lips. Its mouth was moving but she didn't hear anything for a moment. At last, sound started to penetrate her senses.

"Sophie. Sophie. Can you hear me?"

It took a moment for reality to set in.

"Nate?" she finally gasped.

"Sophie, are you okay?" He hovered over her, his hands quickly searching her body for broken bones. When they reached her ankle, she let out a groan of pain. She hurt so many places she hadn't even realized yet that her ankle was throbbing.

"Sophie, don't move. You might be hurt."

The concern in his voice touched her even through her veil of pain. Nate. She'd met him when her best friend Darcy got involved with a murder investigation. Darcy had fallen in love with his brother, Nick, a cop who hid her away from the killers, and Sophie made Nate take her to her friend. Sparks flew immediately between Nate and Sophie, and he'd even asked her on a date. But fate interfered. Nate was a cop, too, but he worked undercover. He was ordered on a job that sent him deep undercover for several weeks, and she hadn't seen him since Thanksgiving, a month ago.

The cop in Nate took over. He leaned down and peered into her eyes, looking for signs of concussion. He pulled out his phone and quickly called dispatch and requested an ambulance. All the while, his gaze peered into hers until she shivered with the effect of those laser-blue eyes staring at her.

"No, Nate, no, I don't need an ambulance. I don't want to go to the hospital." Her voice rose in panic. She'd been laid off from her teaching job and didn't have insurance. She couldn't afford that.

"You're hurt, Sophie. You need to be checked out." He tried using his stern voice and gave her his most serious cop face. "Just let them take a look."

"No," she growled. God, she hated to admit why she didn't want to go the hospital, but an emergency room bill now would break her. She had plans for her money. Sophie struggled to sit up but a wave of dizziness rocked her back.

"See? You are hurt," Nate scolded gently. "Just lie still until help gets here."

"No, Nate, I can't. I can't go to the hospital." She shook her head hard enough that her soft pink beret flew off her short cap of feathery sable locks.

"Why not, Sophie? Are you scared?" he asked quietly.

"No, I'm not scared." Her cheeks reddened at the idea. "I'm not a child, you know."

"Oh, I do know that." He cracked a grin and ran his gaze over her sprawled-out body. "No doubt in my mind. You're definitely a full-grown woman."

"Well, it's not because I'm scared. I can't afford to go." She finally spat out the words. "I don't have any insurance. Besides, I'm fine."

"Don't worry about money right now. Your health is priceless."

"Easy for you to say. You're not the one who's going to have the bill collectors after them." Once again, Sophie moved to sit up, and this time she made it. Nate immediately slipped his arm behind her to support her, and admittedly she had to lean into him just a bit.

"Sophie—" He started to speak but she cut him off.

"No, no way, no how. Just help me up, please."

Nate slipped his arm tighter around her waist and lifted her to her feet. A wave of dizziness swept over her as pain shot through her ankle, and she leaned against the sturdy support of his broad chest.

Wow. She drew back. If she hadn't, she'd have wound up staying pressed against him for quite some time just because it felt so good.

"Call them back and tell them to cancel the ambulance, Nate. Please." She turned her gamine face up to his, her big brown eyes pleading with him.

He reluctantly reached into his pocket and pulled out his phone and made the call then studied her, shaking his head.

"You are stubborn, you know that?" His mustache twitched above his mouth, a dimple dancing in his cheek. "Okay, if you're not going to the hospital, I'm taking you home."

"That's not necessary. Really." She stiffened in his arms. "I'm fine. I can make it home."

"Give me a break, Sophie," he ordered. "I won't be able to rest if I don't see you home. Now, come on, my car's right over here."

"I walked here."

"Well, you're going to ride home." He wrapped his arm tighter around her waist and helped her hobble to his black

122

SUV. She had to allow him to practically carry her to the vehicle before bundling her inside. The pain radiating from her ankle was throbbing, making her feel slightly nauseous.

"Hang on, Sophie. We'll have you home in just a minute," he promised as he pulled his door shut.

He wasn't wrong. Five minutes hadn't passed before he was pulling into the parking lot of Felix's Bar and Grill. Sophie rented the apartment above the neighborhood pub. It was small and could be a little noisy, but she'd decided on it the moment she'd seen the south-facing wall of windows. As an artist, she found the light irresistible, and the price was right.

"Thank you for bringing me home," Sophie said as she reached for the door handle.

"I'm coming in with you," he said firmly.

"What? I'm fine. Please don't put yourself out."

"Sophie, I was planning on coming to see you, anyway."

"You were?"

"Yes. Now let's go in." He climbed from the vehicle and hurried around to open her door. She got out and immediately inhaled with pain as she applied weight to her foot.

Nate didn't waste time. He simply swept her up in his arms and pressed her to his leather-jacket-clad chest.

Sophie gasped and instinctively wrapped her arms around his neck.

"What are you doing?"

"What do you think I'm doing? I'm carrying you upstairs." He bounced her gently in his arms, settling her more comfortably. "We're going through the inside entrance. No sense in taking a chance on both of us falling on the ice this time."

Sophie gasped and buried her flaming cheeks in Nate's neck as he toted her inside through the main room of the bar. Mayzie, the redheaded bartender, gasped when she saw Sophie being carried by the handsome guy who held her so carefully.

"Sophie. Are you okay?' The girl hurried from behind the bar, drying her hands on a bar towel as she scurried forward.

"She took a fall," Nate answered for her as Sophie managed to nod her head. She felt the eyes of half a dozen customers on her, and the color in her cheeks deepened. God, how could he embarrass her like this? "She'll be fine."

He didn't hesitate, simply strode toward the door that hid the staircase and headed up, leaving Mayzie standing behind them with her mouth hanging open. Sophie buried her face in Nate's collar and didn't say a word.

Nate carried her effortlessly into the small living room. Sophie's Bohemian style was immediately evident from the beaded curtains to the fringed tablecloth. In the corner sat a large bird cage on a stand that held a huge white cockatoo. At the sight of Nate carrying Sophie, the bird stuck out his golden crest and squawked, "Lord a mercy, kiss my ass." He repeated the phrase over and over until Sophie hollered at him to shut up.

"Eat shit," the bird hollered back.

Nate burst out laughing as he sat down on the couch, still holding Sophie. "I think he means welcome home."

"I don't think he does," Sophie chuckled. "I think Angel means exactly what he's saying." She'd basically inherited the bird from an old woman who used to hang out at the bar downstairs, and she'd soon discovered his vocabulary was wide and colorful. Sometimes he was a pain in the butt, yet in reality she loved his company.

"Sophie, you are full of surprises." Nate turned his gaze on her and she was caught in the web of his silver-blue scrutiny. She looked deep into his hypnotic eyes and a spear of lust shot directly into her crotch. Her breath caught in her throat, her nipples hardened, and the world began to spin. Time moved in slow motion as Nate lowered his head and captured her lips.

Chapter 2

Sophie slowly melted into Nate's embrace, collapsing like a balloon losing air. She'd always thought a kiss making your toes curl was just an expression, that you would never actually experience it. But now she literally felt it happening as the tingles spread right down to her feet. My God, she suddenly felt so hot she thought sparks would fly from her hair.

A guttural groan came from Nate's throat, and Sophie felt a distinctive ridge growing beneath her thighs. The proof of his desire turned her on even more and her hands delved into his thick, luxurious hair and pulled him even closer.

"I missed you, Sophie." He raised his lips long enough to murmur the words. "I hated being away this time."

"I worried about you the whole time, Nate," she confessed.

"Stop it!" Angel's angry squawk burst through the air and he fluffed his golden crest impressively.

They both started laughing at his antics.

"Thanks for bringing us back to the present, Angel." Nate chuckled. "Here I am, enjoying your woman while I should be taking care of her."

"I thought you were," she couldn't resist saying in a teasing voice.

"Not the way I should be," he retorted. "I need to check your head and see to your ankle."

"I should probably get off of your lap then," she sighed.

"Much as I hate to say it, yes." He kissed her again then moved her to the other cushion on the love seat. "Now, let's see that head."

Sophie allowed him to fuss over her for the next few minutes. He felt the lump that had risen from her scalp and she winced.

"You've got quite the goose egg there."

"Ouch. I can tell."

"I'll get you some aspirin in a minute. I want to look at your ankle first."

Nate gently slipped the leather bootie from her foot and pressed the flesh of her tender ankle. He turned her ankle this way and that, watching her face for reflections of pain.

"I don't think it's broken," he finally announced. "Let's soak it in ice water and see what happens." He strode into the kitchenette to prepare a pan to soak her foot in. She only had one tray of ice cubes, so he ran down to the bar and got some more from Mayzie. Soon he was back carrying a pan of water, then set it down on the floor in front of her.

"Now just put it in the water," he directed, easing her foot into the frigid liquid.

"Oh, that's freezing!"

"I know, sweetie, I know. Here, maybe this will help." He picked up an afghan from the back of the loveseat and wrapped it around her shoulders, tucking it in under her chin. "Better?"

"Not really," she moaned. "It's like having my foot in a blast chiller."

"Shh, let's try to take your mind off it. Tell me why you were out in the weather today."

"I needed some supplies for my framing business."

"Oh, you're pushing ahead with that idea?'

"I am. This place is so small, though. I really don't have room to keep many supplies here or much workspace, either. I wish I had someplace bigger." She waved her hands toward her dining room table which was buried under framing supplies.

"I see what you mean." He eyed the cluttered space and took in the piles of wood, mounting materials, and several pictures waiting to be framed. He scratched his chin thoughtfully. He could see she needed more room if she was going to start framing as a full-time career. He knew she was an art teacher but budget cuts had caused her to be laid off. She was also a skilled framer, however, and had picked up quite a bit of work freelancing. Now it looked like she had grown out of her space.

"So why were you coming to see me?" Sophie couldn't help but be curious. She thought there had been an instant chemistry between the two of them. They had even spent Thanksgiving together, helping serve a huge dinner for needy neighbors at his parents' home. She hadn't heard from him since. If it weren't for his brother, she wouldn't know he'd been working undercover.

"Hmm?" He asked as if she'd interrupted deep thoughts, casually draping his arm around her shoulders.

"You said you were on your way to see me," she reminded him.

"Oh, yeah. I was coming to ask you to forgive me for not contacting you the last month. I was off the radar for work." He smiled, his silver-blue gaze locking on to hers. "And I wanted to ask you to go out with me."

"Really? Then the answer is yes to both questions." She didn't hesitate. She wanted to go out with this handsome man. "Nick let me know about work and gave me your message."

"Thank goodness for brothers," he laughed. "So, how about going with me to the movies tomorrow night? Then we can catch a bite to eat afterward. If your foot's functioning by then," he added.

"Sounds good," she agreed. Sounds great, she thought to herself. Cuddling in a dark theater with Nate? Oh, yeah, it sounded good to her.

"Great. I'll come by around six and see if you feel up to going. If not, we'll stay in, okay?"

"It's a plan."

"Great. Now, do you have everything you need to get by for the next 24 hours? Plenty of food?"

"I do. I just went to the store yesterday."

"Terrific. So would you like to take your foot out of the ice water now?" A twinkle appeared in his eyes.

"Absolutely," she agreed with enthusiasm.

"Okay, but you're going to have to do it again soon."

"Damn." It was her only response.

Nate took the towel he'd brought from the kitchen and wrapped it around her ankle as she pulled her foot from the water. His fingers against her bare skin felt like a cool breeze slipping over her flesh. She shivered as the tingle ran through her right down to her frozen toes.

"Don't worry. I'll be here to make sure you do," he promised, a humorous tic pulling at the side of his mouth. "So, why don't we talk more about your business? What would you say if I told you I knew where there was a place for rent that I think you could afford, with plenty of room for your framing business?"

"That would be great, but I need a place to live and work," she reminded him. "Not just a workspace—I can't afford both."

"This place has that, too. It's small—but efficient." Then he told her the rent and she gasped.

"You're kidding. Where is this place?"

"Just a few blocks away and on a well-traveled street. I think it's perfect for what you need."

"Tell me how to get ahold of the landlord," she urged.

"Well, that's the problem. I don't know if you'll like him. They say he's kind of a rough guy, pretty hardnosed."

"I don't care. For a deal like that, I can put up with him."

"He's not the easiest guy in the world to get along with," he warned her.

"Darn it, Nate, tell me."

"Okay, but don't say I didn't warn you." He paused and looked her straight in the eyes.

"It's me."

Chapter 3

She sat, stunned, her chocolate brown eyes wide with surprise. Him? Nate was the landlord? She didn't know why she was so shocked. He might look like a tough guy, but Sophie knew him as he really was—a cop, a guy who loved his family, and a kind, responsible man. Kind enough, in fact, to offer to rent her his property at a dirt-cheap price. She couldn't let him do it. He could get much higher rental fees from someone else.

"No." She said it quietly but firmly.

"No? Because I'd be your landlord?" He tipped his head and looked at her quizzically.

"Yes. Because you'd be my landlord who was practically giving me the place rent-free. I'm not a charity case." Her chin firmed with conviction, a spark of anger burning within her.

"Sophie, I never said you were. I just think you'd be the perfect tenant. I'm not home a lot and I feel I could trust you. I hadn't decided what I wanted to do with the carriage house yet. I've owned the place for a year and have never rented it out. But when I saw how overwhelmed this place was with your work, I thought of the carriage house and knew it would be perfect."

"Oh, come on. Do you really expect me to buy that happy crap?" She shook her head. "If not for charity, then maybe it's because you think I'd be a really convenient booty call? I mean, in your backyard and all?"

"Geez, Sophie, what kind of man do you think I am? Some sort of predator?" His voice held an angry edge. "I hadn't even thought about that. I just thought it might be a good solution for both of us. The building would be occupied instead of sitting empty, and you'd have a place to establish your business. I am so sorry for trying to be a nice guy."

Nate rose to his feet, a cold glint in his eyes. "I thought we were more in tune than that. I guess not."

"Can you blame me for thinking it?" she shot back.

"Forget it then, Sophie. Maybe you aren't the answer to my prayers after all." With that, he turned and walked out of the room, slamming the door behind him. A second later, it opened again and he stuck his head in. "Make sure you soak that foot again."

Then he slammed the door and was gone; this time he didn't come back.

Well. He did have a temper, didn't he? She couldn't condemn that, though. She was quick to anger as well. Obviously. But she kind of liked the fact that he stood up for himself. She couldn't stand a wishy-washy man, one who was apologetic and passive-aggressive. She preferred a man who spoke his mind. There was something more honest about a man who lost his temper occasionally. Something exciting.

If she were truthful, she had to admit that Nate Baker was exciting in many different ways. She was intrigued by his rugged good looks. He was a police officer but he didn't look like one. His deep chestnut-colored hair was long, past his shoulders, threads of gold running through it. He usually wore it pulled back in a ponytail, but it was well kept and neatly groomed.

He was built like a Greek god, his muscular frame well outfitted in a tight t-shirt and faded jeans that fit his long, muscular thighs like a second skin. His face was square, his cheekbones high. He had a thick mustache above firm lips, and she loved the sun-kissed glow of his skin. Even though it was December, he had a tan.

But the most intriguing thing about Nate was his eyes. Silver-blue, intense, and startling against his dark complexion. She thought she could drown in those icy pools.

Sophie shook her head and ordered herself to stop thinking about the hunky police officer. She wasn't after a long-term relationship. Oh, she wasn't against commitment. She just didn't have time for it now. Instead, she forced her mind to the orders her clients had placed. Even if she couldn't do any actual work, she could plan.

The next day, Sophie woke with an all-over-body ache and an extremely swollen foot. She hobbled through getting dressed and fixing herself a bowl of cereal for breakfast. Every step was painful but she found an old walking stick that she started using and at least was able to function.

She took it easy that day, doing a lot of sitting with her foot propped up, and she was actually getting pretty good with the walking stick. Then she heard her phone ring and picked it up. Huh. It was Nate. She didn't think she'd be hearing from him since he'd left so angry.

"Hello," she answered tentatively.

"Hi, Sophie. I called to see how you're feeling...and if you're still speaking to me." His voice held a hint of sheepishness and she had to fight back an urge to giggle. She couldn't resist taunting him.

"Hmm. Well, the answer to your first question is I'm okay except I have to use a walking stick to get around. As for the second part of that question, I haven't decided yet. Do you think I should be talking to you?"

"Definitely. I do admit I can be a little hotheaded, but so can you. After I thought about it, though, I decided I couldn't blame you for questioning my intentions. You have to look out for yourself. I just felt offended that you thought I had ulterior motives."

Her heart melted at his honest words. She couldn't stay mad at him. She might even owe him an apology, but she wasn't ready to give in on that point yet.

"I understand, Nate, and I forgive you." She made her voice as prim as she could, considering there was a big grin spreading across her face.

"Great. Then we are still on for tonight?"

"I don't see why not."

"Okay. It sounds like you'd prefer to stay in, am I right?"

"If you don't mind."

"That's cool. How do you feel about Chinese?"

"I love it."

"Great. Then Chinese and a chick flick are on the menu. Okay with you?"

"That's perfect."

"See you at seven?"

Since it was only two, Sophie decided to spend some time on her quest. She had gone into the foster care system when she was only eight years old, after he mother was killed by a drunk driver as she walked home from work. She'd died without ever telling Sophie who her father was, and now she wanted to know. Her birth certificate hadn't offered any clues, so she was on a search to discover who he was.

She sat in front of the computer scrolling but not getting anywhere. She had to admit she wasn't really into it today. Her mind kept flowing to Nate Baker. He was an intriguing man. Handsome, kind of mysterious, yet friendly and helpful. An odd combination of traits.

She couldn't help thinking about his eyes. Their silvery-blue color was a shade she'd never seen before except on Nate, his siblings, and their mother. It was hypnotizing. His piercing gaze was surrounded by thick, long, sable lashes. Lashes a woman would sacrifice a kidney for. She could definitely drown in those cool pools.

Sophie jerked her thoughts back to her internet search. She didn't need to be wasting time mooning about Nate. He was just another man, after all. She had no interest in marriage or even a long-term relationship. She couldn't count on a man. She had to stand on her own two feet. If anybody should know that, she should. She may have been just a little girl when her mother died, but she'd learned at least one lesson from her: just because you love a man doesn't mean you can count on him.

Chapter 4

Later that evening, Sophie was feeling relaxed, having been pampered by Nate all evening. He took care of her every need, from bringing her drinks to getting the dishes for their supper. The food was delicious, the movie sweet and funny, and now they were lounging in front of the TV, watching an old rerun of Friends. She lounged against his shoulder, enjoying the citrusy, spicy scent of him.

She found it easy to talk to him. They'd already discussed their childhoods and found they had very different backgrounds. Nate had been raised in a traditional home, his dad a cop and his mom a teacher. He had two brothers and twin sisters. Sophie had been shuffled about through the system, moving from family to family, not really fitting in anywhere. She kept her sanity through her art.

Art had always played a vital part in her life. She'd sketched, drawn, and painted her way through her childhood. She'd started making frames for her own artwork and had managed to work her way through college using her framing skills. Now that she'd been laid off, she was once again drawing on those skills to support herself.

She was feeling all warm and cozy cuddled up against Nate as she enjoyed the television show. That's when he brought up the subject of the carriage house again.

"Have you thought any more about my offer for the carriage house?"

Sophie felt him tense against her, like he was holding his breath.

"I have, actually," she told him. "I might consider it if you'd let me pay a more reasonable price." She tossed out a number and felt her body reflect his tension in her own body. Would he agree to her counteroffer? She wouldn't accept it at the ridiculously low price he was offering.

He tossed back a slightly lower number. Sophie couldn't resist. "Okay. I'll at least look at it."

"Good, good. You know, I really would feel better with someone I know living out there. I really don't want a stranger, or to go through the hassle of showing the place, checking references, all that stuff. I just don't have time."

"Nate, you don't know me well. We just met a bit over a month ago. I could turn out to be a serial killer myself."

Nate tried to hide his chuckle. "I don't think so, Sophie. For one thing, Darcy wouldn't be your best friend if you were."

Darcy was Sophie's very best friend and was now madly in love with Nate's one-year-older brother Nick. Although Darcy and her cop had only known each other slightly longer than Nate and Sophie had, they already knew they were soulmates, meant to be together forever. Sophie ignored a twinge of envy as she thought about her friend. A long-term relationship was the last thing she wanted.

"Well, that is a pretty good reference," she conceded, grinning up at him. "Darcy is the crème de la crème. But you don't know her all that well, either."

"My brother's in love with her. That's good enough for me." Nate nodded firmly as he spoke.

"Well, I question your judgment, but in this case, I'll have to admit that it's right. I'm not a serial killer." She managed to keep a straight face as she answered him solemnly.

"I'm so glad to know that." He grinned at her, the dimple in his left cheek dancing. Suddenly he looked so desirable he felt irresistible. She clenched his face in her hands and drew his mouth to hers, surprising them both with the ferocity of her kiss.

His lips were firm and dry, yet soft and supple. Perfect. She lifted her mouth for a moment then went back for more. His tongue traced along her lip line then slipped into her mouth, dancing with hers, stroking, tasting. Oh, wow. He tasted delicious. Like the wine they'd been sipping, blending with Nate's own special flavor. She felt herself melting against him, his arms sliding around her, pulling her close.

Holy hollyhocks! What was happening? Electricity pumped through her at a crazy rate, her heart raced, and every nerve felt alive and pulsating. This instant attraction had never happened before. Oh, sure, she'd been with men, she'd enjoyed sex, but she'd never felt like this before. Sensations overwhelmed her and she broke free from his embrace.

"I'm sorry," she gasped. "I practically attacked you."

"That's definitely something you don't need to apologize for." His voice was husky, raspy.

"I don't usually throw myself at guys." She folded her hands primly in her lap, trying to keep them from shaking. "I don't know what came over me."

"Well, whatever it was, I hope it's habit-forming." He grinned at her and touched the end of her nose with his finger. Her dark brown eyes met his silver gaze and she felt herself getting lost in their depths again.

She jerked herself away from those fascinating orbs and spoke quietly. "I wanted to say that I would take a look at your place if the offer's still on."

"Of course, it is. Why wouldn't it be?"

"Because I'm a masher?" she asked innocently.

"Hardly. Besides, if you're a masher, I think I'd like that."

"I think you're nuts," she laughed. "Anyway, when should I come by?"

"How about tomorrow? Say around three?"

"Sounds good. Tell me the address again."

A few minutes later, Nate said good night. She walked him to the door and couldn't resist kissing him again. This time, it was even harder to separate from him. Lord, she wanted him. Stop it, she ordered herself. She wasn't a lust-drunk wanton woman. Stop acting like one. Though she had to say, Nate acted almost as reluctant as herself to part. His lips lingered over hers, his hand gently cupping the back of her neck. His eyes looked deep into hers before he turned and disappeared into the night.

The next morning, Sophie's ankle felt quite a bit better. She could walk with just a slight limp if she didn't stay on it too long. She did some framing work then took a break to return to her internet search for her biological father. She wasn't having much luck and was growing impatient. She'd even thought about giving up the hunt.

Her growling stomach reminded her that she hadn't eaten yet that day, so she hobbled to the kitchen to grab a yogurt. Once she was finished, she headed to the shower to get ready to meet Nate. She couldn't deny she was getting excited about seeing the carriage house. It might seem too good to be true, but hey, when opportunity knocks...

She dried her short cap of feathery hair and lightly applied makeup before slipping into jeans and a coral-colored sweater. She gave Angel a piece of orange and listened to him thank her profusely then grabbed her purse and jacket and headed out the door.

Nate's place was just a few blocks away and Sophie was pulling up in her Prius in just a minute. She was impressed with the big house. It was a Victorian style, pale blue with white gingerbread trim and a wraparound porch. A portico extended out over the drive that led back to the guest house.

Nate appeared on the porch as soon as she pulled in the drive. He strode to her car and opened the door before she'd even turned off the engine.

"I'm glad you're here," he greeted her. "Let's go take a look."

Sophie stepped out of her car and turned toward the back of the house. There was an expansive garden, now buried beneath a few inches of snow. Sophie was enchanted by the secret hideaway. At the back of the house stood the smaller structure she'd come to see. It had been updated sometime in the past with a wide concrete porch and four white pillars. She knew the moment she saw it that she loved it.

"This used to be the carriage house, then it became the guest house," Nate told her. "And for the last 30 years, it was an insurance agency."

Sophie drank in the history of the place and admired the look of it. Could this place really be what she'd been dreaming of?

"Come on in." Nate held the door and she walked into one big workspace with a room partitioned off on one end. A staircase ran along the other end. The floors were old wood, and the walls were wood painted white. A large window dominated the front south-facing wall. Outside was a fairly busy street that would offer good traffic for her business.

"Oh, my God. It's perfect." She barely breathed the words but Nate heard her.

"You think? Maybe you should wait to form an opinion until you see the living space." Nate's voice sounded a little worried.

"Okay. Let's see it." Sophie refused to be deterred and headed for the stairs. Nate quickly followed her.

She opened the door and stepped into another wide open space—one big space. One wall was taken up by a kitchen, small but functional. Another wall held two doors into what she presumed was the bathroom and a closet. The space in between would have to hold both a sleeping and living area.

"It's efficient,' she murmured. "It's small, but that balcony is great."

She walked over and looked out the sliding glass door to the broad balcony above the back porch. It would be excellent. She already pictured herself sitting out there in the summertime, sipping some iced tea, looking into the peaceful garden of Nate's house. She could imagine watching him as he worked in the yard, damp t-shirt plastered to his brawny body.

Quit. She shouldn't be thinking about that. Besides, hopefully she'd be too busy in the shop to spend much time lounging on the balcony. This was a chance she couldn't afford to pass up. She'd tried doing things the conventional way and ended up being laid off. She wanted control of her own life, and this looked like her best opportunity.

"I'll take it." Her voice was firm. She wouldn't allow herself to doubt this was the right move.

"Are you sure?"

"Absolutely. It's perfect."

"Shake on it? He extended his hand.

"Shake." She took his hand in hers and couldn't help feeling she might have just sold her soul to the devil.

Chapter 5

Everything happened quickly after that. Within two weeks, she and Angel had moved. Nate and his brothers Nick and Noah helped her move her furniture, and she was settled in a few days before Christmas. She worked furiously to get her business up and open. She had customers that followed her from the shop where she'd been working part-time and a few customers she'd picked up working freelance. Online framing was gaining ground, but there were still people who appreciated custom framing. Business was already growing and she felt happy and contented with her decision. The only shadow on her life was Christmas. She hated the thought of spending it alone.

Sophie usually spent Christmas with Darcy, but this year Darcy would be with Nick. That was something she would have to get used to. She and Darcy had spent most of their spare time together, and now Darcy was no longer as readily available. It was a reality she had to face. She wanted Darcy to be happy, and Nick made her happy.

Sophie named her little shop Sophie's Custom Framing. Not very original but it said it all. It told who she was and what she did. She divided the downstairs space into a showroom and workroom, the divider acting as a cash register area. The walls showcased framed paintings and photographs for sale, by artists she had previously dealt with and a few of her own as well. There was still work to do, but so far, she was happy with her new place.

Now she sat curled in her loveseat, looking out the window over the garden. Snow was falling lightly, the flakes glimmering in the glow from the light in Nate's backyard. It was six o'clock on a Sunday evening and Sophie was wrapped in hope and content. This, truly, was a new beginning for her. Being laid off from her teaching job at the school had knocked her off balance, upset her equilibrium. Her well-laid plans had been thrown completely off track.

She should have expected it. Sophie had spent much of her life in chaos. Her mother had died when she was just a child and she'd gone into foster care. She was never really considered for adoption. She wasn't a dimple-faced baby. She was skinny and gawky, very quiet, and she kept her mind focused on the future...when she would be in control. But getting laid off had made her realize that she would always be dependent on someone else for her living unless she took charge of her own future.

She'd already done that years ago. It hadn't taken her long to realize she was alone in the world and it was up to her how she would live her life. She focused on her education and used art to escape the harsh realities of life. She kept to herself as she was growing up and traveled from family to family. Most of the time, she was just shuffled in amongst the other children already living in the home.

But then there had been the other homes, the ones where she was worked like a dog and others where family members stared at her in a lustful manner. She'd had to fight for her virtue twice and lost the third time. Her foster father, who insisted she called him Daddy, overpowered her one day when she was unprepared for his attack. She was home sick from school, and he snuck up behind her as she returned to her room from using the toilet for the fifth time that morning. The man had brutalized her, raping and sodomizing her until she puked and crapped all over the floor. It wasn't the way she'd imagined losing her virginity, and it sent her spiraling downward.

But somehow, she managed to claw her way back. She stiffened her spine and reported her foster father to her caseworker and dealt with the courts to become emancipated. It messed with her psyche but she refused to let it destroy her. She'd kept on her path and forged ahead. That meant concentrating on her grades, earning a scholarship, and putting herself through college. She'd accepted the fact that people had sex to satisfy natural urges, had even learned to enjoy it a bit, but she hadn't learned to trust others yet. Darcy was about the only one she trusted completely. She'd been burned too many times in life.

As though thinking of her had conjured Darcy up, the phone rang and it was her.

"Hey, girlfriend. What's up?"

"Hi, Soph. What ya doing? Are you busy?"

"I'm being shamefully lazy at the moment."

"Do you feel like company?"

"Of course, if that company is you."

"Well, it's me and Nick."

Of course. No girls' night tonight. That was okay, though. She liked Nick.

"Sounds good, Darcy."

"Great. Okay if we come by in about an hour?"

Sophie ran downstairs to open the door when the bell rang. She hugged Darcy and turned to greet Nick when she realized Nate was standing there, too. She hadn't seen him the last couple days and was again struck by his handsomeness. As usual, her knees felt a little weak at the sight of him.

"Hi, guys. Come on in." She hoped her voice didn't sound as shaky as her knees felt.

"I still can't believe how much you've accomplished, Sophie," Darcy exclaimed as she stepped into the shop area. "It looks great."

"Thanks. I wish the upstairs was as in as good of a shape," she laughed. "Come on up, but enter at your own risk. I'm still unpacking."

She headed to the stairwell and led the way. They walked into the large open room and the four of them nearly filled the space.

"It looks really cute." Darcy clapped her hands in excitement. "I love it."

"It's still pretty messy." She couldn't help but feel proud, although there were still a few boxes to be unpacked. She liked the space. The kitchen was light and airy with its white cabinets and butcher block countertops, and she'd added a pub style table. Her navy-blue furniture looked good against the white walls. She'd hung red-and-white checked curtains at all the windows, and she'd even partitioned off a bedroom with the same fabric in a frame.

"It's adorable," Darcy stated staunchly as she took a seat at the table.

"May I get anybody a beer or some hot chocolate?" Sophie offered.

"Perfect," Darcy agreed. Both men gladly accepted a beer and joined Darcy at the table.

"I bet you're wondering while we're all here," Darcy started. "It's not just to check up on you. We wanted to ask you to come to Christmas dinner at the Bakers' house."

Sophie gasped with surprise. She wasn't prepared for the unexpected invitation. She didn't want to be alone but she didn't want to be an extra wheel, either.

"No, really, I wouldn't want to intrude." Color rushed to her cheeks, staining them crimson. God, this was awkward.

Nick reached across and covered her hand where it lay on the table. "Sophie, you and Darcy are family. That makes you part of my family as well. Christmas is for families. Please don't say no."

Before she could respond, Nate took her other hand in his. "Sophie, I really want you to come." He looked into her eyes, and she felt herself cave. How could she say no?

"Are you sure?"

"Absolutely. Will you come? Please?"

Sophie had to fight the tears in her eyes. She had been worried about spending Christmas by herself and now she was honored with this invitation.

"Thank you so much, you guys. I don't know how to tell you how happy I am to accept." Her voice was weak, overwhelmed with emotion.

"Oh, Sophie, I'm so glad." Darcy wrapped her arms around her neck and squeezed. "I hated the thought of not spending Christmas with you."

Sophie couldn't help the swell of joy that welled up within her. She felt blessed despite all that she'd been through.

Chapter 6

Sophie suddenly had the Christmas spirit, something she'd definitely been lacking. She hadn't done any decorating yet, so she went out the next morning and bought a small tree and a wreath for the front door of the shop. She picked out a pretty bracelet for Darcy and selected a crystal bowl she'd fill with fresh fruit to give to the senior Bakers. She even bought herself a gift: a deliciously scented candle.

On Christmas Eve, she spent the day baking. She made cookies and fudge and then started a batch of banana nut bread. She had just put it in the oven when the doorbell rang. It was the bell to the door facing the garden, so Sophie knew it was someone she knew, probably Darcy. She dusted off her hands and dashed down the stairs. Her heart skipped a beat when she peeked out the window and saw Nate standing there.

He looked incredible. A light dusting of snow dotted his dark hair and speckled the shoulders of his black leather jacket. Shadows danced across the plains of his face and he somehow took on a mysterious look.

"Nate, hi. What are you doing here?" she asked as she pulled the door open.

"I was lonely. I thought you might want to share some Christmas cheer with me." He held up a bottle and waved it in front of her nose.

Sophie was suddenly aware that she still wore a ruffled apron over her faded jeans and she probably had flour on her nose. Well, it couldn't be helped. She hadn't been expecting company, after all.

"Sure, come on in. But you'll have to excuse the mess. I was doing some Christmas baking."

"So I see," he said, reaching out and gently rubbing a white smudge off her cheek with his thumb. Her skin burned at his touch and a little worm of desire wiggled in her pelvis.

"Come on up. You can help me decorate the cookies." She hoped her voice sounded calmer than she felt. Something about Nate Baker unnerved her. She didn't feel like her normal, confident self around him. For some reason, she felt vulnerable.

"Did you say I can help you eat the cookies? I'm good at that."

"I might let you have one...after we decorate them." She spoke sternly, trying to conceal a grin as she led the way into her aromatic apartment. Christmas music played softly in the background. The smell of spices and freshly baked goods perfumed the air. Nate drew in a deep breath.

"This must be what heaven smells like," he groaned.

"You might be right," she chuckled. "I'll get some glasses for the wine and you can open it."

Sophie took out her only two wine glasses and set them on the table. Nate popped the cork and poured the white wine into the crystal. He raised his glass and toasted her. "To your new venture. Merry Christmas, Sophie."

"Merry Christmas, Nate." Her voice softened and she tapped her glass gently against his. Their eyes met for a long moment as she sipped the delicious wine. It was like an electric current shot from his eyes to hers and she had trouble swallowing.

Finally, she broke the spell. "Well, let's get to work, okay? These cookies won't decorate themselves."

They spent the next couple of hours icing the sugar cookies she'd made and cut out with cookie cutters, laughing a lot and consuming a few glasses of wine while they were at it. Sophie felt herself relax as she enjoyed his conversation. He reminisced about his own childhood Christmases shared with his four siblings and his parents. She couldn't help imaging him as a little boy, those charming dimples and sparkling eyes adding mischief to his expression.

They sang along with the holiday songs playing and critiqued each other's decorating skills. It took Nate a bit to get the hang of piping frosting, but soon he was decorating like a pro. She actually thought he was better at it than she was, and she was an artist.

At last, they decorated the last cookie. Nate sagged against the bar stool at the pub table. "Whew. You're a hard taskmaster."

"I promised you a reward. Here it is." She held a cookie a few tantalizing inches away from his mouth.

"Mmm, I want it," he said and licked his lips. Sophie's gaze fastened on his tongue. Damn, she wanted that tongue against her flesh.

Nate reached out with his mouth toward the cookie, but Sophie playfully pulled it back.

"Indian giver," he accused and wrapped his arms around her waist and pulled her closer. "Give me that, you."

Sophie let him win the battle but held the cookie as his perfectly straight white teeth sank into the star-shaped treat. She watched him chew then swallow slowly, and he closed his eyes in ecstasy.

"That is so good," he moaned and took another bite as his arms tightened around her waist. He nibbled away until it was gone and then he sucked each of her fingers into his mouth, slowly licking the last bit of flavor off with his tongue.

Sophie shuddered as sensations ran through her. Her fingertips felt electrified, alive. His tongue slid smoothly around her shell-pink nails and he suckled each one to the knuckle. It was a good thing he had his arms around her because her knees grew weak and her legs threatened to give out on her. She couldn't control the tremble that rippled through her.

"Delicious," he murmured, his mustache brushing against the delicate skin of her hand, his warm breath caressing her fingers. When a tiny moan escaped her lips, he pulled back and gazed down at her heart-shaped face, flushed and delicate. Without hesitation, he lowered his head and captured her mouth beneath his.

Sophie pressed into Nate, scorched by the heat of his body. She savored the taste of him and the sweet vanilla icing, her tongue licking his lips then sliding into the damp cave of his mouth. She felt him suck on her tongue, and it seemed there was a nerve that ran directly from its tip to her pelvis. The goosebumps that appeared on her arms surprised her. No man had ever given her goosebumps before.

But Nate Baker was like no other man she'd ever met before. He was handsome; he exuded sexiness. But it went farther than that. She felt drawn to him, to maybe even like a part of his soul. There was a connection that she'd never felt, a tie that was strong. It wasn't all about sex, pleasurable as it was. It was all about the special, unique feeling that she shared with him. A harmony that had been absent from her life.

But that harmony was suddenly broken by the blast of a gun and shattering glass.

Chapter 7

Sophie barely had time to scream before Nate pushed her to the ground and threw himself on top of her. They lay there for several moments without moving. Sophie trembled and shivered, fright flushing through her. She felt his body sprawled on top of hers, so close she could feel the ripple of his tense muscles, and it calmed her. He had automatically moved to protect her. She felt buried beneath him, sheltered from danger. What a strange feeling after a near-death experience.

"Stay down," Nate ordered as he rolled off her. He pulled his gun from his waistband and crept to the now glassless window. He peered out over the sill, his pistol at the ready. He looked one way and then the other before pulling out his phone and calling the police station. He turned back to Sophie, who had rolled over and sat up.

"I don't see anybody but the cavalry's on the way." He put his gun back in and reached out to pull her to her feet, gathering her in his arms. "Are you okay?"

She nodded and buried her nose in his chest. Her heart was still hammering like mad, uncontrollable tremors running through her body. She couldn't stop her teeth from chattering as the cold wind whipped in the broken window.

"Here," he said and reached over to pull an afghan off the couch. "Maybe this will help." He wrapped it snugly around her shoulders and held her close. She burrowed against him, drinking in his strength, soaking up his courage. It was okay. They were safe now. She pressed her ear against his chest, listened to the steady thumping of his heart, and breathed in a slow, shuddering breath.

"Easy, Sophie. It's okay now." He ran a soothing hand down her back and kissed her forehead. "You're safe."

"And you are, too." Sophie felt a sob catch in her throat. "I was scared you'd been hurt."

"Oh, baby, I was terrified you'd been hit. Thank God you're okay."

Sirens broke through the night air, screaming their way toward the house, a kaleidoscope of lights flashing through the room. In seconds, footsteps were pounding up the stairs, and suddenly the room was filled with cops. Sophie stepped away from Nate and collapsed on a bar stool, trying to stay out of the way.

A minute later, Nate's brother Noah came striding into the room. Although he was the youngest of the Baker brothers, he was also the biggest, though none of them were small, by any means. He was in uniform, a frown tugging at his features. He headed straight for Nate and pumped his hand and clapped his shoulder.

"What the hell happened, bro?"

"Somebody took a shot and put out the window," Nate answered curtly, his voice gruff and tense.

"I see that. What exactly happened?"

As Nate and Noah talked about the experience, Sophie took the time to try to pull herself together. What the hell had happened? Why had someone shot at her home? She buried her face in her hands, confusion washing over her. She just didn't understand.

She didn't see Nate approaching her. When he dropped his hand on her shoulder, she jumped. Her nerves were taut, but when she realized it was Nate touching her, she relaxed. Thank God he'd been here. She couldn't imagine what she would be like if she'd been alone when that shot rang out.

"Sophie, the officer needs to talk to you." Nate rubbed his hand soothingly along her spine.

"Oh, okay. Do you want me to talk to Noah?"

"No. This isn't his call. He recognized the address and headed over.

He introduced her to an older officer by the name of Joe Johnson, and Sophie told him what little she knew. Everything had happened so fast it didn't take long to make her report.

Finally, the officers started leaving. They'd investigated inside and out and found nothing. Not another clue. She was frustrated by the lack of evidence. She wanted to know who did this.

Sophie took out her irritation with the broom as she swept up the broken glass while Nate and Noah fitted a piece of plywood over the broken window. She swept up the last pile of debris just as the men finished hammering the wood into place over the hole in the wall.

"Who wants a beer?" she asked as she washed her hands. "I know I do."

They all took a seat at the table and talked quietly. Sophie listened more than she spoke, letting the two brothers discuss the strange turn of events.

"It is possible somebody just randomly fired the gun off," Noah said as he took a long pull off his bottle.

"Yeah, I suppose. Or it could have been a drive-by gone bad." Nate ran a finger across his thick mustache. "I can't imagine what else it would be."

"I hope it was just a fluke. Why the hell would someone shoot at this place?" Sophie's voice sounded tense, reflecting the sudden fatigue she felt.

"I'm sure that's all it was." Noah smiled confidently and laid his hand on her shoulder. "Don't worry about it, Soph. It was just a freak accident."

She nodded, but still chewed on her bottom lip. She wasn't quite convinced, but there really was no other explanation.

"Well, let's put it out of our minds right now. It is Christmas Eve, after all," Nate noted. "Merry Christmas, you two."

He raised his beer and they all clinked their bottles, but none of them felt the enthusiasm they normally would have. Getting shot at took a bit of the merry out of Christmas, she thought sarcastically.

Well, she wasn't going to let it ruin her Christmas, she decided. She had so much to be grateful for. Her life was turning around and she had a new path in front of her. She had her frame shop and her art, her good friends, and a charming new home. By God, she wouldn't let this get her down and keep her down. She tossed back the last swallow in her bottle and slammed it on the table.

"Merry Christmas, guys. Now let's eat some cookies."

Noah said good night shortly after, and Sophie and Nate were left alone. Nate sat on his chair and looked at her for a long time, trapping her in a sad gaze.

"I'm sorry this happened tonight, Sophie. I'm afraid you'll have to wait until day after tomorrow for me to get the glass replaced. Nobody will be open tomorrow."

"I understand, Nate. It's not a problem."

"Well, I guess I better go. I'll see you tomorrow, right?'

"Of course. I wouldn't miss it." She grinned and felt a rush of elation. She may not have a window but she had tomorrow to look forward to. Tomorrow when she'd see Nate again.

She walked him to the door but hated to see him go. A part of her wanted to beg him to stay with her. She felt lonely, she admitted, and her hormones were in high gear. She hadn't forgotten the sweet appeal of his kiss earlier.

He paused at the door, seeming just as reluctant to leave as she was to have him go. He turned and wrapped his arms around her waist. She didn't hesitate to step toward him and wrap her arms around his neck. He looked down at her and she felt herself dissolving.

"I know you'll be all right, but if you need me, call. I don't care if it's three in the morning." He dropped a kiss on top of her feathery hair. "I mean it. Even if you just can't sleep."

"I promise." She tipped her head back and met his gaze. And then he kissed her. An explosion of feelings shot through her, sending tremors racing through her body. God, what was happening? Her world was centering on her desire for this man. She wasn't used to that. She'd always been the one who men desired, not the one doing the desiring.

"I'll see you tomorrow. Sleep well, princess." She didn't know where that endearment came from. She certainly didn't feel like a princess. But she couldn't help feeling a shiver of pleasure slip through her at the tender tone of his voice, and she had to believe he just might be Prince Charming.

She wrapped her hand around his neck and drew his lips down to hers. It was a sweet kiss, filled with meaning, loaded with emotions. Was this really happening?

Nate reluctantly drew away and turned to leave. Sophie watched him go, a sharp pain hitting her right in the chest. It felt wrong, letting him walk away. So wrong.

Chapter 8

Christmas morning dawned bright and sunny with a nip in the air, and the snow-covered world sparkled beneath the glow. Sophie couldn't help but give thanks for such a beautiful white Christmas moment.

She gathered up the goodies she had made to share with the Baker family and took her time preparing for the day. She took a leisurely shower and put on a red sweater dress made of a soft angora material that showed off her curves and set off her dark hair and creamy skin. A pair of heeled black leather boots encased her slender legs, and a pair of hoop earrings sparkled on her lobes.

She headed out wearing a black coat and arrived at the Baker house right at noon. She was welcomed into the noise and chatter with open arms. She'd met them all at Thanksgiving and enjoyed every one of them. Nate's parents were charming, his twin sisters, also police officers, were warm and witty, and his brothers were just as handsome as he was and quite nice. She was pleased to see Darcy and hugged her warmly.

"I'm so glad you're here, Sophie," Darcy said as she squeezed her. "It wouldn't be Christmas without you."

Her words touched Sophie so deeply she felt tears sting her eyes and gave Darcy a tighter-than-normal embrace. "I feel the same way."

The women seemed to automatically collect in the kitchen as they put the final touches on the dinner, and there was plenty of laughing and joking on the menu. When everything was ready, they all gathered at the table in the dining room and feasted on ham, sweet potatoes, broccoli casserole, and more. They moved into the family room for dessert, everyone groaning that they were too full but indulging anyway.

"Could I have everybody's attention?" Nick raised his voice and stood up. Darcy stood next to him. "Attention please. I have an announcement to make."

He waited until the room quieted then wrapped his arm around Darcy's waist. "We want you all to be the first to know that Darcy and I are getting married."

Noise erupted in the room as everyone gasped then started hollering congratulations. Nick beamed and Darcy glowed. She pulled Sophie close and whispered, "I hope you'll be my maid of honor. Please."

"Oh, Darcy, of course. Did you even have to ask?" Sophie answered with a hug. She would have been sorely disappointed if Sophie had chosen anyone else.

Nick asked Nate to be his best man and Noah to be his groomsman, bestowing the honor on Nate because he was the older of the two brothers. After talking about the wedding, they spread out into the basement and played pool and pinball. They indulged in eggnog and enjoyed Sophie's cookies. By that time, Sophie had a gentle rum buzz. She'd had a wonderful day but the stress from last night was catching up with her. Nate caught her yawning and pulled her close to him.

"You look like you're getting tired." Nate stepped up beside her and spoke quietly in her ear. "What do you say we head home?

Sophie nodded and they quickly said their goodbyes. They decided to walk the few blocks to their home since they'd indulged in some alcoholic beverages, but Sophie didn't mind. It was a beautiful evening, chilly but still. Snow fell gently from the sky, and Christmas lights twinkled from many of the houses. A big full moon shone overhead, peeking from behind heavy clouds.

They walked in comfortable silence, hand in hand. Sophie tossed her head back and caught a few icy snowflakes on her tongue and giggled. Nate paused to look at her then pulled her close.

"You look so cute I just have to kiss you," he whispered in her ear. He placed his lips on hers and she forgot all about the cold. There was nothing cold about her now. Heat raced through her body like flames licking along a fence row. He kissed her lips, stopped and looked into her eyes, then kissed her again.

Geez, she wanted this man. She couldn't think of another man who had ever had this effect on her. This time when he pulled away from her, she pulled him back and kissed him again. Her knees were weak when they finally stepped apart, and suddenly she wondered if she had the strength to finish the walk.

When they came to Nate's property, Sophie didn't want to say goodbye, so she asked Nate if he'd like a nightcap.

"Sure," he answered. "But this time, let's go to my house."

Sophie was surprised by his words. She'd never been in his home before. They always went to hers. Now her curiosity was piqued.

Nate unlocked the front door and they entered a big foyer with arched doorways on each side and a grand staircase winding upward. Hardwood floors gleamed throughout and she spotted a massive brick fireplace to the right.

"The downstairs reno is almost done but there's a long way to go yet upstairs." His voice sounded like her opinion mattered to him. "Come on out and see the kitchen."

The kitchen was breathtaking. He'd chosen dark cherry cabinets and beautiful ivory countertops. It flowed directly into a family room that boasted a comfortable, brown suede sectional and several bright yellow and orange chairs. A fireplace dominated the end wall and a wide screen TV perched above it, and bar stools sat at a large island. A feeling of home pervaded the air.

"It's beautiful," she announced. A look of relief washed over Nate's face. He actually cared about her opinion, she realized with shock. Most men could care less what she thought of their place.

"How about an Irish coffee?"

"Sounds good." Sophie hopped on a bar stool while Nate made them a couple of cups of spiked java topped with thick whipped cream. She wrapped her hands around her mug and took a sip.

A smile slipped over Nate's face.

"You've got a mustache," he said and leaned over and ran his tongue across her lips, licking the cream from them. An electric shock ran through her and she melted against him. Sophie put down her mug and wrapped her arms around his neck.

At last, he lifted his mouth and pulled on her hand and led her to the sectional. To her surprise, he picked up a remote and flicked a button, turning on the gas fireplace. It was a beautiful sight with the Christmas tree next to it. She sank onto the sofa and snuggled into his arms.

"Now this house feels like home," he murmured. "I knew it was missing something."

His words touched her heart. She turned to face him and gazed into his eyes. That's when she saw the future looking back at her.

Chapter 9

Sophie didn't know how it happened so fast, how she knew it was going to be. She just did. A feeling of satisfaction and sureness settled in her and a smile played across her face. They had a long way to go. They needed to get to know each other, spend time together, to confirm her instincts. But, oh, she was going to enjoy the journey.

Nate's hand slipped up to cup her cheek and his lips moved to claim hers. The kiss ignited her, driving her closer to him. He tipped her head back and possessed her, branding her with his heat. His tongue traced her lips, then plunged into her mouth and savored the taste of her. She sucked the fleshy probe deep into her damp cavern, feeling it slip across the roof of her mouth and a flame of desire burned within her.

Sophie let her hands roam across his neck and over his shoulders, feeling the ripple of muscles. She slid her palms downward and caressed his chest, the warmth of his skin heating her hands. Nate leaned forward, pressing against her, and she tilted backward, allowing him access to her neck. His lips ran the slender length of the column, nipping and tasting, his breath fanning across the sensitive skin. He nestled against the hollow between her neck and her shoulder, his tongue flicking over her flesh. She couldn't stifle a moan that escaped her mouth.

Sophie tensed a little bit when she felt Nate move his hand down to her breast, rubbing softly across the material of her dress. She'd been introduced to sex roughly, manhandled by her foster father, but she'd learned to get past that and had grown to enjoy the act when it was on her terms. She was always a little leery at first.

She was glad when that little leap of fear and anger that sometimes flared didn't happen. Somehow, she knew it wouldn't with Nate but she couldn't help being wary, even with this man who had a way of casting a spell over her. She felt enchanted, bewitched, like they were crossing the border into another world as they kissed and cuddled. His thumb ran over her nipple beneath the soft fabric of her dress, stroking, circling the sensitive bud. Sensations exploded within her, curling outward from deep in her belly.

Kissing Nate was addictive. She craved for more, drinking in the flavor of him. She leaned even farther back against the sofa and Nate cradled her against him. Her breasts rubbed against his chest, her nipples puckering even more. She could feel them growing, extending, and the sensation drove her wild. Her hands scrambled at the buttons on his shirt, pulling the tails out of his jeans. She grappled to open the fabric and expose his skin to her fingers. When the material fell away, she ran her palms through a thick mat of dark hair and tangled her fingers in the curls.

Nate dropped kisses across her shoulders and gripped her arms with near desperation. Then his hand dropped to her thigh and slid up her leg beneath her dress. He slipped his fingers underneath the thin band of her panties and stroked the place where her thighs and pelvis joined.

Sophie was burning with hunger, longing for his touch in an even more intimate way. She squirmed beneath him and struggled to pull the sweater dress over her head. She couldn't wait to be naked beneath him, welcoming him into her body.

Nate helped her pull the dress off and gazed at her, hunger apparent on his face. The firelight flickered over her golden skin and enhanced every curve and hollow of her body. He reached out and touched her breast, flicking open the front closure of her lace bra. His palm slicked across her skin, cupping her flesh in his hand. His thumb traced her nipple and Sophie shuddered as a burn of desire raced through her.

His gaze pinned hers as he massaged her breast, studying the emotions on her face. She knew he saw passion, dreaminess, and even a little pride there. She wasn't the most beautiful woman in the world in her opinion, but she was shapely and firm. Her breasts were full on her petite frame and, clad in just a tiny pair of coral-colored silk panties, her curves were on full view. She'd drunk just enough alcohol tonight that she felt sensuous.

"You are golden. So lovely." He breathed the words then dropped his mouth to her nipple, sucking the tender bud between his lips. His tongue flicked across the sensitive tip and her hips bucked in response. He continued, drawing the erect nub deep into his mouth, his tongue swathing the pliant flesh. He gently bit down and a shock ran from her nipple to her uterus, every nerve in her body tightening with an electric charge.

She was all too aware of his hand gliding across her abdomen, slipping across her hypersensitive flesh. She couldn't stop her hips from jerking upwards as he dipped his finger into her navel. A moment later, his fingers slid around the tiny string that held her panties in place, pulling it downward. Sophie raised her hips to ease the removal of the panties, raising her knee as he slipped the scrap of material downward. Then she was naked, completely exposed to his scouring silver gaze.

"Perfection," he moaned, his lips sliding down her abdomen, his tongue dipping into her navel and streaking downward toward her mound. He kissed the flesh across her pelvis, his mustache adding a sensuous touch. Sophie squirmed and desire ran rampant through her. Nate ran his hand down her thigh, gliding along the velvety skin, then let it travel back up. When he slid his palm between her legs she spread them farther apart and released an erotic groan. His breath whispered across her mound and she raised her hips in response.

His fingers slid between her damp folds, rubbing and caressing the tender flesh. He used his thumb to trail across her clit, making her suck in her breath with a gasp. As sensations built within her, she tensed, pressure building within her every second, the threat of explosion growing with every moment. When his tongue swept into the valley between her puffy lips, she couldn't stifle her moans. The sensations were too intense, too stimulating.

He lapped the juices flowing from her center and she felt herself giving in to the emotions swelling inside her. She was absorbed in the swirling feelings building within and dissolved into the moment. Shudders grew within her and fireworks exploded in front of her eyes. She fell into a world of completion, a sphere of satisfaction that left her gasping for breath.

And suddenly she couldn't breathe at all as an earth-shattering orgasm swept over her. Her back arched as spasms of ecstasy convulsed her, her hands gripping his hair, pulling him closer to her as his tongue played against her clit. Just at her peak, his teeth teased the swollen bud and Sophie exploded. Wave after wave of sensation flooded through her as she sailed across a sea of sensuality.

As she started to float back to reality, it suddenly occurred to her there was more to come. But first, she needed to get the rest of the clothes off Nate. Her hands slid across his abdomen under the waistband of his pants, fumbling to release them. She wanted them gone.

Nate shared her urgency and stood to slide his pants and boxer briefs down his legs, slipping a foil-covered pack out of his pocket. Sophie reached for it and ripped it open. She rolled the latex down his thick, throbbing shaft, her hands shaking. Her lips trailed across his rock-hard abdomen and she heard the guttural groan he emitted. As she lay back, she spread her legs and said, "Now, Nate, please. I need you."

Nate looked down at her for a long moment before dropping his lips to hers. Her engorged nipples sketched across his chest, the hard heat of his maleness pressing against her stomach. Her hands roamed freely, across his back, down his sides, and clutching his ass. Then she reached around and took hold of his cock, aiming the head toward her center. She desperately wanted him inside of her; her body cried out for the joining.

Nate reached down and tickled her clit, slicking the moisture up and down, then replaced his fingers with the head of his dick. He slipped inside her and paused, giving her time to adapt to his oversized cock. Then with a mighty push, he entered her completely, filling her to capacity. He rocked back, then forward, and she responded thrust for thrust. She felt another whirlwind building within her, swirling, growing, engulfing her. They pumped faster and Sophie felt herself spiraling over the edge as she wrapped her legs around his waist and dug her nails into his back. God, help her. She'd died and gone to heaven.

A few moments later, they collapsed and lay still on the sectional. Sophie's head rested on Nate's chest and his arms cuddled her close. She draped one of her legs over his muscular thigh and they lay still and content.

Sophie dwelled in the wonderment of what had just happened. It almost felt miraculous, the way she had melded with Nate, and how it seemed the two of them became one at that moment. She would have sworn she heard a chorus of angels singing a hallelujah chorus in the background. She'd had sex before but nothing that compared to this. This had been more than just physical, much more.

Nate propped himself on his elbow and gazed down at her for a long moment, then moved swiftly to cover her mouth with his, his hand cupping her cheek. She kissed him back, running her hands through his long, silky hair.

"You are amazing," he whispered.

"You are incredible," she whispered back.

They kissed slowly, longingly. This time, they made love. They took it slowly, savoring every moment. Every touch, every caress, felt filled with meaning, emotion that neither of them could put into words. When their bodies came together, she felt complete, whole. It was a shock, but it was welcome. Somehow, she knew her life would be shared with this man from this second on. It was beautiful and it rocked her world.

Chapter 10

A couple of days later, Sophie sat in front of her computer, trying to focus on her search for her biological father. She knew she was getting close; she knew she would soon have the answer to her question. Now that she and Nate were drawing together, she really wanted to know her health background. She knew she wanted to be a mom, but she didn't want to pass on bad genes. Maybe it was time to take the next step. A private investigator? Could they fit the final pieces of the puzzle together? It was a big expense but it might answer a lot of questions about her life. Like why her father didn't even acknowledge her privately, if not publicly.

She reached out and impulsively grabbed the yellow pages. She picked the biggest ad and dialed the number. A few minutes later, she had an appointment with Grace Henderson, a private investigator with 20 years' experience, and heaved a sigh of relief. It would take a big bite out of her savings but it would be worth it.

She still had the phone in her hand when it rang. It was Darcy, full of wedding news. They'd chosen the date, the first Saturday in June, and she wondered if Sophie could go wedding dress shopping with her this Saturday.

"That sounds exciting, Darcy. I can't wait."

"Great. I'll see you then, okay? I'll pick you up at 11."

Maybe Sophie might see something for herself while she was at it. Just for future reference, of course.

It really was fun shopping for dresses with Darcy. She looked beautiful in everything she tried on. Nick and Nate's twin sisters accompanied them on the shopping trip and they spent the afternoon laughing and oohing and aahing over the various creations Darcy tried on. But when she walked out wearing a chiffon dress with an off-the-shoulder neckline that skimmed gracefully over her figure, they all turned serious. She looked breathtakingly beautiful, joy radiating from her face as she looked at herself in the mirror. This was definitely a bridal moment. Darcy thought they all had tears in their eyes as she said yes to the dress.

Darcy dropped Sophie off in front of her shop later that afternoon. Sophie asked if she wanted to come in but Darcy declined, telling her she had to meet Nick at five. Sophie climbed out of the car and waved goodbye then headed up the walk to the store door. Since today was Saturday, she'd had her assistant close at three, so she approached a darkened shop. She unlocked the door and walked in, almost missing the piece of paper on the floor. When it rustled under her foot, though, she looked down and picked it up.

She had to strain to make out the words that consisted of cut-up newspaper print. When the message became clear, her heart almost stopped.

Enjoy your life, Sophie. It's almost over.

Sophie felt herself start to shake and quickly spun around. Who had brought this note? Was the delivery person still around, watching her as she read the threat? A shudder ran down her spine as she gaped at the paper.

Sophie pulled her phone from her purse and called Nate. She babbled so badly he couldn't understand what she was saying but he appeared at her side in no time. He read the note and raised his silver gaze to pin hers.

"Who have you pissed off?" he asked in a serious tone. "Somebody seems pretty mad at you."

"Nobody," she shouted. "I'm a sweetheart. You know that."

"Somebody apparently doesn't agree."

Nate went behind the counter and grabbed a bag. "That note is now evidence."

She placed the paper in the bag he held out, blood thumping through her veins. Who the hell had done this? Why?

Nate wrapped his arm around her and pulled her against him. "Don't worry, babe. No one is going to hurt you. No one."

She heard the protective growl in his voice, sensed the threat in his words. It was scary, but she couldn't help but feel comforted. She had no idea why someone was threatening her and she couldn't imagine what she would do if she faced her unknown enemy alone. Somehow, knowing Nate was there gave her courage.

"It could just be someone's idea of a joke," she suggested.

"Well, if that's the case, they've got a sick sense of humor."

The next couple of weeks sped by. Sophie worked long hours in the shop, and she and Nate spent every possible moment together. There were no more threats, so Sophie finally started to feel safe again. She and Nate and Nick and Darcy spent several evenings together, making plans for the wedding, playing cards, or eating dinner. Then one day, Darcy announced she'd hired a wedding planner.

"I really just want to help her out," Darcy confessed. "I met her at that bridal fair I went to last weekend. She's just getting started and can really use the business. And," she confessed with a blush in her cheeks, "I can really use the help."

Darcy, like Sophie, had no family left to help her, so Sophie wasn't surprised at her decision. Neither one of them had much experience with wedding planning.

"Her name is Jenna Harris and I've got an appointment with her late Tuesday afternoon. How about going with me, Sophie?"

Sophie paused as she dried a dish. "I think that's okay. Why don't I drive this time and I can chauffer you around?"

"Sounds good to me."

Sophie had another meeting with the private investigator. She told Sophie that she was almost certain she would have the answer quickly and was following a lead now. Sophie felt expectation building within her. Would she finally have the answer to her question? Would she finally know her true backstory?

She talked about it with Nate one night as they cuddled on her sofa and ate popcorn while they watched a movie. He popped a kernel into his mouth and eyed her ponderously.

"What?" she asked.

"I was just wondering if there could be a connection with the threat and your hunt for your dad. None of this happened before you started getting serious about finding him, right?"

"Right," she agreed.

"It just might be a link." He ran his finger across his mustache in a thoughtful gesture, pondering the idea. He rubbed her neck as he fell into cop mode, tossing and turning the puzzle pieces in his mind.

Sophie shook her head. It was all so confusing. Nothing else had happened so far. Maybe it had been a sick joke.

Or maybe Nate was on to something.

Chapter 11

Sophie worked long hours in the shop, slowly building her business. She and Nate spent as much time together as their demanding schedules allowed. Nate went off the grid occasionally, his work as an undercover cop compelling him to be gone some of the time. Thank goodness she was so busy, because she'd be worried sick about him if she wasn't burning up every minute.

She still couldn't squash the niggling worries in the back of her mind. She had known Nate barely two months but now she couldn't imagine being without him. He had become a major part of her life. She thought about him a lot; he was always at the back of her mind. Would he actually come home this time? Was he in danger? God, she shouldn't even think like that. She'd already lost her mother—she couldn't lose Nate, too. It was hard to comprehend how important he'd become to her.

It was Nate who had made her shop possible. Nate who made her laugh and her heart sing, and love like never before. He made her come alive. She knew she was a goner when they spent New Year's Eve together. Not because it was an elaborate evening or because they'd done anything luxurious. They'd actually spent the evening entertaining Darcy and Nick at Nate's house. They had dinner and drinks, played games, and danced until midnight. It was magical. But the rest of the night was even more enchanted. That's when the magic really happened.

Now here, it was Valentine's Day already. Nate had been on assignment for the last few days, so Sophie hadn't heard from him, but she still had high hopes he'd show up. She looked up as the door to the shop opened and felt her heart sing. A delivery man carried a vase of long-stemmed roses into the space.

Sophie took the vase with a smile and sniffed in the fragrant aroma of the flowers. She took the card and read it. Hope to see you this evening, love, so I can show you how much you mean to me. She felt her heart skip a beat, her breathing pausing for a moment. Now it really felt like Valentine's Day.

She shoved the thought aside as a customer came through the door. Time to get back to business. Tonight would be here soon.

But when the sun had sunk and Sophie had closed the shop a couple of hours before, she was still alone. She'd closed the store a few minutes early and hurried upstairs to get ready for the evening. She'd showered and dressed in a slinky red dress and sprayed perfume in all the appropriate (and inappropriate) places. She'd made a salad and had steaks thawed and ready to go as soon as Nate arrived. All she needed now was Nate.

Maybe he'd gotten held up at work, or maybe he had car trouble. So why didn't he call?

When the phone finally rang at ten o'clock, she heaved a frustrated sigh. At last. It was really too late to spend much time together but at least he was contacting her so she could quit worrying. But when she answered, it wasn't Nate.

"Sophie, it's Nick." Warning bells immediately went off in Sophie's head. Why was Nick calling so late?

"Don't panic, but Nate's been shot."

A roaring started in her ears, and for a moment, she couldn't hear anything else Nick was saying. At last, she pulled herself together and was able to make out his words.

"He's in surgery right now at the hospital. He's going to be okay, they say, but he's lost quite a bit of blood."

"I'm on my way." She didn't wait for him to reply. She just hung up, grabbed her coat and purse, and ran.

She didn't remember the drive to the hospital. She just knew she got there and dashed in to find Nate's family. Darcy was waiting for her near the front door and pulled her into her arms. "It's okay, Sophie. He's going to be okay."

"Where is he? What happened?"

"He's in surgery. We'll go to the waiting room. Come on, I'll tell you the rest while we walk."

Darcy told her Nate had been conscious enough to tell them that he stopped to get a bottle of wine to take to Sophie's place. When he came out of the store, he heard someone shout his name. He turned to see who it was but was shot before he even turned around. He couldn't remember if it was a man or a woman who had called his name. He'd been hit in the side and had a broken rib or two and a lot of internal damage, but he would live.

By the time they reached the others, Sophie was sagging with relief and worry. Thank God he was alive. Pray God he would stay that way.

The hours crept by. Several of the others were nodding in their chairs while some officers who came to check on Nate roamed around, talking quietly and drinking coffee. What was taking so long? It was now three o'clock in the morning and still no word.

Sophie once again ran her hand through her feathery hair, wanting to scream with impatience. When a reporter stuck his head in the door and asked for news, Sophie wanted to charge at him and scream in his face that Nate wasn't a news story: he was a man, a man whom people loved. Darcy saw the look on her face and dropped an arm around her shoulders, breathing in her ear, "He's not worth it, Soph."

Sophie drew in a deep shuddering breath, knowing Darcy was right. Then her attention was drawn to a white-clad doctor walking into the room. She held her breath until he hollered for the Baker family.

"First of all, know that Nate will live unless something unpredictable happens. He's in recovery, starting to wake up. Now, who's Sophie?"

Sophie gasped and stepped forward. "That's me."

"He's asking for you. Come with me."

Sophie's heart leapt to her throat as she moved to follow him. He walked fast and Sophie nearly stumbled as she hurried to keep up. He finally stopped at a door and pushed it open.

"In here."

Her breath faltered when she first saw Nate lying there. He looked so pale, so still. There were tubes running in and out of him, and the sheet had been turned back to expose a chest swathed in white bandages. His eyes were closed; it looked like he was barely breathing. She couldn't stop the strangled sob that escaped as she bit her knuckle to try to hold it back.

Nate's eyes fluttered open. "Soph." His voice was a bare whisper.

"Oh, Nate," she cried and tried to find a way to hold his hand without interfering with an IV.

"Sophie," he struggled to talk. "I have to tell you something." He paused, drawing in a breath. "I love you. All I could think of when it happened was I needed to tell you."

His words bit into her soul. He was drugged, under the influence, he didn't know what he was saying. My God, they had only known each other for a couple of months. But she knew at once that he was telling the truth...and she knew she loved him, too. It seemed impossible but her heart wouldn't deny the fact.

"Oh, babe, I love you, too."

"I'm glad," he said and smiled faintly. "I had to tell you."

"I know now. Close your eyes and sleep, okay?" She dropped a kiss onto his forehead and felt her heart swell. She had come so close to losing him just as their lives were getting started. She understood Darcy's fear of loving a policeman now, the fear of losing him too soon. But she could face that fear to spend any amount of time together.

When a nurse came in and told Sophie they were moving Nate to a private room, she reluctantly laid his hand down on the bed, leaned over, and placed a kiss on his brow, whispering a prayer to thank God that Nate had survived. She knew that from now on she would cherish every moment of their newfound life together.

Chapter 12

Sophie refused to leave Nate's bedside when the others finally decided to go home. She didn't want him to wake up and be alone. She curled in the recliner the hospital provided, pulled her tablet from her purse, and turned on her Kindle app. She couldn't concentrate on the words in front of her, though. Her eyes kept drifting to Nate's still form. He moaned in pain occasionally and Sophie tensed each time. She hated that he was hurting, hated whoever had shot him. They had talked about the dangers of his job before but Sophie had refused to think about it. Now she had no choice.

She understood why Darcy had fought her relationship with Nick. Darcy's father, Forest Campbell, had been a policeman who was killed in the line of duty. After his death, Darcy's mom, who had been totally dependent on him, went off the deep end and she soon died, too. Darcy had sworn she would never fall in love with a policeman. The worry, the pain, was too much stress. And if the worst happened...well, Darcy would never put herself in a position where she had to find out what happened.

And then she met Nick.

Darcy had to come to terms with loving a police officer, and Sophie would have to do the same, it seemed. If tonight had taught her anything, it was that she truly did love Nate. If he had died... Tears stung her eyes at the mere thought. The pain that spread through her when she'd heard he'd been shot was heart-stopping. The fear felt like it was suffocating her. She had just found him and she'd almost lost him.

Nate groaned again and his eyes fluttered open. He was much more lucid now than he was when he was still in recovery. His gaze focused directly on her as she bent over him, reaching for his hand and gathering it close to her chest.

"Hey. I'm glad you're awake. How do you feel?"

"Like I've been shot," he said, smiling with a grimace. "And hungry."

"They said you could have some clear liquids if you were hungry."

"Yuck. I'll have to feast on you to satisfy my hunger." His lips brushed across the back of her hand as he pulled it to him. "You're beautiful."

"Oh, no. I think that bullet affected your vision." Sophie felt a blush blooming in her cheeks. She knew she probably looked a wreck. She still wore the red dress with the deep V-neck, which was mussed and wrinkled, and her strappy black heels. She could feel her hair was standing on end from where she'd curled up in the recliner and vainly tried to catch a nap. She was sure her makeup was streaked and worn.

"You're wrong. You're the most beautiful sight I could wake up to."

Sophie felt the sudden sting of tears in her eyes. She knew he actually meant it. Feeling a love like that was an amazing emotion for a girl who had grown up alone and adrift amongst a chain of foster families. She'd lost her virginity to a cruel foster father, fought back in the only way she could. She reported his abuse, testified at his trial, saw him imprisoned, and earned her emancipation at the age of 17. Since then she'd learn to accept that her foster father was sick and hadn't let the experience warp her attitude toward sex. Yet sex with this man was different from what she'd experienced with anyone else. It was magical.

Now is not the time to be thinking about sex, she sternly ordered herself. Looking into his magnetic eyes, though, it was hard to turn her thoughts.

"You are a silver-tongued devil, you know that, right?"

"Not me. I never lie. Now come down here and kiss me, woman."

Somehow, she ended up lying down in bed with Nate and they both fell asleep, her head on his shoulder and her arm draped across his chest. When a nurse came in about two hours later, she found them like that and tried to tiptoe around without disturbing them, but they both woke up. That was probably a good thing because just a few minutes later Nate's mom showed up. Thank goodness she had gotten out of bed before her arrival.

The feisty woman shook her head when she looked at Sophie in her rumpled dress. "Girl, you look absolutely tuckered out. Why don't you go home, take a nap and a shower? I'll stay here with him."

Sophie resisted at first but finally admitted she was exhausted. Her bed suddenly sounded very welcoming, so she gave in to Mrs. Baker's persuasion. When she climbed behind the wheel of her car, she suddenly realized just how exhausted she was. She sagged into the seat of her Prius, her shoulders drooping. She almost felt too tired to drive home. Drawing in a deep breath, she gathered her strength and started the engine. The sooner she got going, the sooner she'd be there.

Fortunately for Sophie, traffic was light and she covered the few miles from the hospital to home quickly. She breathed a sigh of relief as she slid the key into the lock of the shop. It was still early; her assistant wasn't due for another two hours. She would leave him a note and go upstairs and collapse.

The moment she entered her living quarters, though, something felt off. Angel was silent, not screaming a greeting as he normally would, and there seemed to be a faint odor in the air. She couldn't figure out what was wrong though. She gazed around the open space until her eye caught the sight of something on her bed. Oh, my God, it was a pair of her panties and a bra. A piece of paper lay between them.

Sophie rushed across the room and grabbed the paper. There were words made out of newsprint pasted on its surface. The message read:

I was here, Sophie.

A wave of nausea washed over her. Someone had been in her home.

Chapter 13

Sophie stood there in shock, unable to move for several minutes. Then she looked around the space as if searching for someone still there. She was alone, completely alone. She looked at Angel, who cowered in his cage. The cockatoo looked as if he was scared shitless.

What should she do? She couldn't call Nate—he was in no condition to get this news. Maybe she should just call the police. No, she needed to call Nick. Nate's brother would know what to do. She pulled her cell phone from her purse and hit the call button.

Nick didn't waste time. He was there in a few minutes, gathering evidence and speaking soothing words of reassurance to Sophie. She was deeply disturbed, her security completely compromised. They hadn't found any signs of illegal entry, any clues to who might have been responsible for the break-in.

The most disturbing thing to Sophie was the idea that the perpetrator had gone through her dresser. He'd sorted through her lingerie and selected a matching pair of bra and panties of midnight blue lace. Her skin crawled at the thought of his hands touching her intimate clothing.

"Think, Sophie, is there anybody who would want to threaten you for any reason?" Nick's eyes, so much like Nate's, gazed straight at her.

She tossed and turned thoughts over in her mind but she couldn't think of anyone. The only one who might have a reason to hold a grudge against her was the foster father she had sent to prison. But he'd been out of prison for almost two years and hadn't caused a problem. Why would he start now?

"No, there's no one."

"Well, we're checking for fingerprints, talking to neighbors, doing everything we can do. Don't worry, Sophie. We'll get this guy." Nick laid his hand on her shoulder. "Now, why don't we call Darcy and see if you can stay at her house today?"

Once again, exhaustion washed over her. She didn't feel like going anywhere else. Resentment burned in the pit of her stomach because her life was being disrupted like this. But she didn't want to stay here by herself, either. She finally nodded and sat dejectedly on the arm of the sofa.

Damn. Sometimes, life just sucked.

Darcy grabbed two cups and poured hot water over the tea bags. She set the cups on the table and took a chair across from Sophie. She didn't say anything, just eyed her friend with empathy. Not only had her apartment been broken into, but she had Nate to worry about, too. Sophie hadn't admitted it yet but Darcy could tell Nate and Sophie were meant to be. She couldn't imagine what a wreck she would be if their positions were reversed. She was terrified every minute Nick was at work but had decided she would take whatever time they had together. She just prayed it was a good long time.

Darcy had welcomed Sophie with open arms that morning. She wanted to talk but she could tell Sophie was exhausted. She hustled her into a hot shower and made omelets and toast and was setting it on the table when Sophie came out. They talked a little but Sophie's eyes were drooping, so Darcy sent her off to bed. She had just gotten up a little while ago and Darcy was ready for a nice long chat. Sophie, however, had other plans.

"I'm heading to the hospital in just a little while," Sophie said as she took a sip of tea.

"Oh, okay. I don't blame you at all. I wanted to have a talk but I know you're worried about Nate."

Sophie nodded. "I am. I know they said he'd be okay, but I worry about unexpected things, like infections."

"He's on massive doses of antibiotics, Sophie. He'll be okay. After all, he's one of the Baker boys."

Sophie gave her a tired grin. She'd heard the brothers refer to themselves jokingly as the Baker boys more than once.

"You're right. Being a Baker boy is equal to being Superman, according to them."

"Yeah, they're pretty full of themselves, aren't they?"

"Well, actually, they are pretty special."

"I know Nick is." Darcy smiled into her tea cup. "I think you feel the same way about Nate."

Sophie felt a blush climbing in her cheeks. "I can't believe it. It's happened so fast."

"I knew it. I knew you were in love with him."

"I am. I still can't believe it."

"Those Baker boys are hard to resist."

"You got that right."

"Sophie, I just wanted to tell you, it's worth it. We may live on the edge but we live. We love. Living with a cop, loving a cop, is a challenge. But it's worth it."

"I believe you, Darcy. I believe you."

Sophie stuck her head around the door of the hospital room and peeked in. Nate's mom sat in the recliner, some knitting in her lap but with her head tilted to one side and her eyes closed. Nate lay in bed with his head turned toward the window, but he was awake. He heard the door and looked her way, a smile spreading across his face.

"Sophie. Come on in."

She went straight to his bed and wrapped her arms around him. "I'm so glad you're doing well. And I know you are because you aren't pale or groaning or anything. Thank God."

"I'm doing great. I'm ready to get out of here."

"Oh, I think you're going to be here a few more days. You may look like it and you may think you are, but you are not Superman. You're human and you need time to heal."

"Truer words were never spoken." Mrs. Baker spoke from across the room and Sophie looked up with startled eyes. She didn't know they'd woken her. "You better listen to your lady, Nate."

His lady. Sophie felt fire burn her cheeks. But it was true. She was his lady. An inner glow began to ignite within her.

"Whatever you say, Mama," Nate reached out and touched his mother's hand. His silver-blue eyes warmed to a heated grey as he turned his gaze on Sophie.

"Yeah, just remember that," his mother answered with a grin. "Now, Sophie's back and I'm going home. Your dad and I will come back this evening. Rest, and heal." She dropped a kiss on his forehead, gathered her purse and knitting, and was gone. Sophie looked at the door speculatively after it shut behind the woman. How did she do it? How did she remain so calm when she was not only married to a high-ranking police officer, but all five of her children served the Chicago Police Department? She had remained calm throughout Nate's crisis, and Sophie knew she could be as strong as stone no matter what happened.

"Your mom is amazing." Sophie shook her head in wonder. "Does she ever get upset?"

"Don't let her fool you. She'll go home and fall apart for a while. She'll cry and stay in her room a couple of hours, but when she comes out she's calm and optimistic again. She is a strong woman."

"I wonder if I could be that strong."

"Babe, you are that strong. You've been through so much and you keep fighting to succeed. You've lost your mom, you don't have a dad, you put yourself through college. You are one of the strongest women I've ever known."

Sophie allowed herself a smile at his words, but she could still hear the little voice whispering in her ear. After being broken into and threatened, she didn't feel strong. She felt scared, and defenseless, and vulnerable. She didn't feel strong at all.

But Nate didn't need to be worried about that. He needed peace, to heal and get well. The best thing she could do for Nate now was to keep her mouth shut and not tell him about the invasion of her privacy. So, she drew on what strength she could and kissed him until she forgot all about her intruder.

Chapter 14

Nate was released from the hospital four days later on the condition that he would rest and have someone with him most of the time. Sophie, of course, volunteered to stay with him. It made sense, after all. She was already on the property with him. Besides, Sophie knew nobody else could take care of him the way she would.

"I can make it, bro." Nate shrugged off Nick's offer of a shoulder to lean on. "I just want to get inside and be home."

Nick ignored his brother's refusal and continued to patiently help him inside. Nate moved stiffly and his face wore a set expression. Moving was still hard for him but he didn't want to admit it. Sophie already knew he was stubborn like that. She felt a grin tugging at her lips. She was just glad he was home.

As soon as he was inside, Nate turned and pulled her to him, kissing her soundly. "Thank you for being here, Sophie."

His words were soft, the look in his eyes hot. Sophie felt a shiver of desire slither through her.

"There's no place I'd rather be," she answered, kissing him back. "Now come sit down and I'll get you some tea. Nick, how about some tea or coffee?"

"No, thanks, Sophie. I've got to get back to work. Take care, bro."

Sophie wanted to ask him about her break-in, if he'd learned any more, but she didn't want Nate to hear them talking. She reluctantly said goodbye and hurried out to the kitchen to get the tea and throw together some chicken salad sandwiches.

A few minutes later, Nate rubbed his belly and groaned in satisfaction. "That's the best food I've had all week."

"What? You didn't like the hospital food?" she teased.

"No, I didn't like hospital food." He rubbed his nose against hers. "And they sure couldn't satisfy my other appetite."

Sophie looked up at him coyly. "Oh, and what other appetite would that be?"

"My hunger for you."

"Ah, babe," she sighed and leaned into him. "I can't believe I almost lost you."

"No way. You're not getting off that easy." His hand cupped her chin and drew her lips to his. The kiss started out light but quickly deepened. Sophie melted into his embrace and started to fall under his spell. And then she remembered.

"Nate, honey, you need to stop. We can't do this yet. I don't want to hurt you."

"Darlin', the only way you could hurt me is to deny me your heart. I love you."

Tears stung her eyes and she had to blink to hold them back. "I love you, too. I don't know how it happened so fast but I'm grateful that it did."

"I know. I was to the point in my life that I thought I wasn't going to find love. I found girlfriends, and sex, and fun, but I never found love. Not until you." His hand slipped through her hair, his eyes like molten silver as they studied her. "What is it about you, pixie? Do you have me under a spell?"

"No magic, no spell. This is real." She murmured the words as she pulled him closer, her breath whispering over his lips. A quick movement brought their mouths together, melding and melting into one hot, steamy pit. Sophie tasted him with wonder, drinking in the flavor of Nate. It was heady and intoxicating, sending her mind spiraling.

Nate groaned and cupped her neck in the palm of his hand, rubbing it gently over her skin in a slow, undulant motion. His thumb found the hollow behind her ear and began making tiny swirls, every movement sending a melody of vibes down her spine. She felt alive, alert, on fire. She slid her hands into the long, silky locks of his hair and deepened the kiss even further. She couldn't get enough of him.

Pressing against her, Nate tilted her back on the couch to allow him access to her body. His hands roamed freely, naturally, stroking the surface of her with possessive strokes. His palm glided across her breast, caressing the budding nipple. He paused and playfully tweaked the extended flesh and a sizzling sensation shot from her nipple to her pelvis. Lust built within her, crying out for satisfaction.

Sophie's hands dropped to his chest, fumbling with the buttons of his soft gray flannel shirt She wanted to feel him, needed to feel him. Her palm stroked his chest, her flesh burning at the touch. She slipped her hand downward, sliding it over his muscular abdomen, roaming across the rock-hard muscles. She slid her hand down even lower, delving beneath the waistband of his black jeans.

Nate slid his hand beneath her top and sent it crawling to the hook of her front-closure bra and flipped it open. Her breasts bounced free, jiggling as they were released from the restricting bonds. He dropped his lips to her protruding nipple and suckled the sensitive pebble in between his teeth. His tongue flickered across the surface of the delicate nub and Sophie lost it. Desire burned through her. She ran her hands down his sides then froze when she encountered a swath of bandages.

"Oh, God, Nate. I almost forgot about your wound. You're not ready for this." She felt a sense of shame rising within her. How could she have gotten so wrapped up in her lust she'd forgotten his serious injury?

"Hey, I'm fine. I'll take it real easy," he promised before once again swirling his tongue around her nipple.

"I know you will, big boy, because from now on I'm doing all the work. Just lay back and let me handle everything."

He stretched out on the couch and opened his arms. "Handle away, darlin'."

She gave him an impish grin and slid the shirt off his shoulders then ran her hand sensuously down his abdomen. She held his gaze as she undid the button of his jeans and slowly, slowly, ran the zipper down.

Then Sophie stood and shed her own clothes. Naked, she stood before him and felt the heat of his silver gaze stroking over her. She reached out and put her hands in the waistband of his pants and tugged, pulling off his pants and boxer briefs at the same time. He used his toes and kicked off his shoes and socks.

And then he was naked. He lay before her in all his glory. His bronzed skin glistened in the sunlight spilling in through the window and he looked completely at ease except for the turgid shaft springing from a mound of dark curls.

Her breath caught in her throat at the sight of him. He was perfect; he was beautiful. She needed to feel him, to taste him. She lowered herself to her knees on the floor beside him and leaned over and kissed his stomach. She followed the arrow of hair down to his navel and ran her tongue around its rim then dipped into the shallow valley. She reached out and slid her hand around the heated flesh of his huge erection, sliding it up and down the shaft. White droplets oozed from the organ and she ran the ball of her thumb through the wetness.

Nate groaned and squirmed but Sophie placed her palm on his abdomen to hold him still. She kind of liked being in charge. She liked controlling this man with all his physical strength, a man who normally was in charge, an authority.

Sophie lowered her head and flicked her tongue across the head of his dick, then slid the meaty tube into her mouth. It was so big her lips stretched to enclose it. She ran her tongue up and down the flesh and sucked gently.

Nate arched and moaned, his hands clutching her hair. He writhed as she continued to manipulate his cock and cupped his balls in her palm.

Without warning, he roared and pushed her away.

"Stop, baby, you've got to stop. I can't take it anymore."

"What would you like instead, hmm? Do you want me to sit on your lap? To take you inside me and make love to you until you're screaming?" She looked at him with wide, innocent eyes and ran the tip of her tongue over her lips.

"God, baby, you know I do. I want you right now."

Sophie reached over and opened a drawer in the end table and pulled out a condom she had stashed there earlier, just in case. She held it up teasingly and waved it under his nose.

"Do you think we'll need one of these?"

"Let's play it safe."

He snatched the foil pack and ripped it open. Sophie took the coil from him and ran it down his cock, smoothing it around its hairy base. When she was finished, she looked up at him with a shy smile and opened her arms.

"Come here, baby," he ordered as he helped her off the floor. She settled her knees on either side of his thighs and kissed him deeply, slowly, before lowering her hips down so his dick barely touched her slit. Then, without hesitation, she impaled herself on his steely rod. It filled her up completely, her insides stretching to accommodate his girth. For a long moment, she didn't move, just enjoying the heat of his flesh.

She slowly raised her hips then slid back down. Again and again. They fell into a rhythm, slow and sweet at first then moving faster and faster. The swirls of color built in Sophie's mind, a roar becoming louder in her ears. Nate clutched her hips and helped propel her bobbing behind, drawing her closer each time.

He threw back his head and hollered as a massive orgasm overtook him. Sophie's voice joined his as she, too, came with an explosive force. They rocked together and smothered each other's cries with kisses. It was magic.

Chapter 15

Nate and Sophie fell into a bit of a routine the next few days. She spent the night with him, they had breakfast, and Sophie went to the shop. She ran back to his house a couple or three times a day to check on him. As soon as she closed the store, she returned and they had dinner together, watched TV, or played games. They had a steady stream of visitors that included Darcy and Nick, Nate's parents, his sisters, and his brother Noah. But the week wasn't even over when Nate was hit with cabin fever.

Sunday afternoon, she watched him pace around the room, unable to settle in front of the TV or take a nap. He stopped and talked to Angel for a minute when he thought Sophie was out of earshot.

"I'm trapped in here, Angel. I want out."

"Get out!" the bird screamed back.

"Hey, I want to," Nate countered. "But Sophie's been watching me like a hawk. She thinks I'm not healed up enough to go anywhere."

"I heard that," Sophie said, coming up behind him and wrapping her arms around his waist.

"I'm sorry, babe. I love being here with you, but I'm just feeling restless. I need fresh air."

Sophie hugged him close as she thought about his words. She didn't blame him for feeling cooped up. He was used to

186

being on the go, active and physical. She imagined she could feel him quivering, burning to be running or playing basketball or doing anything besides lounging around the house.

"I'll tell you what," she whispered. "We'll walk over to the pub for a little bit. Maybe that will help."

Nate's smile lit up his face and she decided not to worry. He could walk three blocks. He was definitely healing.

"Sounds good, babe. Let's do it."

"Okay. Just give me a minute to freshen up and we'll go."

A few minutes later, they walked out the door and headed toward O'Connor's. It was a loud and boisterous place with pool tables and dart boards. They had spent a few evenings here before and always had fun. Tonight, as usual, was busy in the pub and they pushed their way through the crowd to find a table in the back of the room. In a couple of minutes, a young waitress showed up, took their order for two beers, and left them alone again.

They settled back and just enjoyed being out amongst the rowdy crowd and happy patrons. They cheered and booed the ballgame on TV and chatted with friends who stopped by their table. They indulged in hot wings and cheese sticks and had a couple more beers before Sophie announced she needed to visit the powder room. Nate stood up to let her out and she wriggled out of the booth.

"Hurry back," he murmured in her ear as she eased past him. A warm flutter flickered in her heart at his words and she touched his hand for a second. He was so sweet.

She made her way to the ladies' room and used the facilities. She washed her hands and combed her hair, then reached into her purse for her lipstick. She'd just started applying it when the door opened and a bleached blonde in black leggings and an off-the-shoulder, long floral sweater walked in. Her eyes were kind of glazed and she stumbled a bit when she walked, but she spotted Sophie and moved directly toward her.

"Here. Some guy asked me to give this to you." She stuck her hand out and handed Sophie a folded note. Sophie opened it and sucked in her breath as she read the message.

"Who gave this to you?" Sophie demanded to know. She sounded mean but she couldn't help it. The words in front of her shocked and frightened her. She had to get to the bottom of this.

"I don't know, man. Just some guy." The blonde shrugged her shoulder and flicked her gaze away from Sophie's.

"What did he look like? Where did he go?" The words burst out of her. "Do you know him?"

"Chill, sister. I don't know anything. I was just headed in here and this guy I've never seen before asked me to give this to the girl with short, dark hair wearing jeans and a white sweater. I said okay. That's all, all right? Back off me, woman." The blonde threw up her chin belligerently.

"Okay, sorry. But it's important to me to find out who it was. He's threatening me."

"Sorry 'bout your luck," the woman tossed back, walked into a stall, and closed the door firmly.

Geez, what a bitch, Sophie thought as she looked again at the paper she held in her hands and reread the typed message:

Looking good, Sophie. I'll be seeing more of you soon. Much more.

Sophie's eyes widened in panic and she glanced around frantically, as if the author would appear right here in the women's room. Her heart thundered so loudly she thought she could hear it. She trembled all over. Damn, she had to walk out of here and find Nate, but the man could be watching her. He could be waiting for her. God, she didn't know what to do.

It took her a moment to pull herself together enough to think. The only thing she could do was walk out that door. She couldn't stay here hiding in the bathroom. Taking a deep, shuddering breath, she pulled the door open and peeked out. The hall was empty.

She slipped the note in her pocket and made her way back as quickly as she could to their table. Every step she took, she felt as if someone was watching her. By the time she reached the table, her breath was coming in gasps, her eyes taking on a panicked look.

"Sophie, what is it? What's wrong?" Nate took her arm and eased her down to sit in the booth. "What happened?"

With shaking fingers, she held out the note for him to read. "Some woman gave it to me in the bathroom. Said she didn't know the guy and to get over it."

Nate's silvery eyes turned to hardened steel. "Come on. We're going to find that woman and make her tell us what this guy looks like."

He didn't give her time to answer, just grabbed her elbow and pulled her back toward the ladies' room. He didn't knock or anything, just slammed his palm against the door and shoved it open. The woman screamed a little and the hand applying the scarlet lipstick jerked and it smeared up her cheek.

"What the hell. You can't come in here, buddy."

Nate flipped his badge out of his pocket and showed it. "This says I can when I need to find a person of interest."

"Well, I'm the only one in here."

"Then you must be who I'm looking for. Sophie, is this the woman who gave you the note?"

Sophie peeked out from behind him. "Yes, that's her."

"I need to know everything you noticed about this guy, okay? You say you didn't know him."

"No, I didn't know him. I never saw him before. I told your woman there that."

"Okay, you didn't know him. What did he look like? What was he wearing? Any little details you can think of will help."

"I don't know. Just an average looking guy. Tall height, a little weight, medium coloring. Wearing jeans and a hoodie. That's all I know. Now I need to get out of here." She moved as if to shove past him.

"Hang on. I need your name and information. The man who gave you this is under investigation."

"For what?"

"Breaking and entering, stalking, etcetera. Now tell me your name."

The blonde crossed her arms over her chest and gave an irritated sigh. "Donna Harper." She followed up with her address and telephone number, each syllable tighter than the last. Nate jotted everything down in a small notebook that appeared in his hand.

"Thank you for your cooperation, Ms. Harper. Are you sure you don't remember anything else? Any moles, facial hair, scars, anything?"

"No, I wasn't paying attention."

"All right, but if you do remember anything, here's my card. Give me a call."

"Sure, yeah, okay." She took the card and stuffed it down her top, flipped her hair, and left.

Sophie stared after her, shocked at her callousness. How could she be so uncaring?

She felt Nate's hands on her shoulders. She closed her eyes, breathing in his presence. It felt as if her world was tilting and everything was swaying. Nate was the only solid thing in her life. She turned, wrapped her arms around him, and buried her face in his chest. They stood without speaking and held each other.

The bathroom door opened suddenly and a group of three young women squealed at the sight of a man in the room.

Nate gave them a smile and said, "Excuse me, ladies. We were just leaving." He led Sophie calmly past them and they giggled as they stepped back to make room.

They walked back to their booth but Nate paused and looked at her solemnly. "Let's go home, baby."

Chapter 16

They decided that night that Sophie wouldn't be going back to stay in her apartment anytime soon. She packed up Angel and moved in with Nate. She loved living with him but couldn't help but feel stressed. Someone was out to scare her and she didn't know why he was doing it. Her mind was plagued with questions. How had she pissed somebody off so badly that they would torment her like this? What was next? She did the best she could to keep calm, though, and kept moving through her days.

The shop kept her busy, and helping Darcy plan her wedding took up time, too. Darcy and Nick had chosen the venue and met with the wedding planner, but now it was Sophie's turn to accompany Darcy to the next meeting while Nick was working.

They met with Jenna Walker at her office. Jenna was a Rubenesque redhead with warm brown eyes. She greeted them with a smile and led them into a small conference room. They sat down at the round table and soon had cups of tea in front of them.

"Okay, let's get down to business," Jenna said and the three of them began discussing the wedding. They soon found themselves laughing together almost as much as they were doing any actual wedding planning and Sophie felt a kinship with Jenna beginning to grow.

They did eventually make some decisions about the wedding. By then, the three women had bonded and a friendship had been formed. They hugged as they said goodbyes, Sophie and Darcy giggling like schoolgirls as they left.

Snow was spitting from the clouds as they walked. Sophie pulled her collar closer around her neck and tugged her knit hat down around her ears. The wind whistled around them. Sophie put her head down to avoid its bite, Darcy clutched the hood of her coat around her face, and together they trudged toward the car like the true Chicagoans they were.

As they approached the car, it was Darcy who first spotted the paper on the window. Probably an advertising flyer. It was odd, though, because there was something else besides just an advertisement for a pizza restaurant. They drew closer and realized it was a dead rose pinned under the windshield wiper.

"What the hell?" Darcy muttered.

Sophie's stomach dropped to her toes as she stood staring at the paper and the rose. Snow fringed the brown edges of the flower, outlining the deadness in stark white. She grabbed Darcy's hand as she reached for the rose.

"Don't. I don't want to know what it says." She started to tremble as she stood there.

"Sophie, I have to take it off so I can see to drive." Darcy's voice was gentle yet firm as she reached out and plucked the rose off the windshield and picked up the paper. Her eyes ran over the newspaper print message.

"Okay. I changed my mind. Tell me what it says." Sophie's voice had an icy edge, a strangled tone.

"Are you sure?"

"Tell me."

"It says 'In memory of Sophie Cruz.' Darcy's words were barely audible but Sophie heard them clearly. At first, a giant icicle formed in her gut, then a flame of anger melted it away. Frustration burned through her, igniting an angry outburst.

"Damn. Damn, damn, damn." Sophie stomped her booted foot and almost screamed in frustration. "I don't understand. Who the hell is doing this? Why? Why, why, why?"

Darcy wrapped her arms around her and held her shaking body. "I don't know, Sophie. It doesn't make any sense."

"It's driving me nuts. I just don't get it." She paused and looked around her. "He's watching me, Darcy. He knows where I go, when I go."

"I know, girl. It's wacky." Darcy squeezed her shoulders. "But you've got to be tough. Don't let this lunatic get to you."

"Huh," she snorted. "Easier said than done."

"I know, I know. But Nate and Nick will figure it out. They'll keep you safe."

"I'm praying you're right."

Nate's face hardened like concrete when Sophie told him what had happened and showed him the rose and the note. His eyes were like flint, his jaw set and firm. He ran a frustrated hand through his hair and swore under his breath.

"Nate, I'm scared," she confessed. "This guy is getting more obsessed every day."

Nate pulled her close, dropping a kiss onto her silky hair. He held her for several long moments without saying anything, rocking her like a baby up against him. Finally, he spoke.

"Hold on, honey. I'm going to get this guy. I promise you that." His voice was grim. "I swear it."

"I know you will. But—" she hesitated a moment. "I think I want to get a gun."

"I hate that idea. I hate that you feel the need to arm yourself." He slammed his fist on the counter. "Damn. I hate this whole situation."

"I know you do, and I do, too. But I'll feel better if I have a gun. I'll take lessons, learn how to use it. I want to do something, something that makes me feel stronger." She jutted her chin upward, a look of cold determination on her face. "I'm tired of feeling like I'm doing nothing to fight back. Will you help me?"

"Ah, babe. I'll be happy to help you. I just wish I didn't need to."

Sophie insisted they go gun shopping the very next day. She tried holding several different models of handguns, testing their heft and their balance. At first, it felt strange to hold a pistol in her hands but she forced herself to get used to the feel of the weapon in her palm. This might be all that stood between her and the maniac that was stalking her.

At the end of the shopping trip, she left as the owner of a Glock 43, a Luger that was small in size but big on power. Somehow, she felt empowered to know she would be able to defend herself.

"Now you need to learn how to shoot," Nate spoke seriously, his arm around her waist.

"I will. When can you teach me?"

"Just as soon as you can legally bring that Glock home."

Chapter 17

The next couple of weeks passed quietly. Nate was still recuperating and they spent quiet evenings at home. Her stalker hadn't made any other moves; nevertheless, Sophie felt more confident now that she was armed.

Nate's shooting investigation made some progress as CCTV footage captured the image of the shooter. It wasn't a good video, only showing a figure clad in dark clothes, a dark hood pulled up covering the face, but they could see it was a person of bigger-than-average build. It was probably a man but the details were skimpy.

As far as Sophie's case went, there were few leads. They found no fingerprints on the notes, no fingerprints anywhere. There had been no more threats or advances, and life went on as if nothing had ever happened. It felt strange but Sophie was grateful for the peacefulness.

She had just finished tossing a load of whites in the washer when the phone rang early one Monday morning. She was happy to hear the voice of Grace Henderson, the private investigator she'd hired to track down her father.

"I'm pretty sure I know who your father is," she announced without preamble. "I just need to check out a couple more details but I'm sure I'm on the right track."

"Who is it, Grace?"

"I don't want to say until I'm absolutely positive. I will tell you this, though. If this is your dad, you're going to know who he is."

"You're killing me here, Grace."

"I'm sorry. I just don't want to make a mistake. I'll be back in touch soon."

"Okay, I'll be waiting to hear from you."

She hung up and hugged herself excitedly. She was so close to finding her answer. It wasn't a matter of life and death but it was important to her. She wanted answers, needed answers. She had been old enough when her mother died to know that her mom had no family. Cruz was her maiden name because she never married, so that part was simple. She'd found her mother's birth certificate online and discovered that both her parents had died when she was 17. She'd had an older brother who was killed in gang violence when he was 18. Other than that, she had found no other relatives.

She'd felt alone her entire life. Now she had Nate to fill that void. But she still would have enjoyed having a blood connection, someone who could tell her stories about family forefathers, someone with a shared association. Oh, she realized, just because she found her father wouldn't mean he would want anything to do with her. After all, he hadn't cared for the last thirty years, why should he start now? But maybe, just maybe...

She couldn't deny the part of her that dreamed of a joyful reunion, maybe that her father had been searching for her, too. She couldn't help but hope that she was wanted.

"Want to watch NCIS?" Nate asked as he settled down on the couch after they had finished the dinner dishes.

"Sure. I'll be right there." Sophie finished wiping her hands on the dish towel, straightened the vase of fresh flowers on the table, then walked in and curled up on the couch next to Nate. His arm dropped around her shoulders and she sighed in contentment. This felt so good, so right. A peace settled around her as she fit herself against his side. The warmth of his body surged through her and a burn of desire flamed to life.

Sophie's hand trailed across Nate's thigh, sliding down toward his knee and back up the muscular plain.

"Sweetness," he groaned.

"What, love? Don't you like it when I do that?" she asked innocently.

"You know I do, you little minx."

"I thought you might."

"You thought right." He dipped his head and trapped her lips beneath his. The kiss was deep and tender, slow and lingering. Warmth spread throughout her body, heating her from the inside out. Her hands slid into the thickness of his hair, her fingers combing through the length of the silky locks. He hugged her to him, his hands sliding down her spine, setting off fireworks everywhere his fingers touched.

His hands tunneled under her sweater, stroking her back sensuously. She shivered against him and wrapped her arms around his neck, sighing as his hand cupped her breast. His thumb slid across her nipple, taking advantage of her braless state. When she'd arrived home from work, she'd slipped into black yoga pants and a pink sweater, no underclothes. Now she was glad she had decided to go for that comfort.

His lips tasted sweet and tantalizing. She let her tongue tickle against his mustache before slipping into the damp cavern of his mouth. His fingers played with her nipple, tracing the tip, tweaking the hot flesh. Nerves lit up clear down to her pelvic region.

Before she knew it, Nate had pushed her down on the couch and started pulling her sweater over her head. In response, she began to claw at the buttons of his flannel shirt to expose his chest. She ran her hands across the steely plains and tweaked his nipples as she explored. He dropped his lips to her breast, suckling and tasting, teasing and taunting her with his nipping kisses.

She felt a groan burst from her lips and she bucked her hips with desire. His lips slid from her nipple to trail along her rib cage, his fingers replacing his mouth on her nipple. His mouth traced down her abdomen and found its way to her navel. His tongue plunged in the small space and lapped at it eagerly. Spasms caught Sophie, her hips writhing, undulating with desire.

Nate slipped his fingers beneath the waistband of her yoga pants and began pushing them downwards. Sophie raised her hips to help him and in just a moment she was naked. She shivered both from the cool air and the heat of desire. His lips were still exploring her lower abdomen, kissing and tasting each inch of exposed flesh. His hand slid down to the v between her legs and she automatically opened for him, liquid flowing in her valley.

His finger slid between the damp folds of flesh, magically stirring her emotions. She felt herself gasping for breath, trying to breathe through the sensations. She threw her head back and curved her neck, a groan of desire bursting from her throat.

Nate slid his lips lower, slipping toward her epicenter. He used his hand to thrust her legs farther apart and buried his face in her depths. As his tongue flashed out and zeroed in on her clit, she couldn't contain a scream. His hands held her legs far apart as his tongue lathed the sensitive bud. Oh, God, God, God. The hunger for satisfaction overwhelmed her, her appetite for fulfillment soaring. The world spun around her and explosions tore apart her reality. Her hips bucked as rockets launched in her groin.

Nate caught her fluids on his tongue and lapped it up like it was liquid gold. He buried his nose between her legs and breathed in the essence of her.

Sophie finally released her clench on his thick, silky hair. She floated downward, still drifting in the aftermath of satisfaction when she felt Nate's fingers replace his lips. He raised his mouth to meet hers, capturing her lips so she could taste her own flavor. Her palms cupped his sculpted cheekbones and drew his face closer to hers. Her arousal returned as his fingers manipulated her clitoris, swirling the flesh until she felt another surge of desire running through her. Her valley flooded with more liquid and she gasped at the resurgence of desire that ignited within her.

His steely prick pulsed against her pelvis and she yearned to feel him inside her. Her uterus hungered for the heat of him, the meaty feel of flesh on flesh, hotness meeting hotness. She moved her hips invitingly, welcoming him into her warmth. He pulled down the zipper of his jeans and freed his pulsing prick. She felt the length of his flesh and heaved her hips toward him. Her hands fought frantically to remove his shirt and fully expose his chest. She shoved his jeans down and grasped his hard cock, running the ball of her thumb across the hot head of his dick. Slick liquid spread out beneath her digit, dispersing across his prick. She ran her hand lovingly up and down the shaft, enjoying the feel of his heated flesh against her palm. Lord, she wanted him like nothing she'd ever wanted before.

In one motion, he'd donned a condom and prepared himself to plunge into her depths. Her legs spread and her hips lunged to welcome him in.

They came together slowly, exquisitely. Sophie floated, soared, and sailed as her body celebrated their joining. Ribbons of color swirled through her mind and she felt her nails bite into Nate's back. She wrapped her legs around his waist and dug her heels in as he gripped her butt cheeks and aided her hips to rise and fall.

They melded into a collage of arms, legs, and torsos, straining to get closer, closer. The feel of Sophie's vagina stretched to capacity, his balls slapping against her ass, the head of his dick bumping into her cervix, all served to send her spiraling over the edge. She felt as if she were flying, rising above the earth, and Nate was flying with her.

As she floated back to reality, a thought struck her. Life was sweet, and love was sweeter. Stalker or not, she wouldn't change a thing about her life.

Chapter 18

"I like this one," Sophie declared firmly, eyeing herself in the dressing room mirror. She was trying on maid-of-honor dresses for Darcy's wedding and this was the fourth dress she'd tried on. The sky-blue color was vibrant and the fit was nice. Off-the-shoulder neckline and slim flowing skirt finished off the look. "What do you think?"

"I don't like it," Darcy spoke firmly. "You'll look better than I do."

Sophie's mouth dropped open, then she noticed the grin on Darcy's face. "Now you know that's impossible, girlfriend. You're going to be the most beautiful bride ever."

"And you'll be the most beautiful maid of honor." Darcy reached out and hugged Sophie. "I love the dress."

"Okay, then it's decided?" Jenna asked. The wedding planner had accompanied them on this shopping trip. Nick's sisters were also standing up with Darcy but they had to work, so left the choice up to Darcy and Sophie, confident in their taste. Now that that task was out of the way, the next stop on their list was the florist.

"Yes." Sophie and Darcy spoke in unison.

"Okay, then. Onward and upward."

The girls finished dress shopping earlier than expected, so decided to stop for lunch before going on to check out the flowers. They picked a nearby sports pub and sat at a round table in the back corner of the room. In just a few moments, they were munching hamburgers and eating fries, talking and giggling as if they had all been friends for years.

"So the bride says 'Are you sure?'" Jenna ended the story she was telling about a lady wearing her veil backward, and they all laughed. Jenna had kept them all in stitches and Sophie's eyes were damp with tears. The redhead had a natural talent for storytelling and did great imitations.

"You are so funny, Jenna. How come you aren't married, and here you are, planning everyone else's wedding?"

A light seemed to turn off in Jenna's deep blue-violet eyes. Then she seemed to force herself to shake it off and said softly, "I was married. It just didn't take."

Her confession took them by surprise. Both women had just assumed Jenna had always been single.

"Now, let's go take a look at flowers, ladies. What do you say?" Jenna reached for her purse and pulled out some bills. "I've got the tip."

Sophie and Darcy exchanged a quick look as they prepared to leave. Obviously, Jenna was not comfortable talking about her former marriage. They silently agreed to let the subject drop, quickly got up from the table, and headed out.

Three hours later after an intense time at the florist's, Sophie was happy to go home. She was tired, her feet hurt, and a headache was beginning to throb behind her eyes. Darcy was anything but a bridezilla, yet she and Sophie had argued a bit over the flowers. Darcy leaned toward sunflowers but Sophie thought they were too fall-oriented. Darcy had finally agreed to forego the sunflowers, then they had to discuss everything from daisies to orchids. They'd finally chosen a selection of orchids, pink roses, and lilies of the valley. Not only would they be beautiful, their smell would be intoxicating.

Sophie waved goodbye to Darcy at the curb to the shop. It was a couple hours after closing but she wanted to check on the business they'd done that day. She was so lucky to have the assistant that she had. He ran the store exactly as she wanted and always left meticulous notes.

She entered the silent building and went straight to the register. She knew she'd find notes there fully outlining the happenings of the day. They were right where she expected and she looked them over carefully. Business had been fairly steady throughout the day and she was pleased. She'd never expected her little shop to actually make it, but it looked more and more like she was going to pull this off. A smile slid across her face as she read the notes.

Okay, that went well. Now she just needed to run upstairs and get Angel's extra bag of bird food and she could get back to Nate. Her smile grew broader at the thought.

She unlocked the door to her apartment and pushed in. Daylight was fading fast so she flipped on the overhead light. A deep silence greeted her. The place felt deserted, empty. Maybe it missed her, she mused as she glanced around.

Then she froze. There was something scattered across the table top. Squares of paper. What the hell?

She forced herself to walk slowly over and picked up one of the papers. It was a picture. A picture of her. It must have been taken earlier today. She was still wearing the same slacks and sweater that she was when she arrived at the dress shop.

The next picture was also of her. This one was taken as she walked from Nate's house to the shop. She thought back and realized it had to have been taken yesterday. That's what she'd been wearing.

Another one showed her at work in the shop. One of her sweeping the sidewalk free of a dusting of snow. A snap of her climbing into her car, another of her running into the grocery.

It was the last picture that stole her breath. Oh my God, no. No, it couldn't be. She looked again, nausea waving across her. It was her, naked. It looked like she had just emerged from the shower, because she held a towel barely covering her privates in front of her and one hand ran through her wet hair. She looked like a fricking porn star.

There was one more slip—a paper with newsprint taped across it read, "Looking good, Sophie. See you real soon."

The horror of reality washed over her. The world dimmed a bit, a gray haze covering her eyes. Damn. He'd been watching her. Stalking her every move. Taking her picture. God, he might be watching her right now.

She sat in stunned silence, letting her eyes take in the pictures once again.

And that's when she heard it.

The door closed downstairs.

No. She'd heard wrong. No one was down there.

Then there was a thump as someone bumped into something.

Oh, God. It was him.

A shaking started deep within her and worked its way out to her limbs. Her teeth chattered as chill after chill ran down her spine.

Wait. She had her gun in her purse. Sophie grabbed her leather hobo bag and reached into its depths. She ran her hands through the contents until her hand wrapped around the handle of the pistol and pulled it out. It felt heavy in her hand and she had trouble balancing and aiming it at the door. Fear made her want to fire right away but that would be stupid. You had to see your target to hit it.

Her hands steadied as she waited. Waited to see the face of the person coming toward her.

She heard the familiar creak of the third step from the top and she held her breath. Her fascinated gaze stared unwaveringly at the door. She could do this. She could shoot an intruder who was there to hurt her.

The doorknob turned slowly, achingly slowly. The door began to swing open and a figure stepped inside.

Chapter 19

"Sophie. What's going on?" Nate asked, his voice tinged with concern.

She couldn't speak for a moment, so overcome with relief at seeing Nate. Thank God she hadn't shot. Her finger had tensed on the trigger, ready to fire. If she'd given in to panic, she could have fired the gun. She could have killed him! The realization washed over her like a bucket of cold water thrown in her face.

"Oh, Nate, I almost shot you." Her voice broke as tears started rolling down her face. "My God."

"Hey, hey, what's wrong? What happened?" Nate hurried across the room to take her face in his hands and tip it toward him. "Tell me what's going on."

Sophie tried to explain but she was too upset to talk straight. "I found...I was scared...you didn't say anything..." Her voice broke off in hiccoughs as she wrapped her arms around him and buried her face in his chest.

Nate reached out and carefully slid the pistol away from her, then placed his hands on her shoulders. His grip was firm, tense. He didn't speak, didn't move, just held her against him. She couldn't tell if he was angry or upset, if he was stunned or in shock.

"God damn it, Sophie," he finally shouted. "This has gone too far. I've got to make him stop."

She no longer had any doubt how he felt. His anger was palpable, a wave of heat radiating from him. He fisted his hands, a dark scowl on his face. He breathed deeply, tension pulsing through his body. At last, he grabbed a small vase and hurled it against the wall. The china shattered and rained to the floor.

"Nate, don't." She cried, scared by his reaction. She was angry, too. She wanted to know who was behind these insidious threats just as much as he did. But she'd never seen this side of him before, never felt such anger.

"We've got to stop this shit. Enough is enough."

"I know, baby, I know." She moved to wrap her arms around his waist. "But how?"

"We'll start by calling the cops again. But I'm taking this personally. I'll find the bastard. I'll kill him"

The cold certainty in his voice made Sophie's stomach clench. She didn't recognize this Nate. This angry, angry man. This man who almost scared her.

"Nate." Her voice sounded pleading to her own ears. "You're frightening me."

"I'm sorry, honey. I don't mean to scare you. I'm just so mad."

"I know, babe. I'm mad, too. I don't know what to do about it, though."

"Well, we don't just sit back and take it. We fight."

"How?" She choked out the word as she clung to him.

"I've got to think about it, Sophie. I'll come up with something."

He bent his head and captured her lips, drinking in their sweetness. "We'll get through this. We'll do it together."

Once again, Sophie lived through the experience of having cops swarm her home, evidence technicians roaming around the premises. Both of Nate's brothers were on the scene, digging into the photo collage. Sophie's face was scarlet as they eyed the picture of her naked.

She'd almost grown cold to the events. She was getting used to the arrival of police cars, the presence of law enforcement officers. She had grown so immune to the events that she was hardened against the chaos.

Nate was obviously still stressed. A vein at his temple visibly throbbed and his body was whipcord taut. He spoke with his brothers, and Sophie could see the angry glare on his face. Was he mad at her for putting him through this? She wasn't sure and felt a kernel of doubt sprouting in her.

She called Darcy and filled her in on the latest events, her voice cold and hard. She was angry and beginning to grow numb to the fear that engulfed her. Worry about Nate's reaction to this was starting to consume her. He looked so dangerous, so cold and angry. This wasn't the kind, loving Nate she was used to. This was a person who almost scared her.

Darcy tried her best to soothe Sophie, but Sophie was too stressed to hear it. She spoke to her a few more minutes, then excused herself and said goodbye. She didn't feel like giving details over and over again after already having done so with the police.

It was nearing midnight by the time Nate and Sophie finally found themselves alone. Exhaustion ate at Sophie and she was heartsick. Not only was she being stalked by a stranger, but Nate was locked in his anger. They walked silently together from the store to his house.

"Welcome home." They were greeted by Angel, squawking and dancing across his perch, screeching his greeting over and over. Finally, Sophie snapped.

"Oh, shut up," she hollered.

"Fuck you," Angel responded. "Fuck you, fuck you, fuck you."

"Don't worry, I'm already fucked." Sophie bit out the words.

"I know it feels that way, but you're not. Don't say it." Nate grit the words out, his mouth a grim line.

"Why not? Why hide the truth? I'm being stalked, threatened, followed. I don't know who, why, or anything else. I'm fucked."

"Sophie stop it." He took her shoulders and gave her a gentle shake. "I know you're angry, so am I. I know you're scared. I am, too. But this asshat will not win, do you hear me? He won't."

Sophie searched his face, desperate to believe him, desperate to see he wasn't mad at her. She knew she'd become a pain in his ass, probably more trouble than she was worth. Suddenly, she knew she had to be willing to walk away, to free him from the danger she was bringing him.

"Nate, I think I should leave. I need to get out of here, get away from you. I'm putting you in danger. If something happened to you, I couldn't take it. I need to go."

Nate didn't say anything He just stared at her. His eyes were storm-cloud gray, fierce and piercing. His mouth formed into a hard line.

"Are you insane?" he finally spat out. "The hell you are going anywhere. Don't even think about it, Sophie."

His determined tone made a flame of anger shoot through Sophie and she stiffened her spine. She spoke in a cold, hard tone. "Don't tell me what I can and can't do, Nathan Baker."

He ran a frustrated hand across his face, trying to hide a look of anguish unsuccessfully.

"This is not your fault, Sophie. Don't even try to save me. I won't let that bastard destroy us. Do you hear me? It's not happening. We're in this together."

The fierce growl in his voice somehow reached through Sophie's agitated viewpoint. She lifted her gaze to his and let herself get lost in its pewter depths. There was so much emotion in those eyes, so many feelings. She saw his heart in his eyes. A lump grew in her throat.

"Sophie, I love you. I can't imagine being without you. Please don't say you'd leave me." His voice was soft, warm, smooth like hot chocolate. "I do love you."

Chapter 20

She whirled around and clutched her waist. A shiver ran along her spine as reality set in. She couldn't leave Nate. Not now that she'd finally found love. She'd have to stay and fight. He was worth fighting for. Love was worth the fight.

He stepped up behind her and wrapped her in his arms, pulling her back against his heated torso. His lips feathered her hair with kisses and she couldn't resist him any longer.

"Oh, Nate, I love you, too." Tears filled her eyes as her voice choked.

"It's true, Sophie. I love you and I won't let that bastard take you away from me after waiting all my life to find you. We will resolve this situation...and then we can get on with our future."

They didn't make love that night. Instead, they went to bed and held each other, just kissing and cuddling until they fell asleep. Sophie woke up early and immediately felt Nate's hard dick pressing against the crack in her ass. Hot and hard, prodding her, rubbing against her. She felt a sleepy groan escape her throat as Nate pressed harder against her. In a dreamlike state, she pushed back. She didn't want to move from her comfortable position cuddled up against him, but she ached with wanting him. This was the man she loved. She needed him. The moisture pooling between her legs was proof of that.

Sophie didn't open her eyes. She stayed in her dream-induced state and let herself melt into his presence. He felt so safe, so secure, so sexy. She had to still be dreaming.

Nate's hands slid over her naked body, dwelling on her breasts. His fingertips delicately brushed the swollen buds and she rolled her hips as desire stirred her. His lips gently kissed a path beneath her ear and down her neck. One of his hands continued to play with her nipples while the other slid down her torso, over her ribs, and on to tease the dark curls crowning her pubis. A sleepy smile slid across her lips as she moved just enough to open her legs to him and felt his finger slip into the damp canal.

He rubbed the folds of her flesh, his thumb stroking and swirling her clit. Then his finger plunged into her depths, then two. They pumped and caressed her tissues and she spiraled up and into space, soaring through the stratosphere, flying outside her body and journeying into unexplored worlds. Her body clenched around his fingers, spasms of delight rippling through her.

While Sophie floated slowly back to earth, Nate pulled away long enough to reach in the drawer of the nightstand and grab a condom. He quickly slipped it over his throbbing dick and pushed against her entrance. She only had to wiggle a little for him to gain access. She gasped and threw her head back as his bulk filled her completely. Their joining felt so complete, so thorough, that Sophie felt overcome with emotion. Tears rolled down her face as she was caught in the whirlpool of orgasm.

"I love you, darlin'," Nate whispered. "I cherish you."

"You are my heart." Her soul ached with feeling as she confessed. Lord, she didn't know what was going to happen in the future, but she knew she was going to enjoy every minute leading up to it.

Nate was in the shower when she was awakened a second time by the ringing of the phone. Sophie reached over and grabbed it off the nightstand. "Hello," she mumbled, her voice hoarse with sleep.

"Hi, Sophie. It's Grace. I'm sorry to call you so early but I couldn't wait. I needed to tell you, I'm sure I have found your father."

"Really? Who is it? Tell me, don't keep me in suspense."

"That's what's going to blow your socks off. Hang on...it's Ephraim Farris."

"Excuse me? I thought you said Ephraim Farris."

"I did say Ephraim Farris, Sophie. Ephraim Farris is your father."

"Holy crap." Her voice was weak with shock. Ephraim Farris was the celebrated artist who had won the world over with his computer-generated art, producing amazing artwork in surrealistic settings.

"There is no doubt, Sophie. I had a DNA test run. You'd already offered up your DNA for testing and I just happened to pick up a coffee cup he had used. It's the real deal."

She'd wanted to know who her father was. She had hoped for a normal man, somebody not a criminal or a maniac. Just a man who went to work every day and bowled on a league or played cards with his buddies on Thursdays. Just a normal man.

But her father was anything but. Her father was Ephraim Farris. Hell, he'd been on the cover of People magazine. From what she'd read, he was quite the swinging bachelor. He'd been seen with some of the most beautiful women in the world in his arm. He was wealthy, handsome, and charismatic.

And he was her father.

"My God, Grace. What do I do now?" her voice quavered weakly.

"That's up to you, Sophie. You have to decide if you want to confront him, or at least meet him. You have to figure out whether you want to do it yourself or have a lawyer contact him. Those are decisions you have to make."

Sophie knew Grace was right. She had to think about it. You would have thought she'd have already planned out the next step, but she didn't think she'd ever actually find out who her father was. And she certainly never thought it would be someone like Ephraim Farris.

"Thank you, Grace, for everything. You don't know what this means to me. It's life-changing."

They talked a moment longer and hung up, Sophie agreeing to call her in a couple of days. Her mind whirled with questions and thoughts. Would Ephraim Farris be happy to know he was a father? Or did Ephraim Farris already know? Could it be him stalking her? She didn't know what to think. She just needed time to consider the situation.

Sophie became aware that she no longer heard Nate singing in the shower and turned just in time to see him emerge from the bathroom wearing only a towel slung low on his slim hips. His hair tumbled around his pale face and her gaze was drawn to the still raw-looking hole in his side. Damn, Nate really wasn't healed yet. Circles shadowed his eyes and he looked like he'd lost weight. He didn't need the added stress of worrying about her. She made a sudden decision to conceal the news about her father for the moment. He had enough to worry about without adding a dramatic parental reveal. The news could wait a couple of days.

Chapter 21

"We do appreciate your business, Mr. Cheek. I hope you'll allow us to serve you again." Sophie reached out and warmly shook the hand of the twinkly-eyed, middle-aged man at the counter. He was a first-time customer and seemed to be extremely pleased with her work.

Calvin Cheek shook her hand and grinned with satisfaction. "Nice work, Sophie. Very nice. I'll be sure to recommend you to my friends." Gathering up his newly framed picture, he waved as he left the shop. Sophie was happy Mr. Cheek was satisfied but breathed a sigh of relief as the talkative man departed. She was flooded with work and her assistant had gone home early after barfing twice. She ran her hands through her short hair and returned to her workspace. Back to the frame she was building for a client.

Sophie was frazzled by the time she closed the shop. She'd kept busy answering phone calls, fielding clients' needs, and trying to finish her latest project. She couldn't remember when she had been happier to call it a day. Yet she was hesitant to go home. Nate had a doctor's appointment and wasn't back yet. He didn't even know she had been alone most of the afternoon. She'd tried to call Darcy to come over but she and Nick were checking out a reception venue. Now the thought of being alone had her spooked.

What if the stalker was watching her? What if he was hiding nearby and realized she was alone? He hadn't ever made physical contact with her but Nate thought that might be his next step because his taunts seemed to be escalating.

She thought about the pictures the stalker had taken. How had he gotten close enough to take them without her noticing him? She knew how he'd gotten the one of her coming out from the shower. Nate had torn the apartment apart looking for hidden cameras and he'd found two. One of them had been aimed directly at the bathroom door. A shiver slid through her as she thought about that. It was too disgusting to consider.

Sophie flipped through the mail that had come earlier and she hadn't had time to look at yet. Bill, bill, bill...hey, not a bill. It was a postcard announcing an exhibit of Ephraim Farris's artwork, and the artist himself would be present. When was it? Should she go? Her heart fluttered as she pondered the situation.

Darn, the showing was going on now. She looked for the postmark on the card so she could see when it had been mailed but it was illegible. This was awfully late coming.

Was she brave enough to go there and confront the man? Could she tell him he was her father? Could she ask him where the hell he'd been for the last 27 years?

She didn't have to do that. She didn't have to barge in and make a scene, as much as she might want to. She could just go there and take a look at the man who had been there at her conception. See him for herself. She didn't have to say anything to him. But, if everything felt right, she could talk to him if she wanted to.

She wished Nate was here to go with her. She picked up the phone and called him but it went straight to voicemail. Noah had driven him to the doctor's because Nate hadn't been cleared to drive yet. Maybe he knew more.

She dialed Noah's number next and was relieved when he answered.

"Hi, Noah. It's Sophie." They chatted for a couple of moments before he told her he hadn't heard from Nate for about three hours.

"I dropped him off and he said he'd call when he was ready. I haven't heard from him yet."

Sophie's eyebrows pulled together in a frown. This was quite a lengthy doctor's appointment. Well, she'd just get ready and go to the showing for a little while and hurry back home. She'd leave Nate a note.

Thirty minutes later, she was dressed in a simple black sweater and skirt and headed to the gallery. Though it wasn't yet six o'clock, the sun was gone and dark clouds scudded across the sky. Traffic was heavy and moved sluggishly over snow-slick streets. With a sigh of relief, Sophie pulled into a public parking garage and locked her vehicle. She didn't feel safe being out alone, not with the stalker lurking, but she wanted to look at her father so badly that the need overrode her fear. Now her nerves were doubly irritated—once because of her fear of the stalker and twice because she was about to see her father for the first time in her life. A lump sat in her stomach like a brick.

The gallery was right across the street from the parking garage, thank goodness. Sophie pulled the red angora knit scarf tighter around her face and hurried to get out of the weather. When she walked into the gallery, it was like walking into a different world. Classical music tinkled softly through the air that smelled pure and fresh. Uplights and downlights in different shades of colors were directed at works of art displayed on pedestals, in crevices, and on the walls. Stylishly dressed women and men roamed the space and murmured quietly as they admired the art.

Sophie checked her coat and grabbed a glass of champagne from a passing waiter. She wanted to blend in as most people had drinks in their hands. She took a sip for courage then began to mingle amongst the crowd and study her father's work.

He was very talented in a weird sort of way. His use of color was amazing, shocking. There was a surrealistic feel to his work that captured her attention and drew her in. She was studying a picture that she thought showed a woman standing in a rainstorm, looking out over a cliff facing an angry ocean, when she felt a presence at her side. She turned and recognized the tall, lean frame of Ephraim Farris standing next to her.

"What do you think of the Lady on the Edge?" he raised dark eyebrows over coffee brown eyes as he questioned her. She had to swallow...twice...before she could answer.

"I think...she is troubled." She was surprised by how normal her voice sounded.

"You are right. She is. Greatly troubled." He turned his scalding gaze on her and said, "You remind me of someone. Someone I knew years ago."

Tell him. Now's the perfect time. But somehow, she couldn't form the words, couldn't get it out. She stood there, silent, as their eyes clashed. She looked into his face, seeing eyes the color of her own, seeing a narrow chin just like hers. This man was her father and she saw herself reflected back at her.

A man in a suit walked up to them, leaned in, and whispered in Ephraim's ear. Ephraim frowned and then turned back to Sophie. "If you will excuse me, I must attend to business. I'd like to continue our conversation in just a few moments, if you will wait."

She nodded, still not speaking. She watched his slim figure as he walked away with his dark head bent toward the gray-haired man's.

Now she was scared to tell him. She hadn't brought the DNA proof. He would probably think she was just some crazy woman trying to cash in on his fame. She shouldn't have come here. She needed to go.

Sophie glanced around, her eyes searching for sight of her father. When she didn't see him, she hurried to retrieve her coat and make her escape. She didn't think she drew a full breath until she was outside in the frigid air.

She breathed a sigh of relief when she got back to the car and was locked safely inside. Now all she had to do was get home. Nate would surely be there by now.

She started the car and proceeded to back up just as the phone rang. She stopped, checked the caller ID and breathed a sigh of relief. Nate. Finally.

"Hi, Nate. Are you home?"

"Hello, Sophie. I'm afraid this isn't Nate, and he's not home. He's with me."

Chapter 22

A cold pit opened in Sophie's stomach.

"Who is this? Where's Nate? Why the hell are you on his phone?" Sophie spat the words out. If this was a joke, it wasn't funny.

"Ah, ah, ah, Sophie. Watch your temper. After all, your man's life is in my hands. I caught up with him as he was coming out of the doctor's office." He gave an evil laugh and added, "Poor guy got a little shot that sort of knocked him out."

"Who are you?"

"You'll find out very soon. Now, you are going to come to me."

"What do you mean?"

"If you want to see your Nate alive again, you'll follow my directions exactly. I have him here right now."

"I don't believe it," she gasped. "Let me talk to him."

"I knew you'd say that. I've awoken him enough to let him say a couple words. Here. Talk to your lady, cop."

A groan transmitted across the line. "Don't do it, Sophie. Don't."

She heard the sound of a fist smacking against flesh and a bellow of anger. "I told you not to say that."

Her heart thundered in her chest. Nate. He had Nate.

"Damn it, don't hurt him. What do you want? What the hell do you want?" She choked out the words, pushing them past the lump in her throat that felt like it was choking her. She couldn't stand hearing how weak Nate's voice sounded, how pain-filled it was.

"Haven't you figured it out yet, Sophie?" His voice slithered across her raw nerves. "I want you."

Sophie recoiled at his words. She didn't know what to say, couldn't talk even if she had an answer. Her breath was stolen away.

"What...what do you want me to do?" she finally managed to whimper.

"Come to me, Sophie. Come and find me. When you get here, I'll let your man go."

"Where?"

He spat out an address that was close to Nate's house. She couldn't believe it. If she was right, it was just around the corner.

"Come alone. Don't call anyone. In fact, don't hang up. Just stay on the phone with me as you drive here. So, get going. Now."

Her mind was roiling. What should she do?

"I...I don't drive and talk on the phone. It's dangerous."

"Stupid bitch," he roared. "Dangerous is doing anything other than what I tell you to do. Now put me on speaker and drive, damn it."

"Okay, okay, give me a sec," she shouted back as she followed his instruction. "There, you're on speaker."

"That's better. Now start driving."

Sophie was shaking so bad she wasn't sure she could steer but managed to back out of the parking space and head out of the parking garage. What the hell should she do? She couldn't call anyone while the maniac had her on the phone. She didn't just want to drive into the stalker's trap. God, help her. She didn't know what to do.

"Are you looking forward to seeing me, Sophie? I can't wait to see you. It's been a long time." His voice sounded eerie as it came across the speaker.

"So I've seen you before?"

"You have. And I've seen you. All of you." Crudeness tinged his words.

"Shut up, you sick bastard," She couldn't stop the angry words from spurting out of her.

"There you go again, Sophie. What did I tell you about that nasty temper of yours?"

Lord, she had to make a plan. What? What?

Wait. She could text while she was on the phone. She needed to let somebody know what was going on. The last she knew Noah was available and waiting for Nate to call. She'd text him.

Fingers shaking, she managed to type out a hasty message and give him an idea of what was going on. She added the address where she was going and the word help in capital letters. That's all she could do. Please, please, let him get the message fast.

Fear swelled within her as she neared the address. She didn't want to walk into that house. She didn't want to confront the man who tormented her. God, she didn't want any of this to be happening.

But most of all, she didn't want Nate to be hurt...or worse. A sob rose in her throat at the idea of losing him. She could do this...she had to do this. She wouldn't let him kill Nate.

She spotted the address and realized the house was directly behind Nate's. A shiver ran down her spine. He'd been so close the entire time.

He'd told her to go to the garage. There it was—a compact two-story building set behind the darkened main house. She switched the car engine off and hesitated. Come on, Noah, text me back. Her phone remained stubbornly silent except for the sound of the stalker breathing into it.

"I'm here." She tried to put a tone of bravado in her voice but was afraid she failed miserably.

"Come into my parlor, said the spider to the fly," he taunted. "I'll open the door for you."

It was all she could do to make her legs move. They felt like two giant icicles too stiff to move. Somehow, she managed to climb out of the car and walk forward. She had to get to Nate. That's all she could focus on.

A side door to the garage swung open and revealed what looked like a gaping black hole. There were no lights on inside the first floor. She moved toward it cautiously, her heart pumping. When she got closer, she could see a looming, shadowy figure. Someone who looked big. Very big.

The sight caused her to hesitate but it was too late. The man reached out and grabbed her wrist, jerking her into the garage and slamming the door shut. Pain shot through her arm where he gripped it with tight fingers. She whimpered and shivered in the pitch black of the garage.

He dragged her toward and up the stairs, hauling her up like she was a bag of garbage. At last, they reached the top and he flung open a door and shoved her inside with a meaty palm on her back. She stumbled and fell onto the floor, scraping her hands across the rough carpet.

She lay there and blinked for a moment, adjusting her eyes to the pale light filling the room. She raised her head and looked around. Where was Nate?

Then she spotted him. He sat on a saggy couch, a dirty cloth stuffed in his mouth. His eye was swollen and purple, blood caked around his nose. His feet and hands were bound and he didn't even look conscious.

"God, what have you done to him?" she cried, rising up on her hands and knees and scrambling toward him. "Nate, Nate, wake up, honey. Come on."

She threw herself on the couch and took his face in her hands, patting and stroking it. His eyelids flickered and for just a moment he looked at her. He tried to speak but the gag blocked his words. She saw him try to focus but in a moment that dazed look returned and his head sank on his chin.

The chuckle of the man behind her drew her attention. It was time to find out who this monster was. She turned her head slowly in his direction.

She should have known. Mac McKinney. The foster father who had raped her when she was a teenager. She recognized him as soon as she saw his face. Oh, he was older, broader, and more muscular now than ever before. He'd never been a small man but now he looked pumped, beefy. His hair had almost disappeared except for a skinny tail at the back. He stood there, hands planted on his hips, feet apart. A snarl on his face. She'd hoped to never see him again but there he was, her worst nightmare come to life.

"You," she breathed.

"Are you glad to see me, little girl? I've been waiting for this reunion for over ten years."

"Why? Why now?" Confusion flew through her mind like autumn leaves in a gust of wind. "You've been out of prison for two years."

"Hell, yeah. It took me that long to get set up. Find a job. Find this place with the lovely old landlady who spends the winters in Florida. And then, I couldn't believe it. You moved in right next door. Wowee, that was perfect. I had to make my plans, do this right." He looked down on her and grinned. "And now I have plans for you."

"What plans?"

"I plan on making you pay, Sophie girl. You're going to pay for making me lose everything. My wife, my kids, my business, my freedom." His voice escalated with each word until he was shouting. Spit flew from his blubbery lips and landed on Sophie. "I want you to hurt like you hurt me, to lose it all."

"I hurt you?" She lurched to her feet. "You raped me when you were supposed to be taking care of me. You stole my virginity and threatened to kill me if I told anybody. You put your slimy, drunken hands on me. You tortured me. The price you paid wasn't anything compared to what you did to me."

She didn't see it coming. His meaty fist connected with the side of her face and pain rocketed through her head. She fell to her knees, trying to blink away the stars dancing before her eyes, the tang of blood filling her mouth.

Chapter 23

"Shut the hell up, bitch," he roared. "I don't want any lip out of you. Now get your fucking coat off and get in that kitchen and fix me some eggs. Kidnapping makes me hungry."

He guffawed after he said it and Sophie gaped at him. He actually thought this was funny. She shook her head and slowly drew herself to her feet, tears stinging her eyes. She fought them back with determination. She'd be damned if he saw her cry.

"You said you'd let Nate go."

"I lied. Now shut the hell up and cook. I only gave him a little medicine. I can up the dose, you know."

She fumed silently as she did what he told her, her mind spinning the entire time. She weighed and considered different options, rejecting each of them. There had to be a way to get them free. But with Nate out of it, she didn't know how she'd move him even if she managed to somehow trick or overpower Mac. He'd been drugged and would be dead weight.

She slammed the plate of scrambled eggs on the Formica table where the big-bellied man sat. He immediately started shoveling the food into his mouth and ordered her to sit her ass down.

She went to the couch and sat beside Nate, picking up his hand and squeezing it. To her surprise, he squeezed back and she cast a quick look at his face. He winked at her! Oh, my God, he was playing possum. Hope surged within her. He was awake. Thank God.

Mac finished his meal and leaned back in his chair and scratched his belly. A loud belch erupted from his throat. He turned his gaze in her direction, a lewd smile on his face.

"Let the games begin," he said, slapping his hands on his knees. "I've been looking forward to this for a long, long time. Stand up, Sophie. Now."

Sophie didn't move. She couldn't. Her legs refused to function.

Mac lumbered to his feet. "Now that's bad, Sophie. You're supposed to do what I tell you. When you don't, this is what's going to happen." He lunged forward and punched Nate in the chin, snapping his head back.

Sophie screamed. She threw herself over Nate to try to protect him from any further blows.

"You want me to hit him again?"

"No, don't. Please, don't."

"Then stand the hell up."

She stood on trembling legs and couldn't hide the shiver that ran down her spine when he reached out and took her chin in his hands. He tilted her head up and scorched her with his gaze.

"You are still the prettiest little piece of ass I've ever seen. I'm going to get me some of that, then I'm going to fuck you up. Then I'm going to let you watch as I kill your boyfriend. Kill him slowly." He chuckled maniacally and pulled her mouth toward his and kissed her.

She couldn't help it. She gagged, bile rising in her throat. God, she couldn't stand it.

"Let's get some of those clothes off you, girlie." He growled the words and reached for her sweater.

"Wait," she shouted, trying to get away from his hands. "I've got to go to the bathroom."

He ran a paw across his whiskery chin. "Hmm. I could be a hard ass and say no. But I'm not an unreasonable man, so go ahead. Just make it snappy."

Sophie didn't wait. She made a dash for the bathroom to escape his presence. Lord help her, she couldn't handle this. She braced her arms on the sink and hung her head, her breath rasping. She needed to keep her shit together.

Look for something she could use for a weapon. That's what she needed to do. She shot her gaze frantically around the small room. Shaving cream, a toothbrush, and a pocket-sized comb. Shit. Nothing. She reached up and opened the medicine cabinet. Pepto-Bismol, a half-used tube of toothpaste, deodorant, a razor...a razor! She could remove the blade and slip it into her pocket. It wasn't much but it was a whole lot better than nothing.

Her hands shook as she grabbed the razor and removed the blade. She was just putting the handle back on the shelf when she heard Mac yelling for her to get her ass back out there. She slipped the razor blade in her pocket, quietly shut the cabinet door, then remembered to flush the toilet. She drew in a deep, shuddering breath and opened the door into the kitchen.

Her feet refused to move more than a few steps. She stopped just inside the kitchen, her stomach churning. She would throw up if he touched her, she just knew it.

"Get over here, bitch," Mac growled. "I've waited long enough to have you again. Only this time, I'm not going to be so nice about it."

God. Did he actually think he'd been 'nice' the first time he raped her?

She inched closer to him, dreading the moment he would lay his hands on her. Wave after wave of nausea rolled over her. It felt like all she could do to not faint, but that would be like an open invitation. Like saying come and get me, I'm helpless.

She moved another inch forward then lurched back as he lunged to his feet. He grabbed her upper arms and pulled her up against his body. Rank breath forced its way into her nostrils and she gagged. She jerked and her knee banged into a coffee table, sending a big, overflowing glass ashtray spinning off its surface. His beer dumped over, liquid spilling onto the floor.

"Stupid, clumsy bitch," Mac bellowed and brought his palm up and cracked it against her cheek. The blow stunned her and a red handprint flamed to life on her face. Anger blazed inside Sophie but she forced it down. He had to think he was in control, that she was too frightened to fight back. She needed the element of surprise on her side.

Mac wrapped his meaty fist in her layered haircut and pulled her to him, jerking her head back so she was staring right at him. "You're going to give that pussy up one way or another. My life is over. Getting back at you is the only reason I've kept going this long."

He stopped talking and kissed her, pressing her head hard against his. He plunged his tongue down her throat and she couldn't breathe. She felt the pressure of his teeth bearing down on her lips and she tasted a hint of blood.

"I'm going to fuck your brains out, bitch," he said as he fumbled for her breasts and pawed at her sweater. "But first, you're going to give me a blow job."

The idea overwhelmed her. She'd wanted to wait for the perfect moment to attack him but she knew time was up. She would never put his dick in her mouth. Not even if her life depended on it.

"Take those fucking clothes off." He grabbed the neckline of her sweater in his fist and jerked. She heard the fabric rip and felt the flesh of knuckles brush against her skin. God, she wanted to take him out now but she had to be careful. She'd only get one chance.

Mac focused on ripping the sweater the rest of the way, jerking and tugging her roughly. Sophie fought to get her hand in her pocket and get hold of the razor. She had to hold it just right or she wouldn't have a prayer of making this work.

The corner of the razor stuck her finger as she fumbled for the blade. Her hands were shaking so badly she had trouble grasping it properly. There, she had it.

Fueled by fear and fury, Sophie jerked her arm up and rammed her fist into his eyebrow and brought the blade slashing downward. She screamed as blood flew.

Time froze for a moment. Then Sophie went flying across the room as Mac bellowed and tossed her. She landed with a crash, pain instantly shooting through her left side, pain so intense she nearly blacked out. She was afraid she couldn't get up. But she had to get up. He was coming toward her, blood pouring down his face.

"Fucking bitch," he roared, lunging for her.

Sophie rolled over and fought to get to her feet. Agony ripped through her as he grabbed her hair and slammed her face into the floor. He shoved his other hand into the middle of her back and used the one gripping her hair to raise her head up and ram it down again. Pain exploded behind her eyes.

She wanted to give up. She wanted to collapse and let him win but there was still a spark of fight left in her. She reached around frantically searching for a weapon. Anything she could hit him with, hurt him with. Then her hand bumped into something. The heavy glass ashtray she had knocked off the coffee table earlier. Her fingers grasped it as he grabbed her and turned her over and slammed her on her back. His hands wrapped around her neck, shutting off her air. Darkness swirled before her eyes.

She used her last bit of strength to bring the ashtray crashing against his temple.

Chapter 24

He hung suspended over her for a minute then came crashing down like a dead tree. He landed on top of her, pinning her beneath him.

His weight knocked what little air she had left out of her but at least his hands loosened from around her neck. She lay there, stunned, and heard Nate trying to talk around his gag. At last, she managed to draw a deep breath, then another. She finally was able to gasp, "I'm okay, Nate. I'm okay."

She looked over at him where he lay on the floor. He had rolled off the couch trying to get to her and his eyes were frantic. She imagined hers looked the same way as she was trapped beneath Mac's heavy body. Agony shot through her like flaming arrows and the smell of her former foster father made her sick. God, she had to get out from under him before he came to. They were still in grave danger.

She tried to move, to free herself from beneath him. Every motion sent new waves of pain searing through her. She managed to get her arms up beneath him and he moved a few inches. Now, a few more.

She paused to catch her breath then began the struggle again. She was almost free when the sudden crash of the front door exploded through the air. Feet rushed in.

"Police! Freeze!"

"Nick, Noah, and their brothers in blue flooded into the room.

It was over.

Two days later, Sophie struggled to zip her jeans one-handed. She was excited. She was getting out of the hospital this morning and couldn't wait to get home. She and Nate had been brought in by ambulance that awful night. Nate had a broken nose and fearsome-looking bruises but was allowed to go home to recover. She, on the other hand, had a couple of broken ribs, torn ligaments in her left shoulder, and a concussion, and was ordered to remain in the hospital for at least twenty-four hours.

Her arm was in a sling and her face sported rainbow-hued bruises, but she was alive. She was alive, and Nate was alive. That's all that mattered.

The door opened and Nate walked in. He still had two black eyes but Sophie had never seen anyone who looked better.

"Hey, honey, you look like you could use a helping hand." He moved to her and reached for the zipper and pulled it down. "After all, I'm going to be taking your pants off for years to come."

He grinned and cupped the back of her head with his hand, leaning down to sweetly kiss her lips. She wrapped her one good arm around his neck and kissed him back.

"That may be true, babe, but not this time. I'm in a hurry to go somewhere."

"Oh? Did you have any place special in mind?"

"To the only place in the world I want to be right now. Home...home to you and Angel."

"That bird will be happy to see you, too. He's been hollering for Sophie for the past day and night."

"Is he the only one who's missed me? She looked up at him from beneath her lashes and he laughed.

"No, you little minx, he's not. It feels like you've been gone for a month. I can't wait to take you home." They kissed again, Sophie sliding her palm along his cheekbone. She loved this man. Nothing else was important anymore. Just Nate. She'd told him about finding her father and running away. He'd been silent, just held her and kissed the top of her head, rocking her as he sat on the edge of her hospital bed. Then he told her how Mac had come up behind him as he was leaving the doctor's and stuck him with a needle. The next thing he knew, he was out of it.

They had both made mistakes.

A nurse came in just then and handed Sophie a list of instructions.

"Ready to roll?" she asked.

"You bet," Sophie answered and let Nate help her into her coat. She took a seat in the wheelchair and her lap was loaded with flowers and balloons from Jenna and Darcy. Nate carried everything else.

"Okay, Miss Cruz. Let's cruise on home."

"Darcy's here," Sophie announced as they pulled in the drive. "There's her car."

"I imagine she and Nick wanted to make sure you get settled in. I thought that was my job."

"Well, Darcy's always been a mother hen."

Nate came around the car and helped her out, holding her close for a long moment. The March breeze rippled through her hair and Sophie suddenly felt free.

"I love you, Soph. I don't know what would have happened if I lost you."

"I love you, too, Nate, more than I can say."

"You know I want to marry you. Will you be my wife?"

Tears stung her eyes as she nodded. She couldn't believe it. She'd waited all her life for somebody to love her. She'd never dreamed she'd hit the jackpot and wind up with her perfect soulmate.

"Yes, yes, of course."

"Then let's pretend it's our wedding night and I get to carry you across the threshold. With those words, he bent over and scooped her up in his arms. Her laughter tinkled through the air as he carried her onto the porch and the door swung open.

Darcy was waiting on the other side, her eyes filled with tears as Sophie was carried in.

"Sophie, welcome home," she squealed. "How are you? Do you feel okay?"

Nick came up and joined his fiancée. "Yeah. Did this guy hurt you again? Is that why he's carrying you?"

"No, no, we're practicing."

"For what?"

"For when we get married and he has to carry me over the threshold," she announced, joy filling her voice.

A chorus of cheers erupted.

"But if I don't set her down soon, I won't be able to function." Nate groaned as he pretended to drop her.

"I've got a place ready for her in the family room. Can you make it that far?" Darcy didn't wait for an answer, just set off at a brisk pace toward the back of the house, and Nate followed. But when he walked around the corner, Sophie got a surprise. Not only were Nick and Jenna here, but there by the fireplace stood her father.

Ephraim Farris took one step forward then hesitated. Nate gently sat Sophie down on her feet and she just stared at the man standing before her. My God, what was he doing here?

"Hello, daughter," he said quietly and held out his arms. Sophie stood motionless for a moment then flew into his embrace.

"How...who?" she stammered.

"Grace told me. I didn't know, baby. I didn't know you existed." His voice cracked as he stared into her eyes. "Can you ever forgive me?"

She didn't know what to say. Emotions tumbled through her. She needed to know more, had to find out what had happened. But she knew one thing. Her father was here now, accepting her, holding her. There was nothing to forgive. And that's exactly what she told him.

"Sophiiiiaaaa!" A loud squall broke through the air. Angel was tired of being ignored. They all laughed and Sophie cried a little. She wrapped one arm around her father's waist and another around Nate's. It had been a fight but she'd won. She was surrounded by love.

Noah

Chapter 1

God, I'm going to die.

The thought slammed through Jenna Harris's mind as she writhed against the man who held a gun against her temple. With his left arm wrapped around her neck, she fought for air. Officer Noah Baker stood across from them, his weapon trained at her captor's head.

How the hell did I get myself in this position?

Her mind rewound as she thought back to earlier in the evening. She was a wedding planner and had overseen a wedding that afternoon. She still wore the chic navy-blue sheath dress that was almost a uniform for summer weddings. The wedding had gone smoothly, and she left the reception cleanup in the hands of the catering company. She left the venue at about nine o'clock. As she was driving home, she remembered she was out of diet cola. She wasn't a coffee drinker but was addicted to diet cola. She would be a total grump in the morning if she didn't have one.

That's why she decided to stop at the convenience store closest to her home on the west side of Chicago. She just wanted some Diet Coke. She pulled into the parking lot and closed her eyes for a moment. She had a headache that was killing her and exhaustion overwhelmed her. She'd almost felt too tired to walk into the store.

But walk she did. She dragged her tired body into the building and headed to the soft drink aisle then moved toward the cash register. She'd been distracted by the bakery case and stopped to grab a gooey brownie. She hadn't had time to eat at the reception, and her stomach growled in protest.

She'd moved to the line at the cash register and stepped behind a man who didn't have any products in his hands. He was probably getting a lottery ticket or a pack of cigarettes. She patiently waited for him to finish his business.

That's when she saw the pistol in his hand. It was aimed directly at the belly of the small, bald man behind the counter who stood like a frozen statue. The bandit stared him down, the clerk visibly shrinking before him.

Just then Noah had walked in. He was off duty in plain clothes and had understood what was going on at once. In one quick move, he pulled his pistol and shouted, "Police! Drop your weapon!"

The man turned on his heel and yanked Jenna toward him. "Get out of my way, cop, or this lady gets it."

Jenna's hands clutched at the man's forearm that pressed against her throat pipe, tugging at the iron hard flesh with no results. Panic swelled within her, and she fought harder for her freedom. The man barely noticed, just holding her firmly in place and pressing the gun barrel a bit harder against her temple. Ribbons of fog started swirling around Jenna's eyes, and she couldn't breathe. She wasn't sure if it was from the pressure of his arm on her throat or pure panic.

Her eyes flashed around the room and landed on Noah Baker. The young police officer was the brother of two of her clients. Both his brothers were marrying friends of hers. She personally thought Noah was the best looking of the three Baker boys, and he looked incredible in his jeans, standing there, pointing his weapon at the man who held her captive.

Stop it, you fool. She scolded herself for thinking about Noah Baker's looks at a time like this. God, what's wrong with me?

Her gaze locked with Noah's, and then a strange thing happened. Fear receded, and a sense of quiet washed over her as she gazed into his crystal blue eyes. He communicated with her without saying a word. It was as if she could hear him talking to her, telling her to stay calm and trust him.

The picture suddenly became clear to Jenna. She wasn't a little girl. She was almost as tall as her captor with her low-heeled shoes on, and she had been called Rubenesque. That meant she wasn't a stick girl. Surely, she could use that to her advantage.

Instead of fighting to stick her chin out, she tucked it beneath his arm instead. She moved her hand and grabbed his thumb, pulling it back as hard as she could. At the same moment, she lifted her foot and stomped on the arch of his foot with as much force as possible.

A howl burst out of the man as she allowed herself to go limp and become dead weight. He fought to maintain his grip but the pain weakened him, and she slipped down his body. She heard him pull the trigger on the gun just before a shot rang out.

God, she was dead. Noise reverberated in her ears. She waited for pain to overwhelm her, the blackness of death to smother her.

Then she was falling, crushed beneath the man who held her. He landed on her back, pinning her to the cold tile floor. She couldn't move, couldn't even wiggle.

It took her a minute to realize she was still alive.

It was the man who was dead. Dead, collapsed on top of her, holding her down. She felt wetness soaking into her hair and onto her skin. Dear God, it was blood.

Shudders ran through her, and she closed her eyes in horror. God, get him off her, get him off her.

It seemed like forever, but in reality, it was only seconds later when Noah rolled the body off of her.

"Jenna, are you okay?" His voice was barely audible above the ringing in her ears. His hands landed on her shoulders, and he gently turned her over. Her eyes were clenched shut, and she didn't want to open them. She didn't want to see the aftermath.

She heard him calling her name, calling her back to reality. God, she didn't want to go there. It was too much, too horrible. She couldn't face it.

And then he slapped her.

Oh, it wasn't a hard slap. It barely stung, but it was enough to shock her out of her nightmare. Her eyes flew open, and her gaze slammed into the concerned stare of the man kneeling beside her. Time stood still as the world collapsed to contain just the two of them. Nothing, no one else existed.

Then suddenly she was gasping for air like a fish out of water. The bulky body of the man had knocked the wind out of her when he collapsed on top of her. Noah held her shoulders as she pulled air into her lungs, her mouth an O shape as she sucked for oxygen.

And then reality slapped her in the face. No, not reality. Noah.

"You hit me," she squawked, glaring at the handsome man before her. "I can't believe you hit me."

Chapter 2

Noah stared at her as if she were nuts.

"Really, Jenna? After all that has happened, that's what you're worried about?"

"I won't allow any man to lay a hand on me," she sputtered. She tossed her head, only to realize there was a huge wet spot on the side of her head. She glanced down and saw blood soaking the front of her dress, the skirt riding high on her thighs. A wave of nausea swept through her.

"You were going into shock, Jenna. It was the quickest way to bring you out of it."

"Of course, I was in shock. I'm still in shock. My, God, you just killed a man."

"To save a life, Jenna. Your life."

"I was trapped under a dead man." She shuddered, and her teeth began to chatter. Noah saw the signs of shock returning, and a worried look clouded his face. She shivered uncontrollably and saw it all happen again and again.

"Jenna, come on, honey. It's all over. You're okay. Let's see if we can get you on your feet."

Noah wrapped his arms around her and pulled her to her feet then simply held her. He felt the tremors running through her and the shakiness of her breathing. His hand slid to the back of her head and cradled it against his chest.

Jenna fought to overcome the flood of emotions shooting through her. She was horrified, traumatized, and devastated by the events that had just taken place. But she'd been traumatized before and lived through it. She knew she had to slow her breathing, calm her body and mind.

She leaned her head on Noah's chest, focusing on feeling the rising and falling of each breath he took, trying to match the rhythm of her breathing to his. She flattened her ear against his muscular rib cage and listened to the steady thump, thump of his heart beating. An unexpected feeling of peace flooded through her.

Her head snuggled in the middle of his chest, she realized, dumbfounded. She wasn't a little girl. She stood five feet and nine inches tall and had a full, curvaceous figure. There were very few men who could make her feel dainty or protected, but to her astonishment, she felt both as she snuggled against his broad chest.

Then her mind made another quick turn. What the hell was she doing, thinking about Noah Baker's machismo at a time like this? She needed to stop. And she would in just a few more seconds, after she'd drawn on his strength for a little bit longer.

The sudden squawk of sirens tore through the air and Jenna was jerked back to reality. She drew in one long, shuddering breath then pushed away from Noah. She wanted to appear as a sane woman when the rest of the police officers arrived, not as a clingy, hysterical girl. Now that the worst of the shock was over, she felt somewhat embarrassed by her display of emotion. That wasn't like her. She always managed to keep her cool and maintain a warm, friendly, yet professional attitude.

Officers swarmed into the store, and noise swept through the place. It was organized chaos for the next while, and Jenna felt shakier as the evening wore on. Noah made his reports and Jenna talked to the police, too. Finally, she was allowed to go home. Noah laid his hand on her arm and stopped her as she started to go.

"Jenna, I'll call to check on you."

Jenna raised her eyes to his. Their gazes locked. He stared deeply, and Jenna felt a melting in her bones. She didn't know why but she felt a connection to this man. She'd felt it from the first moment she'd laid eyes on him at his brother's home. She didn't trust men in general, but there was something about this one...

Jenna forced herself back to the present and gave him a quick nod. She really couldn't speak right now and quickly walked away.

The storm that had been threatening all evening finally broke as Jenna drove home. By the time she pulled into the driveway of the home she'd inherited from her maternal grandparents, rain was cascading from the sky and lightning flared spasmodically through the dark night. Jenna's mom died when she was only seven, and sometimes it seemed as if this house was the only thing she had that tied her to her mother.

Jenna pulled into the detached garage, gathered up her briefcase, and dashed for the back door. By the time she got there, she was soaked even though it was just a few feet. She let herself into a kitchen with the lights on and a mess on the counters. The smell of pot filtered through the air. Damn her half-brother Lucas.

She heard the stereo blaring and voices coming from the living room. Her little dog Leon came out of the corner to greet her, the terrier mix obviously scared by all the commotion. She felt a flare of anger flow through her. Jenna wasn't happy to come home to a houseful of noisy party-goers. This was more than she could deal with after everything that had happened tonight.

Before she could make her way to the front of the house, Lucas came stumbling into the kitchen. His dark hair tumbled around his sculpted face, dark with beard stubble. He staggered into the wall and gave his sister a smirk.

"Hey, Sis, you're home early."

Anger burned inside as she gazed at her brother, an empty beer bottle waving in his hand. He had just turned 21 two months earlier, but he'd been giving her trouble ever since his mother and their father had been killed in a plane crash when

240

he was 16. She loved him, but she hated the attitude he'd developed. It was only growing worse as he got older.

"Early? Early? It's after midnight. I'm tired, I'm exhausted, and I come home to this mess. And you're drunk! I can smell you from here." She waved her hand in front of her nose. "Who the hell do you have in there anyway?"

"Just a few friends. We're just chilling."

"You're chilling at top volume, Luke. I can't even hear myself think."

"That's how you need to listen to that music, man."

Jenna drew in a deep breath, willing herself to remain calm. She didn't have the energy for another fight tonight. It seemed that's all they had done lately.

"I'm sorry, Luke, but your party is over. It's late, and I have to work early tomorrow. Either you tell your friends to leave or I will."

Lucas glared at her with his burning dark chocolate eyes. He looked just like their father standing there, angry, commanding, and stubborn. He tilted his chin at her defiantly, and she glared right back at him. She wasn't in the mood for any arguments.

Lucas finally backed down. He tossed the beer bottle into the trash can and strode into the living room. "Hey, guys, let's cut on out to Harry's place. My uptight sister is home and wants to go to bed. She has to work in the morning."

Jenna followed him into the room and felt the hostile glare of a dozen eyes on her. One pair, in particular, scorched her with its heat. She felt her own gaze drawn to that of Louis "the Bull" Garcia. He was a new friend of Luke's, older than most of the others. He didn't go to college like many of Luke's friends but was a "working" man instead.

She didn't like Bull Garcia. His looks were swarthy and macho. He had piercing black eyes, broad shoulders, and a smirk on his handsome face. A tattoo coiled down his neck and disappeared beneath a sleeveless white shirt that accented his bulging biceps. There was something about the man that set warning bells off in Jenna.

Bull took a final gulp of beer and eyed her up and down insolently, not making any move to leave. Jenna pulled herself up to her full 5'9" and refused to be stared down. The man might be built like a bull, but as far as Jenna was concerned, he was a punk. Nothing but trouble.

She held his gaze until her cell phone rang. She reluctantly looked away to pull the phone out of her pocket and saw it was Noah Baker calling. Perfect.

"Hello, Detective Baker." She spoke in a loud, clear voice and saw the flicker of alarm in Bull's eyes before the mask of arrogance fell back in place. She moved over and defiantly turned off the music. "What can I do for you?"

Bull shrugged and started for the door. "Let's get out of here, guys. Sis is talking to her cop boyfriend on the phone. See you soon, Sis." He raked his gaze challengingly over her as he sauntered across the room and left. The others followed him, and in a moment, she was left alone with only a clutter of beer cans, overflowing ashtrays, and Noah Baker on the phone.

Chapter 3

"Jenna? Are you there? Is everything okay?" Noah's anxious voice brought her back to the phone pressed against her ear.

Jenna breathed a sigh of relief and drew air deep into her lungs. She felt much better now that Lucas and his friends were gone.

"I'm fine, Noah, thanks. I was just distracted because my brother and his friends were leaving."

"When you answered, it sounded like a party going on."

"That's how I found it when I came home. My half-brother lives with me, and right now, things are a little, oh, let's just say strained."

"Oh, brother trouble. I understand that. I've got two of them, you know."

"I do know."

"Well, I hope it's not serious. Anyway, I called to see how you're doing after your traumatic evening."

She paused and thought about it for a moment. She hadn't had time for it all to sink in yet. "You know, I actually haven't had time for it to hit me yet. I guess it probably will, now that I'm alone."

"I wanted you to know I was thinking about you. I don't know if that helps, but I didn't want you to think nobody cared."

His soft words froze her heartbeat for a moment. How long had it been since she felt somebody had actually thought about her, her feelings, her emotions?

"Thanks, Noah. That does help."

Jenna smiled as she spoke and moved to curl up in her favorite big chair. She remembered sitting here with her grandma, listening to her tell her stories. She always felt better when she sat in this chair.

"You've got my number now. If you want to call me, please do. I know after something like this happens, I find it hard to sleep. If you have trouble, I'm here to lend an ear."

"Thanks, Noah. I think that might be asking you to go above and beyond the call of duty, though. I'll be okay." She managed to disguise the surprise she felt by the offer. Was he just being polite or did he honestly care about her?

That thought made a lump the size of a softball swell in her stomach. She didn't want him to care about her...or did she?

"I wasn't thinking about duty, Jenna. I was thinking about you. The offer still stands. If you need to talk, call me. Any time." His tone was serious, his voice quiet. "I'll say good night now. Sweet dreams."

"Noah," she said his name but didn't really know what else to say. Finally, she just told him good night and disconnected. She sat there for a long time, just holding the phone on her lap.

Noah was right. She did have trouble sleeping that night. Her thoughts pinged back and forth between reliving the nightmare attack at the store and trying to decipher Noah's real message. Every time she almost fell asleep, another image would appear in her head. Sometimes it was of Carl Williams, as the assailant had been ID'd; sometimes it was of Noah.

She didn't want to think about either subject. They both terrified her. Williams for obvious reasons, Noah for more subtle ones. It seemed every time she closed her eyes, she felt the cold metal barrel of that gun pressed against her temple. She'd jerk awake and lay there shivering. Then her thoughts would switch back to the concerned tone of Noah's voice. Was it more than a professional interest? That thought sent the fear of God shooting through her as well.

Jenna let her thoughts drift back in time. She'd only been seven when her mother died in a carjacking. By the time she turned eight, her father had remarried, and Lucas was on the way. Her father was an ambitious man who had little time for things that didn't make him money, and that included Jenna and Lucas. Frank Shepherd and her stepmother Vivica died in a plane crash when Jenna was 23. Lucas had been almost 16, and she had taken custody of him. That was probably not a good decision on her part, Jenna knew now. She'd been too young to be in charge of a hotheaded teen like Lucas. She was also already mentally stressed from her marriage to Jackson Harris.

Jackson Harris. A charismatic, beautiful man on the outside—a narcissistic, mean, abusive man on the inside. She'd met him when she was just 18 years old and been swept away by his good looks. He was almost eight years older than her and seemed suave and sophisticated. She fell under his spell immediately, but soon after their marriage, she began to feel suffocated. He picked apart everything she did, everything about her, that she was fat and ugly, stupid and clumsy. He didn't like her friends. He picked at her incessantly, and toward the end, he became physically abusive. He bullied her and harassed her until she was almost at a mental breaking point.

Why had she stayed with him? Because she had no place else to go. Because her father was distant and uncaring. Because she didn't have any job skills to support herself. All the typical reasons why abused women choose not to leave. Because they don't feel like they have a choice.

Jackson thought he was intelligent, even when he chose to drink too much and when he started to dabble in drugs. Jenna knew he drank, but he kept the drugs secret from her. He didn't let her know when he decided dealing drugs was a good way to make money. He kept her at home while he was often away "on business." It wasn't until the cops came around that Jenna had an inkling what he was up to.

They wanted to talk to Jackson about a shipment of drugs. He wasn't there when they showed up, but Jenna was terrified. What would she do if Jackson were arrested and went to prison? When he came home, Jenna confronted him. She soon discovered that was a stupid move as Jackson drove a fist into her stomach and smacked her across the face.

He went wild because the cops were on to him, and he accused Jenna of squealing. She hadn't. She couldn't. She didn't know anything to tell. He knew that, but being a typical narcissist, he couldn't believe anything was his fault. He tossed her aside like a rag doll and hurried to his office and began shredding papers. When she tried to talk to him again, to find out what he was planning, he pushed her against the wall and ordered her to stay out of his way, emphasizing his point with a slap across her face.

Jackson left her slumped on the floor and hurried to the bedroom. He reached into a closet and pulled out a bag Jenna had never noticed that he'd packed in case of emergency and then turned to the nightstand. He pulled a gun from the drawer and stuffed it in his waistband.

Jenna watched him in shock. She hadn't known he had a gun, had never inspected the suitcase in their closet. She'd been ordered to leave his stuff alone, and like a good little wife, she'd obeyed him.

"Jackson, what about me?" she'd finally asked. She couldn't believe he was walking out on her, leaving her to face the music.

"You're excess baggage, baby," he growled.

The moment she heard the words, she knew she had been a fool. She'd fallen under the spell of this con man, allowed him to manipulate and control her, let him lead her into danger. And now she was just excess baggage to be tossed aside.

"Then go. Get the hell out and don't ever come back!"

He sneered at her and replied, "Don't worry, baby. I'm gone from here to someplace better, someplace where you'll never be. You think I didn't plan ahead? You really are a stupid bitch." He tossed the words over his shoulder as he headed for the front door.

She followed him as he walked out and stood at the walk as he headed toward his car. That's when cops leaped out of the shadows, guns drawn, and ordered Jackson to raise his hands. Jenna's heart froze when she saw in his eyes he wasn't going to comply. Instead, he pulled his gun and began to fire. A moment later, he was dead with a bullet through his heart.

Chapter 4

Sometimes it was like it had all happened yesterday. Other times it seemed like a long, long ago bad dream. At the time, she had been thoroughly traumatized. Not only was she a twenty-two-year-old widow who had witnessed her husband's violent death, but she also had to prove her innocence—that she knew nothing about Jackson's drug deals. She had no means of support and was desperate. The police had seized their bank accounts, and she couldn't make the house payments. Then her grandmother died, and she inherited the house she lived in now. And her Aunt Cherie had come and slapped some sense into her.

Cherie was her father's sister but nothing like him. She was vivacious and optimistic and an avid animal lover. She owned the event planning business that was now Jenna's. Jackson had only been dead three months when Cherie confronted Jenna. She told Jenna that she couldn't just roll over and give up. That she had it in her to fight. Cherie needed a new assistant, and Jenna was going to be it.

That's when Jenna's life turned around. She threw herself into learning the business and found she truly loved it. She was a quick learner, and her confidence grew daily. She felt better about herself than she had at any other time in her life.

Then her father and her stepmother died. Lucas came to live with her, and she became an instant mother figure. Lucas had been a sweet, adorable child but had grown into an angry, rebellious young man. He kept his grades up but defied her in so many other ways. He constantly broke curfew, smoked, drank, and refused to do chores. She didn't like the friends he made; most of them were overindulged teens with a bad case of affluenza.

Lucas had a trust fund his father left him, but Jenna was the administrator. Lucas wouldn't gain control of his finances until he turned twenty-five, and he rebelled at her refusal to let him blow his money on fancy cars, hot girls, and other luxury items. He received an allowance of $75 a week and Jenna thought that was generous. She'd bought him a decent car and paid his insurance and college expenses from his fund. But it seemed he'd grown angrier at her every day that passed.

Her life had taken another turn when Aunt Cherie announced she wanted to retire nine months ago and made Jenna a deal for the business. Jenna would be paying for it for a long time to come, but if she could keep the business going, it would be worth it.

She shook herself back to the present. God, she needed to sleep. She rolled onto her stomach, punched the pillow, and vowed to get at least a few hours' sleep. At last, she fell into a restless slumber and awoke feeling exhausted.

If she didn't have to work, she'd lay there all day and indulge in a big old pity party, but she had a wedding to supervise in just a couple of hours. She stumbled through a shower and headed to the kitchen for a Diet Coke. She'd just taken the first cold, refreshing sip when her phone rang. It was Noah.

"Hi, Noah."

"Hi yourself. How are you doing this morning?"

God, his voice was sexy. She felt a shiver slide down her spine just from the sound of it.

"I made it through the night somehow."

"I'm glad. Was it rough?"

"You could say that."

"I know it wasn't easy. You went through a lot." He paused a moment before continuing.

You were really brave last night, you know."

"No, I wasn't. I was scared to death."

"Being brave doesn't mean you're not scared, Jenna. It means you overcome it to do what needs doing. You did exactly that."

She closed her eyes and drew in a deep breath. She didn't feel brave. Not about facing homicidal maniacs or even facing the obstacles in her life. Lucas was becoming a major problem, she was under pressure to make sure her business remained successful, and she didn't trust men. She was a mess, she thought.

"Thanks, Noah," she finally answered. No sense in telling him her troubles.

"I just thought you ought to know."

"If I was so brave, why did you slap me?"

"I didn't slap you. I tapped you."

"Semantics. Why did you do it?"

"Because you were about to lose it. You were a courageous warrior while the danger was on, but you got overwhelmed in the aftermath. That happens sometimes, and people need just a little tap to bring them back to reality." His voice was patient as he explained it to her. "Forgive me for having to do it, but it did snap you back."

She had to admit he was right. She didn't want to, though, because after what she'd gone through with Jackson, she had sworn no man would ever hit her again. She knew Noah hadn't done it maliciously, but she still felt a little resentful. Or was it just part of her general grumpiness today? She questioned herself, and that pissed her off, too.

"You're right. But that's the only situation where a man will ever get away with slapping me again." She growled out the words.

Silence hung in the air for a couple of moments before he said, "Again?"

Damn. She hadn't meant to make that slip. She didn't want to talk about the past, not now or ever.

"Hey, Noah, I really have to go. I've got a wedding in just over three hours, and I have to be there shortly." She avoided the question and disconnected the call. Coward, she chided herself. Well, she did have to get going. This bride was a nervous wreck, anyway, and Jenna didn't want to add to her stress. Besides, that part of her life was none of his business. She didn't want to talk about it, and that was that.

Jenna tried to shove him out of her thoughts as she did her makeup and got dressed. She slipped into another navy-blue dress with short sleeves and added a pair of nude pumps. She swept her auburn hair up in a loose knot and headed out the door.

The first person she saw at the church was her assistant, Penny. The dark-haired beauty with big green eyes was a bundle of energy. When she saw Jenna walk in, she dashed toward her and started rattling off a list of things that she'd finished and those that still needed accomplishing. Jenna had no time to spend another minute thinking about Noah.

Until the wedding was over and the reception well underway, she had no time to think about anything but wedding details. But as soon as she started home, Noah popped back into her mind. Just picturing him made Jenna sigh. He was hauntingly handsome with his dark, silky curls and the dimples in his cheeks. And his eyes, a clear silver blue, were hypnotic. His shoulders were broad, and his biceps bulged. She didn't know if she'd ever seen such a good-looking man up close and personal before.

And being held against his chest yesterday was definitely personal. He felt strong, safe. It surprised her that she felt that way. Men, in general, did not make her feel safe or protected. She didn't trust them. Look what had happened with Jackson. He was a beautiful man, charismatic and charming...at first. Reality hid beneath the perfect exterior. How could she trust after that experience?

Jenna pulled into the driveway of her home and sighed. Noah Baker might be delicious eye candy, but he wasn't on her diet.

Chapter 5

Jenna's last meeting of the day on Monday was with Sophie Cruz and Darcy Campbell, the two women engaged to Noah's brothers. Jenna liked them both, and the three of them had become good friends. Darcy's wedding to Nick Baker was in just two weeks, and they were meeting to hammer out last-minute details. Jenna had suspected the meeting would end just as it did...at a nearby pub offering apps and alcohol.

The three women sat in a curved booth and indulged in wings and margaritas. It was happy hour, and the place was crowded with after-work revelers. The girls had already placed their orders and gotten their strawberry margaritas. They made an interesting picture—they were all so different. Jenna with her auburn hair, Sophie, brunette and elfin with a feathery, short cut, and Darcy with golden curls. Men couldn't help but look twice at the attractive trio.

Jenna raised her glass and made a toast. "To my friends, the happy brides."

"And to you, Jenna, for helping make our weddings perfect," Darcy added.

"Thank you." They clinked glasses and took a drink.

"Hopefully, we'll be drinking to your wedding one of these days," Sophie said.

"I don't know about that," she replied. "Men and I don't get along that well."

"Well, I know one man you've made an impression on," Darcy said with a mischievous grin.

"Me, too," Sophie chimed in. "Do you want to know who it is?"

"It's Noah." Darcy didn't wait for Jenna to answer. "He's been asking about you."

Jenna's cheeks instantly flamed and she felt her stomach clench. She fought to maintain a cool exterior, but a strange excitement flared within her.

"Did he tell you what happened the other night?" Noah's brothers were also police officers, so she assumed they knew of the shooting.

"He did. My God, Jenna, you must have been terrified." Sophie reached out and laid her hand on Jenna's. "He said you were great, though."

Jenna snorted. "That may be what he said, but it's not the way it happened." She went on to tell them about her moment of hysteria and Noah slapping her face to bring her back to earth.

"Wow. He didn't tell us that part. He said you were brave, cool, and calm. He also said you are a beautiful woman."

"Are you kidding? I had blood in my hair, blood on my dress. I was a mess."

"Well, apparently, Noah didn't think so."

"Well, apparently, Noah's nuts."

"He isn't, Jenna. You are beautiful." Darcy jumped to her defense.

"That is so true, girl," Sophie agreed. "You are a stunning woman. Lord, I wish I had your height."

"I wish I could give it to you. I'm always the tallest woman in the room."

"And I'm always the shortest. Which is worse?"

"Sophie, you're like an elf or a pixie."

"And you're like a queen."

"Okay, enough of this talk. Let's change the subject."

"All right, but I still think you are a beautiful woman. And so does Noah."

An hour later, Jenna waved goodbye to her friends and climbed into her minivan with Elegant Events painted in a beautiful scroll on the side. She flipped on the air conditioning and pulled out into the traffic, headed for home. She'd only gone a few blocks when she saw the flashing red and blue lights behind her.

Jenna quickly decelerated and pulled over, muttering under her breath. What the hell had she done wrong? She wasn't speeding, she had her seatbelt on, and she'd signaled her lane change. Damn, just her luck.

She knew it was silly, but also natural, to feel nervous as hell. She hadn't done anything wrong but still felt a twisting in her gut.

She lowered her window and waited for the officer to approach. She plastered a smile on her face, tossed her hair over her shoulder and turned to face...Noah.

He leaned his handsome face down toward her, a serious expression painting his countenance but a twinkle in his eye.

"Good afternoon, Miss, I'm Officer Baker."

"I see. Can you tell me why you pulled me over, Officer Baker?" She decided to play along with the "we don't know each other" game.

"I'll tell you after you give me your driver's license, registration, and proof of insurance." He spoke in a serious tone.

"Sure, officer, I'll get right on it." She dug in her glove box first and pulled out the registration and insurance papers, then pulled her license from her wallet. She handed them to him then sat with her hands on the steering wheel and a mutinous look on her face.

He took her license and headed back to his patrol car, leaving her fuming in her vehicle. She liked to think she had a sense of humor but this seemed like crossing the line. He was pushing her nerves now. She didn't appreciate it.

In a few minutes, he returned to her car window and handed her back her papers.

"Thank you," she said tersely.

"The reason I pulled you over is that you have a brake light out," he finally told her, and she felt a bit ashamed of her anger. What made her think this was personal? Probably because Darcy and Sophie had been on a roll about Noah. She felt a burning in her cheeks as they pinkened. It was the curse of the redhead to blush easily.

"I'm not going to give you a ticket, just letting you know you need to get that fixed."

"I will. I'll get it done ASAP."

"Make sure you do. The next cop who stops you might not be as friendly as I am."

"I said I would." She felt her ire rising again. He didn't have to talk to her like she was a child.

"Okay, I'm just saying."

"I get it, all right? I'll have it done tomorrow."

"Great. How are you doing, by the way? I mean, after what happened the other night."

She finally turned and faced him and looked him straight in the eye. "It's been a fucking nightmare. I haven't been calm or cool. I can't sleep. And you lied. You told everyone how brave I was. I was a mess."

Noah tilted his head and stared at her with intense pewter eyes and finally spoke in a quiet tone. "I have to disagree. Yes, you were nervous and upset. Who wouldn't be? But if you were a mess, you were a brave, beautiful mess in my eyes."

Jenna felt a small, sharp constriction in her chest at his gentle words. She had been married for over three years and couldn't recall Jackson ever saying anything so lovely. Once again, her anger faded away. Geez, Noah certainly could make her moods swing. She almost felt bipolar around him.

"I appreciate you saying that, even if it isn't true."

"I don't lie, Jenna. Ever."

Their eyes met for several seconds until Jenna finally spoke.

"Then we have something in common."

He gave her a grin, dimples flashing in his cheeks. "I bet that's not the only thing, redhead."

She stiffened in her seat. Was he flirting with her?

The radio on his shoulder squawked to life, and he tilted his head to listen to it.

"Hey, I gotta go," he announced abruptly. "I'll see you soon, red. After all, I've got your address."

Chapter 6

Lucas was sprawled across the couch playing a video game when Jenna came home. She called out a greeting to him, and he grunted in response. She was getting used to his sullen attitude, so she just let it roll off her shoulders and bent to say hello to Leon. He nearly bent his furry body in half as he welcomed her. Well, at least somebody was glad to see her.

Leon's nails clicked on the floor as he followed her to her bedroom and observed her as she slipped out of her business suit and into a pair of pink capri leggings and a white tank top. Oh, it felt good to get that bra off.

She padded barefoot to the laundry room and stuffed a load of whites in the washer then headed to the kitchen. Lucas didn't seem to care if he ate or not, but she was a little hungry. She rummaged through the fridge and finally decided on a carton of yogurt.

She took the yogurt and a spoon back to her room and curled up in an old quilted armchair. She switched on her TV and enjoyed the first bite of the yogurt, letting the cold concoction slide down her throat. She settled back and let herself get absorbed in a movie. She thought she heard a knock at the door—it was late for that—but figured it must be for Lucas.

Though it was still early, she was starting to nod off in her chair when the sound of voices roused her. Lucas was yelling at somebody. What the hell...

Jenna flew toward the living room and stopped dead when she saw Bull Garcia grasping her brother's shirt in his meaty fists.

"Stop it!" She ran forward and skidded to a stop by her brother. "Let him go. This is my home, and I won't allow you to disrespect it."

Bull turned and leveled his gaze at her steadily. He still held Lucas by the shirt, her brother's toes stretching to touch the floor. Bull turned and stared at Lucas before finally shoving him away.

"Okay, mamma, we'll have it your way this time." His eyes roamed boldly over her, and the telltale red crept into her cheeks. She hated how dirty he made her feel. "But don't let me catch you outside, boy."

Jenna drew in a sharp breath as she heard the threat. At first, she thought the pounding she was hearing was her heart thumping in her ears until she realized someone was knocking at the door. She lifted her chin in a haughty gesture as she passed Bull and hurried over to open it. Noah stood on the other side.

Jenna couldn't stop the emotions the sight of him released. Thank God he was there, in case Bull wouldn't leave without trouble. What the hell was he doing here? And, most of all, God, he looked hot.

"Detective Baker." She spoke clearly so Bull could hear his title. "Come in."

Noah strode into the room, his eyes taking in the scene before him. You could tell he felt the tension in the air as he turned his gaze on Jenna.

"Is everything all right?" He queried as he stared intently at her.

She sucked in a breath and nodded. "Our...guest was just leaving."

Noah turned his glare on Bull, a cold recognition on his face. "Garcia. What are you doing here?"

"Just visiting my amigo here. Like the lady said, though, I was just leaving." He wore a sullen look on his face as he moved past Jenna and out the door. Lucas took off to his room before the door closed behind Bull.

"Pretty rough company you're keeping," Noah commented once the thug was gone. "I arrested him on a possession of meth charge a while back."

Jenna wasn't surprised to hear it, but she was disappointed. She'd hoped Lucas had better sense than to be involved with somebody like that.

"Believe me—he's Luke's friend, not mine." She felt herself shiver a little as she thought about the muscular jerk. There was something about the man that she found repulsive.

"Your brother doesn't have very good taste in friends."

"In this case, I have to agree with you." Jenna rubbed her hands down her upper arms. "So, Noah, what brings you here tonight?"

"Would you believe I was in the neighborhood?" He grinned mischievously as he said it.

"Not really, no." She answered without cracking a smile.

"Well, I was. In fact, I live in an apartment just around the corner and decided to take a walk."

"Oh, and your walk just happened to take you right to my front door. I see." She fought to maintain her serious countenance.

"Guilty as charged, your honor." His lips quirked at the corners, and his dimples dared to dance. "What sentence are you giving me?

"Hmmm." She tilted her head and tapped her pointer finger next to her mouth in a thoughtful gesture. "Since it's your first offense, I think I'll show some leniency and just put you on probation."

"Thank you. I appreciate your mercy." And then he reached out, took her fingers in his, and bent to kiss the back of her hand. It was like a lightning strike against her flesh.

Noah seemed to feel it too. He looked startled, all the humor flying out of his eyes. Jenna jerked her fingers away, barely able to stop herself from shaking off the burn.

He straightened up, his large hands sliding down the legs of his jeans while his gaze locked into hers.

"Actually, I wanted to ask you if you like to dance."

She loved to dance. She wasn't one to go jogging or do calisthenics, so her workouts consisted mainly of dance. That was her exercise of choice. She'd loved to dance since she was a little child. Her father and stepmother had always thought it silly, but Jenna didn't care. When she heard music, she felt the rhythm in her soul.

"As a matter of fact, I love to dance." She tried to maintain a cool tone to her voice.

"Then how about joining me at The Boogie Club for Jive Night Thursday evening?"

"Jive Night?"

"Yeah. It's great, especially if you like the swing sound. "He wore a hopeful expression on his face.

"You dance jive?" She couldn't disguise the shock in her voice.

"Yeah, I do. It's a great stress reliever." He spoke a bit defensively.

"I don't have much experience dancing jive."

"It's great fun. You'll catch on. After all, I'll be your partner." He winked at her and grinned.

Jenna tipped her head thoughtfully, studying him unblinkingly. "Why?"

He looked at her, confused. "What?"

"Why? Why are you asking me out?"

"Well, heck, Jenna. I guess for all the usual reasons. I like you, I think you're gorgeous, and I'd like to get to know you better. Anything wrong with that?"

"You think I'm gorgeous?" she asked incredulously.

"I'm not blind. Of course, I think you're gorgeous. Don't you?"

She barely suppressed a snort. Jackson had blasted any such silly notions out of her head. She was a ginger, a big woman, and she had freckles on her nose. Gorgeous? Hardly.

"Hey, if I didn't think you were beautiful, would I do this?" his voice dropped to a deep timbre, and he stepped toward her. His arms went around her waist and pulled her to him, his mouth lowering and capturing her lips beneath his.

Jenna froze like a mouse beneath the intense glare of a hungry cat. Her eyelids flew open...until they began to drift slowly closed, her body melting against his.

Chapter 7

Oh my God! What the hell was happening to her? Her knees were weak; she sagged against the heated plains of his body. Her blood began a slow boil. She felt totally disoriented.

Noah's hands roamed across her rib cage, cutting a trail along charged nerve endings. His thumbs stroked the sensitive skin there, and she thought steam might be coming from her ears. Lord, was the world spinning?

Jenna couldn't stop her arms from twining around his neck. His lips felt like hot velvet, tasted like ambrosia, opened just enough to allow his tongue to slip out and trace the outline of her mouth. Her neck tipped back to allow him better access. It was a foreign feeling. Most men weren't tall enough that they towered over her, but Noah did.

He slid a hand up to her face and trailed his fingers along the crest of her cheekbone. She breathed in a small gasp, stunned by the effect of his touch. "Please. Stop."

Noah took a shuddering breath and let his hands trail down to her waist. "I don't want to stop, but I know I have to."

"Yes."

"Well, I hope that answers any doubts you have about why I want to take you dancing. Shall I pick you up at seven?"

"Okay," she answered in a dazed voice.

"Okay. See you then."

And then he was gone. She felt the cold the moment he took his hands off her. Part of her wanted to call him back; the other part was relieved to see him go. What had she just done? Damn, she'd agreed to go out with him. That was a stupid decision on her part. Now she was obligated to go. Why the hell did she say yes?

Jive dancing. Who the hell did that? Jenna shook her head, still kicking herself for her temporary insanity. Well, she wasn't going to waste any more time thinking about it. Now she needed to confront Lucas and find out what the hell was going on with him and Bull.

Jenna checked herself in the mirror one last time. She wore a simple periwinkle blue dress with a fitted waist and a circle skirt, paired with a pair of nude sandals. Her auburn hair swung in a high ponytail, and her cheeks flushed pink. It was time for her date with Noah and her stomach churned like a fully loaded washing machine. It was too late to back out now, she admitted, as she heard a knock at the door. Lucas wasn't home, so she had to answer the door herself. Lucas had been absent most of the time lately, so she hadn't been able to pin him down about his argument with Bull. This wasn't the time to think about that, though. She was going dancing.

Jenna took a deep breath before pulling the door open. She heard the pounding of her heart in her ears as her gaze took him in. His burnished locks glistened in the fading rays of sunlight. He wore a white knit shirt which showed off his bronzed skin and jeans that fit him like a second skin. She was so caught up in looking at him she didn't even notice he was looking at her with the same appreciation.

"Hi," she finally managed to squeak out.

"Hi. You look amazing."

"Thank you." She bit back the urge to contradict him. "Would you like a drink before we go?"

"No, thanks. If it's okay with you, I'll wait until we get to the club."

"Sure. Are you ready to go then?"

"Let's do it."

With that, they were off. They spoke little on the way to the club, just exchanging small talk about their work and families. It wasn't long before Noah pulled into the parking lot of an old-fashioned style brick building.

Noah hustled around the car and opened the door for her just as she reached for the handle. She wasn't used to the polite gestures he always seemed to bestow on her. Was he actually real?

The thought was still tossing about in her mind as they entered a lively scene. The crowd wasn't thick yet, so they easily found a red leather booth in the corner with windows surrounding them. Music from the big band era filtered through the air as they took their seats. Only a moment later, a waiter appeared at their table and took their drink orders. Jenna watched eagerly as a few dancers took the floor, her toes beginning to tap beneath the table.

She was fascinated by the movement on the floor. There was every level of dancer accounted for, from professionals to obvious beginners, which made Jenna feel better. At least she wouldn't be the only one learning steps and fumbling through the routines.

Noah seemed to read the relief on her face and reached out and touched her palm. "No need to worry, Jenna. You're not the only one here who's doing this for the first time."

"Thank goodness. Some of these people are really good, though. Look at them." She pointed at a pair of dancers that moved in perfect synch. The man was tall and slender, his legs fluid and skilled. The woman was beautiful with platinum blonde curls and a short red skirt. They moved together like one person with perfect precision, yet their personas radiated fun and lightheartedness. Jenna didn't think she could ever dance with that type of joy and enthusiasm. She took another sip of her peach wine and watched in awe.

They watched and talked a few minutes longer before Noah grinned. "Ready to give it a try?"

Jenna's heart flew into her throat. Was she ready? Well, she guessed she better be. She nodded slowly and took another huge gulp of wine. She needed fortification.

Noah led her on to the dance floor, his hand at the small of her back, burning into her flesh where it made contact. They turned and faced each other, and Noah took her hand in his and put his arm around her waist.

"Okay. Start with your right foot and do a rock step. Like this." He demonstrated, and she followed his movements carefully. Okay, she could do that.

He continued patiently showing her each step. Soon she was actually dancing. She loved the lively music and the happy vibes that filled the room.

"It's all in the legs," Noah said as he twirled her around. "That and learning to relax."

Before she knew it, she was having a ball. Once she got the rhythm of the music, she found herself following Noah's lead almost effortlessly. He was a wonderful dancer, and they moved well together. It was a joy to let go of her inhibitions and throw herself into the dance. She couldn't help but feel her troubles float away and her hormones charging up as she watched his gyrating hips.

Noah was probably the sexiest man she had ever met. She'd been swept away by Jackson, handsome devil that he was, but not like this. When she'd been with Jackson, she'd been so young, so naïve. She'd like to believe she was older and wiser now but she didn't have confidence in that. What if she'd only been hiding from the danger for the past few years? What if she really was just naturally stupid about good-looking men?

Her negative thoughts started to bring her down, but she pushed them aside and refused to think about it. She only wanted to enjoy this evening of dance and Noah. She laughed as he swung her around his hip and her feet bounced down. This was the most fun she'd had in ages. She was going to follow Noah's advice and just relax. It wasn't often that she indulged in recreational time, so she was going to make the most of this evening.

They danced several dances then made their way back to their booth. Jenna glowed, damp with exertion, and Noah grinned as she gulped at her wine. The flush on her cheeks accented the sparkle of her periwinkle blue eyes, and he couldn't disguise his delight in her happiness.

"So, you're having a good time?"

"I'm having a ball," she confessed. "I didn't expect to have such a good time."

"Did you think I'd be terrible company?"

"Not at all. I just expected to be so nervous I wouldn't be able to enjoy myself. By the way, you're a great dancer. And a great teacher."

"It helps when you have a natural for a student."

The sincerity in his voice made Jenna blush, and she ducked her head in response. She didn't want to feel these conflicting emotions involving Noah. She wanted to deny the flicker of hunger that ran through her when she looked at him. She didn't want to admit that goosebumps broke across her skin when he touched her. She wished she could pretend he didn't have any effect on her...but she couldn't.

"How long have you been dancing?" She wanted to turn the conversation away from herself.

"I've always loved to dance. Even as a kid, I was always dancing. It helped with football and other sports, I think. It enhanced my agility, I guess you could say. It didn't hurt my standing with the ladies, either," he chuckled.

Jenna figured he would have had to have halitosis from hell and massive zits to turn off the ladies whether he could dance or not. Dancing ability was a bonus.

"Hey, I love that song. Ready to dance again?"

"Sure." She took another invigorating sip of wine and let him lead her to the dance floor.

They danced a couple of lively numbers, then the music suddenly dropped to a slow, sultry number. It wasn't a jive tune, but many of the dancers seemed to enjoy the change of pace. Noah drew her close, and Jenna leaned into him for support. Her knees weakened when he was this close.

A magic spell began to weave its way around her. The rest of the world retreated, her existence narrowing down to just the area that held the two of them. She felt his arms pull her closer and her hips pressed against him. Her breasts pushed against the solidness of his chest and her breath caught in her throat. She was floating, following perfectly with his every move. Were they dancing or flying? She couldn't tell, but she was sure her feet weren't touching the floor.

The dance became even more heated as the music's beat became more seductive. The tension rose as her nerves throbbed. It was almost like sex, the anticipation of a climax, building, building...

When Noah ended the dance with a deep dip and their gazes met, the world exploded.

Chapter 8

"Are you ready to get out of here?" he whispered into her ear while she still bent over his arm.

"Yes." She breathed the word against his cheek.

It seemed like it took forever to gather her purse and pay their bill. She wanted to be alone with Noah, alone to drink in the sexiness of him, drown in the passion he produced in her. She needed to kiss him, and she didn't need an audience.

Thank God the fresh air smacked her in the face when they left the building and knocked some common sense into her. Had she lost her mind?

Noah was an intoxicating drug, as addictive as heroin or cocaine. He went to her head, muddled her senses, and made her hallucinate. She'd almost believed for a moment that she could have a relationship with a man that didn't end in disaster. That maybe happy endings really did come true.

She knew better than that. She may make her living helping other people plan perfect events, fairytale weddings, and blissful engagement parties, but that was for others, not for her. She knew better than to hope for something that just wasn't destined to happen.

Noah, unfortunately, hadn't come back out of the trance yet. He held the car door as she slipped in, his hand trailing warmly across her back. When he climbed into the driver's seat, he turned and looked at her, his eyes serious and piercing. She tried to look away, but it didn't work. She was pinned.

"Jenna Harris, I think you are special." He spoke softly, warmly.

"No, Noah, I'm not. I'm not special at all. I'm just an ordinary woman with a brother to finish raising and a business to run. I don't have time for dancing, and fun, and, and..." Her breath ran out and she burst into tears.

"Hey. Hey, hey, hey, what's wrong, Jenna?" He sounded worried as he swiftly gathered her into his arms. "You seemed so happy just a minute ago."

"Oh, Noah, it's stupid, but I'm afraid of you."

"Afraid of me? Why, Jenna? What have I done?"

"You haven't done anything wrong. That's just it. You're too perfect. I'm waiting for the other shoe to drop." She knew she was wailing, but she couldn't seem to help it. Tears scorched her cheeks and her nose plugged up. She wished she knew how to cry prettily but instead she turned red and couldn't talk.

"What do you mean, Jenna?" He ran his hand across her hair, soothing the length of her ponytail.

"You're not real. You're too perfect. I'm afraid of what I'll find out about you." She buried her tear-soaked cheeks in the hollow of his shoulder. She felt like a fool. What girl cried because a man was too perfect?

"Oh, Jenna, I appreciate your flattery but believe me, I'm not perfect. I've been called pigheaded, I'm kind of a slob, and don't tell anybody but I've heard people say I snore like a freight train. Believe me, I'm not perfect."

She had to laugh as she sniffed. "That's not the imperfections I'm worried about." Her voice sounded wet, gurgling. God, she didn't want to do this right now.

"Tell me, Jenna," his voice soothed her.

"The only man I ever trusted almost killed me," she whispered the words. "He died when the cops shot him."

She heard him suck in his breath through his teeth and felt his arms tighten around her shoulders. "That wasn't a man. It was an animal," he growled.

She didn't know what to say. He spoke the truth, but she didn't want to admit it. Jackson Harris seemed like a good man when she'd met him. She'd felt mesmerized, hypnotized, just like she felt with Noah. Could she possibly walk that road again and expect a different ending? The thought made her cry even harder.

"I don't know what to tell you, Jenna, except that judging all men by the actions of one is confused thinking. I'm not Jackson. I'm not my brother. I'm me. All I can ask is that you let me stand on my own merits or fall because of my own faults." He tipped her chin up with his finger and looked into her eyes, running the ball of his thumb over a silver teardrop. "That's all I ask."

She closed her eyes for a moment. He was right, of course. But it was so hard to close out the memories, to let herself trust this man. Even her father had turned against her mother before her death, focusing all his energy on work and finances. He'd immediately replaced her after she died, like it didn't even matter who his wife was as long as he had one who lived up to his high standards. Of course, Jenna had been held to the same criteria.

Even Lucas was turning out to be a disappointment. He'd been a sweet, loving little boy who adored his big sister, but now he didn't seem to care about her or anything else. It seemed to Jenna that all the men in her life were narcissistic assholes. God, Noah was right. She was confused.

"I'm sorry, Noah. I know it's twisted thinking. I'll try to overcome it."

"Honey, you can't help the way you feel. I just hope you'll give me a chance before you close the door on me."

"I'll try, Noah. I promise." She sniffed, feeling like an idiot for letting her emotions overwhelm her.

"I'll do my best to prove to you all men are not alike."

They didn't really talk anymore as Noah guided the car toward her home, but he did reach over and take her hand in his. His palm covering hers was a combination of comfort and electricity. He pulled the car into her drive, the headlights flashing across the back porch.

"Stop," Jenna ordered abruptly, squeezing his arm. "I saw something."

Noah put the car in reverse so the lights hit the porch fully. He saw it, too, then. A figure huddled on the steps.

"Luke." The cry broke from her throat as she threw the car door open. Her feet scarcely touched the ground as she flew to her brother's side. "Luke. What happened? Are you all right?"

Lucas lifted his head and looked at her through bleary eyes. She saw discoloration marring his cheekbone, and his lip was fat. He tried to grin at her but ended up wincing in pain instead.

Jenna groaned and dropped to her knees beside him, reaching out to stroke his hair off his forehead. "Who did this to you, Luke?"

"I fell," he said, a waft of alcohol reaching up to Jenna's nose. "I fell down the porch steps."

She glanced up and caught Noah's eye as he stood over them. His face showed no expression, only a wooden countenance, his sharp gaze taking in the scene.

"Well, you are drunk." Jenna looked back at her brother, tilting his face toward her. She still felt suspicious that he had had a run-in with someone. After all, there were only three porch steps and, more importantly, he sounded like he was lying.

"Do you need to go to the hospital?" she asked.

"No. I'll be fine. No hospital."

"Are you sure?'

"I said no hospital, damn it. I'm okay. Back off." He snarled at her and staggered to his feet. "I'm going to bed."

She watched him stumble through the door with her heart sinking. Something was wrong. She knew it. Lucas was in trouble. She wished he would talk to her, but it didn't look like that was going to happen.

Jenna felt like all the happiness had left the evening. She'd had an amazing time tonight, but it had been temporary. Reality wasn't near as enjoyable. She still had to make a living, still had to take care of Lucas, and still had to deal with the everyday problems of life.

She turned and looked at Noah sadly before telling him she needed to check on Lucas.

"I'll call you," he said quietly before reaching out and grasping her shoulders. His crystal blue eyes pinned her as he lowered his head and let his lips capture hers. Her blood throbbed through her veins, her pulse pounding. Her hormones begged her to ask him to stay, but her common sense drowned them out. This was not the time to add more complications to her life.

"Good night, Noah. Thanks for a wonderful time." She pulled away from him reluctantly but with determination. She couldn't afford to have Noah in her life.

Chapter 9

The wedding season was in full bloom, and Jenna was kept busy with nervous brides, anxious mothers, and even some fuming fiancés. She came in early, worked late, and weekends were packed. It seemed like she put out fires all day, every day. Darcy's wedding was less than a week away, and she was the calmest bride Jenna had. She was surprised by Darcy's serenity.

Jenna was so busy she didn't have time to see much of Lucas. She'd confronted him about his injuries the next day, but he still denied any trouble. Just a tumble down the stairs, he insisted.

Noah, too, had to take a back seat. They talked on the phone, and he often sent funny texts. She appreciated the fact that he didn't pressure her to see him again and that he didn't come on too strong. She needed to tread carefully where he was concerned, and he seemed to understand that. Thank God.

Jenna finished another phone call and laid her head on her desktop. Her temples pounded and stiffness enveloped her shoulders and spine. She was exhausted. She just needed to rest for a minute.

She groaned as a knock at her office door disturbed her stolen moment of peace. She straightened up and hollered "come in" and turned to see her assistant, Penny, enter the room. She knew as soon as she looked at her that something was wrong.

"What is it, Penny? What's wrong?"

"You won't believe who's out there." She gasped and leaned against the closed door. "You won't believe it."

"Okay, I won't believe it. So, who is it?" Jenna couldn't help but feel impatient. She didn't have time for guessing games.

"It's Marcus Moreno."

Marcus Moreno, the hot, hot singer from here in Chicago? No way. He must have at least four platinum records.

"Holy shit, Penny. What the hell is he doing here?"

"He said his sister is getting married and he wants you to plan her wedding. And he's not alone. He's got two big thugs with him."

Good God. Planning a wedding for Marcus Moreno's sister? This could truly help solidify her business. Or break it, if she screwed up.

Jenna clasped her sweaty palms together. Well, there was only one thing to do. Talk to the man and see if she could get this job...and if she wanted it.

"Give me two minutes, then send him in." Even as she spoke, she was straightening her desk, hiding the Diet Coke that sat there and shoving files into drawers. She took a second and ran a comb through her hair and dashed on a bit of lip gloss. By the time Penny knocked on the door, she was drawing deep breaths and trying to calm her shaking hands.

"Mr. Moreno. I'm Jenna Harris. I'm so pleased to meet you." She extended her hand to one of the best-looking men she had ever seen. He was tall and slender, his hair as black as a raven's wing. His dark eyes sparkled, and he sported a lush, thick mustache over full, sensuous lips.

"Ms. Harris, the pleasure is all mine." His speaking voice was as lovely as his singing voice, and Jenna stood mesmerized as he raised her hand to bestow a kiss on the back of it. "Thank you for seeing me without an appointment."

"I have a few minutes free. Won't you sit down?" She waved a hand at the floral upholstered chair in front of her cherry wood desk and took her seat.

"I apologize for not calling ahead, but I am only in town for a day before I go back on tour. I need to talk to you about my sister Elena's wedding."

"Of course, Mr. Moreno. I'd be happy to help."

"My sister attended a wedding last week and was delighted. She insists that you are the only wedding planner she wants."

"Which wedding was it?" She'd coordinated three weddings last weekend. That was one of the reasons she was so exhausted today.

"Sylvia Cortez's."

Jenna had suspected as much. The Cortez wedding had been the splashiest she'd done yet; the other two had been fairly simple. The Cortez wedding had taken place on a yacht on Lake Michigan complete with Mariachi band, champagne fountain, sumptuous sit-down dinner, and fireworks.

"That was certainly a beautiful wedding. So, Mr. Moreno, I don't mean to seem blunt, but usually, it is the bride and groom who contact me. May I ask why Elena didn't come?"

"Please, call me Marcus, and of course that is a legitimate question. I'll be happy to tell you in just a moment, but first I must ask you to sign a non-disclosure agreement. In my position, I cannot afford to have anyone who works for, or with me, knowing my business. No matter who you are, the tabloids will harass you and offer you money for any dirt you can give them. I'm sure you understand the necessity of the NDA." He smiled charmingly and slid a paper across the desk to her.

She read it carefully. It was a standard NDA with no extras, so she went ahead and signed it. She kept all her clients' business confidential anyway, so it wasn't a problem.

"Thank you, Jenna. May I call you Jenna?" He cocked his head and gave her a warm smile.

"Of course." She couldn't help but blush beneath his steady gaze.

"Okay. I will tell you. My little sister Elena is in kidney failure. She is at dialysis today. If she doesn't get a transplant soon, she will die."

His words hit her like a fist to her stomach. The thought of a young woman facing such a bleak future hurt.

"I'm so sorry."

"Please, don't be. Elena doesn't want anyone to feel sorry for her, but she and her fiancé want to have a wedding and be together whatever happens, and I want to make it magical for her. Cost is not a factor."

Jenna blinked back tears but tried to speak in a professional tone. "What is the date of the wedding?"

"It's in three months."

Jenna's head jerked up at his words. Three months? Holy smokes, that wasn't even time to order a dress.

Marcus held up his hand to stop her before she spoke. "I know, it is very short notice. But there is no time to waste. Elena may not live another six months. She will wear my mother's wedding gown, and the wedding itself will take place at our church. That makes it much easier, right?"

But that still left the reception venue, caterers, flowers, entertainment, and so many other details. And this was the busy season. She was booked nearly solid for the next six months. Could she even do this wedding justice in such a short time?

"Mr. Moreno —"

"Marcus," he interrupted with a smile that showed off his beautiful white teeth.

"All right. Marcus. I don't know if I can do this and do it right. I've got weddings booked for months ahead. People usually come to me a year in advance."

"Oh, Jenna, please do not say no. Elena has her heart set on you planning her wedding. Sylvia was impressed with you. Look, here is my Elena's picture." He pulled his phone from his pocket and brought up a picture to show her.

A feminine version of Marcus grinned back at her. Black, satiny hair tumbled past slim shoulders; large, dark eyes shined and a blissful smile spread across her slim, angular face and radiated happiness mixed with mischief. She had her head propped on her hands and head cocked, looking like an impish fairy. How could she say no to that adorable face?

"I will pay you five times your normal fee." His face hardened with a look of determination.

"It's not about the money. It's about giving this wedding the attention it deserves."

Marcus drew in a deep breath and his gaze bored into hers. "Jenna, this is my sister's wish. It could be her dying wish. Please, is there no way possible you can find it in your heart to do this?"

His pleading tone and intense eyes reached in and tore her heart out. It might consume every bit of her time, but she couldn't refuse him.

"If your sister would be willing to take evening appointments and make some other concessions, I'll do it."

"Ahh, Jenna, thank you so much." He reached across the desk and took both her hands in his. "You have a beautiful soul. Thank you."

Jenna was stunned to see a glint of tears in his eyes and felt wetness well up in her own. She was honored to be asked to do this, but at the same time, she wondered what the hell she had let herself in for.

Chapter 10

Penny went into shock when Jenna told her about their new client. Jenna knew she would be asking her assistant to work a lot of overtime but silently vowed to share the extra pay generously with her. They already had an overloaded schedule, and now she had just made it much worse. Like the trooper she was, though, Penny soon calmed down and began strategizing.

Jenna put in a call to Elena and arranged to meet her and her fiancé the next evening after her regular work schedule was finished. It would be the only way she could work on planning her wedding with the load she already had.

When Jenna met Elena, she was enchanted by the petite girl. Elena was happy, excited, and optimistic, impressing Jenna with her positive attitude. She knew she would be struggling to maintain any semblance of cheer if she knew she would be dead unless she found a perfect match for a kidney transplant and found it fast.

Elena's fiancé's name was Ramon Rosetti, and he was completely in love with Elena. It was obvious as soon as you saw them together. They had known each other since they were children and were not only in love, they were best friends. Ramon wasn't overprotective but kept a close eye on Elena.

Elena was fragile-looking, with high cheekbones and large eyes. When she spoke of her wedding, that face lit up like the sun. She had been dreaming about a fairytale princess wedding since she was a child and yearned to make her dreams come true. She looked trustingly at Jenna.

"I know you can make it happen."

Jenna wanted that, too. She wanted to help Elena have the wedding of her dreams. She vowed to do it regardless of how much extra work it made her do. Ideas rolled through her mind long after she'd gone to bed that evening.

The rest of the week flew by until suddenly it was the night of Darcy's rehearsal dinner. Jenna felt on edge, knowing she would see Noah for the first time since they'd gone dancing. She tried to push down the nerves that squirmed inside her, but she didn't have much luck. She just needed to push Noah Baker out of her mind, damn it. She was so busy taking care of other people's relationships there wasn't time to even consider one of her own.

Jenna gave herself one last glance in the mirror and straightened the slim skirt of her sleeveless black dress. Tonight, she was not only the wedding planner but a guest as well. She and Darcy and Sophie were close. It was as if they had known each other for years instead of a few months. She was happy for both girls. Their chosen men seemed great, which spoke well for Noah, since they were his brothers. Darn, she was doing it again. Stop thinking about Noah and keep your mind on business, she reprimanded herself.

The church where the wedding was scheduled to take place was beautiful, an old red brick traditional with a giant white steeple and the sun beaming behind it when Jenna pulled into the lot.

She entered and was greeted by Reverend Ford, a jovial man in his 60s. He'd been the Bakers' pastor for many years and was excited to be performing the ceremony.

"We're here," Jenna heard Darcy sing out as she and Nick entered. She gave them each a quick kiss on the cheek and turned to greet Sophie and Nate as they trailed in behind the first couple.

"Okay, we just need the rest of the wedding party, and we can get started," Jenna announced. Darcy clapped her hands with excitement. Jenna smiled at her friend's enthusiasm.

In the next few minutes, Nick's parents arrived. His twin sisters, who were the other two bridesmaids, the groomsmen, the flower girl and ring bearer and their parents had all gathered. Everyone was there except Noah. Jenna glanced at the slim gold watch on her wrist and sighed. They were already fifteen minutes behind schedule. Where was he?

People were starting to get antsy, and she knew Reverend Ford needed to get things moving. He'd stressed to Jenna earlier that he was on a tight schedule this evening. Had something happened to Noah? He was a cop, after all. She decided reluctantly to go ahead and start the rehearsal without him, but worry still niggled at her mind.

With a nod at the minister, Jenna clapped her hands for attention.

"Okay, people, let's get started. We've waited as long as we can for our missing groomsman."

"Sorry!" A deep voice boomed from the back of the room. "I'm here."

Jenna's knees trembled with relief. Thank God. She had a sudden vision of what it would be like to be in a relationship with a police officer. There would be constant fear whenever he was gone or a few minutes late. She didn't like that feeling.

A smile lit up Jenna's face as she met Noah's gaze. He did look fine. His dark jeans outlined muscular thighs, and he'd added a white button-down shirt and a navy sports jacket. His sable curls tumbled across his forehead, the only sign that he'd had to rush. He smoothed the stubborn locks back as he made his way directly to Jenna.

"Hi, wedding planner. I got held up at work. I'm sorry, but I'm ready to go now. Do with me what you will." He grinned, making his dimples dance.

His words conjured up visions of what she'd like to do with him and she fought to control the blush creeping across her cheeks. Not now! She scolded herself.

"Let's just start by running through the processional," she said in the sternest voice she could muster.

"Aye, aye, captain." He gave her a salute and a wink as he spoke.

Damn him. He made her forget what she was doing. She turned her back on him and spoke to the group, trying to ignore his distracting presence.

The next half hour was spent going through the rituals, with everyone laughing and joking. They all seemed to have a grasp of what was expected of them, so Jenna declared them wedding-ready and sent them all to the restaurant where the Bakers were holding the rehearsal dinner. Noah was the last to leave besides Jenna.

"You are coming to the dinner, right?" he asked as they headed toward the parking lot. The twilight fell softly around them, and they were all alone. Everyone else had already left.

"Definitely. I don't think Darcy would forgive me if I didn't." Jenna fumbled for her keys as she spoke. "I'll see you there, then?"

"You bet." He smiled and opened her car door for her. She climbed in and gave him a slight wave as he turned and walked to his car. She heard him start his truck as she stuck her key in the ignition and turned it. It only greeted her with a tired grinding. It didn't start. She tried again with the same results.

"Well, damn," she hollered and slammed her fist against the steering wheel.

Chapter 11

"Trouble?" The familiar voice broke into her thoughts, and she jerked with shock.

"I'm sorry. I didn't mean to scare you."

"Oh, I was lost in thought. My car won't start. I'll just call my auto club."

"I'll wait until you get in touch with them."

"Oh, you don't have to do that," she hurried to say. She didn't want to seem like she couldn't take care of herself. She was almost thirty years old, after all.

"But I will," he said sternly.

She didn't reply, just pulled her card from her purse and called the auto club. She was shocked when they told her they were extremely busy and it would be over an hour before they could get someone to her.

"Are you sure someone can't get here sooner?"

"Hey, ride with me to the restaurant. They can come and take care of things while we're gone." Noah spoke up when he saw her face fall.

Jenna thought fast and decided to take him up on his offer. She told the woman on the phone the plan, and they agreed to call her when they completed the service call. She hung up and tucked the keys under the mat, then climbed out and joined Noah in his truck.

Thank goodness the restaurant was only a few minutes away because Jenna felt like she couldn't breathe. The air conditioning was cool and kept the air circulating, but there seemed to be a band around her chest. Being this close to Noah had a definite effect on her, and she wasn't sure she liked it.

The other party-goers greeted them enthusiastically when they entered the private room where the dinner was taking place. Darcy hugged Jenna and said, "I was worried about you. I'm so glad Noah was there with you."

"Mmm, yes, he was very helpful. But he makes me nervous."

"Jenna, I think the word you're looking for is horny. He makes you horny."

Crimson stained Jenna's cheeks. "Darcy, you're nuts. Just because you're in love doesn't mean everyone is."

"Oh, but believe me, those Baker boys are irresistible when they've chosen their woman. And I can tell Noah's chosen you."

"You're silly. How many drinks have you had?" Jenna frowned at her friend and her assumptions. She was glad when Nick joined them and the subject changed.

The restaurant was beautiful. The room they were in opened onto a terrace that overlooked a pond. Potted plants stood strategically around the dining room, and fairy lights twinkled amongst them. It was an indoor/outdoor setting that felt peaceful and inviting.

She didn't know how she ended up seated next to Noah at dinner, but somehow it happened. She was nervous, but his easy conversation soon had her feeling more at ease. By the time the entrée was served, she found herself laughing at his jokes and enjoying the easy camaraderie at the table.

After dessert, a few couples started dancing on the terrace. Jenna hated to admit it, but she wanted to dance with Noah. She felt her feet tapping under the table and started swaying to the rhythm. Noah grinned at her, and her heart stopped as he asked her to dance. She couldn't say no.

It wasn't a jive dance but a lively tune that encouraged them to wiggle and shake. Noah moved naturally, his hips keeping time with the beat. Jenna allowed herself to relax and moved her own hips in a sexy motion. Color stained her cheeks by the end of the dance.

The next song was a rendition of I Will Always Love You that had Noah gathering her in his arms. Jenna found herself lost in the moment as their bodies fit together. The match felt seamless, perfect. They melded into one person as they swayed to the music. The sensations that swirled through her left her awestruck. Her breasts pressed into his muscular chest, her hips fit snugly against his. It felt like they were the only two people present on the terrace, moonlight spattering across them.

When the song ended, Jenna swallowed disappointment. They stayed together for a moment before Noah reluctantly separated from her but wrapped his arm around her waist as if he didn't want her to stray. It was a magical moment that was interrupted by her cell phone. Dang, what bad timing.

She pulled it out of her pocket and saw the caller ID said the name of her auto club. She answered it, and in a moment her happy smile was replaced by a worried frown. She covered the phone and said, "They say it's the starter. They can tow it somewhere for me, but I won't have a ride home."

"You know I'd be happy to take you." His smile was warm, promising.

That's exactly what she was afraid he'd say. But what choice did she have?

"Are you sure? I don't want to put you out."

"I'd be happy to do it. We're practically neighbors, remember?"

She smiled her thanks and finished making arrangements with the auto club. When she hung up, she felt breathless.

"It looks like the party's breaking up. Are you ready to go?"

She nodded without speaking. They said their goodbyes and walked out to the parking lot. She was all too aware of his hand at the small of her back as he led her to the truck and helped her in. She settled onto the leather seat and tried to get her heartbeat to slow down. It was silly to be this nervous just because she was getting a ride with Noah Baker.

Those Baker Boys are irresistible. Darcy's words kept echoing in Jenna's ears. No, it wasn't true. She could resist. She mentally stamped her foot.

"I've enjoyed spending time with you tonight," Noah said quietly. "You're good for my spirit."

"Thank you," she said. "That's a beautiful compliment." And she meant it. No one had ever said anything more meaningful to her.

"You know, Jenna, I think I'm falling for you. Falling hard and fast."

"Maybe too fast," she murmured.

"I don't think so. I think when it's right, you'd know it."

"Sometimes it doesn't pay to move fast. Sometimes it backfires." She spoke around a big, fat lump in her throat and felt the sudden sting of tears behind her eyelids.

"Jenna. I know something happened to you. But that doesn't mean it will happen again." He reached over and took her hand, clasping her fingers in his.

"I didn't think it would happen the first time. Jackson seemed so perfect when I met him."

"He was an idiot," Noah muttered.

"I think I was the idiot. I should have left him long before the end."

"It's easy to see that now," he said logically. "You know what they say about hindsight."

"I was a fool,' she snapped.

"No, Jenna, he was a fool. Too blind to see you just wanted to be a good wife and have a happy life."

The sincerity of his tone sent a single tear rolling down her cheek as they pulled into the driveway of her darkened house. He put the truck in park and gathered her in his arms, his hands cradling her head.

"Jenna, honey, don't let one bad experience dictate the rest of your life. You're shutting the door on all kinds of joyous experiences, don't you see?" He used the ball of his thumb to blot away the solitary tear on her cheek. "It's like dancing. You were scared to try jive at first, but you did, and you loved it."

"I was betting an evening of my time, Noah, not my heart. I don't know if I could stand to have it broken again." She buried her head in his shoulder and shuddered.

"Shh, babe, it's all right. You're not a coward. You're brave, courageous, and beautiful. You're made for love. Let me love you." He spoke with conviction, determination ringing in his voice. "I'll even make you a bet."

"What kind of bet?"

"I bet you'll fall in love with me in the next month."

Chapter 12

She pulled back and stared at him. "Arrogant, aren't you?"

"No, just confident. I feel this is right. It's meant to be. I don't think you'll be able to resist the magic of love. It will cast a spell on you."

"I don't think so. I'm in control of my own emotions. I won't allow myself to love again. It's too dangerous. It hurts too much."

Noah didn't say a word. He simply drew her to him and kissed her, deep and hard. His arms wrapped around her back, one hand sliding up her neck beneath her hair. She started to push away in protest but found her hands melting on his chest. They slid across the surface, reveling in the hot, solid feeling. God, he was irresistible.

No, he isn't, she silently shouted. She had just said she was in charge of her emotions and now she was acting like she had no control.

"Stop," she gasped. "Please stop."

He pulled away reluctantly but kept his arms around her and leaned his forehead against hers.

"You don't play fair," she whispered.

"You know what they say. All's fair in love and war."

Jenna didn't reply, just breathed, trying to calm her inflamed nerves. Being with Noah was like playing with fire. Hot and dangerous.

When she finally had her breathing almost back under control, she said, "Well, tomorrow's a big day. I better call it a night."

"You're right. Let me walk you in and make sure everything's okay. It doesn't look like Luke is home."

She protested, but he insisted. He helped her from the truck and took the key from her and unlocked the door. He walked through the house and returned to where she waited in the living room.

"Are you satisfied, Officer?" she inquired tartly.

"Not really. I'll only be satisfied when we're spending our nights together, and I'll be with you to keep you safe."

"It's not going to happen, Noah."

"We'll see." He grinned at her and winked. "Now, will you need a ride to the wedding?"

"No. I'll use my personal car. I can get by without the work van."

"Okay, I'll see you in church tomorrow." He leaned down and kissed her forehead tenderly. "Until we meet again."

"Such a drama queen," she teased and walked him to the door. He took hold of her shoulders and dropped another quick kiss on her lips and then he was gone.

Jenna found herself leaning on the door and smiling after he left. He was like no man she'd ever met before. Stubborn, determined, and funny. Maybe she would lose this bet.

Yeah. And maybe she'd get her heart broken...again.

Jenna was happy. It was Darcy and Nick's wedding day, and it couldn't have been more beautiful. The weather was perfect. A light breeze tickled the air, and the sky was sapphire blue with ribbons of white lace trailing across it. Best of all, the humidity was low, a rarity on an Illinois summer day.

It was only moments away from the ceremony, and Jenna gazed at Darcy in awe. She was an incredibly beautiful bride. She looked like an angel in her flowing white gown and long veil.

Jenna swallowed. She wasn't a true believer in happily after, but she knew if anyone could make it come true, it was

Darcy and Nick. She reached out and took Darcy's hands in hers.

"It's time. You know I wish you the very best, Darcy." Her eyes unexpectedly filled with tears. She wasn't usually emotional at weddings.

Darcy hugged her and pressed her cheek against Jenna's. "I know. You've been so much more than a wedding planner. You are a dear friend."

Jenna hugged Darcy close then turned to go and supervise the wedding. It was a beautiful ceremony. Sophie was the maid of honor and looked amazing. Nate was the best man and stood handsomely next to Nick. Nick's twin sisters were bridesmaids, and another good-looking police officer named Joe was a groomsman.

And then there was Noah.

Her breath froze when she first saw him standing at the altar. The black tux fit him perfectly, highlighting his muscular body. The white shirt emphasized his tanned complexion and his pewter blue eyes, so like those of his brothers and sisters, were spellbinding. Damn, just looking at him made tingles spread through her body.

As soon as the ceremony was over, Jenna had to head to the reception space to make sure everything was ready. She didn't even get a chance to speak to Noah. She left an assistant at the church to see to the finishing details and drove to the beautiful club the Bakers had rented.

There was a hubbub of activity going on when Jenna arrived. Penny was overseeing the setup for cocktail hour, and the catering staff was buzzing everywhere. It was controlled chaos right on schedule.

"Hi, boss," Penny greeted her. "I think everything is under control, but the photo booth people aren't here yet. I called them. They said they're on their way but had a flat tire. They should be here any second."

"That's great, Penny. People will probably start showing up in about fifteen minutes or so."

"Sounds good." Penny went back to supervising the setup, and Jenna checked on the DJ. Time flew as she took care of myriad details.

It seemed like only seconds before guests started filling up the space. The photo booth got set up, and people donned crazy accessories and took pictures, sipped cocktails, and munched on finger foods as they waited for the bride and groom and their wedding party to arrive.

Darcy and Nick arrived amidst grand fanfare, and they took their place at the sweetheart table flanked by their bridal party. Jenna caught a glimpse of Noah and then turned her attention to Penny's anxious voice crackling through the headset Jenna wore. When she looked back, he was gone.

Nick and Darcy's first dance was beautiful, and dinner was served right after. As the meal wound down, the DJ started playing rhythmic music. Jenna heaved a sigh of relief as she decided her work was almost over.

"Don't look so serious." The voice came from behind her. Jenna recognized Noah's voice instantly. The distinct baritone timbre tipped her off right away.

"Hi," she managed to reply, turning to face him.

"You look beautiful."

The sincerity of his tone almost made Jenna believe him. She felt color stain her cheeks, and she spoke quietly when she thanked him.

"Tell me, is it against the rules for the wedding planner to dance with a groomsman?" He tilted his head inquisitively, a warm, sexy, smile sliding across his lips.

She knew she shouldn't, but she found herself unable to refuse. She let him lead her to the dance floor and felt the familiar magic take over. Why was it whenever he moved to music with her in his arms, she fell under his spell?

They only danced one dance then moved on to the photo booth. Noah chose to don giant spectacles and a black fedora, and Jenna put on a violet feather boa and a floppy white garden hat surrounded with a band of roses. They stepped into the booth and began making silly faces and hitting wild poses until suddenly Noah pulled her into his arms. He kissed her sweetly, pulling off his hat and using it as a privacy screen. That was her favorite picture of them all.

Their lips melded as the curtain surrounding the booth hid them from sight.

She thought her ears were ringing until she realized it was her phone. She reluctantly pulled it from her pocket and glanced at the caller ID: Luke.

"Hi, Luke." She answered rather shortly. He knew he wasn't supposed to bother her at work except in an emergency.

The color left her face as Jenna listened to his frantic voice before she snapped, "I'm on my way."

"What's wrong, Jenna?" Noah asked, his face concerned.

"My house is on fire."

Chapter 13

"Let's go. I'll drive," Noah immediately responded. Before Jenna had a chance to protest, he'd taken hold of her elbow and begun steering her across the room. She didn't have time to argue. She just notified Penny she was leaving, and why, then grabbed her purse and headed out. Her breath caught in her chest, panic welling inside her. God, not her house. It was the one part of her life that had good memories attached. She would be lost without it. Please, don't let it be destroyed.

Noah drove skillfully through the streets and called into the station to get a report. They couldn't tell him much, just that the call had come in at 9:02 and a patrol car and fire trucks were dispatched.

"Breathe, Jenna. It's going to be all right."

"You don't know that, Noah. That house is the only stable thing in my life."

"I know, babe, but whatever happens, you are strong and will make it come out right."

His words penetrated her soul, and she suddenly felt calmer. It would be all right. But she prayed she didn't have to deal with catastrophe.

When Noah swung his truck onto her street, the number of flashing lights in front of her home immediately set off panic alarms. Fire trucks and police cars were everywhere. Dozens of people filled the yard. It was so crowded Noah had to park about a block away, and they ran the rest of the way to her house.

The first thing she realized was the house was still standing. Thank God. Her eyes searched for Lucas, at last spotting him standing off to the side, talking to a firefighter. She gratefully noticed Leon in his arms.

"Luke, honey, are you all right?" She grabbed his shoulders and scanned his body for injuries. He looked okay. Next, she turned her gaze on her dog, accepting his wiggling body into her arms and his slurping kisses on her face.

"I'm okay, Sis. I'm sorry." His voice reverberated with apology.

"What happened, Luke?"

"I don't know. I came home, went into the kitchen to get something to eat, and smelled smoke. It started in the garage."

"We contained it mainly to the garage, ma'am. It did spread slightly to the back porch." The firefighter waved his arm at the house as he talked, sweat beading on his forehead beneath his helmet.

"I'm so glad. How did it start?"

"We're still trying to figure that out, ma'am."

Jenna's knees sagged with relief when she realized her garage was destroyed bur her home was relatively untouched. The back porch was gone, but the house itself stood in one piece. Lord, she was grateful for that.

The fire was just about out by then. They milled around with the first responders and the neighbors while final details were looked after. The crowd began to dwindle, and Jenna felt the adrenaline seeping out of her body. Exhaustion overwhelmed her and Noah took notice right away, wrapping his arm around her waist and supporting her. She sagged against his strength, drawing energy from him.

A moment later, another firefighter approached and talked quietly to the first one. They conferred for several minutes, then one of the firefighters turned to face her.

"Ma'am, I hate to say this, but they found evidence that this fire was deliberately set. There is evidence of arson."

His words punched Jenna in the gut. Who the hell would start a fire at her house? Why would someone do it? Fuck. She didn't understand why this was happening.

"So you're saying someone intentionally set the garage on fire?" Noah questioned.

"Yes, sir, that's what I'm saying."

His arm tightened around Jenna's waist, and she felt anger scorch through him. Moved by his emotional yet calm response, she felt tears sting behind her eyelids. It was obvious he cared someone had harmed her, or at least her property.

"Thank you, officer. I assume you'll be in touch with Miss Harris?"

"Definitely."

"Thanks. May we go now?"

"Certainly."

Noah directed Jenna and Lucas into the house, Jenna starting to shake beside him. When they stepped in the front door, Jenna put Leon down and turned and buried her face in Noah's chest.

"Why? Why did someone do this to me?" Her voice sounded harsh to her ears.

"I don't know, babe. But I promise you something. I'm going to find out."

His words rang forcefully through the room, resonating with determination.

Lucas stood to the side and watched his sister cry then turned his gaze on the policeman at her side. Without a word, he strode out of the room, his shoulders hunched.

Jenna noticed him leaving and tried to stop him, but Noah prevented her. "Let him go," he said. "It looks like he wants to be alone."

"But he shouldn't be right now."

"I think maybe he's got some thinking to do."

She shot a look at Noah. "You don't think he had anything to do with this, do you?"

"I don't know, Jenna, but as I said, I'm going to find out."

His words cast a sinister shadow on her heart.

The next day Jenna had another wedding to supervise. It was hard to get into the wedding spirit, but she did her best. Penny hovered around her all afternoon, worried that her boss was so stressed. Darcy, Sophie, and Noah all called to check on her as well. Thank goodness it wasn't an elaborate wedding, so Jenna found herself back home by six p.m. and lowering herself into a hot bath minutes later. Once again, Lucas was out, so she settled in for a long soak.

The long soak was cut short when the doorbell rang.

"Damn," she muttered, grabbing a towel and climbing out of the tub. Who the hell was that?

She wrapped a short pink terry robe around her and pulled the belt tight then scurried to the door and squinted through the peephole. Noah. What was he doing here?

She pulled the door open, and Noah stepped forward and presented her with a pizza box and a bottle of wine.

"I knew you'd be too tired to cook, so I cooked for you."

"You shouldn't have."

"No problem."

"No, really, you shouldn't have. I was in the tub, and I'm not hungry."

"You need to eat. You'll wither away."

She chuckled and patted her curvaceous hips. "I don't think missing one meal will do any damage. "Well, you're here now, so come on in. I'll get dressed."

"Don't bother on my account," he teased. "You look pretty in pink."

Jenna blushed as he appreciatively eyed her figure under the robe. This man was nuts. Didn't he see she wasn't a dainty little lady but a woman with too generous curves? He didn't look like that bothered him at all.

"Nonetheless, I'll change."

"Suit yourself. I'll get some plates and glasses."

Jenna returned a few minutes later dressed in blue cutoffs and a yellow T-shirt to find that he had set the table and even plucked a rose from the yard and set it in the center of the table in a crystal vase. Pale blue candles flickered on either side of the vase.

"Wow. What's all this?" Her eyes took in the special touches as she tossed her hair behind her shoulders.

"You pamper people for a living. Now it's your turn."

His words sent warmth slipping through her. He pulled out her chair, and she took a seat, too moved to say anything. He took the chair opposite her, a smile lighting his face.

Jenna's appetite had suddenly returned, and she took a bite of gooey pizza, savoring the zesty flavors. Noah poured the wine, and they spent the next half hour eating pizza, sipping wine, and laughing over stories they exchanged about their jobs and childhoods. By the time there were just crumbs left on the pie plate, she felt better than she had in a long time.

"Let's move to the couch," she suggested. "Bring the wine."

Once they settled in, Noah turned to look at her with a serious gaze.

"Jenna, I did some snooping today. I found out a neighbor spotted someone who looked like Bull Garcia outside your house last night."

"Bull? What would he have been doing here? Luke went to the gym last night."

"I don't know, but we're going to question him as soon as we can. Right now, he seems to be amongst the missing."

"I don't understand. Why would Bull have anything to do with setting my garage on fire?"

"It appears someone was making meth inside of it."

His words were like a punch in the stomach. Meth. Oh my God.

"Don't worry, babe. They know it wasn't you. You were at Nick and Darcy's wedding all day."

"Luke?"

"They'll have to talk to him about it."

"Oh, God. Surely, he isn't involved in making meth, Noah. I can't believe it."

"I know, sweetie, I know. It will all work out." He pulled her head to his shoulder and let her close her eyes for a minute. She felt bad. Cuddling up to him helped soothe the worry and made her feel stronger. She didn't know why. She didn't question why. It just felt right.

The next thing she knew, she had turned her lips up to his and began devouring them. The kiss sent shivers racing up and down her spine, and suddenly she couldn't get enough of him. It had been so long since she felt like this; in fact, she wasn't sure she ever had. She'd been so young when she married she'd been caught up in the excitement, the newness. Now she'd had offers to date, but turned most of them down. No other man made her feel feminine, feel that burning desire for a man. No one but Noah.

Noah groaned and slid his hands down her back, pulling her close. He kissed her as hungrily as she kissed him, his tongue dancing with hers. She pressed against him and marveled as her nipples hardened into tight, protruding buds. Her fingers slid into his hair and slipped through the silky curls, loving the feel of the thick mop. Her lips trailed to his ear, his jaw, and his neck. He tasted better than a hot fudge sundae with nuts on top.

Noah's hands kept moving. They slid up her ribs and hovered there before sliding over to cover her left breast. This time, Jenna moaned as sparks shot through her entire body.

Noah's thumb stroked the sensitive nipple that bulged against her cotton bra. She arched her back trying to get even closer. Heated blood pumped through her veins, warming every place his body touched. She let one hand slide down to cup his jaw in her hand.

"Jenna, sweet Jenna," he murmured in her ear.

"Don't stop, Noah. I need you."

"I need you, too, babe, like a soul needs a mate." His lips ran up to her ear, whispering the words to her.

"Please, let's go to my room." She couldn't believe she said that, shocking even herself. Her desire for him was too overwhelming. Darcy was right. The Baker boys were irresistible.

Before he could answer, the front door opened and Lucas strode in.

Chapter 14

Talk about a mood killer. She tried not to glare at her brother as he strode into the room. What the hell was he doing here? He was supposed to spend the night camping with his buddies.

Then again, it might be a good thing. A cooling off period. She didn't want to rush into this, and if Lucas hadn't come in, she could have done something she might regret.

"We called the trip off. Joey's truck broke down." He tossed the words over his shoulder as he headed to the kitchen and began rummaging through the fridge.

Noah quietly accepted the disappointment and gave Jenna a gentle kiss on her forehead.

"Want to watch a movie?"

They spent the rest of the evening watching Runaway Bride, cuddling on the couch. When the movie was over, Noah reluctantly moved to go. She walked him to the door and lifted her face to accept a kiss that had her nerves tingling clearly down to her toes.

"Tomorrow night, my place for dinner. I'll pick you up at seven."

She nodded and watched him walk away. God, she thought she had just made a date to have sex with Noah Baker. Now she knew for sure: she was out of her mind.

Jenna's nerves were raw the next day. She jumped at every little noise and snapped at Penny when she made a minor mistake. That was odd because she made more than a couple herself that day.

A little after four, she decided to give up. There was nothing else absolutely pressing that had to be done today, her head was aching, and her stomach felt jumpy. She gathered her things and went out to let Penny know she was leaving.

"Good. You seem on edge today like something's bothering you."

"Don't worry, Penny. It's just a headache."

"Well, take it easy then. I hope you feel better tomorrow."

"I'm sure I will. Sorry I was short today. You know I think you're the best." She gave the girl an impulsive hug before walking out the door.

She lectured herself all the way home. She was acting silly about this. Hell, she was almost 30 years old. She'd dated a bit after Jackson's death, even had sex with a couple of guys. But none of them had made her feel safe or special. They all seemed self-interested, selfish, and she never felt like she could trust any of them. Noah was different—she was almost sure.

But what if he wasn't? What if he turned out to be like all the rest? She guessed she would do as she had done before— put it behind her and move on. But somehow this felt more important, more life-changing.

She entered a house silent and still except for Leon's happy wiggles. Lucas was missing in action as usual. That was okay. She wanted to take a long hot bubble bath and try to compose herself. It was good to be alone right now.

She soaked for nearly an hour then began to get ready for the evening. She rubbed lotion all over her body and wiggled into a pair of lavender lace panties and a matching bra. She added a generous spray of vanilla-scented body spray and swept her hair up in a loose knot. She fretted over what to wear but finally slipped into a pair of snug dark jeans and an off-the-shoulder grape knit shirt that made her eyes look even more violet. She was adding a pair of opal earrings when an

299

aggressive knocking at the front door caught her attention. What the hell?

She peered through the peephole and saw Bull Garcia. She didn't want to open the door to him, but in a minute, he started hollering Luke's name. She didn't want him to disturb the neighbors, so she flung the door open at last and jutted her chin out angrily.

"What?" she demanded.

"Hello, sis. You're looking hot tonight." He ran his gaze over her in a way that made her feel naked.

"I'm expecting Officer Baker. You know, the cop who arrested you last year."

"Yeah, well, I was framed." He shrugged and eyed her insolently.

"Look, I don't have time for this. Luke's not home. What do you want?"

"Give him a message for me, sis. Tell him I'm looking for him. And tell him I'll find him. And when I do..." Bull drove his fist into his palm.

"You want me to deliver a threat to my brother?" Jenna felt her maternal instinct kick into high gear. Lucas might be a pain in the ass, but she loved him. She wouldn't stand for threats of bodily harm.

"I'll tell you what," she sneered at him. "Why don't you stick around and tell Officer Baker all about your complaints?"

"Oh, I don't think you want me to tell your cop boyfriend what I know about your brother."

"What are you talking about?" she demanded.

"Ask Luke."

"Don't think I won't. Now I think you better leave."

"Don't get your panties in a bunch," he said and had the balls to wink at her. "I'm going, but remember this—I'm going to get to know you better, too, if you know what I mean."

She took pleasure in slamming the door in his face. His wicked laughter floated through the door as he walked away.

Jenna was still shaking when Noah came to the door a couple of minutes later. He could see as soon as he walked in that she was upset and so wrapped his arm around her shoulder.

"Hey, what's wrong? Come here and sit down." He led her over to the couch and sat beside her.

"B...Bull," she stammered.

"Bull Garcia? What about him?" His voice hardened as he spoke the thug's name.

She told him what Bull had said, and he smacked his fist into his palm. He grabbed his phone and called the station to advise them Bull was in the neighborhood. When he disconnected, he ran his hand through his curls.

"Damn. He is bad business. Jenna, I think it's time I talk to Luke."

"You can't."

"I have, too, honey. I know he's your baby brother, but finding out what's going on is the best way to help him."

"I mean, he's not home right now."

"Okay, but I don't want to put this off for long."

"I know. I want to know what he's got himself involved in, too. Right now, I'm going to call him and warn him about Bull."

The call went directly to voicemail, so all she could do was leave a message. She told him about Bull then added, "I need to talk to you, Luke. ASAP. Call me."

She heaved a sigh of frustration as she disconnected. What kind of trouble was Lucas in now? Worry ate at her heart, a frown etched on her face.

"Hey, we'll work this out. Now let's put it out of mind for a moment and say hello the proper way." He leaned down and caught her lips under his. It was a kiss filled with an odd blend of tenderness and sensuality. His arms pulling her close made her feel warm and protected, his kiss full of passion and promise, almost dangerous. She ran his hands through his curls and thoroughly kissed him back.

"I've got dinner in the oven," he murmured, lifting his mouth. "Why don't we move this party to my place?"

"I'd love to." She grinned as he stood up and extended his hand to her. "It will be my first time in your lair. Promise I'll be safe?"

"As a babe in arms." He chuckled and winked. "In my arms, that is."

Noah's place was a spacious two-bedroom apartment on the third story of a big Victorian house. Overstuffed couches and lots of potted plants filled the living room. A fat black-and-white cat curled up in the bay window beneath a massive philodendron and a huge fern hanging from hooks above.

They ate in his bright, cheery kitchen at a table with a crisp, yellow cloth and a vase of daisies in the center. Noah made lasagna, and it was delicious. She was surprised how at much she loved the dressing he had created for their salad, and now she sat, sated, sipping at a glass of wine.

"I hope you have room for dessert," Noah said. "I made a chocolate mousse."

Jenna couldn't suppress a giggle. "You are a man of many talents."

"I haven't even shown you my best ones yet." He leaned over and gave her a kiss that made goosebumps stand up on her skin.

Suddenly she wasn't laughing anymore. She was drowning. Drowning in sensations. Heat rushed from her cheeks down to her pelvis, sparking a wildfire in her middle. She slid her hands around his neck and relished in the feel of his bronzed skin, the graze of soft stubble on his cheek. His scent invaded her senses. He smelled of soap and citrus, fresh and inviting. It was intoxicating.

"Jenna, my sweet. I can't get enough of you." Suddenly he swept her up in his arms and carried her across to the sofa. His strength took her by surprise, and she felt more feminine than she ever had in her life. He laid her on the sofa and snuggled in next to her, his lips tracing her ear then sweeping down her neck.

The groan that escaped from her came from deep within, erupting involuntarily as hunger exploded inside her.

"Jenna, if you're not ready, we'll quit now. While I still can."

He looked at her with those hypnotic blue eyes, and she knew she couldn't stop the storm brewing inside her.

Chapter 15

"Please, don't stop, Noah." She hated that she sounded like she was pleading but she couldn't help it. She wanted this, wanted him, like nothing ever before. Touching him set her on fire, tasting him made her feel intoxicated. There was no way she could stop.

"Thank God. It would have been incredibly hard to tear myself away from you." He sounded relieved and kissed her again. "You taste so sweet."

"You're my favorite flavor."

Her words had him running his hand across her abdomen, sliding under her soft, cotton shirt. Jenna arched her back, trying to get closer to his touch. Her own hands slid across his shoulders, noting their solidness and width.

She turned her lips to his neck, kissing the length of it as she let her hands travel down to his chest. Her fingers plucked at the buttons of his pale blue cotton shirt then delved beneath its surface to explore his muscular chest. It felt like hot velvet steel. Her nipples hardened as she ran her hands across the smooth plain.

Noah nipped hungrily at her shoulders, tickling the hollow at her collarbone with his tongue. He sipped and tasted, devouring her skin with his ravenous lips. Her shirt skimmed higher up her sides, and his hands roved over the exposed silky surface. When his fingers traveled to her breast, her breath caught in her throat and sparks shot through her.

Her lips trailed down his chest and across his rock-hard abs. She swirled her tongue around his navel and traced the dark swirls of hair down toward the top of his jeans. Her hands played across the bulge that throbbed against the denim fabric at his crotch.

Noah whispered her name and her top disappeared over her head, landing somewhere on the floor. His tongue traced a pattern around her nipple beneath her bra before he unsnapped it and pitched it aside.

The air skimmed across Jenna's exposed skin, and her nipples jutted even more. Shivers ran down her spine as his lips closed around a sensitive nub and his tongue flipped across the tip, her muscles spasming in the heart of her feminity.

Noah pulled her close, their bare flesh melding. Her breasts, his chest, fusing in a blaze of sensations. Both of them were groaning now.

Noah's fingers reached for the snap of her jeans and urged the zipper down as his tongue swathed her breasts, flickering and tickling across her nipples. One hand slipped beneath the waistband of her jeans and brushed against the curls nestled at the apex of her thighs. Her breath caught in her throat and she braced in anticipation. When he ventured further and his digit dipped between her lips and rubbed across her clitoris, she felt herself begin to spiral out of control.

Noah pushed her jeans and panties down her legs, and Jenna lifted her hips to help dispose of them as fast as possible. She was completely exposed, naked and vulnerable. Somehow she felt powerful, though, as she watched the awe appear in his eyes as he gazed at her figure.

He dipped his head and kissed her navel, slipping his tongue into the tiny cavern and swirling it. Matching cyclones erupted in her pelvis, and her legs began to shake. His fingers continued to work their magic, caressing and massaging her sensitive nub. Her hips thrust upwards, urging him on.

When he slid a finger deep inside her, then a second one, she felt the pressure building from the pit of her pelvis to the top of her head. She tossed her head back and forth as sensations flooded through her, and Noah placed one palm on her belly to steady her. She couldn't stop the cries emitting from her throat. Suddenly, he crooked his finger and found a magic spot inside her, and the ball of his thumb pressed down on her clit. Spasm after spasm shook her like a volcano disgorging hot lava.

Her cries turned to near sobs as her head exploded. Her body rocked, ransacked by the force of her orgasm. Time stood still as she climaxed with an eruption of vibrations.

It might have been seconds—it felt like minutes—that she hung suspended in a sea of sensations. The waves finally receded, and she slowly floated downward. Then it struck her: Noah still had his clothes on. He needed to be naked. He needed to bare himself to her so she could ravish his body. She pushed the shirt off his shoulders and down his arms, trailing kisses along his stony biceps. Her fingers found a nipple, and she gave a playful twist to the hardened bud. She stroked his abs, delighting in their firmness.

Her lips slid down his chest, her tongue stopping long enough to twirl around his tiny hardened nipple. Her finger dipped into his belly button then traveled downward.

When her hand encountered his huge erection, she hesitated. The thick muscle bulged beneath her fingertips, and the length of it left her nerves quaking. She'd never encountered a man with such a big dick. She wasn't sure she could accommodate all that maleness.

She wrapped her hand around the oversized hard-on and ran her thumb over the crest of its mushroom head. A bubble of pre-cum appeared, and Jenna spread it around the scorching flesh. She felt him convulse as she stroked the length of his pulsating rod.

She pushed his jeans down and took his boxer briefs with them. In a moment, he kicked them off his feet, leaving him as naked as she was. She pumped her hand along the length of him, thrilled by her ability to make him so hard and moan so hoarsely.

"Jenna, Jenna, you're driving me crazy. I want you."

"I want you, too, Noah. I need you like lungs need air." It was true. She wanted him desperately. It was like she would die if she didn't have him in her. Now.

Noah grabbed at his jeans and fumbled a rubber out of the pocket. She took the coil and slid it down the length of his cock, cupping his balls before she released the shaft.

Noah groaned and imprisoned her lips with his mouth, kissing her long and hard, and then he raised on his arms above her. Their eyes met and held, and silent communication zipped between them. Noah used his thigh to push her knees apart then placed the head of his dick at her entrance. He pushed into her slowly, and she felt her canal spreading, opening to accommodate his girth. God, he was huge but somehow managed to enter her, inch by inch. As his penis slid in, she felt like screaming with the sensations. She felt full, complete, not just physically but emotionally as well. She'd been waiting for the pain she normally experienced but it didn't come. Only sensations of pleasure washed through her.

Once Noah managed to impale her on his pole, he began to rock back and forth. Her hips instinctively matched his movements, each thrust harder than the last. She spread her legs wider and drew her knees up, allowing him even deeper access. She felt the head of his dick knock into her uterus, the sensation swimming through her.

Her arms wrapped around his neck and pulled him to her. God, she couldn't get close enough.

Noah moaned as he ravished her neck with kisses and his hands caressed her breasts. The sounds of his pleasure made Jenna's reactions even more intense, and she felt another massive orgasm building within her. In another moment, she was out of control, her head thrashing back and forth, wild cries emitting from her throat. She wasn't sure she was on Earth anymore. She felt as if she were sailing through space, unfettered and floating free through space. She opened her eyes and looked into Noah's incredibly heated pewter gaze and felt herself spinning, spinning. Suddenly, the world imploded.

Chapter 16

Sunbeams crept through the window and played across Jenna's eyelids as she began to waken.

A feeling of warmth and safety filled her as she snuggled up against the solid body pressed against her back. Noah's arms wrapped around her rib cage, one hand resting on her abdomen, the other just above her breast. Satisfaction thrummed through her. She couldn't remember ever feeling this content.

Then reality slapped her in the face. What was she doing? She had guarded herself against men, commitment, for so long—she wasn't ready to give up that self-protection. She shivered with trepidation, and that slight motion started to wake Noah. He tightened his grip on her, his hand roaming down to cup her breast, his thumb sliding across the tip of her nipple. Another shiver ran through her but for an entirely different reason. This time, it was caused by erotic, sensual feelings that immediately engulfed her. She felt his member harden against her butt cheeks, proof that he desired her again.

After they had sex the first time last night, they had made love two more times. The second time was more of an exploratory mission. He'd taken her from the side and the rear, sending her to a place she'd never been before. The last time had been slow, sensual. Their kisses were longer, their caresses more heartfelt. Now she found she wanted him again. She rolled over to face him and meet his lips in a passionate kiss. Could she imagine waking up to this every morning? Oh, yeah.

Noah reached into the nightstand drawer and grabbed a condom and slid it on to his ready cock. She opened to him and felt him plant his pole within her, claiming her, branding her. She let herself get lost in the sensations, crying out as they came together.

A few moments later, she wiggled against him, happy and satisfied. Why couldn't she indulge in these magnificent feelings without commitment? She didn't have to fall in love with Noah, did she? She could keep her sex life and her romantic life separate, right? Hell, she could indulge in sex like this on a regular basis without obligating her heart to him.

"You know we have to get up and get ready for work, right?" she asked.

"You don't know how much I wish we could just stay here in bed all day making love."

"Duty calls, babe."

"You're right. But maybe we can shower together and see what happens?"

"Maybe."

And of course, they did.

He drove her home so she could get ready for work. She was surprised by how painful kissing him goodbye felt. She wasn't prepared for how sad leaving him made her feel, but she shoved those thoughts aside and smiled cheerfully as she waved him off. She promised herself she wasn't going to grow dependent on him.

The day was hectic. She spent much of it on the phone finalizing details for upcoming weddings, then turned her attention to the Moreno wedding. She had just finished arrangements for the mariachi band when Penny tapped on her door.

"Come in!" Jenna called out.

Her assistant stepped into the office, her face lit with curiosity, holding a crystal vase filled with a dozen long-stemmed red roses.

"Someone sent you flowers. Fess up, boss. Who's the guy?"

Jenna's face turned as scarlet as the roses. "There's no guy. Let me read the card, silly."

"I've got it right here. You want me to read it to you?" She waggled the little white envelope teasingly in her fingers.

"No. Give it up, Penny." Jenna held her hand out for the card.

"Okay. You can read it to me."

Jenna took the envelope and slipped it open.

Thank you for the magical night was scrawled across it in bold handwriting. No name, but she didn't need one to know the flowers were from Noah.

"Well? Penny asked encouragingly.

"Just a grateful client." Jenna squirmed at telling the little white lie, but she didn't want Penny to think she was involved with Noah.

"Okay, if you say so, but I don't believe it." Penny shot her a pained glance and turned and left the room.

Damn. Now she'd hurt Penny's feelings. This was all Noah's fault. Darn him.

Still, she had to admit the flowers were beautiful. She buried her nose in the blossoms and breathed in their rich fragrance, a small smile playing across her lips.

Jenna pulled up in front of the Moreno home after she'd left the office that evening. There were several things she needed to discuss with the beautiful girl and her fiancé, so she had made the appointment for tonight.

She ran up on the broad porch and rang the bell. She was shocked when Marcus Moreno opened the door.

"Mr. Moreno. I didn't expect to see you."

"I am in town between shows. Elena told me you were coming, and I wanted to see you." He leaned in and kissed her on the cheek. "Please come in."

He led her to the living room, and she sat down in a wing-back chair. He took the chair across from her and looked deep into her eyes.

"Jenna, I have to ask a favor of you."

Uh-oh. What now, she wondered.

"I have talked to the doctor. She tells me Elena is failing fast." His voice choked up as he spoke.

"Oh, Marcus, I am so sorry." She blinked, realizing her own eyes had teared up. Elena was such a sweet girl, so full of life.

"You know, what she wants most is to be married to Ramon. She might not make it until her scheduled wedding date. We have to move the wedding up and I need your help. We want to have it on her birthday in just over two weeks on a Thursday."

Jenna was stunned by the news. She had never planned a wedding so quickly. It had been a near miracle she had accomplished so much already for the original date. She felt stress winging through her, but at the same time, she didn't want to give up. This might be Elena's last chance for the wedding of her dreams. She had to to get it done. She would pull in every favor owed her.

"I'll do everything I can," she vowed.

"I cannot thank you enough. Thank you, dear Jenna." He took both her hands in his and squeezed them. She pressed his fingers back as they shared a moment. A fleeting thought shot through her mind. Why didn't she react physically to this handsome man the way she did when Noah touched her? She frowned as she pondered the question.

"I know we are asking a lot, Jenna, but it's for Elena. I will do anything to make her happy."

"I understand, Marcus, and I will do the very best I can."

"I know you will, Jenna. I've already talked to the priest at the church, and fortunately, he and the building are available that evening. That's one good thing."

"It is. We'll pull this together. I promise."

"Again I thank you. Unfortunately, Elena is not feeling well this evening, so won't be able to meet with you. What can I do to help you?"

They spent the next hour going over details, everything from Elena's favorite flavors of cake to what foods she liked best. At last, Jenna couldn't suppress a yawn, and Marcus glanced at his watch.

"I know you are probably exhausted. I won't keep you anymore." He stood and held out his hand to help her from the chair. Jenna rose and gathered her notes and her purse before heading to the door, Marcus's hand at the small of her back.

"You are a very special woman, Jenna. I will never forget your helpfulness." He gathered her in his arms and dropped a soft kiss on her forehead. "Good night, Jenna. Please drive carefully."

Jenna returned his hug and got in her car. Once again, she was pondering why Marcus Moreno, superstar, didn't wow her. He was rich, handsome, suave, and sophisticated. Any woman would be thrilled to be with him.

The only thing she could figure out was he just wasn't Noah Baker.

Chapter 17

Jenna's life was a whirlwind of activity over the next few days. She had a slew of details to go over for upcoming weddings, and she also had two anniversary parties to plan. Despite all of her obligations, she spent a lot of her time focusing on Elena's wedding. She begged the florist and the caterer to take on the project, playing on their hearts and explaining the reason for the time crunch. She made arrangements with all the rental companies and even talked the mariachi band into changing the date.

She'd just finished a marathon phone call with the manager of the reception venue and finally worked out all the kinks. She was amazed at how much was coming together.

Her phone rang, and she smiled when she saw Noah's name on the caller ID. She hadn't had time to see him since their night of passion. She had to admit she missed him. A pang of hunger shot through her groin as she smiled at her phone.

"Hi there, Officer Baker. How are you?"

"I'm lonely, that's how I am. I miss you, Jenna." His tone touched Jenna's heart, and she confessed that she missed him, too.

"Please, may I see you tonight?" He almost sounded like a little boy, pleading for dessert. She couldn't help but give in.

"I'm not going to be finished here until about seven. But maybe we could get together after that."

"Sounds good to me. How about Chinese takeout?"

I'd like that. About 7:30 then?"

"See you then."

Jenna disconnected and grinned. She was exhausted. She was way too tired to do anything but go home, take a bath, and go to bed.

But she couldn't convince herself of that. She wanted to see Noah more than she wanted to rest.

She'd just changed into a pair of white shorts and a navy tank top when he knocked at the door. Tingles danced in her stomach as she raced to let him in. He gathered her in his arms, boxes of takeout dangling from his hands.

"Wow. That was worth the wait." He kissed her once again then moved to set the takeout down.

"I'm glad to see you, too," she said pertly. "I'm also glad to see that food. I'm starving."

"Well, what are we waiting for then? Let's eat."

She grabbed plates and a couple of beers from the kitchen, settled down at the coffee table, and dished out sweet-and-sour chicken, house fried rice, and egg rolls. They both took chopsticks and made quick work of the meal before them, taking turns feeding each other chunks of food and giggling like children.

Then disaster struck. Her hand hit a beer bottle and knocked it over. Beer flowed out and off the table straight into Noah's lap. For a moment, she froze. When she was married to Jackson, such an accident would have earned her a beating. The color drained from her cheeks, and she cringed, waiting for the blow.

"Hey, Jenna, it was a silly accident. Don't worry about it." He took her chin in his fingers and forced her to look at him. "I will never hurt you. Never."

Her gaze met his, and somehow, she knew he was telling the truth. But deep down, fear still lingered. Would she ever be completely comfortable with a man again? Dare she expose her heart to potential agony again?

"Honey, there are many things to fear in life. Happiness is not one of them. When it comes your way, reach out and grab it. If you don't claim happiness when you can, your only other choice is misery."

She let his words settle into her soul as she gazed into those hypnotic ice-blue eyes. They made sense. She knew that but was still hesitant. She was just about to tell him so when the door burst open and Lucas slammed into the room. His eyes were wild, his hair standing on end.

"Noah, thank God you're here. He's going to kill me." He leaned against the door, panting for breath.

"Who is, Luke? Who's going to kill you?" Noah strode over and grabbed Lucas by the arm. "What's going on?"

"It's Bull," Lucas said grimly. "He thinks I ripped him off."

"Come in here and sit down. I think you better start from the beginning." Noah led him to a chair and pushed him into it. "Now, spill."

Lucas leaned his head against the chair back, guilt flooding across his face.

"I didn't know what was happening at first. Honest."

Noah didn't speak, just stood, waiting patiently for Lucas to continue.

"Bull seemed so cool, you know? He always had money. Women swarmed around him. He was always ready to party." Lucas shook his head sadly. "I was so stupid."

"What happened, Luke?" Noah spoke softly but in a no-nonsense tone of voice.

"At first, he just asked me for a favor. He needed a package dropped off to a friend, he said, and didn't have time to do it himself. He told me he'd give me a hundred bucks if I'd do it. So I did."

Lucas gave a wry chuckle. "I was a gullible fool. He asked me to do the same a couple more times. It was easy money, so why not? I was starting to get suspicious because the guy I was taking the stuff to was a big shot, you know. He had a fancy office and all. I went to the building once to take him the stuff. Usually, I met him at a café or something. The last time was at a park. It was dark, but I didn't think anything about it. When I was carrying the package to him, I tripped over a tree root,

314

and the package went flying. It split open. There was a bunch of packets of meth and heroin in there. I about shit."

"I knew it," Jenna shouted, jumping to her feet. "I knew Bull was no good the minute I laid eyes on him."

Noah wrapped her arm around her waist and hugged her to him. "Okay, honey, let's hear the rest of the story. Go on, Luke. So, Bull was using you like a mule."

"Well," Lucas continued, "I started to scramble away, but I looked up and Ace was snapping pictures of me and the dope. He told me to hold up some packages of it. I said no, and he pulled a gun on me. He made me pose with the stuff. He showed me the pictures and then sent them to Bull. Now it looks like I'm the dealer."

Lucas ran his hands through his hair then buried his face in his palms. "Bull made me start delivering packages to other creeps, threatening to turn those pictures over to the cops if I didn't do it."

Lucas drew in a deep, shuddering breath. "Then I got jumped one night when I was making a delivery. They jumped me from behind, beat the crap out of me, and took the stuff. That's the night you found me out back."

"Oh, Luke." Jenna couldn't hide the sympathy in her voice.

"I tried to tell Bull what happened but he didn't believe me. He said I had to give him $20,000 or else. He gave me some time to come up with the money but, of course, I couldn't. Now he says time's up and somebody took a shot at me tonight while I was walking home."

"Oh my God, Luke. Are you sure?"

"They barely missed. I ran the rest of the way home through the alleys."

"Okay, we're going to get this resolved. Luke, will you be willing to testify against Bull?" Noah turned to the younger man, placing his hand on Lucas's shoulder.

When Lucas hesitated to answer, a look of fear in his eyes, Noah looked him in the eyes. "If you testify against Bull and any of the people you delivered to that you can identify, then we can probably keep you out of jail. You'll be testifying for the state so that we can get you immunity. You'll be okay."

"Yeah, but what about the other guys who will be out to get me? Bull's buddies."

If we do this right, we can take them all down. Now, how about it? It's that or spend the rest of your life looking over your shoulder. What's it going to be?"

Chapter 18

Jenna spent a restless night while Noah and Lucas went to the police station to talk to a detective. Fear for Lucas engulfed her. Every little noise made her jump. She tried to take a nap on the couch, but sleep evaded her. Was this her fault? Had she not given Lucas something he needed? Lord, she didn't know what to think.

Lucas and Noah finally returned in the wee hours of the morning. The moment the door opened, she was on her feet and running to wrap an arm around each of their necks.

"I've been so worried."

Noah kissed the top of her head. "It's going to be okay, honey. We've got a few more details to work out, but it's going to be okay."

"Bull?" She tilted her head enquiringly.

"There's a warrant for his arrest. We'll get him."

"But you don't know where he's at, do you?" she tried not to sound accusing but knew she did.

"He won't go far."

"I hope you're right, Noah. Luke's in danger until Bull is captured. Are the police going to protect him?"

"We just don't have the manpower, babe. Besides, it's best if Luke just acts normal, like nothing's going on."

"That's not good enough. Luke," she said, turning to look at her brother, "you've got to get out of here. Go somewhere."

"No, Jenna. I'm not going to run away." He looked at her determinedly. "I'm tired of feeling like a coward. I'm going to do what's right."

"And if that includes getting yourself killed?"

"I'll be careful."

"Famous last words," she shot back. "Noah, tell him to go."

"He knows what he's doing, Jenna."

Tears shone in her eyes. Anger shot through her. Anger at Lucas, at Noah, and anger at the whole situation. Damn! She wanted to cuss, to shout, and to demand they do what she wanted. It would do no good, though, she thought with resignation. Both men jutted their chins.

"I think you're both idiots." She jammed her fists on her hips and glared at them before turning on her heel and striding out of the room.

Somehow Jenna managed to get her work done the next day despite the pounding in her head and the churning in her stomach. She was actually glad she had so much to do because it kept her mind off the situation at home.

She met with a couple of new clients and, as usual, made an abundance of phone calls. By the time she finished, she was so tired she was shaking.

Home had never looked so good as she pulled into her driveway. She parked the car and was headed for the door when she spotted something on the porch and walked over to it. She couldn't help but coo when she figured out it was a soft, fuzzy teddy bear holding a bouquet of daisies. She picked it up and hugged it to her as she read the card: Hugs and kisses. Please bear with me through this.

She felt her heart smile as she held the sweet gift. Noah was indeed someone special.

Jenna found Lucas at home, hanging out in his room and surfing the web.

"I'm glad you're here. At least I know you're safe."

"I'm going to be okay, Sis. This is something I need to do."

"I know, Luke, but I'm afraid."

"I'm scared, too, Jenna, but I've got to do this. Bull used me. Ace threatened to frame me. Don't you get it? Besides, those are bad drugs. I want to help get them off the streets."

He looked at her so seriously that she knew he was determined to see this through. Her chest tightened and she had to blink back tears.

"I'm proud of you, Luke. I really am." She spoke quietly but meant every word she said. Lucas was growing into a man.

Sophie and Nate's cake tasting took place the next afternoon. Jenna smiled as she watched the two together. They held hands and exchanged glances, almost as if they had a secret, silent language. Jenna almost felt a thread of envy running through her.

"Jenna, I love this lemon rosemary cake," Nate said as he munched on a bite. "It's unique but delicious."

"Really, honey? I like the chocolate chip and praline." Sophie turned pleading dark eyes on Noah's brother.

"That's an easy problem. Have a layer of each and another flavor for the third layer." Jenna wished all her problems were so easily solved.

"Okay, then what about the chocolate cherry cake for the third layer?" Sophie asked. "I loved that."

"Then you shall have it, my lady." Nate smiled and leaned in to give Sophie's lips a quick kiss."

"Okay, decision made." Jenna made a note on her laptop and grinned. "That was quick. You guys are so easy to work with."

"Say, Jenna, when you and Noah get married, will you plan your own wedding or use another wedding planner?"

"Whoa, Nate. Who said I was going to marry your brother?" Jenna almost choked on the water she'd just taken a sip of from her goblet.

"I know my brother. He's in love with you, and just like Nick and me, he's the marrying kind."

Marriage. Was she willing to entrust her heart to a man again? The thought terrified her, even though she thought Noah was genuine, not hiding another nature beneath his endearing manner. But she didn't trust herself. She didn't trust her judgment. Part of her yearned for the fairytale ending that seemed so elusive. Another part felt paralyzed with fear. Did fairytales ever come true?

And yet she kept hearing Noah's voice telling her if she feared love then she was choosing misery.

"We'll see, Nate, but don't hold your breath." She winked at him as she wiped her lips with a napkin. "We'll see."

By the time she got home that evening, the sun was gliding down behind thunderclouds building in the west. She watched lightning slice across the sky and heard the clap of thunder that followed. She hoped she could get home before the storm broke.

She just barely made it. The first fat raindrops plopped earthward as she ran into the house and shook droplets off her hair. A few seconds later, rain was pounding down.

She looked around for Leon and realized he wasn't there yapping his usual greeting. The house felt eerily quiet. What was going on?

She walked into the dining room and froze at the sight that met her eyes.

Lucas sat at the table bound to a chair and Bull held a gun to his head.

Chapter 19

Her heart stopped beating for a moment. Shock ran through her, the look on her brother's face filling her with fear. She wanted to turn and run, but she couldn't leave Lucas at the hands of the asshole that flashed a wicked grin at her.

"Hello, sister. We've been waiting for you."

"What do you want, Bull?" She was amazed by the strength in her voice. She was surprised she could speak at all, but she wasn't going to let this jerk intimidate her.

"I want my money...and I hear you hold the key to the bank." He chuckled and shook the gun at Lucas's temple. "You're going to unlock it, sis, because I know you want your baby brother to live."

"How much money?" She already knew the answer but didn't want to let Bull know Lucas had squealed on him.

"$25,000."

She almost snapped that she thought it was $20,000 but managed to bite her tongue in time. "And just why am I going to give this money to you?"

"Because Lukey boy here stole it from me, that's why." Anger masked Bull's features, his lips curling into a snarl. "I told him to pay me, but he didn't listen. I didn't know he was a trust fund baby until I had him checked out. I guess you hold those purse string pretty tight, though. That's why he stole my shit."

"You're crazy. Luke's not a thief," she told him coldly. "Now where's my dog?"

"Your mutt's locked up out back. Sit down and shut up or I'll shoot the little fleabag first."

"I even tried burning down your garage, you know. But little Lukey didn't get the message.

Jenna's fists clenched at her sides, but she plopped into a dining room chair and glared at Bull.

"Just how do you think I'm going to get you this money? The banks closed hours ago, and ATMs don't spit out $25,000, you know."

"That's why we're all going to wait here until morning," he said smugly. "Just you, and me, and little brother. Now give me your cell phone."

Heart sinking, she pulled the phone from her pocket and slid it across the table. Damn. She hoped he would forget that and she would get a chance to use it. Now she felt cut off from the world.

"I'm not going to tie you up, pretty girl. I've got plans for you later." He flashed her a crooked grin and slid his gaze across her bust. Jenna shivered as she felt burned by the look that pinned her against the chair.

"Besides, I'm hungry. Get your ass in the kitchen and cook me up something to eat." She thrust her chin defiantly in the air and glared at him. "Now. Or I'll take a little trip to the garage and get rid of the yapper."

Damn his hide, threatening a little dog like Leon. Bull was a piece of shit, but she knew she better go along with him or he'd follow through on his threat.

"Stay put, bro. I'm going to keep an eye on your sister. Come on, babe. Move it." He turned the gun in her direction and she stood on shaking legs. It felt like the kitchen was a hundred miles away. Her hand trembled as she reached for the light switch and walked into the room, Bull right behind her.

"What do you want to eat?"

"Hmm, I could use some of you." Bull wrapped his arms around her and ran his lips across her neck. The feeling made her squirm and jerk away from him, turning a furious stare in his direction.

Laughter bubbled from his throat. "You look like an angry red hen. Okay, okay, time enough for that later. Got any steak?"

"No. I've got hamburger." She'd be damned if she'd feed this asshole steak.

"I guess hamburger will do then. And make me some French fries to go with it."

Jenna moved to the fridge and got out the meat then opened the freezer door to retrieve a bag of fries. Her mind flew, tossing around ideas for escape or revenge, but everything led to a bad ending in her mind. She wanted to poison the meat, or at least put a load of hot sauce in it. She wanted to throw the pan of hot grease in his face, but she wouldn't be able to move fast enough to free Lucas and get away before Bull could catch them, burnt or not.

"Put some lettuce, onion, and mustard on there, woman," Bull ordered and poked the gun in her side. "And get me a beer."

It was all she could do not to slam the bottle into his smirking face. Let him have the damn beer. She hoped he drank so much he passed out.

She carried his plate, and he took the gun and the beer, and they returned to the dining room. He waved the gun at a chair, and she sat, her shoulders hunched.

Bull ate like a pig, lips smacking loudly, mustard trickling down his chin. She shoved a napkin at him just as her cell phone rang. She jumped and reached for it.

"Ah, ah, ah," Bull waggled the gun at her. "I'm handling the phones. Oh, look, it's your boyfriend, Officer Baker. Too bad, too sad." He laughed and clicked the refuse button.

Jenna didn't say a word, just prayed that Noah would think it strange she didn't answer and come to investigate.

"Go turn on the TV, bitch," he demanded.

She did as he ordered then turned and looked at him.

"I have to go to the bathroom."

"Not until I finish eating. Then I'll go with you."

What an ass, she thought disgruntledly. If he thought she was going to hike up her skirt and pee in front of him, he was wrong. There was no way.

Bull leaned back in his chair and belched, rubbing his stomach in satisfaction. "Not bad cooking, sis, not bad."

She didn't answer him but jerked when her phone rang again. This time, he didn't even bother to look at the caller ID, just cut the ringer off.

"I'm shutting this phone down, got it? I'm not going to listen to this bullshit all night."

Please, Noah, please, please, know that something's not right, she prayed. It was their only hope.

"Okay, let's go to the bathroom now," Bull said, rising from his chair.

"I don't have to go anymore," she told him, setting her chin stubbornly.

"Tough. I do." He reached out and grabbed her upper arm, pulling her to her feet. She stumbled but caught herself then let him jerk her toward the restroom. "If you don't have to go, then you can either hold it or piss your pants. I don't care which."

Jenna ground her eyes shut as she listened to him unzip his pants and start to pee. She had no desire to see his penis.

The sound of him urinating ended before he spoke. "Look here, bitch. Look what's going to be up in ya before this night's over." She squealed as she felt his dick against her hand, her stomach rolling over and threatening to spew its contents.

"God, don't touch me," she screamed, jerking away, her eyes flying open.

"Oh, I'll touch you all right. I'll do more than touch you, ice princess." He took his dick in his hands and waved it at her. "But first, a little more beer and TV."

"You are disgusting," she spat before heading back to the dining room.

"Disgusting, is it? Well, you ain't seen nothing yet." The sound of his evil chuckle followed her as she sat back down at the table. Damn, what was she going to do?

Chapter 20

The evening dragged on with Jenna and Lucas watching each other across the table and Bull laughing loudly at a comedy on TV. She knew Lucas had to be aching from having his arms tied behind his chair and his face showed his unhappiness. He eyed her, silently begging forgiveness.

"I love you, Luke," she told him softly.

"Can you ever forgive me for getting us into this mess?"

"It wasn't your fault, Luke."

"Yes, it was. I was a fool who fell into that goon's trap. He used me." He barked, "I should have never been hanging around him in the first place."

His words hit Jenna hard. It sounded like her talking about Jackson. She'd called herself a fool a thousand times because she'd let Jackson manipulate her, use her and abuse her. Yet she knew she could forgive Lucas for his mistake. Shouldn't she be able to forgive herself as well?

Bull drank all the beer in the house then pulled a flask from his pants pocket. "I'm down to my emergency reserves," he muttered, tipping the bottle to his lips. "Gotta drink straight whiskey now."

"Why? Because you're an alcoholic who can't go an hour without a drink?"

"I've about had it with your mouth, woman," Bull roared, coming to tower over her. "Shut your face, or I'll shut it for you."

His hand slapped her across the face, snapping her head to the side.

Lucas hollered and struggled, threatening to kill the bastard. Bull didn't waste any time, just turned and fired his gun at Lucas. The bullet struck him in the arm and blood flowed onto his shirt sleeve.

Jenna screamed and jumped up, rushing toward her brother. Bull stopped her with the gun.

"Leave him be. He'll live."

"But he's hurt."

"He's going to be hurt a lot worse if you touch him, bitch. Now, I think it's time for you and me to have some fun. Get in your bedroom."

"No. I won't do it." She planted her feet and refused to move. In response, Bull simply whacked Lucas across the cheek with the gun. The skin busted open, and Lucas groaned out loud.

"Stop it. Stop hurting him."

"Then do what I tell you and get in that room."

She didn't want to do it. She knew what would happen once they entered the bedroom and the thought sickened her. God, how would she stand this animal mauling her?

She didn't have a choice, though. She couldn't take him hurting Lucas anymore. Luke, her baby brother. Luke, sitting there with blood on his face, his arm bleeding, and a look of pure horror on his face. Slowly, she started toward the bedroom, one sluggish footstep after another.

"Don't do it, sis," Lucas pleaded.

"It'll be okay, Luke. I'll live."

"God, don't go. Please."

"Shut up, you," Bull ordered, pointing the gun at him again, "or I'll shut you up. I don't need you to have her go to the bank and withdraw the money, you know."

Jenna chewed on her lip as she entered the bedroom. She could take this, she really could. As long as Bull didn't kill Lucas. If she could stand the beatings Jackson had dealt her and the rapes she incurred at his hands, she could stand this. She forced herself to believe that. She had to.

As soon as they walked into the bedroom, Bull slammed the door. He laid the gun on the dresser and grabbed her head in his hands, mashing his lips against hers. The smell of the booze on his breath gagged her, and she fought to keep from retching.

"Ah, pretty mama, I been wanting a piece of that big ass of yours for a long time now." His hands slid down and clutched her butt cheeks through her dress, squeezing hard. "The time has come, baby."

Once again his mouth assaulted hers, grinding against her, his lips so hard she felt his teeth bruising her delicate skin. His tongue forced her lips open, and he used it to probe inside her mouth. His hands cupped her ass, rubbing and pressing her into his pelvis, pinching her flesh. The bulge of his dick burned against her like a torch, searing her right through the fabric of her dress. When his hands moved to the zipper at her neckline, her knees threatened to buckle, and a hoarse cry broke from her throat.

"Come on now, baby, show Daddy your titties." He laughed harshly, pulling her sleeveless bodice down her shoulders. "Let's see them big old boobies."

Lord, he was crude. She needed to fight him, to get away. She twisted her head to avoid his slobbering lips, and her gaze landed on the gun on the dresser. It was so close. Maybe she could maneuver him just a little bit closer.

Jenna curved her body sideways, one step closer to the gun. His hand grabbed a handful of hair and jerked, stopping her in her tracks. Tears welled in her eyes.

"I said I want to see them titties." His hand took hold of the bodice of her dress and ripped downwards, the material splitting from the force.

"You bastard," she hissed. She saw the blow coming and turned her face, his fist blasting into her ear.

"I don't want no more bullshit out of you, woman," he roared, throwing her down on the bed and towering over her, his hands planted on his hips. "You and me are gonna fuck, so get used to the idea."

He grabbed the gun off the dresser and began to wave it wildly. "If you don't give it up willingly, I'll start shooting. First your dog, then your brother. You got that?"

The maniacal gleam in his eye told Jenna he meant it. She couldn't fight anymore. She didn't have any other choices.

He saw the look of defeat come over her face and gave her an evil grin. "So, you see it my way, right?"

He waited for her to answer then shoved the gun under her chin. "Right, bitch?"

Tears streamed down her face as she tried to nod, then she spat the word back at him. "Right."

"That's my girl. Now I want you to take your clothes off, nice and slow."

Just do it, she told herself. Don't think about it, just do it.

She rose on shaking legs and shook the ruined dress off, drawing herself up to her full height and jutting her chin. Clad only in bra and panties, she stared him in the eyes.

"Do with me what you will. I can't stop you."

"But I can." The door swung open and Noah stalked in, gun raised and pointed directly at Bull's head.

Chapter 21

Jenna didn't even have time to celebrate Noah's arrival before she found herself yanked back against Bull's body. His left arm coiled tightly around her neck, the gun pointed directly against her temple.

Bull jerked his arm and pressed against her windpipe so hard that black spots began to dance before her eyes. She clawed at its brawny width, desperate for air.

"Get the hell back, Baker or she gets it right now." Bull spat the words out angrily. Jenna saw spittle fly from his lips as he yelled.

"Let her go, Bull. It'll go a lot easier on you if you just let her go." Noah's voice was steady, cool. His hands didn't shake, and he stood steady on his feet. Jenna couldn't help but admire his courage. He didn't quake in the face of fear, didn't weaken against his enemy.

And he was doing it for her. A sudden flood of love crashed through her. He did love her, he wouldn't hurt her, or he wouldn't risk his life for her. He calmly stared death in the face and stood his ground. Because he loved her.

God, she wanted a chance to tell him she loved him. She wanted to spend every night in his arms, every day laughing and loving with him. She couldn't die now. She had to be as brave as Noah was.

Then she remembered that night just a couple of months ago. She had been in this same position, held captive in a big man's arms, a gun pressed to her temple. Noah had stood there like an avenging angel then, too. She thought back to that night and remembered what she had done. Her eyes frantically sought Noah's. He looked steadily at her, and she wondered if he could read her mind. Did he remember that other night as well? When he gave a slight nod, she knew they were thinking the same thing.

"You know I'll kill you if you hurt her, don't you, Bull? Put the gun down and make the choice to live."

"Fuck you, cop. Just back off and let me go."

"Give up the girl and I'll let you leave."

"No way, man. She's my shield, my ticket out."

"She's your ticket to hell."

That's when she acted. She twisted her head down and back and then let herself turn into dead weight, collapsing her legs and forcing her mass into drawing his arm down. Noah fired and Bull staggered, dropping the gun. She felt his arm loosen its grip and she sprang away from him before he fell, his eyes wide open, staring glassily at the ceiling. A bloom of red grew in the center of his forehead.

It was a few hours later when the place settled down. There had been cops and the coroner, ambulance drivers, and crime scene investigators swarming all over the house. She stood dressed in a pair of gray yoga pants and a purple tank top. Thank God she'd had time to change before Noah's backup arrived. Having all those people see her in her underwear would have been too much to bear on top of everything else.

Noah stayed after everyone else left. She sat on the sofa, his arm wrapped around her, and listened to the silence. It sounded strange after all the hectic activity of before.

"Tell me how you came to be here just in the nick of time."

"When you didn't answer your phone, I got worried. I called three times before I decided to investigate. I saw your car was here and knew something was wrong. I peeked in the windows and saw Luke in the dining room. Then I saw Bull dragging you to the bedroom." His tone went cold at the memory, his teeth clamping at the recollection. "I knew I couldn't wait. I called for backup and came in through the window."

"You're my hero," she whispered, laying her head on his chest and running her hand over Leon where he lay on Noah's lap.

She thought about the talk she'd had with Lucas as two men loaded him onto the ambulance gurney.

"Jenna, I am so sorry for everything. You could have been killed, damn it, just because I was a fool." Self-recrimination reverberated in his voice, his face pale and drawn. "I don't blame you if you never forgive me."

Jenna felt like someone had reached into her chest and squeezed her heart in their fist. She brushed a hand across her stinging eyes.

"There's nothing to forgive, Luke. Believe me, we all make mistakes. I love you, little brother. That's all that matters." She took his hand in hers and squeezed it. "I love you."

"I love you, too, sis."

She'd wanted to go to the hospital with him, but there was so much to do here at the house. The EMTs assured her it was just a flesh wound and she wouldn't be allowed in while they treated him, anyway.

She sighed wearily, and he raised his hand and smoothed her hair.

"Noah, what's going to happen to Luke now? You know, now that there's no Bull to testify against."

"I've already talked to Detective Jakes about it. If he takes us to the people he delivered the packages to, he'll get the same deal. Hopefully, this will all be over soon."

Jenna couldn't agree more.

"I was so scared when I saw you wrapped in Bull's arms, his gun to your head." Noah's words were whispered as he leaned his head against hers. "You're the most beautiful, bravest woman I've ever seen."

"Didn't you see my legs shaking?" she asked.

"No. All I could see was you, wearing just your bra and panties, and Bull pointing his gun at you. I thought my heart would pound out of my chest. That's the second time I had to shoot a man for you."

"Oh, Noah. I hate that. You don't know what I would give if neither one of them had died." She buried her head in his neck, tears trickling from her eyes.

"I know, babe. But I couldn't lose you. I love you. There was no choice."

The words melted her heart. She had wanted the chance to tell him she loved him. She couldn't believe she was getting it.

"I love you, too, baby. Noah, I had lots of time to think tonight. I thought about what you said about fearing love. You're right. Life is too short. You can't fear happiness, or you'll never have it. I love you, Noah. I'm not afraid anymore."

Their lips met in a kiss so passionate Jenna felt liquid forming between her legs. She knew this was her happiness. Being with Noah, loving Noah, was what happiness was all about for her.

Chapter 22

She'd done it. She'd managed to pull together a fairytale wedding for Elena and Ramon in less than four weeks. A few minutes ago, a snowy white carriage pulled by a white stallion rolled up in front of the church, Elena stepped out, and Marcus helped her down. She looked incredibly beautiful, like an enchanted princess. The flowing white dress and her pale complexion framed by raven-black hair made her appear ethereal and fragile.

Marcus and Ramon both looked handsome as well. Ramon had been nervous, pacing back and forth as they awaited Elena's arrival. Marcus clamped his shoulder and reassured him once again. Nothing would go wrong.

It had been touch-and-go for a while. Elena's health had deteriorated, and they didn't know if she'd be well enough to be at the wedding or if she would be in the hospital. Or even if she would be alive. They had gone so far as to put the hospital chapel on hold just in case. Fortunately, Elena had perked up the last few days and insisted she could handle the wedding.

Now the last notes of "Ave Maria" faded and the chapel doors swung open. She watched as Marcus walked his sister down the aisle. Harp music played softly, and Marcus couldn't keep from smiling proudly. His white teeth sparkled against his bronze skin, his black eyes gleaming. The tux he wore fit him flawlessly.

Ramon watched his bride gliding toward him, and you could see his eyes welling up. He couldn't tear his gaze from her as she drew closer. When Marcus and Elena reached the altar, Ramon shook Marcus's hand then took both of Elena's hands in his after she passed her bouquet of roses and gardenias to her maid of honor. Jenna read his lips as he whispered "I love you" to his bride.

She turned and looked at Noah, standing next to her. Noah was working security for Marcus, who had encouraged her to bring a date with her so she could enjoy the dancing, and Elena insisted on it. Noah looked even more handsome than the men in the wedding party. His custom-made suit fit his body to perfection, outlining his brawny shoulders and showing off his long legs in crisp, black fabric.

Noah looked into her eyes while Elena and Ramon exchanged vows. She couldn't look away, held prisoner by the love she saw shining there. He had asked her to marry him last week. He had surprised her with a romantic picnic in the park, complete with wine and cheese. They had settled on a blanket next to the lake and fed each other strawberries and grapes. The storm had come up quickly. They had been so involved with each other they hadn't noticed the clouds scudding quickly across the sky. Noah had just gotten down on one knee when the first raindrops fell, dampening his hair. He ignored the droplets and took her hand in his and kissed it.

"Darling Jenna, we've been through storms together before. Please say you'll marry me so we can share sunshine and storms together forever."

The heavens had opened as she said yes. Rain poured down on them, but she didn't care. Her hair was soon soaked, hanging around her face and blended in with her tears of joy. They kissed, her arms wrapping around his neck, his hands spanning her waist and lifting her off her feet.

The memories swept through her, and Jenna reached out and took Noah's fingers in hers. Nothing had prepared her for love. She hadn't really believed in it before.

But it was real and its existence amazed her. She met Noah's gaze and silently vowed to never be afraid of happiness again.

The ceremony ended with the traditional kiss, and Jenna joined in the cheers of the crowd as Elena and Ramon practically danced back down the aisle.

In a few moments, Ramon and Elena climbed into the rose-bedecked carriage and headed the few blocks to the reception venue. Marcus had rented out an entire restaurant that looked like a castle. The gated garden had a magical air, with fairy lights twinkling everywhere, and the tinkling of a fountain drew people to it. The mariachi band strolled through the garden, the sound of guitars filling the air.

The cocktail hour took place outside with flowing champagne and a bevy of appetizers. The doors swung open to the reception area as darkness fell, and an audible gasp from the guests went up as the room came in to view. Tables were covered in cloths of white and runners of mauve brocade. Eight chairs were pulled up to each roundtable and centerpieces of tall crystal vases filled with pink roses and white orchids graced their surface. Ribbons of silver tulle draped the ceiling and held a bevy of blossoms in their folds.

The most beautiful moment came when Ramon and Elena had their first dance. Marcus took the microphone and serenaded them with his song, My Love. The love between the bride and groom was visible, palpable.

Jenna swayed against Noah as she watched the happy couple from the rear of the room where she could supervise the happenings when Penny came running up. She skidded to a stop, her face wreathed in smiles.

"You're not going to believe it, Jenna. Oh, my God. It's unbelievable."

"What is it, Penny? Spit it out."

"They have a kidney for Elena."

"Are you serious? Elena's getting her transplant?" Jenna's heart sang at the news.

Penny nodded, clasping her hands together in delight.

"We've got to get word to her. Go tell the DJ and he can make an announcement."

Jenna would never forget the look on Elena and Ramon's faces when the DJ called for a drum roll. He was a family friend and choked up as he told everyone the good news.

Jenna turned to Noah and raised her lips to meet his, letting him dip her in his arms. God was good. Life was beautiful.

And fairytales really do come true.

About The Author

Simone Carter is a passionate Romance Author. She initially started writing in her spare time after University, and 10 years later she's managed to turn it into a full time venture.

She loves to write promiscuous stories that feature strong, sassy women, in an array of different settings and scenarios.

Simone lives in Colorado with her husband and two children. When she's not creating steamy story lines, you can find her spending time with her family, hiking trails, or at home on her balcony with a book and a nice glass of wine.

You can download a FREE book from Simone "A Women's Prerogative" and join her exclusive mailing list. You'll receive notifications of huge discounts, FREE promotions, and hot, new release dates. Sign up to Simone's mailing list here:

simonecarterbooks.com/free-book

Other titles by Simone Carter

If you enjoyed reading *"**Brothers in Blue: The Complete Series**"*, you might want to check out my other titles:

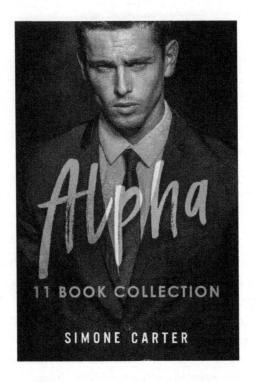

Alpha: 11 Book Collection

11 Books for the price of 1

Enjoy the complete Alpha Collection by bestselling author
Simone Carter

Romance, Lust, Suspense, Uncensored Scenes and No
Cliffhangers

Made in the USA
Monee, IL
20 May 2023

34112553R00198